I0778148

SWORD OF RUIN

SWORD OF RUIN

The Ruined Destiny Series: Book Two

S. H. Blodgett

Dedication

First and foremost, none of this would have been possible without my husband, Ian Blodgett. I'm entirely blessed to have such a supportive life partner. I love you to the moon and back!

To my Dad, thank you for reigniting your love for reading and diving into my work with such enthusiasm. Your feedback during the final edits truly made this book better, and I'm deeply grateful for your support throughout this journey.

To my Mom, my greatest cheerleader, thank you for sharing the news about my book and believing in me every step of the way.

To Gramme, who encouraged my passion for reading, thank you for all of those visits to the local Books and Bagels shop! I forever have a place for each book you gifted me on my shelves and an even bigger place in my heart for all of those memories.

To my family who shaped me into the person I am today, I will always be grateful. The support you all have given me has made this journey possible. Thank you all from the bottom of my heart!

S. H. BLODGETT

Chapter One

SAYRA

Normally, it took a monumental amount of *dritt* to throw Sayra completely off-kilter, but today it only took her mom being alive—eleven years after being abandoned by her.

"Sayra, wait," Nessika called out behind her.

Sayra's jaw ached from how hard her teeth were clenched, but she knew the moment she opened her mouth, all *helvete* would break loose again. She nearly killed Emrys once by lashing out against her despicable mother Arene von Lykken, and some rational part of her brain prodded her into realizing any further action would only hurt those around her.

And so, Sayra kept putting one boot in front of the other as her mind struggled to process the world-churning information Arene gave her.

She was a living, breathing relic.

A fourth of an ancient artifact that granted people majik, and Sayra was a walking experiment whose goal was to expose the evil underlying the Holy Family's foundation.

Give me a break, she thought, her mouth drawn tightly across her face. Flames flickered in front of her, a ball of light guiding her down the narrow storm tunnels beneath Saint Highburn Monastery. It glowed on her black training leathers.

Another's footsteps echoed behind Nes's—a nickname Sayra coined for Nessika when they became friends.

"We have to wait for Rys," Sylven said, the Arcanist sounding unsure as he paused beside Nes. "Unless you remember how to wind back up in the monastery grounds."

Her feet slowed to a halt, but her heart raced. Burning edged at her eyes, and her throat closed in on itself. The urge to punch something again was overwhelming, but all Sayra could do was tighten her fists as Nes's hand rested on the side of her arm.

"Oh, Sayra." Her voice was thick as her leather-clad arms enveloped her friend.

Sayra's mouth trembled as she returned the hug, a well of plaguing sorrow tearing at her soul. Everything had drastically changed, and the tiny fact that her mother had paved this exact path for Sayra all those years ago devastated her.

For a moment, she stayed there, stealing a deep, centering breath. Then, her gaze rose to see the outline of Sylven's face. Shades of reddish-orange highlighted his pinched brows, and his hazel eyes flicked between hers. So many emotions ran behind them, but he upheld his mental block, which prevented them from escaping into her mind through their link. His head lowered for a second before he ran a hand behind his neck. The rich fabric of his navy academy uniform bunched around his broad shoulders.

Sayra pulled back from Nes as Sylven turned around to the distant spot where her mother and Emrys still spoke. Their words were the faintest of echoes down the tunnel, soon joined by her Arcanist's footsteps as Sylven sought them out. Her spell's flame spurted as Sayra's focus loosened. She returned her attention to that little thing, tuning everything else out.

The chill of the stone wall reached Sayra through her training leathers as she leaned into it, her eyes staring at nothing. She maintained the spell and thought of only it. Minutes ticked by until she heard two people approach, her eyes not meeting either as Emrys took the lead.

It was silent on their way back.

Everything hung heavy in her mind, and judging by the varying levels of seriousness on everyone's faces, Sayra knew it was not just her.

When they met the chilled air of the monastery garden, Sayra didn't pay attention to the frosted evergreens, ornate marble fountains, and lush winter blossoms sprouting from beds of flowers. She ignored Emrys's attempt to talk and walked away with Nes under the arching lampposts, the majik-fueled light warming the pathways winding through the encompassing greenery.

But when a figure shifted nearby, Sayra froze in her tracks.

Every face Sayra dreaded flashed before her. The list was growing exponentially with every secret she had collected in the last couple of months and, with it, the fear of how each could be used against her. However, when a cloaked Arcanist peeled himself from a nearby tree, her haunches relaxed a hair. The majik-user's black cloak billowed dramatically in his sweeping gesture of acknowledgment.

"Vander," Sylven said, his voice disgruntled.

Behind her, Sayra heard the breeze of passing words form a spell of protection around them that would prevent eavesdroppers from gathering their words. Emrys always took care with precautions, even when Sayra was two seconds from damning it all to the wind.

Sayra's mouth pressed into a line as Vander, the crowned prince of Acacea, gave her his most charmed grin. "Let me guess. You also knew the so-called informant was my mother?"

The crowned prince's face turned, and his roguish features came into focus. "Apologies for not sharing. As you may have heard, we have been rather tongue-tied over the details." A hint of regret stole the brightness from his grin.

Sayra made a noise of annoyance, Sylven crossing his arms beside her. A foot tapped as Nes glanced between them, her icy-blue eyes puzzling the unsaid between them all.

"Well, Vander. I'm surprised to find you here, considering I have yet to update you." Emrys's voice sounded cool and even.

Sayra couldn't meet his eyes. Not yet. Not after all she'd learned.

A frown crossed Vander's pale face. "Which I am terribly wounded over. You know I should have been, little brother. Aren't we all to work together?"

She knew Sylven had choice words to share on the matter, but not even the son of a duke could speak in such a manner before his future king. Sayra had no such reserves. After all, she hailed from the empire of Droden, which ruled over her conquered territory of Faenda. "You two can talk all about the most recent development. I, however, have no interest in discussing anything further tonight." She exaggerated her dismissal of them with a flick of her ribbon-laced braid.

"Wait," Emrys said, and not with the voice of a friend. Rather, that of a prince.

Sayra slowed, everything in her wanting to lash out against him. She rocked forward on her heels, swiveling to face him at the last second. "What?" Her sharpness smoothed the emotion from Emrys's face.

The younger prince of Acacea moved with purpose. His gloved hand pulled a leather-bound journal from his trousers. The black fabric of his cloak folded over his navy and gold Arcanist uniform as he held out the small notebook. "This is for you to read. She wants you to have this."

She.

Her mother.

A woman who lived a lie, who brought this all on Sayra.

She swallowed her rage, ripping the journal from Emrys's hands before turning away from them all. Vander's eyes were curious as they watched, but Nes's held an anger for Emrys, as if she viewed it distasteful he would continue to prod the matter. The Valkyrie followed Sayra as they left the men to talk amongst themselves.

Sayra maintained her composure while she paced through the maze of impeccably maintained marble corridors, for once not smelling the earthy tones of incense that burned throughout. By the time she reached the Valkyrie dormitory with Nes, she could only manage a hasty nod toward her friend before climbing up the stairwell to her own room on the fourth floor.

Once there, Sayra locked the door behind her, tossed the journal on top of her armor chest, and climbed into her bed without bothering to change into nightclothes. She buried her face into a cream-shaded pillow, wishing more than anything she was just a Valkyrie.

⸻✦⸻

"*It has been foretold*," a voice whispered in a foggy glen. It was strangely devoid of inflection, the sound undiscernible, as if it came from neither a man nor woman. "*You are the pekelný vyvolávač.*"

Shimmering figures stood around Sayra, the fog far too dense for her to make out anything beyond faint outlines. Her eyes scoured the area. She couldn't detect anything concrete, no matter how hard she tried. She walked, but the distance between her and the figures never seemed to change. Something about the dream felt fractured, as if everything were hanging in purgatory. A place that once had a beginning; however, the end was yet to be determined.

"The what?" Sayra asked, her posture tense as her speed picked up. She began jogging, her bare feet crossing dew-covered grass. Moisture collected on her training leathers. The voice whispered into her ear, but the words were far too faint for Sayra to hear.

"What?" Her tone echoed her frustration, and her eyes squinted in the direction the noise came from. But everything began to fade, and the next time her eyes blinked open, all she saw was her ceiling.

And she just stared at it.

For how long, Sayra didn't know. Her eyes traced the patches of indirect light scattered across the ceiling, but her mind struggled to repress the memories of the last few days. It was all too much.

When knocking sounded at her door, all Sayra could do was close her eyes and grimace. She knew she looked bad. Her eyes felt puffy, and her hair pulled messily from the tight braid that normally ran from the top of her head down to her waist. As she pulled herself from the bed, albeit reluctantly, she readjusted her *slør*, the silk ribbon wrapped around her braid representing an unwed woman from her homeland.

Even *that* was disheveled.

The moment Sayra opened her door, she froze. Her eyes widened in abject horror.

Emrys stood there, cloaked in black and shifting his weight. His eyes leaped from the hall, presumably scanning for witnesses, to hers.

And she was wearing yesterday's clothes.

Sayra's face burned, her mind cursing her for not caring more about her appearance.

His deep voice was quiet when the prince asked, "May I come in?"

"You can't be here," Sayra hissed, waving him in quickly as her eyes searched for any bystanders. Arcanists were forbidden from entering the Valkyrie dormitory. Valkyries were trained and contracted to be their guardians from daemonkind, not their companions. Hastily, she shut the door and retreated against it until her back was flush with the wood. "Why are you here?"

The words came out harsher than she meant, but she was angry at Emrys for withholding the secret of her mother being his informant on the Holy Family. Even if Emrys had been majikally sworn to secrecy.

Pulling off his hood, Emrys's short black hair remained perfectly maintained. The collar of his navy uniform shone, the gold trim edging around his neck. "I spoke further with Arene." His words were careful, an edge of regret lining his face. "She'd like to request another meeting to explain herself."

Sayra had to refrain from smoothing the frizzy edges around her face. Instead, she lifted her chin, ignoring the bizarre mix of anger and butterflies that simultaneously made her nervous and on edge. Emrys's gray eyes, so dark they were nearly black like his hair, marked the worn leather notebook haphazardly splayed across the trunk at the foot of her bed. Then they flicked to her new oak dresser and desk to his right. The previous furniture burned in the dormitory fire that had nearly claimed her life and that of the other Valkyries on her floor.

"I have no interest in speaking with her again."

A slow nod. "She thought you'd say that. Hence the journal. Arene mentioned there were more she'd like to share if what you find leaves you with questions."

Clearing her throat, Sayra couldn't meet his eyes. "Is there anything important I need to know otherwise?"

Silence clung to the air, only interrupted when she heard him sigh. Forcing her gaze up, Sayra's anger dimmed when she saw the conflict etching the Arcanist's expression. Emrys wasn't one to show his true emotions. Only a person who grew to know his tiny tells could see the way a muscle on his brow tensed just so, and how his right hand curling a centimeter showed just how torn the prince was.

However, it also exposed how Emrys was back to masking his reactions in front of Sayra despite being alone.

They'd both had the rug pulled from under them by her mother. Emrys thought Sayra was the only one imbued with the ancient majik relic, but the grave of secrets ran deeper than they could have imagined. After all, Emrys was the original, expendable test subject to determine if it would be safe for Sayra. She imagined that could have stung quite the amount, considering her mother did the same to her.

And...

And that same relic, no matter how tiny the piece Emrys harbored, may have been the underlying connection that compelled them toward each other all along. Sayra had felt that uncanny pull to him the moment they met, and by the way he kissed her, he felt it too. Was it genuine, or was it all a fluke of the relic's threads trying to rewind itself together? It could never work between them. She was a Valkyrie sworn to serve as Sylven's protector, and Emrys had a grander destiny of serving his kingdom by Vander's side. More so, Sayra had to figure out how to topple the Holy Family's corrupt network of power throughout every country before they gained total control, murdering thousands of innocents in the process.

Their feelings, or whatever they were, could wait. Even if it left a bitter taste in her mouth. It seemed Emrys agreed.

"The *proelium* will begin in the coming months for the senior class of Arcanists. I believe it wise for you and Sylven to attend and study the combat techniques between *anima* to best prepare for next year." *Anima*—the combination of a contracted Arcanist and Valkyrie. Saint Highburn Monastery held a yearly competition for students to showcase their talents. "Regardless of what transpired of late, the plan is set for you both to participate and qualify for the *Grand Proelium* between countries next year."

Sayra was supposed to out her majik to the world then, exposing the Holy Family's lies and deceit to everyone in one fell swoop. From there, Emrys's family would take over in the chaos to dethrone the rulers of Saint Highburn Monastery and remove their corrupt roots.

She couldn't shake the sight of the horrors the Holy Family carried out under their very feet. "That shouldn't be an issue."

"Come summer, we will depart for Acacea to formally discuss plans with my family. In the meantime, let me know if there is anything I can be of use for." Emrys's eyes drooped to his leather boots, and he cut himself off before saying something else. He looked up at her, shifting focus. "I do apologize for how the situation has unraveled, Sayra."

Pain crumbled her face, everything far too fresh for her resolve to bear. Still, she remained quiet. If she spoke, she didn't know if that final string of control would snap. She would not break down.

But damn him, Emrys stepped forward, raising a hand to tuck loose strands of her hair behind her ear. His fingers traced a warm path, and her breath caught in her chest.

For a moment, she forgot the betrayal of her oath as a Valkyrie, her mother's years of deceit, the near-death experience against the daemons that nearly killed her and Emrys, and only remembered the feel of his lips against hers. The desire to do it all over again was incredible. His juniper, black pepper, and vetiver-smelling cologne lingered in the air, and she couldn't help but *really* look at the face she'd grown to admire. A chiseled structure. One that caught her breath when he revealed that smile he cultivated only for her.

His deep voice rumbled close to her face, and a sound commonly imbued with authority gave in to something else. "Though I don't regret what happened between us." There were too many undertones, all richly layered in a sentence that left her wanting more. But he withdrew, leaving her skin tingling.

Stunned, Sayra didn't move as he left her room, returning the hood above his head before disappearing into the dormitory floor.

Chapter Two

SAYRA

Cursing, Sayra immediately snapped into alertness at the time. Apparently, she'd slept through most of the day, the lecture with Sylven fast approaching. Her feet sped toward her new drawers, where she grabbed training gear to don and a pale green *slør* from her trunk. It was one of the only good things to come from the dormitory fire. She was given brand-new furniture to replace the burned pieces.

"Sayra!" Lynn called through her door, enveloping her in a bear hug the moment Sayra rushed to open it.

Sayra returned the hug, rubbing her eyes afterward from the jumble of a morning she had. "What's up?"

"Nes wanted me to check in," Lynn explained, her prim face squinching the freckles across her nose as she smiled. "Are you..." She hesitated, searching for the right word. "Well?"

"You could say that." Sayra snorted, deftly beginning to wind a braid down the crown of her head. Emrys's presence stirred to the surface, and her need to deflect the conversation was overwhelming. "But yes, thanks. How have you been? It's been a while since we spoke, just the two of us."

Switching to their native tongue, Lynn responded, *"I'm relieved to hear that."* Leaning against Sayra's bed, she gave her a dreamy smile.

"Everything has been so... unreal. Casber is really special to me. We just have so much in common, from our favorite foods," which Sayra knew to be a roasted pork dish over a bed of greens, *"to our favorite hobbies."*

Casber, a young man who hailed from the northern Yendire Kingdom, was her Arcanist. Their relationship had shocked their cadre of Valkyries, but Sayra, Nes, and Kimimari trusted Lynn in her decision to break tradition to date the man she was contracted to.

"As long as he is treating you well." Sayra dipped her chin, intertwining the final strands at the base of her hair. *"It's great to see you as your old self again,"* she said, tying off the soft green fabric around the bottom of her braid.

"It has been too long, but I finally enjoy every morning again. I finally look forward to the next day to come." Lynn's smile fell, her eyes tracing the lines of Sayra's wooden floor. *"I finally feel whole again."*

A part of Sayra longed for that relief, knowing it would ease her mind each night she slept. But it wasn't her time. Trying for a smile, Sayra said, *"You have no idea how happy that makes me for you."*

It made sense to Sayra, the sudden strength of Lynn's bond with Casber. Lynn found her heart, her purpose. She'd moved on, an ideation her friend had striven to achieve for nearly ten years. Sayra was always pessimistic about the notion of 'when you knew, you knew,' but seeing the way Lynn swooned when Casber was near, the adoration in her eyes, made some lonely part of Sayra desire for that fulfillment. To move on from that shared loss of theirs.

The memory of Emrys's hands on her lower back suddenly entered her mind. Blinking excessively, Sayra repressed the thought before it led to something far too dangerous to consider. Something she refused to admit, even to herself.

Hooking an auburn curl behind her ear, Lynn tilted her head at Sayra. The white slør of Lynn's braid shone. "I hope similarly for you," she said, switching back to the common tongue, which was more difficult for her. "Too long to hold such sadness."

"Too long indeed." Sayra sighed, her hand lingering on the knob of her door.

A part of her begged to turn around and fully share the contents of her mind with her lifelong friend. Besides the minor fact that Emrys requested that knowledge remain secret, wouldn't it be selfish to unload the disaster occurring under their feet? Lynn was glowing with happiness, and the last thing Sayra wanted was to snuff out her friend's happiness so soon. Perhaps one day, but for now, Lynn deserved the precious time of ignorance.

"Come, lateness is almost here," Lynn broke in, pointing toward the clock above Sayra's bare desk. Snagging her arm, she directed Sayra out of the room and to the stairwell. "Happy you are well physically. Though you seem distanced." Worry flashed in the corners of her brown eyes.

"I'll be okay, Lynn. Sleeping in made me feel worlds better," Sayra said, taking care to place her feet on the steps without stumbling. "I've been training for too many hours, I think."

Lynn made a noise of disapproval, eyeing her up and down with sternness. "Get more sleep. No more late nights!"

"Yes, ma'am."

Huffing, Lynn proceeded to give her a lecture on self-care, most of which Sayra nodded placably toward—a smile fighting to rise on her lips at Lynn's sincerity about the importance of yoga. When they reached the lecture hall, most of the class had already taken their seats and flipped their notebooks open.

Emrys somehow sensed the moment she entered the room. He grew still, a pen tucked between two fingers as he held her gaze with no hint of his own inner turmoil. Sayra knew hers was storming, and such deep conflict made her falter behind Lynn. She couldn't allow herself such sentiments, not when her duty fell elsewhere.

She wouldn't act the part of some infatuated schoolgirl.

Lifting her chin, Sayra circled her desk and sat beside Sylven, his side-eye assessing her as she did so. Behind her, Lynn tucked her hand inside Casber's under the table, and her chin rested in her other palm as they whispered to each other.

Breaking the silence between them, Sayra smiled sweetly. "What's the latest on the Sylven angst journey?" It may have been forced, but she wanted nothing more than a sense of normalcy.

He gave a disgruntled grunt, but his face stayed pointedly forward. Sayra prodded him with his own pen. "C'mon. I know there's something." She mocked a gasp, her eyes widening. "You missed me, didn't you? I knew deep, deep down in some long-abandoned corner of your soul you were a softie."

The side-eye came back with a remarkable increase in grouchiness. It only furthered her smile's width. She winked at him, basking in his perpetual moodiness. Monk Ibski floated in the room a second later, silencing the next words she had cooked up to pester Sylven with.

Much to her disappointment, of course.

Their assignment moved from some boring topic to one that intrigued her: learning to block the link. Every *anima* had that majikal link between their minds upon contracting together in the Old Covenant ceremony, and while it didn't use to bother Sayra, the need for privacy was growing fast. Her feelings had to remain her own, especially around

Emrys. Sylven didn't need to know such things, and the mental bond could be used for speaking when necessary.

While she'd gleaned some semblance of an idea to block it out at Astor Manor when Sylven practiced, Sayra hadn't yet given it much rehearsal.

It was fairly difficult to maintain the block, but by the end of the two hours, Sayra had practiced enough to employ it while still and completely focused on it. The moment the instructor clapped his hands, though, the control slipped through her grasp. Sylven was at a much more advanced level than she was, a small piece of knowledge that irked her whenever her block evaporated, leaving the oaf with a slight and satisfied smile.

Nes and Lynn joined her on their walk to their combat lecture, the three of them enjoying a casual conversation about their progress to hold a block and, in Nes's case, being able to communicate with words through their minds. The feat impressed Sayra as she was vastly behind. When Nes attempted to walk them through it, Sayra had to admit it wouldn't be her strong suit until she had plenty of practice. Currently, she was limited to sharing distinctive emotions.

Halfway toward their destination, Sayra noted Sylven hanging further back than Rys and Waylen, walking alone with a metaphorical cloud over his head. An urge to slow hit her, to try to reach out and inquire what it was that was bothering him. After all, Sylven seemed to lend out that olive branch first. When Emrys confronted them with undeniable proof of the Holy Family's daemonic experiments, Sayra would have torn the place apart with her majik if it weren't for Sylven's steading presence. He was concerned for her, and it was enough for Sayra to see if they could work toward a professional relationship.

Sayra's shoulders twisted with her body, but a person behind stopped her in her tracks. Right in front of a broad, thick-skulled, and unendurable Arcanist.

"Sayra, darling." Kenji amicably smiled, gesturing to an alcove in the corridor's corner. "Would you walk with me? I've been meaning to depart some words with you." His upturned eyes were calculating.

Lynn's steps became unsure, and Nes's face asked if they should stay. With a quick shake of Sayra's head, they reluctantly continued onward, Sylven steering clear as he walked around them.

A stone settled in her stomach as she followed Kenji's burgundy cloak, the wafting smell of cedarwood smoking from a nearby incense scone. She switched to an inflection more befitting for those of royalty. She was a princess before Kenji's father conquered her country, after all. "Of course. What is it you need to say?" Sayra asked, keeping her tone neutral.

"I wanted to cement our evening plans for this coming Friday. Will you be in attendance?" His autumn-gold eyes pressed on hers, asserting his desire for her to say *yes*.

A wrinkle appeared between her brows, Sayra having made no such commitment. More so, she wondered why he'd inquire after concocting such plans and what his ultimate agenda was. Knowing the Droden Empire heir, he wasn't up to anything she'd remotely approve of. Kenji always had a tendency to flatter before asking for something from another. The greater the request, the further he would go to get in one's good graces.

"I haven't the slightest clue as to what you're referring to." Honesty was the best policy.

A younger Arcanist, perhaps in his second or third year, rushed past them, causing a small rift between Sayra and the heir before he closed it once more.

"Ah, have you not convened with Sylven yet? I extended a formal invitation for dinner this coming Friday and would love to enjoy the company you two would offer," Kenji explained, his countenance far too casual for the offer to be genuine.

Wistfully sighing, Sayra donned a stressed appearance. "I apologize, Kenji. I already have plans this weekend that I cannot postpone. It would be rude of me to do so." *Let's see how badly he wants this dinner and just how far he'll strive to obtain it.*

Waving his hand, Kenji said, "I completely understand the obligation, and it would displease me greatly to cause you such a burden." A sly gleam sparkled in his eye. "Would the next weekend suffice? It has simply been far too long coming to extend the invitation terribly far into the future."

It seemed honesty would *not* be the best policy in this situation.

"I appreciate your consideration, Kenji." Sayra shared a dazzling smile, hoping to gain some leniency on her next request. "If you'll permit it, I'd best speak with Sylven to clear our schedules to prevent further conflicts. He considers his studies of the utmost importance, and his obligations to Acacea have him quite hurried these days."

A moment's hesitation showed in the small slip of his smile, Kenji's annoyance beginning to leak through. Regaining his composure, he said, "Naturally. I'll cross paths with you again soon to follow up on possible dates to host the dinner. Until then."

The heir dipped his chin in farewell and proceeded to the training arena's entrance, where Akira awaited his arrival. Grinning when their eyes met, the Valkyrie shared a small wave before spinning on her heel to follow her brother's steps. Black locks ended above her neckline, and she accentuated the sway of her leather-clad hips as she flicked her hair behind her head.

Pressing her lips together, Sayra only followed after they had cleared enough distance between them. Her mind was whirling from what Kenji was after.

The arena's fifteen-foot, wood-carved doors stood wide open at the end of the hall. It was a massive dome-shaped marble contraption crafted from the finest materials. Grand arches spanned the ceiling, and mosaic windows rose twenty feet tall in the surrounding circumference. Regular stone lined the floor, easily replaceable in case of damage during combat training. Though wards protected the area, there was always a possibility something may get damaged.

Throughout the entire class, her movements were distracted. Her focus drifted between too many thoughts and too many memories that refused to leave her be. Even Sylven was abnormally absent during the training, his mind encompassing some problem or another that held his innermost attention.

Flames burst around Sayra as her opponent's Arcanist interrupted her sparring with Imani, a lanky Valkyrie in her graduation class who had always been insistent on acting the part of the silent and intimidating guard wherever she went. The warmth had her fist snapping back before it tore through the fiery veil between them.

A clammy sweat broke out on Sayra as her mind returned to the charred, ash-coated clearing where her majik ran rampant—the flames nearly consuming Emrys in the process. Three daemons corralled them, almost killing them if it hadn't been for Sayra diving into forbidden majik—*nefas* majik. The horror of it all soaked into her very bones.

Sayra froze, and the distraction provided all the advantage her opponent needed to slip past her guard toward Sylvan's casting form.

Fy faen, she cursed.

Without thinking twice, Sayra leaped toward him. Already Imani was feet away from Sylven, his mundane capabilities not standing a chance against a Valkyrie's majikally-enhanced speed and strength. His lips were forming a different word as Sayra's elbow drew back, her body airborne and expression furious at her lapse.

Before Sylven's mouth finished moving, Sayra had whispered a word of her own, a whoosh of air flicking between the *anima* before her fist connected firmly with Imani's temple.

Sylven's jaw slackened. His feet were planted by the thin veil of fire where Sayra stood a moment before. Sayra used her majik to trade places with him. Collapsing to the ground, Imani blacked out, and Sayra sprinted at Imani's thunderstruck Arcanist. Majik thrummed in her veins, and her heart raced from the use of the spell Sylven had once cast when they were ambushed by daemons on the way to his family estate.

A ball of flame formed in front of the Arcanist's palm, and Sayra refused to balk in the face of it a second time. Her pride wouldn't allow it.

Layers of light flickered around her the moment the fire enveloped her, a weak barrier summoned by Sylven against the majik. It gave after a second's furtive effort of resistance. Sayra barreled into it, the heat blazing across her chest where it impacted and licked the exposed skin on her neck as it traced around her fighting leathers. It burned fiercely, a gasp sounding from the crowd as she stumbled through the pain. Sylven's barrier against majik only mitigated the spell, decreasing its strength as it burned her.

Within seconds, Sayra's arm was drawn tightly across the Arcanist's throat, and his hand raised in surrender to the round of applause the match garnered.

"Well performed!" Jax Zefare congratulated, joining in on the round of clapping. The instructor's freshly shaven face gleamed with approval, and his abnormally wide mouth curled at the ends.

Sayra released the Arcanist, wincing at the flash of pain burning across her skin.

Jax folded his arms. "Sylven, that was a remarkably executed switch between you. The hours of extracurricular practice you two must have conducted to perfectly execute that maneuver must have been extensive."

Sayra withdrew to the circle of gathered students. Her ears numbed to the array of congratulatory remarks and commentary from the instructors. Arcanist Warden, the monastery's resident healer, tended to the burns on Sayra as she focused on breathing through her nose. A tremor shook her hand, and she swallowed as her other hand clasped it into stillness behind her back. Her mind was blank for the remainder of the class, not registering any other matches following hers.

When their class ended, Sayra left before Sylven could address her dangerous use of majik. She noticed how Emrys was inching toward her after his match ended, and the last thing she wanted was to discuss the subject with either of them.

She could feel Sylven's horror at her actions and his anger at her disregard for secrecy. From a logical viewpoint, Sayra agreed it was rash and completely idiotic. However, some irrational part of her panicked at the situation, her body reacting rather than thinking to ensure his safety. It had felt so real in that moment—the danger, the dire seconds she had to do something before someone else died.

It's okay, Sayra.

Her elder brother, Brevn, had said those words as he died by the claws of a daemon. Because of her. Because she hadn't acted, or rather, because she had acted selfishly. Such haunting words, and she wasn't certain they would ever leave her. Words that plagued her and made her strive to redeem her wrongs. To become the Valkyrie she was today.

So, she walked.

Her feet journeyed across the monastery grounds, mindful of distancing herself from Sylven when she felt him approaching through their *anima* link. Cautious to avoid any faces remotely familiar as the afternoon gave way to a chilly night, Sarya barely felt the difference, immune to anything other than the need to keep moving and avoid thinking. When she slowed, it caught up with her, propelling her forward again until the church's bell rang in the night's darkest moment.

Startlingly close.

Sayra hadn't realized she had unintentionally wandered straight to the top of the monastery grounds where the cathedral towered.

The only word to describe the masterpiece was breathtaking. Sharp spires, seventy-two in all, ranging from the size of her five-foot-four-inch height to twenty feet tall, lanced across the roof, holy guards patrolling along pathways at the top in five-minute intervals. A diamond-shaped, stained-glass window depicting the Goddess beckoned worshipers in over the mighty bronze-formed doors, inscriptions written within concealed crevasses and vine-shaped irons locking the doors in place.

Statues of saints and their stories were tucked away in occasional alcoves on the cream-and-black-layered marble exterior. Circular columns sprouted from the ground and arched upward to merge with the building, a network of vined arches connecting each. The entryway was a staggering hundred steps up from where she stood. Grand arches linked the entirety of the ascension.

Sayra stared at it almost longingly. People from her homeland, Faenda, didn't believe in the Goddess like a majority of the continent did. They believed the land itself was to be worshiped, along with all that grew on it. But at that moment, she was urged to go inside the cathedral and pray for a miracle. For something to mend the pieces of her life into a semblance of a whole.

Only then did the wariness sink into her frozen bones, her fogged breaths merging with the tiny pinpricks of snow falling from the cloud-specked starry sky, convincing her it was time to return to her room. The skin on the back of her neck tingled in the spot where a cross was majikally tattooed. It was the runic spell of an Arcanist that gave her a Valkyrie's gifts, but frankly, Sayra never spared it another thought. Now, it gave her the distinct impression someone was watching her back as she strode from the cathedral.

Unease pricked at her limbs, making her feel jittery. When she glanced over her shoulder, however, there was nothing but a guard in the distance, patrolling the wall around the monastery grounds. As she reluctantly made to return to her room, she wondered if there would ever be a time when she'd be free of the fear of losing another.

An ear-piercing screech split the nighttime serenity, shouts of alarm echoing behind her. Adrenaline bellied the growing wave of fear that rolled into her mind, muddying her senses.

The thing about daemons that caused the most deaths wasn't their deadly maws or claws. No, it was the majikal wave of paralyzing fear that froze those in the vicinity. It made moving near impossible for anyone who wasn't trained. Animals and humankind fell victim to the majik, rendering them defenseless against the vicious, daemonic Horde.

Valkyries were given a slight buffer against them with their training and enhanced abilities, but that guard Sayra saw seconds ago didn't harbor such immunities.

The man buckled to the side of the wall, only his expression of horror reaching her eyes as she darted toward the switchback of stairs leading up to the walkway.

A daemon was attacking the monastery.

Sayra's heart thudded as she crested the thirty-foot wall, finding the fear-ridden man calling out to a metal-clad Valkyrie in the distance. Rushing forward, she braced her hands against the chilly stone, searching for the source of the fear that constricted her lungs.

There.

Majik lanterns cast bright rays of light below the wall in regular intervals, though the one a dozen feet to her right highlighted a ghastly sight. At least fourteen feet tall, the daemon stood on rotting back-bent legs. Its peeling skin was leathery, emanating a horrific stench that rolled her stomach. A whiplike tail was spiked at the end, writhing as its long trunk reached for the top of the wall. Two knobby arms lashed out, seven-inch, razor-sharp claws screeching against a majik barrier covering the stone wall.

Sparks flew as the daemon viciously attacked the barrier like a canine digging for a bone, but the moment Sayra made eye contact with its glowing crimson slits, it froze. A cruel maw gleamed with silva as it opened its triangular head, several curved horns glinting.

It screeched a noise that caused her to flinch just before it launched.

At her.

The daemon went rabid, possessed by a power far greater than any she'd seen before. It leaped over and over, slashing a mere six feet below her against the barrier keeping it from its prey.

"Make way!" a woman's voice shouted, pulling Sayra's attention to a brown-haired Valkyrie with a navy-cloaked man in tow.

Swallowing, Sayra backpedaled, allowing them room to work.

The man's hand rose, a metal, clawlike contraption shining with jewels on the back of his hand. Gauntlets—a powerful device that helped Arcanists draw power from the earth's ley lines to perform majik. "*Infundibulum!*" he cried.

At the same time, the daemon began growling a strange noise.

A funnel of immense fire poured from the Arcanist's hand, the white-hot flames near scorching her skin as Sayra watched. In a final desperate attempt, the daemon did something aberrant. It lurched for Sayra, rather than the Arcanist, right before the flames consumed its decaying body. Its cries of pain were short-lived, and the husk shriveled into a charred, vomit-inspiring pile. The stench made Sayra pinch her nose as the fire died out. The man who was patrolling earlier was long gone.

"Valkyrie Sayra," a voice called out to her left.

Sayra started, her head whipping toward a figure more imposing than any other.

Catara Zefare's hazel eyes were severe, and her platinum hair was pulled back into a perfect bun. Even in the low lighting, her ivory armor gleamed, and her velvet cape flicked in the mild breeze. The monastery's renowned cross was carved beneath her left clavicle. She strode down the walkway, a gloved hand resting on the pommel of her sheathed sword.

"You are not scheduled for patrol until tomorrow evening." It was a statement, though an underlying curiosity seemed to puzzle Catara's tone. Before Sayra could respond, she glanced at the Valkyrie behind her. "Find Arcanist Jefure and ensure the wards aren't weakened." To the Arcanist beside her, she said, "Well performed against the Horde, Arcanist Drenden. Your efforts are appreciated."

Murmurs and bows followed Catara's words before the Valkyrie and Arcanist left. Sayra made to bow, but when Catara's hand raised, she stilled.

Sayra rose from her shallow bend, clasping her hands behind her training leathers. "I've been restless today, Sanctus Catara. I was walking about the grounds and just heading back to sleep when I heard the disturbance."

Catara slowly nodded. "And you've come to lend aid where possible. That is admirable but unnecessary."

Daemons occasionally wandered around their wards, drawn in by majik and those who wield it. Valkyries and Arcanists fended them off often enough, though wards around the monastery and nearby lake protected them from any daemon attacks in the night.

"Get some rest. I fully expect you to carry through your entire shift on the morrow," Catara said.

Bowing again, Sayra raised a fist over her heart. "Yes, Sanctus Catara." An honorific for any of the Holy Family members. Her fist was clenched tighter than need-be.

Sayra's legs ached to run as she descended the stairwell. She knew Catara's eyes trailed her, and she hoped more than anything that no one caught the bizarre abnormality of the daemon's growl.

It sounded suspiciously like it spoke.

Hell Summoner.

Chapter Three

SYLVEN

It flabbergasted Sylven when Sayra dared to majik them in front of Jax and Catara. For crying out loud, did Sayra lose her mind on that journey with Rys? Either way, that night he swore to himself she'd not get away with that reckless nonsense. Sylven struggled to accept the compliments thrown his way for her majik after class, knowing it wasn't his but having no choice but to protect her confidentiality.

He was well aware she'd be killed by the Holy Family if it was discovered she wielded stolen majik.

For an hour, Sylven hunted Sayra down after class, tracing her general direction through their mental link until he gave up in frustration. After enduring the strange glances he received at his sporadic altering of directions and halting movements whenever Sayra would backtrack to a new route, Sylven lost his patience in a freezing garden. After a few loudly spoken choice words, he retreated to his room for the night with every bit the perseverance to try again the next day. Unfortunately, Sayra was assigned to the wall for patrolling and managed to escape him a further day.

By the end of the week, Sylven was restless, his frustration with her growing to a boiling point. If Sayra was going to flaunt her majik so openly, she'd eventually get herself caught. Then what? Rys nor his family would be capable of helping her then. Any resistance or concocted plan would prove fruitless, not to mention Sayra losing her life at best and becoming one of the Zefare's subjects to experiment on at worst.

What a drag.

Huffing, Sylven flung himself from his bed, rushing to put on his dark leather boots before he changed his mind. Clasping his cloak in front, he stormed from his room, down the hall, and into the dormitory beside his without a second thought. He blocked his mind from hers along the way, attempting to prevent her from guessing his intentions. When his fist banged against her door, when those empty jade eyes flashed beyond the crack that opened between them, Sylven pushed past her without asking for permission.

"We are going to have this talk, and we are having it now," he demanded, all his pent-up anger rising like a tidal wave.

A door closed behind him, Sayra still facing the entryway with a hand remaining on the knob. Sylven's words got tangled for a moment as he looked at her, with her blonde hair somewhat mussed from sleep, falling just short of the hips of her tawny cotton pajamas. It was as if she were another person, a strange disconnect his mind was befuddled over before his anger became remembered.

"You were completely irresponsible in class earlier this week," Sylven said, his voice a deep growl. "And you know it too, by your tedious effort to evade me all week. Nothing about that was acceptable. You jeopardized everything, Sayra. It isn't worth your life nor the aftermath of what would occur if they discovered everything."

Sayra said nothing. Did nothing.

"You know you've also placed Rys in the crosshairs, right? And what about me? I'm now complicit in everything." Sylven paced across her wooden floor. "It's childish to act like you have. It was training. *Training.*" Emphasis was heavily placed on the word as he drew it out.

Seconds ticked by. Sayra did not react, and her mind was blocked to his. It seemed she was getting rather good at it and quick. Making a sound of exasperation, Sylven shook his head.

"Have you nothing to say?"

Sayra's hand fell from the doorknob, and her face could not meet his as she retreated to her bed. Sylven watched in outrage as she tucked herself back in, ignoring him in the dark. A huff escaped his lips, but just as he was about to go off on a tangent, he stopped himself.

Sylven braced a hand against his face, breathing deep for a moment. "I'm simply concerned is all. I apologize for my rudeness. It's... it's..." He threw his hand in the air. "You saw what I did under the monastery. You know what could happen. I don't understand why you are taking unnecessary risks." He waited for a minute in silence. Deciding he should give up, Sylven began for the door before his ears caught a soft sound behind him.

"I'm sorry," Sayra whispered.

The words stole the remaining dredges of his anger.

Not once had she ever come close to apologizing, not for the endless tormenting and not for almost getting him killed that first day they encountered the Horde. It had him hesitating, unsure of how to proceed. Sylven believed her, believed those words. Not from anyone other than Waylen and Rys would he ever believe them, but here and now, from Sayra nonetheless, he realized he felt them true.

But why? There was something she wasn't sharing.

"That day, when you promised to share why you hesitated in front of the daemons with me, when the second one nearly killed me... I want to know why," Sylven insisted, his brow pinched as he turned to consider her.

Rather than answering his question, Sayra squeezed her eyes shut. She only said, "I've put off Kenji for some time. He told me about wanting to dine with us. I'll try to postpone whatever game he's playing as long as possible."

"Okay," Sylven said, uncertain.

Then, the awkwardness of their situation crashed down on him all at once. He shouldn't have intruded in her dormitory room, even if he was in a maddening state. Yes, Sayra intentionally avoided him every day, and yes, this was the only method he could think of to talk. But it was clear she still wasn't going to. Being an arsehole wouldn't change anything.

He was there when Sayra was confronted with the truth about the Holy Family and her mother afterward. Sylven knew and felt terrible about the burden she bore. He wished to do something to alleviate a fraction of that weight, but he didn't know what steps to take in such uncharted territory.

Women were terribly befuddling, *especially* Sayra.

"I came off horribly, and for that, I once again apologize. However, I need to know what's going on. I want to help. Let me do so." His voice was earnest, but it didn't seem to work.

She didn't so much as move a muscle.

He racked his mind for ideas on what to say next and what experience he had in such matters of conflict. Truly, he didn't know anyone better at handling such things than Rys. What would Rys do?

Rys gave people space when needed, allowing them to think matters through and come to him when ready. He never abandoned Sylven during hard times, always being a reliable presence and not prodding the matter.

Sylven could do that for Sayra.

"I'll be around if you want to discuss it," he said, hoping Sayra would still talk.

She didn't.

Sensing that was the end of the conversation, Sylven carefully shut the door behind him with a heavy heart and returned to his own room. The coming days bore similar results, Sayra eerily silent and distant during their shared lectures. It grated on his nerves for weeks, especially when her eyes became bagged and her personality a shadow of its former self. Several times, he attempted their usual disdainful banter but to no avail. Not a single punch he threw was returned.

How did Emrys manage to keep from digging into matters for so long? How had he put up with Sylven in such a way for *years*?

It became a prominent concern for Sylven, each week passing in a melancholy way. He threw himself into his studies, occasionally pairing with Waylen to work through their ethics and morality papers. His majik classes thrillingly challenged him, and his mind worked through new methods of majikal delivery and applications. The days were... normal. Except for the lack of Rys's friendship. The prince became an illusion, only showing up during his classes and then disappearing to Goddess knew where. Not that Sylven put much effort into finding him. That last fight had left a bad taste in his mouth.

Ever since Sayra had entered their lives, there had been an imbalance between the three of them. Even Waylen questioned what happened between him and Rys, noting there was some disconnect between Sylven and his Valkyrie as well. Sylven had to shut down the matter, honoring his promise not to discuss Sayra and the situation developing from it. Though it was difficult to justify skipping the small celebration of drinks

Waylen purchased for a night of fun for Rys's twentieth birthday. He had to fake sickness to convince his friend.

Rys harbored feelings for Sayra, a sentiment that disturbed Sylven for one reason or another. The thing was, Sylven could feel the resonating feelings she held for Rys that day in class before she degraded into the current version of herself. Embarrassment, longing, frustration, and resentment all turned into a firm resolution in her mind at the end. Now, she refused to speak with him, ghosting the halls with her presence only when necessary for Sylven's lectures and avidly avoiding any mention or interaction with Rys.

What was Sylven to make of that?

He couldn't decipher his own opinions of the situation, so he chose to bury his nose in books instead. But after a month, Sylven couldn't allow the bystander's guilt to plague him any longer. After their combat class, he managed to snag Nessika's attention, pulling her to an alcove in the monastery hallways where no other students lingered.

"Well, get on with it," she said, her hand circling in a hurrying motion.

A statue of an angel seemed to judge them both as Sylven gathered his resolve. "Is—" He breathed hard out of his nose, cutting his words off and running a hand through his messy walnut-brown locks.

Nessika raised a manicured brow for him to get it out.

"Sayra. Is she okay?" He chewed the words out, reluctant to verbalize them and mortified he did to another, even more so when his face reddened across his cheekbones.

To him, Nessika Onai was intimidating. With her dark skin, high cheekbones, and silky but straight shoulder-length hair offset by the light blue of her eyes, she appeared out of place with her position as a Valkyrie.

Her mouth curved downward. "No. And before you ask, her business is her own."

Scoffing, Sylven lowered his brows. "Am I not supposed to care then?"

Cocking a hip, Nessika folded her arms. "Now, I didn't say that. Only that she'll share if and when she's ready."

"What am I supposed to do then?" He sighed, defeat etching into his face.

The Valkyrie appeared to take pity on him, her brows softening an inch. "I ask myself the same question. For now, just being there is all we can do."

Sylven grumbled, "I don't understand any of this."

"What's holding you back from asking?" She nodded once at a Valkyrie who waved at her in the distance.

"I did. Directly. She didn't respond."

Nessika gave him a side-eye, managing to look down her nose at him even though she was inches shorter than he was. A feat Sayra had similarly accomplished many a time with her even shorter stature. "Try again." When he pressed his lips together, she added, "Also, maybe fix things with Emrys while you're at it. I don't care whose fault it was. I just don't like being iced out more than normal."

Sylven scoffed. "That's of his own making. You know as well as I that he has his own agenda. For once, I don't agree with him."

"Is there something I don't know about?" Nessika's brows bunched.

Chatter in the hallway grew loud as a dozen Arcanists a year behind Sylven left a classroom, their navy cloaks clogging up the hallway.

While Sylven knew better, he truly did, he was sick of secrets. "Rys has affections for Sayra. In a way he shouldn't." Sylven got the words out, but they took a toll as he uttered them. He became intolerably sad and lonely all at once. So much so he missed the marked tension that pulled back Nessika's shoulder blades.

"Does she like him back?"

The question stung, Sylven hating himself for his mistake in spilling something clearly sensitive to Rys but even more than that, how he felt on the matter. "Not in the way Rys does." It was honest at least. Yes, he sensed Sayra harbored some sort of attachment to him, but he knew Rys had fallen much harder.

"I see," Nessika said at last. "And that bothers you. In what way do you like her?"

"I don't." He denied it hastily, the words spitting out of his mouth instinctually.

Nessika's eyes narrowed further on his, a stern look crossing over her pristine features.

"Seriously. She's the bane of my existence! I didn't even want to contract with her to begin with. We couldn't be more opposite. Now I only want to work together," he affirmed.

Nessika held a hand up to stop his ramblings and firmly pushed a finger into his navy overcoat, just next to the cross stitched into his uniform. "Let's get something straight." Her face moved uncomfortably close, Sylven flustered and peeved simultaneously from her questioning and reaction. "You cannot have feelings for her. Sayra will *never* be romantically interested in you or Emrys for that matter. She is a Valkyrie first and foremost, and I will not see her being used and tossed aside by an *Arcanist.*"

The last word sounded synonymous with trash.

Sylven swiped the finger away. "I would never do something so disgraceful. If you knew even a fraction of my character, you'd never question my honor in such a manner." He seethed, squaring his shoulders at the responding look of violence on the Valkyrie's face. "Go deal with your own insecurities elsewhere."

Turning his back on her, Sylven joined the remainder of his straggling class and walked to the central grounds. He was halfway back to his dormitory before realizing he never denied his growing sentiments.

CHAPTER FOUR

EMRYS

Emrys had never held such conflicting ideals in his life. Every day, he warred with himself, the situation deviating onto an inconceivable path. He never intended to act on his affections for Sayra. He couldn't become an obstacle for her, a distraction that could prevent her from carrying out her duty. A selfish part of him wanted to rebel against that instinct to withhold, to damn the consequences and kiss her again, and to fully give in to that incessant need to feel that connection between them once more.

But Emrys couldn't. He wouldn't.

And it was hell.

Every day passed painfully slowly, the evenings lacking without the studies he'd had with Sayra. They hadn't been distracting in the least; rather, he'd found himself becoming... happy. He wanted those eves to drag on, for him to be in her presence as much as possible. It was as if Sayra being near simply lifted the burdens weighing him down, his mouth betraying him with frequent smiles.

Now, Emrys fought to enforce a distance between them to ensure he didn't deepen the icy crack threatening the path laid before him. During the nights, however, sleep became difficult. His mind wandered to the next threat the unknown faction would pose and whether she'd be prepared and to the images of her during their shared lectures and the haunted hollowness that began to cave under her cheekbones.

After the dormitory fire, Emrys visited the sole lead he'd tracked using his personal network of intelligence: Tanner. However, that became a dead end when Emrys learned the Arcanist had disappeared back to the southern Rendevar Coalition before he could follow up on his threat. He was back to nothing. No answers. No leads on who might have tried to kill Sayra and how they knew about her majik.

It was infuriating.

Emrys tried to talk with Sayra after she used majik in their combat class, but Sayra managed to squirrel away. In fact, it was a feat replicated throughout the entirety of that week and the next, each scenario only further ingraining into him Sayra had no interest in conversing with him any further. He wouldn't pursue her any longer to have that conversation, so he chose to receive updates through Nessika. From her, he learned Sylven had talked with Sayra, which reassured him they were amicably talking to some degree. The only bit that had Emrys refraining from further interfering was the knowledge she continued to practice her majik, occasionally with Nessika when the Valkyrie would check in on her friend.

And so, Emrys continued plotting in the shadows, making an effort to expand his network. Slowly but surely, he felt Nikolay Barcov from Zendiya would be a formidable ally in the coming year and went to great lengths to forge an acquaintanceship with him. It would take much time since they were the most reclusive sort of people he'd ever met, but he felt it was a good lead to pursue. Otherwise, he was reaching out to his network of contacts to investigate the whereabouts of Tanner and the impending threat of Thapula. The country across the ocean heard whispers of their majik and would eventually seek to control it if Emrys suspected correctly.

Late at night, he'd disappear to happen across his family's insider agent in the Holy Family's distant circle of associates, writing home often on crisp notepapers in his typical broad-stroked cursive what he gleaned from those interactions and those with Sayra. All in a coded message, of course, protected by destructive majik—a particular spell passed down from his father that served them well over the years.

Emrys tapped the tip of his pen against his leather-bound notebook. Finally, he stood up from his classroom desk and left with the crowd.

As his steps took him toward his room that afternoon, his mind reflected on his brother's inability to contribute. Vander had recently taken up a strange new interest in paintings, going as far as hiring collections to be brought to him and surveyed before purchasing a select handful. Emrys had it on good authority Vander was remarkably impressed by a stunning depiction of the cliffside lake below the monastery, a work commissioned by Aurther Malbeck a few decades before the legendary artist perished fifty years ago.

Otherwise, his brother had been abnormally commonplace with his activities, studying for his final exams that semester before he graduated from the Arcanist Academy and began his duties for real in Acacea as the crowned prince. Any other person would lay aside their concerns at the unusual pattern of behavior, but he'd long since known better.

When Emrys found Vander casually sprawled against his door, a blushing woman from the monastery's staff enraptured by the smooth words of the prince in arm, Emrys's internal warning bells chimed, and his haunches instinctively rose.

"Vander." Emrys greeted him. Their relationship was strained from the lack of interest Vander employed in their plans.

With a quiet dismissal accented with a playboy's charm, the young woman reluctantly turned to leave, Vander's dark eyes trailing her as she did. "Hello, little brother."

His tone was mild, slightly tainted with the condescension the eldest sibling had for the younger, which spoke of Vander's unimpressed perception of Emrys. Rather than responding, Emrys studied the crowned prince. Even after Sayra was attacked and Vander learned of her mother's arrival, the most he did to lend a hand was to send his Valkyrie, Breane, to check on Sayra during sparring sessions.

Emrys shut his door behind Vander, spelling his room for privacy before they spoke.

With a disarming quirk of his lips, Vander turned to raise a brow. "I've learned you've distanced yourself in the last month from our charming Sayra after your trounce into Tern."

It wasn't a surprise Vander similarly kept a close eye on him. After all, they had very opposing views on their parents' agenda. Vander believed they were far too uptight and should take their time to harness the advantage they were gifted with Sayra's position. He went as far as to plan what they would do after the Holy Family was toppled. Vander wanted to bask in the glory of having the first female Arcanist within Acacea to elevate his status among the countries and that of their kingdom.

But they needed to focus on the problem at hand: the Holy Family. Not what came afterward.

Emrys dropped his bookbag on his mahogany desk and sat in his ebony chair. "Have you learned anything of Tanner?" He tried to focus the conversation.

Vander pulled a brass chronometer from his navy trousers, flicking the elegantly carved lid open to tell the time. "I am merely observing that you two were quite close. I do surely hope she isn't neglecting her duties."

Emrys stiffened at that, unable to suppress the reaction in time.

Vander's dark eyes gleamed in the corners, and his styled black hair shifted as his hand tossed the contraption into the air, deftly catching and pocketing it in one succinct motion. "Not to say that I believe her lacking. To that degree, we both can agree."

The joints connecting his jaw ached from the force Emrys clenched his teeth with. Rather than reacting further, he untied his black boots.

"I've been considering stopping by to visit, given your lack thereof," Vander mused, testing Emrys's neat shelves for dust. "I must confirm, after all, her newfound developments. From what I've heard of your Tern trip, she must be quite capable." Finding it spotless, Vander's face crinkled.

Emrys placed his boots beside his desk, on top of his burgundy high-pile carpet. He wanted to loosen a sigh but refrained. Vander was trying to include himself in their plans at least. It was a start, though a rather annoying one at that.

"You know what? I believe I'll do so this week," Vander said, his words decisive. "I rather enjoyed our last interaction, after all. Perhaps I can be of use." He added that last part with a suggestive smirk, flattening his flawless cashmere frock coat before stepping into the hall, his final words striking Emrys as he passed.

It took every ounce of lifelong constructed self-control Emrys could muster to not charge his brother and strike him in his smug face. He wasn't concerned with Sayra falling for Vander's false charms, but the thought of another man making any move on her set his blood boiling. A near minute passed before Emrys realized the death grip he had on his armrests. He flexed his hands, muttering, "*Abiit.*" The privacy spell dissolved in his room.

Emrys was a man of principles. He held his beliefs tighter than most people's convictions. Even now, at one of his lowest points, he wouldn't break his oath to continue doing what he could to find the people looking to harm her. If Sayra wanted to speak with him before their rendezvous with his parents in a couple of months, then she'd do so when she was ready.

After all, he'd already given her all the tools she needed to succeed on her own. It was her turn to move the next piece on their chessboard.

Chapter Five

SAYRA

A master of evasive techniques, Sayra successfully managed to derail Kenji for a total of four weeks before propriety damned any additional plausible excuses. Her personal favorite was Sylven being confined to the porcelain throne, his bowels unfortunately not permitting him any relief for that particular weekend. Though with two months remaining in their semester, Sayra knew she couldn't put it off any longer.

Tonight was her last night to enjoy a Kenji-less evening before their dinner tomorrow. Unfortunately, it was also a night Lynn and Nes insisted on hanging out. So, Sayra pulled some loose strands from her braid to border her slim jawline, donning a nicer pair of Valkyrie-tailored black trousers and a caramel-brown loosely fitted long sleeve under her cloak. A matching brown slør was woven into her braid.

She made to leave her room but hesitated beside her desk. On top, a worn leather journal lay untouched. Her mother's journal. A hand reached out as if to touch it, pulling back on second thought.

Sayra hadn't mustered the courage to open it. Not yet. It seemed she couldn't muster much these days, not even when Sylven had become abnormally kind to her. Everyone was stepping on stones around her, though Lynn was in her own world with her boyfriend, and Kimimari was always a silent presence. Sayra warred with her feelings for Emrys and her oath to Nes to remain faithful to their chosen paths.

A path she'd strayed from.

Then there was her mother's betrayal and the upcoming meeting with the king and queen of Acacea for Sayra to worry over. Somehow, she managed to stay afloat with everything constantly pressing her down. She practiced her majik spells and trained with Breane to hone her fighting skills.

But the nights were restless. Vivid nightmares of tortured Valkyries and daemonic faces woke her often. Then, there was a dark, beckoning lure in the back of her mind, whispering words that made her skin crawl. Her use of *nefas* majik left a mark on her soul, and Sayra could feel it wriggling about when her mood grew somber or fearful.

If only her brother saw the mess she had become. Was it worth trading his life for?

Slowly, her feet padded down the floor to Lynn's room, her mind circling the fact she was dreading the entire evening with every fiber of her being. When she knocked on the door, Sayra mustered a fake half-smile while Lynn squealed within, shushing the others inside.

The door threw itself open, Lynn simultaneously chorusing "Happy Birthday!" with four others sitting around a rectangular maple table draped with a floral tablecloth for the evening's festivities. The walls were decorated with dried floral arrangements, Lynn's hobby on full display above her dresser, around her bed, and beside her window. A rose candle flickered on her desk, the scent pairing with the coloring of her oval carpet. Her daffodil wrist-length gown swayed around her as she ushered Sayra in.

The layout of the table was very reminiscent of Faendan traditions, towering with home-cooked specialties made from the cookbooks of her people. Beautiful lacework placemats were under every dish, the stitching Lynn's signature floral taste with Sayra's initials inscribed into the bottom right corner. A feat that must have taken Lynn months to prepare amidst their other duties and her boyfriend.

Speaking of which, Casber was widely grinning beside Lynn's empty chair, wearing a tidy set of amber trousers and a formal ivory frock coat with accenting colors. Sayra wondered if Lynn selected the variety for him, as he was becoming far more colorful every time she crossed paths with the Arcanist. What astounded her most in the room, however, was the uncomfortably postured guy across from him.

Sylven half-heartedly raised his hand in greeting, his other one holding up his chin over the table as if the situation were boring him to sleep. His typical sour expression and the surprise factor of being coerced somehow into the dinner—which certainly was a horror for the brooding man—tweaked a corner of her mouth, but only just.

Kimimari, seated beside him in head-to-toe black training leathers, rose and gripped her in a stiff bear hug, towering over Sayra. Her narrow face was unusually energized when she pulled back, her upturned eyes bright. "You're nearly as old as me," she teased, lightly punching her shoulder. The ends of her flame tattoo sleeves edged from the collar of her shirt as she took her seat once more.

"Now only Lynn is left as the youngling," Nes hummed, tapping a white-tipped nail against her chin beside Lynn's empty chair.

"Only three months by," Lynn protested, her earthy and innocent eyes widening.

To which, Nes corrected, "Only by three months." She received a stuck-out tongue in response.

Casber laughed, shaking his head. "You have to face it, Lynn. You're the youngest."

Sitting between Kimimari and Sylven—who, frankly, she was still shocked to see and couldn't imagine the bribe that got him to suffer through it—Sayra plucked a handful of bread rolls, each stuffed with a combination of vegetables, meats, and cheeses commonplace to her native country. Lynn eagerly passed glasses of honied wine, a delicacy she must have sent for months ago to have reached them there.

"I am excited to see you use the laceworks the next time you host, Sayra." Lynn beamed, collecting the fine pieces and wrapping a silver silk ribbon around them.

Beside her, Sylven dabbed his mouth with a linen napkin, giving her a longways glance as if he couldn't imagine Sayra doing such things.

Sayra sipped her glass of wine, savoring the sweet notes of honey and berries as it rolled through her mouth. A smile began to peek at the corners. "Thank you, Lynn, for this. It's absolutely beautiful work. You put anything I could make to shame."

Which was true. Sayra was never good with such work, despite her tutors spending hours drilling the process into her mind. It was customary for a lacework piece to be given on female birthdays, a collection to add to over the years to decorate their tables for dinners of importance. It was an honor for Lynn to work so tediously on it, and it lifted some of the glum that had been glued to Sayra.

"It's the least I may do." Lynn squeezed Casber's hand when he looked at her dotingly.

The sight twisted Sayra's stomach. It reminded her of a certain someone, a man cloaked in black with eyes she could never stare at long enough. But was it all a sham? Did she truly feel for Emrys, or was it the relic's influence pulling them together? Their majik blended in ways that were unheard of, and she wouldn't put it past the relic invading their very thoughts.

As they finished eating the delicious meal, Sayra noticed a brilliant new piece of art gracing her friend's wall—a landscape oil painting of the cliffside lake below the monastery, with vibrant coloring and masterful detailing.

Nes helped Kimimari clear the table as Lynn replaced the dishware with fresh trays of finger delicacies.

"Those look most delicious," Sylven said with a polite air. He gestured to the pink jelly candies. "What are those?"

"Faendan rose delight," Lynn answered, immediately grabbing a pair of tongs and loading five pieces onto a delicate porcelain saucer. "Try!"

The Arcanist did, initially perplexed by the texture as he lifted a pink powdered piece to his mouth. As he chewed, his hazel eyes widened. "This is delicious."

Sayra snuck several for herself, lavishing in the subtle rose taste and the combination of the powdered sugar on the jelly. She pointed at the oil painting above the maple dresser. "Where did you find that painting, Lynn? It's stunning."

Lynn gushed, "A friend for Casber gifting it to us! He knew we both love beautiful scenes. He shared the location at a nearby lake where the painting was brought to life. We would like to visit one day." She accidentally got a swipe of powdered sugar on her short auburn braid and the lilac ribbon running through her hair.

Sylven stared at the painting appraisingly, swirling the wine in his glass with a practiced motion.

Sharing a smile with his girlfriend, Casber said, "It was most generous of him. Speaking of..." He paused, pulling out a decorated floral bag from under the table. "Happy birthday from Lynn and I both."

Sayra accepted the gift with a small smile. "You really shouldn't have gotten me more. A lot of effort was put into this gathering. It's too much."

She wished more than anything they had forgotten her birthday; the idea of gifts always made her uncomfortable. Lynn knew that, of course, but always insisted. After multiple gestures and assurances, Sayra relented and opened the bag to find three beautifully woven slørs, a burgundy, seafoam, and mint-hued set. She barely had time to express her gratitude before Kimimari and Nes each placed a wrapped box beside her nearly emptied dessert saucer.

"You'll get good use out of mine," Kimimari promised, her black eyes eager for Sayra to open her present.

Nes polished off her third glass of wine, leaning back into her chair with a strange expression. Her eyes were glued to Sylven's uncomfortable face.

Opening the box, Sayra's mouth parted at the gorgeous work of metal within. A double-sided seven-inch blade rested in black velvet, engrained with the runic old language of her people along the center. Only a handful of the latest generation of Faendans bothered to learn the near-extinct and impractical language, but Sayra read it clear as day.

Strength.

The quality was unparalleled, and the hilt was a work of art in its own right.

Nes pushed forward her gift. It contained a sturdy knife sheath Sayra could attach to her armor at the waist. The two pieces from Nes and Kimimari were a set from the same smith, matching perfectly and crafted with an expert eye.

"It'll pair well with your *spyd*," Nes said, grinning a wicked thing as she tore her eyes from Sylven at last. "Between your personal weapon and that dagger, you'll be an absolute menace."

"Thank you both." Sayra tried for a sincere smile, feeling far too inferior for a knife labeled "strength." Everyone seemed pleased, Kimimari even clapping hands with Nes across the table as Sayra carefully placed the collection of gifts on Lynn's dresser to make room on the dinner table.

Lynn gestured to Sylven, who silently placed a moderately sized paper-clad box beside Sayra. The entire exchange was halting, from the moment he set it down to Sayra opening the gift. It felt out of place. Just months prior, Sylven wanted nothing to do with her, but there he was giving her a birthday gift. He'd been trying for weeks to be kinder, even going so far as sharing stinted compliments in their two shared classes.

She opened the present with slight hesitation. But the moment her eyes pulled out the contraption, Sayra couldn't help but marvel at the beauty within. An ivory-and-gold-inlaid music box was nestled into a cashmere plush box, vines of gold weaving to hold the interchangeable discs in place while spinning. On the side were several cases, each piece of music performed by renowned Faendan artists.

"Nessika mentioned at my family's house how you had an attachment to music and something with your training with dance and whatnot. And, well, I figured this might be something you'd care for," Sylven rambled, folding his arms across his chest and staring at anything but her.

Sayra didn't notice, her eyes drinking in each minute detail of the impeccable design, from the ivory-carved legs to the minuscule leaves occasionally sprouting through the vines. It was simply breathtaking.

"Thank you," Sayra expressed. The thought Sylven put into the gift genuinely moved her. She never would have thought him capable of something so kind, and the gesture made her question her previous perception of him. "I'm surprised you remembered."

Relief broke out on Sylven's face. Nodding once, his eyes brightened, his back straightened, and his mouth opened to speak, but Nes broke in. "That's something your brother would have loved."

All the breath left Sayra's lungs, her heart constricting in a painful ball in her chest. Lynn gasped across the table, and Kimimari glowered at Nes's offhanded comment. Bemused, Casber glanced around at the metaphorical elephant in the room. Sylven frowned at the dramatic shift that had Sayra reeling as she stood from her chair.

"I appreciate you all for putting together this evening," Sayra murmured, a scrape of her chair sounding as it backed onto the wooden floor. She stood quickly, making for the door before the grief and self-loathing became too much.

A hand grasped her forearm, pulling Sayra's attention to Nes's stricken face. "Sayra, I'm sorry. I shouldn't have said that, no matter the reason. I swear, I didn't mean to hurt you. Not intentionally. I just..." She trailed off, her mouth gaping as she struggled to verbalize the words.

Sayra slipped her arm away and turned her face. "It's fine. I'm really exhausted from today is all. Thank you all again." Her words lacked emotion, but it boiled through her and threatened to overtake her if she didn't leave *immediately*.

So without another word, Sayra did exactly that.

CHAPTER SIX

SYLVEN

Sylven knew exactly what Nessika had done, what her intention was, even if he hadn't a clue about the meaning behind that particular method. The Valkyrie was sabotaging his efforts to try to be a decent person to Sayra. After all, he had much to make up for. When the door closed behind her, the room exploded.

"What the hell, Nes?" Kimimari snapped in her quiet manner, her stark brows pinched in anger.

Lynn appeared devastated, Casber clasping her hand under the table. "Why?" Those doe eyes were pinned on Nessika.

"I was trying to do something nice," Sylven complained to Nes, his eyes unflinching at the steel that eyed him back. "After everything she's gone through, I only took your advice to keep trying."

"You know, I can't believe you," Nessika snapped at him, those icy eyes piercing before they trained on Kimimari's glower. "I apologized!"

The muscular Valkyrie leaned forward, fiery with anger. "You know this day is already difficult enough. What you did was messed up."

"What meaning do you have, Nes? What do you not believe?" Lynn asked, her voice mouselike in comparison to the others.

Nessika paled, glancing between Lynn and Casber before turning her icy glare to Sylven. He knew what she was requesting of him. It was painfully obvious then, knowing more context. Nessika disapproved of Valkyrie-Arcanist relationships. That was easy enough to deduce from their encounter the other day. Considering Lynn's relationship with Casber, there would be fallout if Sylven revealed the true cause in front of the entire room. Usually, he wouldn't care less about any of these people, but they were Sayra's friends. He felt a sense of responsibility on her behalf to maintain some kind of peace.

Sylven despised having to do the right thing at times. It was annoying and went against the grain for him to lend a branch to Nessika after what she accused him of. He said flatly, "I have a bit of a history of verbally sparring with Sayra, so Nessika here thought I brought Sayra's hopes up only to dash them once more." His eyes never left her relieved ones for a second. "I can assure you, this is quite real, and I intend to be a better *friend* to her."

"I shouldn't have tried to take away from that," Nessika admitted, facing Lynn now. "I was skeptical and shouldn't have brought Sayra in the middle of it."

Kimimari clucked her tongue. "You'll need forgiveness from her, not us."

Abashedly, Nessika lowered her chin in agreement.

"What happened to her brother?" Sylven asked, glancing between Lynn and Kimimari to see who'd answer him.

Lynn's face fell, Casber wrapping a comforting arm around her shoulders.

Kimimari was the one to speak freely. "He fell to the Horde eight years ago today protecting Sayra. She went beyond her home's wards in the early evening, running into a daemon before her elder brother and his friend, Lynn's brother, found her. It was divergent, hunting her down and preventing her from returning past the wards to safety. Her brother risked everything to save her. He and Lynn's brother fell in the process, giving Sayra the seconds she needed to get back inside the wards."

Sylven's arms fell slack at his sides, and Lynn closed her eyes across the table with a pained expression.

"It was brutal, and the daemon she encountered used tactics to elicit the most fear possible. Sayra nearly died, and if it weren't for the daemon taking its time carving her face, she'd not be here," Kimimari concluded.

The barely perceptible scar across her face...

Addressing Lynn, Sylven said, "I apologize for bringing up such a terrible moment. I didn't realize..." His face contorted into sorrow and sympathy.

Squeezing Casber's arm, Lynn loosened her pent-up breath. "Please, it is not concerning me. I accepted the loss long time ago." Her brows drew up with worry. "I only wish Sayra the same."

It smacked him in the face. That was what made Sayra freeze that night long ago with the Horde. When the second daemon appeared, she must have been reliving that night all over again. The realization hung heavy in his thoughts as he came to understand much of his Valkyrie's discrepancies and her unusual adherence to the ideal of her duty.

Since her return from Tern with Rys, Sayra hadn't been herself. After messing up with Sylven and nearly losing to the Horde with Rys, she probably internalized it all and blamed herself. She felt responsible for them. Much like what happened to her and Lynn's brother. Sayra carried that weight as well. There was only so much any one person could carry before they crumbled, and that made him feel some sort of way.

In summary, he felt like shit.

"Don't take it personally. Sayra isn't one for sharing," Kimimari added, lounging an arm beside her half-full dessert saucer. "In fact, I'd say it's a damn good thing for you to make the effort of showing up at all."

When Lynn had Casber hunt around the halls of his dormitory with her, Sylven almost chose to ignore them. But when it became apparent they'd knock down every door in an attempt to find him, Sylven saved himself the embarrassment and waved them down. They were only halfway down the hall, some bleary-eyed Arcanist a few doors down giving him the stink eye, with the two pestering him for Sylven's whereabouts.

When they asked him to join them for her surprise birthday dinner, he almost gave a blatant no since he didn't want to prove Nessika's argument right. But he grudgingly accepted the invitation, knowing it would mean something to Sayra and... to him. All of that ran through his mind when Kimimari shared the praise, Sylven undeserving of it.

His eyes found the music box, recalling the way hers had lit up with wonder at the contraption. It had given him hope, that look. Sylven would keep trying to bring it back, even if it meant enduring Kenji's dinner on his best behavior and ten more gatherings with her friends.

Sayra, and all they needed to work toward, was worth it.

CHAPTER SEVEN

SAYRA

Preparing herself for a night of verbal gameplay was right in Sayra's forte. For one reason or another, she frequently sharpened that knife whenever Vander would cross paths with her. There was something unsettling about him, that arrogance that hinted at downright gluttony aimed at all his pursuits. He seemed to seek her out purposefully, though he explained he had taken a newfound interest in his family's aspirations and wanted to keep in the loop. Sayra kept their meetings short, lacking any real depth of conversation. It wasn't a challenge, especially since she didn't have the energy or patience to converse for long.

What was not in her forte was her opponent being Kenji. They'd had several years of courtship growing up, Sayra more than familiar with his tactics and, rather unfortunately, he with hers. The only tried and proven method that managed to secure her victory in each instance was to completely overwhelm him with persuading charm, the kind Sayra absolutely and unequivocally detested.

Wisping on a thin layer of mascara, Sayra eyed her appearance for the first time. Only a small portion of her wardrobe was dedicated to the finer dress her station had once demanded. Tonight, she slipped on a dazzling emerald gown with crepe material tightly formed along her arms, loosening to elegant waves below her cinched waist. Accenting pearls lined the deep V down her back, cascading down her sleeves and in elegant lines down the sides of her torso. Simple black heels adorned her feet, a sliver-thin silver necklace spanning her neck with occasional pearls dotted around, appearing almost as if they floated on her skin.

Rather than a simple braid, Sayra swooped her hair into a thick and elegant braided bun at the base of her skull, manipulating the ivory *slør* to pin around the inner circumference. Emerald teardrops hung from her ears, curls of wheat hair trimming her bronzed and blushed face. The scar beneath her eyes was invisible, but she could imagine it beneath the façade.

Her birthday gifts were mostly gathered beside her mother's journal on her desk, the sight making her frown as she left her bathroom. The music box rested on her nightstand, a gorgeous work of art. Lynn had dropped them off last night. Sayra hadn't touched them since, not even the small box someone had left beside her door yesterday. Though she did bring that inside, resting it beside the untouched journal.

Sayra swirled on her finest cashmere cloak, buttoning it down to her hips where the fabric parted to expose a glimmer of her dress. She made for the formal dining hall. As she was crossing the corridor linking their buildings, Emrys emerged from the Arcanist dormitory, his eyes doing a double take at her appearance.

"Good evening, Sayra." He nodded. His eyes were transfixed by her outfit, although he was hesitant to take another step in her direction.

The admiring glint warmed her face. There was an unspoken tension between them from weeks of avoidance, and she'd be lying if she said she didn't miss their evening majik practices. Sayra dipped her chin. "Good evening, Emrys." Her tone was steady, but words were threatening to bubble to the surface. There was much she wanted to say to clear the air between them and erase the awkwardness that had been there too long.

Emrys straightened, his eyes conflicted when meeting hers. He appeared to choose his proceeding words carefully, as if navigating a floor laden with shards of glass. "The timing is fortunate. I must speak with you for a moment if you can spare it."

"Of course." She was unable to tear her eyes from his as he held the dormitory door open. Nervous butterflies fluttered in her stomach.

Two Arcanists studied their textbooks in the lavish common room, relaxing on beige couches beside a warm hearth as they quietly discussed a classroom topic. Zefare banners hung along the cobblestone walls, draped in elegant fabrics and designs. Mosaic windows glowed next to the fireplace, a plush navy carpet beneath it all.

Sayra followed Emrys to his room, nodding her thanks as he opened the door for her. She briefly took in the familiar ebony and mahogany desk and table, his shelves and cabinets as immaculate as ever. Even the downy comforter on his bed was folded to an exact line and his pillows precisely placed.

As the door clicked shut, Sayra heard Emrys whisper his privacy spell—a ward that would destroy any vibrations that created noise as it reached the bubble. None outside would hear him as he said, "My mother wishes to meet you next weekend in Tern." He adjusted his academy uniform, a fitted overcoat of navy lined with gold buttons down the middle, both the collar and cuffs braided gold.

Sayra leaned a hand against his desk, her mind whirling with the implications.

"We'll have a full entourage. It will be an official visit." Meaning they would not be alone to face any of the Horde like last time, nor would they have to worry about any of the Holy Family being suspicious. "Since plans have taken a rather drastic turn, they think it fit to discuss matters in person with you. I happen to agree," Emrys said.

Her mouth pressed into a line. Arene and Emrys's mother, Evangelina Navarre, were some sort of friends. That much was evident. There was history between their families when they aligned to bring down the Zefare line, and Sayra *did* have questions. Namely, how had they faked her mother's death? And if her mother betrayed the Holy Family, then why had they not shown any indication to or mistrust of Sayra? If anything, they came across as indifferent.

There had to be more behind the scenes than Arene had shared in that short meeting, and while Sayra wasn't willing to speak with her mother, she was prepared to talk with the queen of Acacea.

"Okay," she agreed in a quiet voice.

Emrys casually pocketed his hands in his black trousers, the cut of his uniform hugging his muscled form in a way that caught her gaze. That incessant thread between them pleaded for Sayra to step closer, but her stubbornness somewhat held her in check.

It did not seem Emrys could withstand it, however. Twice he stepped closer, and only when they were two feet apart did his control snap back into place. His eyes were guarded, but there was a tenseness between them that spoke more than they could allow.

They both wanted more. Wanted to give in to that desire to explore what grew between them. For Sayra, she wasn't certain if the relic within them was the source of that unnatural affinity or if it truly was something more destined than majik's influence. She couldn't betray the promise she made to Nes so easily, nor her brother. Sayra had to remain faithful to her duty as a Valkyrie and preserve the legacy of her own fate. Even if it wasn't one she chose for herself, she wasn't selfish enough to sacrifice all that others had built for her own shot at happiness.

There wasn't time to deviate from her path, not when it could cost so much more than the world could bear. They had to focus on their common objective.

For Emrys, Sayra wondered if that same resolve held him back.

He had once said, *Though I don't regret what happened between us.* He didn't regret it... but did that mean he thought their connection was solely based on the relic's influence?

No, that couldn't be right. He acknowledged something more than what she tried to force herself to believe. No matter how strongly Sayra wanted to make it a reality, there had to be something more than the artifact's power.

"How are you?" Concern broke through his maintained demeanor, but something else curled in the back of his onyx eyes.

Her chin tilted up at him, and her eyes blinked rapidly. She realized she had been staring longer than proper. "My majik is coming along well. Some spells better than others."

Emrys leaned forward. "That's not what I worried over."

He was bothered then. That did something to Sayra's emotions, and she struggled to block them from the mental bond with Sylven. The less he knew the better regarding their conversation.

There was too much to say, but there was too little she could without threatening that boundary between them. So, she bolstered her best smile and smoothed out her cloak in a nervous way. "Everyone has been beyond supportive. I'm well enough. I'm running late to a dinner that Kenji has forced my hand to accept." She moved toward the door. "I can't be much later."

A warm hand grabbed her upper arm. Catching her breath, she pulled her eyes to Emrys's narrowed ones.

"What is it he wants?" His voice went low, and his nostrils flared.

Inhaling deeply, Sayra shook her head. "I don't know. I'd wager that will be forthcoming this evening." Her frown twisted her face. "Even with my political allegiance formally being with the Holy Family and their Holy Kingdom of Eveline, Kenji still holds power over my family. I'll not risk offending him on their behalf. When the day comes that the Zefare line is taken down, and I'm no longer a Valkyrie, my allegiance will yield back to Droden."

Emrys lowered his hand, his expression displeased. "Be careful with him. I haven't yet discovered anything further on the culprit of the dormitory fire. We can't discount *anyone* yet."

Shadows passed through Sayra's sight. "No. No, we can't," she murmured. "But I can't leave Sylven to fend off the sharks by himself for long. Kenji and his sister will eat him alive."

For a moment, it seemed neither of them had any other words to share. The distance between them seemed so great, yet too close at the same time. Sayra wanted to walk away. Wanted to close that gap. Her majik tingled, calling out for his. She could feel that yearning reach, the push hers made toward him and the pull of his own.

She stepped closer.

Then paused.

She saw how his eyes brightened with hope and a longing similar to hers. He didn't recoil or create more distance between them. It was then she realized just what he wanted, and it was for her to choose. Choose him or honor her oath. He had made his stance clear.

Her heart swelled at his integrity but ached at the same time at the truth of it all. She wanted to forgo the consequences. What could it hurt but her own honor?

"I must be off," she said.

When he didn't immediately respond, Sayra opened his door and began striding down the hall. After a few steps, she heard him speak once more.

"The armor suits you better," Emrys called out, just loud enough to reach her ears over the distant chatter of approaching Arcanists.

Sayra cracked a smile in his direction as he turned the corner of his entryway, the gesture involuntary. He knew of her distaste for *proper* women's attire and all that societal stigma that clung to it.

"Thank you, Emrys."

But why did it have to *hurt*?

Chapter Eight

SAYRA

It took over a dozen minutes to reach the formal hall tucked away close to the cathedral, past several gawking Arcanists and curious Valkyries. Right then, Sayra resembled a court lady rather than one of them, a most unfortunate comparison. While most women in the Holy Family sported such attire, and visitors to the monastery grounds to a lesser degree, the nuns and staff were simply dressed. It made Sayra hasten her steps.

Sylven must have already entered the double-set arched doorway, the wrought iron cold to her touch as she pulled one side open.

Upon first impression, the hall was extravagant in nature in a glorious way. The modestly sized domed gallery was bedecked in shades of gold, ivory, and cetacean blue, the Zefare emblem on display between two pillars of ivory. Brilliant constellations were painted in vibrant hues above, and a table below seated four comfortably. Crystalline dishes and various fine fabrics ornamented each setting. Fresh flower arrangements dotted pedestals around the walls, filling the space with natural floral notes. Serving staff lined the kitchen's entryway, awaiting the call for the first course to be served. A kind nun took her cashmere cloak, hanging it as Sayra made for the table.

Kenji and Akira were dressed in the royal fashion of their homeland, a stunning gold-leaf kimono hugging Akira's curves and a black haori, cobalt nagagi, and charcoal hakama on the prince of Droden. Twisting in his seat, Sylven's eyes widened upon seeing Sayra. While he always dressed in the formal frock coat of men in Acacea, a commonly accepted middle ground of fashion, he had switched tonight to a dashing, velvety maroon vest with double-lined columns of brass buttons. A rust-shaded underlayer peaked before giving way to a pressed white long-sleeve shirt, and his trousers were umber. It all meshed well with the color of his eyes and arranged walnut locks.

Before anyone could steal the first word, Kenji rose to greet her in the formality of her country, his right hand clasped over his heart in a deep bow. "Sayra, darling, well met," he beamed, doing a lingering once-over with hungry eyes. "You look absolutely ravishing this evening." His voice grew husky, and a hand directed her to the seat across from him.

Placing a polite smile on her face, Sayra elegantly folded herself into the chair, managing to respond without disgust in her voice. "As do you, Kenji. Quite the striking sight. It's been some time since we've met like this."

Kenji's smile turned satisfied at the stroke of his ego.

Turning to Akira, she continued, "How was the Droden Valkyrie program?"

A feminine giggle sounded from Akira's red lips, cleavage peeking through the low satin as she leaned forward with a conspirator's tone. "Absolutely dull!" Sending a wink Sylven's way, she confessed, "There weren't any men there for me to tease." Her plump lips pouted. "It was a waste of my years, but the Zefares needed a country to test an experimental satellite program with, and well, it was an honor to be among the first chosen for such prestige."

Sylven frowned beside her, and Sayra was smug that he was immune to Akira's efforts. He even avoided any angle of his eyes that might make it appear he was cheating a glance at her inappropriate posturing.

"Then it was fortunate that arrangements worked out so that you could attend here," Sayra said, sharing a simpering smile in Kenji's direction.

He took the bait.

"Indeed, it was." Kenji smirked, beckoning the servers forward with crystal bowls of soup. "It led me to realize how improved a dynamic could become if the paradigm was altered just slightly."

"How so?" Sylven entered the conversation, sipping on a glass of white wine.

Regarding him with a curator's eye, Kenji smoothly responded, "By adding to my court, of course. Recently, I've learned just how imperative the role of *sicarius* is in the royal court, and we have a prominent position opening up rather soon."

"Oh?" Sayra cocked a brow as she lifted the silver spoon to her mouth.

Kenji was going to offer the role to Sylven. That was the only reasonable conclusion Sayra could make. But the proposition was anything but reasonable. The Astors served Emrys's family loyally. To attempt to poach one of them could incite undue unrest and bitterness between the countries. The slight in no manner could go unnoticed.

Kenji went on to detail how they lost their latest to the Horde just outside the capital limits and how another pair of *anima* were nearing retirement age. He went through the particulars, especially the benefits of long-term employment security, well into the evening. Desserts were served when Kenji divulged the esteemed privilege exclusive to those working in his inner circle, one that would grow within the coming year as he ascended to being crowned emperor. Not that he disclosed any of that during the dinner, not when most weren't aware of his father's rapidly declining health. Not even Sylven knew, as far as Sayra was aware.

Prestige, fame, unlimited funds... all associated with the role. It was dangerous, after all, to work in the royal family's guard, and Kenji sold the idea well. Akira remained silent throughout, likely at Kenji's behest. Sayra wondered when the other foot would drop and if Sylven knew what the heir of Droden was attempting to corral them into.

Did Kenji have any motive beyond attempting to regain Sayra in his court again? Not that she was vain enough to believe it was solely because of her presence being secured, but that Kenji was simpleminded enough to strive for such a pointless endeavor.

As the last of the dishes were cleared, Sayra struggled to maintain an intrigued air. Her fingers began to tap on her thigh before she caught herself. Kenji frequently regarded her throughout the evening, forcing her to ensure her demeanor reflected attentiveness and allowing her feminine charm to disarm him with ease. Once, she even heard Kenji stumble over a handful of words when she tucked a curl behind her ear, holding his gaze through her lashes for just a second too long.

She didn't do it in a flirtatious manner. Unlike Akira with Sylven, there weren't any coy smiles or suggestive exchanges. But she knew the best way to gather information from Kenji was to play nice, and *nice* she did.

"You've come a long way since we last had a formal evening." Sayra tipped her glass toward the Droden prince.

Leaning back, Kenji teased the bottom of his square jaw for a contemplative second. "Indeed. Almost four years, if I'm correct."

Not long enough, she wanted to glower.

"Right before you ran off to become a Valkyrie." Kenji sighed wistfully.

Her back stiffened.

"I often wonder if it was because of your father's arrangement that you fled to this life."

Her hands clasped painfully under the table.

"Ah, yes. I've heard you two were set to be engaged," Sylven said, an awkward smile spreading on his tanned face.

Kenji's narrow eyes shot daggers at Sylven. "A haste arrangement that wasn't meant to be in the Goddess's eyes. I can only imagine what plans she has in store for me yet." His eyes grazed Sayra's. "What comes in time will. For now, I'm rather focused on grander schemes and my studies." His expression was polite, but a warring edge tightened his words.

It felt like something had crawled down Sayra's spine. "It was the Goddess's will that pulled me here. I think she meant for me to devote my life to these works," she said. A heaviness brought her head down for a moment.

Mistaking her reaction, Kenji's hand rested gently on the table. "Eveline calls on us to do the impossible to honor Her. I believe you have brought much glory to your house. Your siblings especially rally behind your accomplishments."

Blinking hard, Sayra couldn't help the slip in her mental bond with Sylven. A wistful sorrow overwhelmed her. With Faenda being a several weeks' journey northwest, she hadn't bothered to return home since she had enrolled at Saint Highburn's Valkyrie Academy almost four years prior. Out of her remaining siblings, Sayra was closest with her younger sister, Sofia, but she had a strained relationship with her younger brother, Leif, due to their father's poisoned words.

"You've heard from them?" Sayra breathed, her hands falling flat on her lap.

Akira leaned forward over the table, and her chest nearly spilled out. "They've been frequenting the capital upon our return. Our fathers have grown rather close in recent years. With your sister's courting period beginning soon, he wanted to introduce her formally into polite society before the season begins this summer."

"How time flies." Sayra's chest hurt. She must write home again soon. It had been too many months, but mail was rare and in between when it came from vast distances.

"Perhaps you both should visit us this summer. I'm certain Sofia would be encouraged by the support of her elder sister." Akira raised a brow. Her face was a portrait of a widow ensnaring a fly.

"Perhaps," Sayra replied as she collected her thoughts. She put on a pleased smile and pulled at the end of her green sleeve.

"Well, I believe I have held you both for quite some time," Kenji said, rising from his chair alongside his sister. "We simply must do this again. If possible, it would please me to continue this enlightening conversation over another elegant evening the following week."

Not if she could help it.

Within two strides and a smooth twist, Sayra looped her arm around Kenji's, the gesture appearing familiar between them when his arm automatically crooked up to receive hers. Sayra tilted her head and lifted a corner of her rosy lips at him, a look with her eyes sealing his attention. "Now, Kenji, I just know you too well to let this linger for long. If Your Highness is willing, I'd be delighted to know what is on your mind."

Sylven balked at her boldness, Akira twirling a lock of hair with a mischievous smile unfurling across her face.

Kenji's lids became heavy, a self-satisfied grin splitting his face. "You certainly would. For you, Sayra, I will be forthright. After all, resisting such beauty is one of life's greatest challenges," he relented, walking forward to stand across from Sylven.

"You're far too generous with praise." Sayra tsked, forcing her eyes to crinkle.

"Not when it's deserved," Kenji said in a way that made her want to punch him. Raising his voice, he addressed Sylven. "An invitation to my court is what I'd like to extend to you, Sylven. If you're willing, I'd have you as a *sicarius* under my direct employ upon graduation. You'd need for naught, everything provided on a silver platter. It would be my honor to have such a prestigious Arcanist within my capital."

High praise indeed.

Sayra would have bet her left hand Kenji knew about the discord between Sylven and Emrys, pouncing because their friendship was in tatters. Smugness coated her thoughts at her success. While she didn't think it would be that simple, at least it was a charade they wouldn't have to continue. Peeking at her Arcanist, Sayra noted the distrust lingering in his multi-shaded eyes. His mind was likely whirling on how best to address the predicament. She wasn't concerned Sylven would accept such a honeyed deal from his country's most prominent adversary.

"Kenji, while your offer is most lavish, one nearly irresistible, I cannot afford to abandon my family and the mantle they intend for me to inherit one day. I must graciously decline," Sylven apologized. To his credit, he managed to sound sincere even though his sentiments through their link were in blatant contrast to his spoken words.

Disengaging her arm, Sayra gifted the Droden heir one last smile before returning to Sylven's side, the distraction of the denial providing her ample time to escape.

Gone was the combination of amusement, covetousness, and cockiness Kenji sported mere moments ago. In their place, a stone-cold expression rested. He never handled "no" well, complaining or storming out whenever he didn't get his way. However, that was the Kenji she knew years ago, and this one appeared more intimidating. His sister peaked a brow at Sylven's rejection, disdain crossing her features.

"I'll permit you time to reconsider. After all, it's a league better than any Vander might bestow when he becomes king. Seeing as you and Emrys aren't the best of chaps anymore, fortune may have it be the only deal you'll ever manage to scrounge. You'll come to my court this summer to see all that I have to offer," Kenji warned, his voice darkening. "I'll have your answer this semester, my friend."

The "my friend" portion was satirical; nothing about their dinner conveyed such a notion.

Without waiting for Sylven's response, Kenji motioned for their coats, then held out a hand to caress the back of Sayra's into a proper kiss. None too gently. He squeezed harder than was polite, and her fake smile became stiff. Her eyes trailed his back as he stormed from the formal dining hall, his twin following with her usual smirk of superiority.

Reigning in her temper, Sayra threw on her dark cloak like a protective layer. Clasping the buttons, she made to leave. Footsteps behind her gave the telltale sign that Sylven quietly followed, likely stunned by the display. But as her feet clipped across the marble floor, Sayra fought not to remember the years of their courtship. The occasional bruises collected on her skin whenever Kenji released his anger.

The hallway was too stuffy for her liking.

Sayra burst open a polished wooden door to the gardens beyond. With the layout of the monastery, anyone could walk almost the entire grounds inside or outside, and right then, she'd never been more grateful for the fresh air.

The memories were flooding back. Sure, there were always mounds of flowers and delicacies showered on her the next day, but the bruises didn't fade any faster. Kenji was a petulant child, lashing out whenever his desires were denied, a fact that concerned her gravely. How would he act out next? She had wrongly assumed she'd ended any association by entering the Valkyrie Academy, a mistake that dragged Sylven down with her.

Most prominent of all was the night Kenji failed to kiss her, Sayra ducking at the last moment. She silently bore those smattering of bruises across her gut for a week and a half.

Her feet slowed over the cobblestone path, now bare of snow or ice. With summer approaching, the weather had become warm during the day, giving way to a lingering chill in the evenings. She never thought about what it would be like once she contracted with an Arcanist and how that would affect her old life. Now that it was thrown in her face, she questioned why she was so shortsighted. For years, she was just happy to be out of Droden and Faenda, and her sole goal was to be a Valkyrie and protect Arcanists. To make up for her brother's sacrifice.

But running away from problems never solved them.

Sayra wasn't a victim and never would be. It wasn't often Kenji used such tactics to express his anger. Over the years, while he packed a harder punch, he also learned some semblance of self-control and had become far less physically aggressive. She simply bided her time, waiting for the opportunity to abandon the arrangement for the Valkyrie Academy. Back then, she'd never balked, never cried.

She wasn't going to start tonight.

Chapter Nine

SAYRA

Sayra walked through the chilly night, her mind reeling from the dinner with Kenji and Akira.

Striding beside her, Sylven asked, "Nothing about Kenji's arrangement is actually about me, I'm assuming?"

Sayra shook her head, her thoughts too distracted to take in the dazzling starlit sky above. Not even a breeze stirred a single evergreen branch.

"He's disgusting." Sylven grunted. He didn't wear a cloak, and his brighter colors stood in stark contrast to the silent night around them.

"He's only the second reason I became a Valkyrie," Sayra murmured, pausing when they reached a junction where Sylven could turn for his dormitory. "Are you walking me to my room, or have you possibly lost your way?"

"I'd like to speak with you out of earshot," Sylven admitted.

Given the Arcanist's determined stance, Sayra gestured to a nearby bench tucked into a cove of trees. The chilly seat gave them a view of the towering marble walls of the Arcanist dining hall. At that hour, the occasional shadow of a passing person went by. She folded her hands and whispered a spell of privacy. "Well then. What is it you have to say?"

Sitting beside her, Sylven stared at a majik lantern hanging across from him before speaking. "I'd like to accompany you should you leave with Emrys again, whenever it might be and for whatever cause."

Sayra frowned. "They told you." She didn't think her cadre of friends would share *that* story of her birthday so casually, but she couldn't find it within herself to be mad.

"They did."

"It makes no difference."

"But doesn't it?" he rebutted, those hazel eyes appearing clearer to her than they had previously.

Sayra shook her head slowly and traced the scar across the bridge of her nose with a hand. "No. Because no matter what you think you know, you'll never truly realize the full extent of what I've done. Of what I bring to others. The Horde only found me that night because they were attracted to majik. *Mine.* If I had never given in during that selfish moment of storming away from my family, my brother would be alive. Lynn's brother would be alive. Instead, I watched as their heads were torn from their bodies. I deserved this scar. My father was right to never heal it. He agreed I warranted it."

"You couldn't have known a daemon would be that close," Sylven argued, his eyes shifting to her.

Her fingers bit into her palms as she lowered them. "It doesn't matter. Every child knows to stay within wards. I was upset at my father's plans for me to marry. I was furious that my mother died, leaving me when I needed her most. I was reckless and childish, wanting to run away from Kenji and that future. It was my fault entirely."

Sayra swallowed back the rising pain. "I froze when you were nearly killed that night, failing yet again when the Horde attacked your family's caravan. Because of me, I almost murdered an entire floor of Valkyries, including my own friend, in the dormitory fire. I nearly killed Emrys had he not dispelled his own majik in time and likely would have razed the world had he not acted. Imagine the one hope his parents and my mother created to combat the Holy Family falling to *nefas* majik." She barked a cold laugh. "It's happened so often that I acted out irrationally during our combat class, thinking for a split second the threats were real when the Valkyrie almost hit you."

Sayra couldn't feel anything beyond a chilling emptiness, her eyes closing so she could avoid seeing his face any longer. She couldn't take seeing sympathy on a face that detested her for so long. "It'll happen again. I'd rather you not be collateral as well," she said.

"My sister died in combat with the Horde three years ago. Her Arcanist survived only because of her sacrifice and was ungrateful for it." His voice was low and raw. "He took his time to use majik to fight back, watching with a sneer as it pulled her apart. Alive." The last word caught in his throat for a moment. "Only after she was truly dead did he burn it. He didn't want to waste his energy unless he absolutely had to, seeing it beneath him. Seeing my sister as expendable."

Sylven's pain echoed in his words, and it stabbed Sayra in the gut.

"I can understand how you feel. I never wanted someone else to be sacrificed for me. Never wanted to contract with a Valkyrie for that sole reason. I couldn't handle it," he said. "Not when my sister saw it as an honor above all, disgraced so horribly at her end. There is nothing poetic or heroic about that."

Opening her eyes, Sayra felt a familiar pang in her chest—that loneliness and pain that had plagued her for months recognizing another's. The lamplight illuminated his sharp jawline, the crook of his nose, and the agony reflected around the golden circle of his irises. They stared back at her with an earnestness she'd never seen from him.

"I treated you horribly. I never thought I'd have to contract with someone and hoped to never cause the death of another. Ever since we became *anima*, I pushed you as far away as possible to keep myself from caring because I was sure that eventual day would come." Sylven's throat bobbed, and his thick brows lowered. "I can't express enough how sorry I am for that."

In him, Sayra could see a part of herself mirrored, the burden of another's life on their hands. They weren't the same, a fact they both were fully aware of, but they could empathize with each other.

"I suppose I could have been less aggravating," Sayra breathed, shrugging her shoulders.

Sylven huffed a laugh, his mouth tilting up. "I don't believe it would have changed my attitude with you in the least."

"I'm sorry for your loss as well," Sayra said softly, resting a hand on his shoulder.

The crook of his smile lowered, his face pinching. "Don't be. I only hope to be better than the Arcanist who worked with her. He couldn't have cared less, and I can't imagine how he valued a life so little. Especially one that saved his," he clipped, face churning with disgust. He gripped the stone bench tightly with his hand. "It's a cruel world, one where people die at the Horde's hands every day. But *you* care to keep that from happening, to go above and beyond to stop them when it was never your duty to do so. You *care* about others, even assholes like me who treat you like dirt."

The shadow of a smile crossed Sayra's face at that.

"You're just like Jess," Sylven said quietly. "I don't want to lose you like I've lost her."

That smile faded as quickly as it had appeared, and Sayra's throat tightened.

Sylven hunched forward, watching as an owl swooped into a nearby tree. "But I see now you have a very different purpose, and it's far greater than being a Valkyrie. If there can be a world where people don't have to sacrifice their lives to save others from the Horde, I'll go to the depths of hell with you to make it happen. The Goddess brought us all together for this purpose, and as crazy as it sounds, I'm in."

Sayra needed a moment to steady her voice. "Queen Evangelina has requested we meet in Tern next weekend, but I can't justify more people tagging along on this next outing. It's an unnecessary risk."

Sighing, Sylven crossed his arms across his chest, tilting his head up at the stars. "Then how about this? Either I join you and Rys, or I shall become tasty Horde fodder when I head out alone to track you guys down."

"Who says you'll be tasty to them?"

Sylven cracked a smile at the normalcy of their banter, hiking a single shoulder in response. "I go by a sense of arrogance. Apparently, mine is high enough that I think myself capable of braving the world alone."

A quiet laugh escaped Sayra's lips, her fingers picking at a nail as she considered. Sylven shuffled his feet. At last, she said, "I'll find out the exact details and share them when I know them. It would be in poor taste to leave you to fend for yourself."

"I'll be there," Sylven promised, standing and offering her a hand up. She accepted without reluctance. "For now, I need to figure out how to get Kenji off my back and how to survive this week's midterms."

"Don't worry about Kenji. I can handle him." Sayra's nose wrinkled at the mention of his name.

Sylven's face grew grave. "I don't think it would be wise to go near him."

Breathing through her nose, Sayra rolled her eyes and tucked her cloak in close. "No need to bring on the overprotectiveness. I know exactly how to keep Kenji away. Didn't I stall this dinner for a month on top of enticing him to spill his secrets tonight?"

"Just… be careful is all I'm saying," Sylven huffed, his mouth drawing taut. "He's very close to the Holy Family, practically a lapdog."

With a word, she dispelled the privacy spell and followed him into the corridor. Lavender wafted from the hallway's burning incense. As two Arcanists walked out of their dormitory, Sylven gave her a hesitating glance as they stopped beside hers.

Sayra raised a finger, her brow pinching as she peered beyond his shoulder.

She had mistaken the second figure for an Arcanist, but it was a woman in a man's black academy cloak. The edges of her dress looked every bit like crimson silk. And was that Vander swaggering beside her?

What was Vander doing with Akira?

"Hey, hey," Sayra said in a hushed tone. She poked Sylven's arm twice and jerked her chin. "Look."

Twisting, Sylven's brow raised to the roof as Vander held open the garden door for his companion. When the door shut behind them, Sylven's eyes were as wide as saucers. "Was that Akira with Vander?" The way he said it made it sound like he asked, *Was that a daemon holding hands with a nun?*

"We're following them, right?"

"Of course!" Sylven nodded, his sight dark with concern.

They paced toward the garden door, Sayra creaking it open with caution. Her eyes narrowed as she watched Vander and Akira disappear into the winding pathway and lush greenery, their whispers carried away too far from her ears. Candlelit windows dotted either side of the path, each dozens of feet from the center.

She edged into the night with care, both hands grasping the emerald material and raising it away from snagging branches as she moved around the marble walls. Sylven gently closed the door behind them. After their weeks of practice, Sayra managed to become proficient at blocking emotions and communicating with her link. For a moment, she thought her words, imagining her mind nudging them in Sylven's direction. *We need to be smart about this. Follow me and stay low.*

After you.

The garden hedges stretched before them, outlining the furthest edges of the outdoor path. In the distance, Sayra could just make out the glint of Vander's onyx hair as he and Akira pulled aside into an alcove of trees. Her training as a Valkyrie kicked in, her senses hyper-aware of every rustle of leaves, every shift of shadows. The earthy smell of freshly turned soil clung to them as they neared the spot where Vander and Akira disappeared.

Stop, she ordered.

She could hear voices, low and urgent.

"Can't keep this up forever," Akira was saying, her tone laced with frustration. "Kenji grows wearisome."

Vander's usually carefree voice was uncharacteristically serious. "We don't have a choice. If the Holy Family finds out..."

Sayra's breath caught in her throat. She exchanged a quick glance with Sylven, seeing her own shock mirrored in his expression. To think there was more Vander could have been involved in, well, the situation was bigger than they had imagined.

"We need to move faster," Akira insisted, allowing some of her usual convincing undertones to warm her voice in an alluring way. "The longer we wait, the more dangerous it becomes. For *all* of us."

Sayra's heartbeat was going wild, but she leaned in further, making out Vander's pacing silhouette.

"You think I don't know that?" Vander hissed, his normal swagger replaced with jerky movements. "For the millionth time. We. Can't. Rush. This. One wrong move and everything we've worked for goes up in smoke. My brother is far too intelligent for his own good."

Akira let out a sympathetic noise, her outline drawing close to Vander's. "The cat mistakes a lion for a mouse, Vander." Her arm grazed his, a hand lifting to cup his agitated face. "You are every bit as gifted as him but far more clever and powerful. They will all see it in time. In the end, your goals align, and all will be settled once we deal with the Holy Family."

Sayra strained to hear his response, but it was too low for her ears.

Akira's hands began wandering across Vander's broad shoulders. "And what about Sayra? She's the key to all of this, yet she hasn't a clue."

At that, the ground dropped out from beneath Sayra. Sylven's face went pale, but his jaw was clenched as he stared down Vander and Akira through the leaves. They pulled further into the alcove where none besides Sayra, Sylven, and any passersby could see.

"I worry about the extent of knowledge my family's informant may know and what she'll share with Sayra. The Valkyrie isn't ready. Not yet. Not until we figure out how to use it."

Leaning back, Akira's face came into view. Her black widow's smile grew wide across her face, something like adoration igniting her black eyes as her hand lowered to the front of Vander's navy uniform. "She could ruin everything. I know. But what if the Holy Family finds out first?"

Sayra's breath caught. What was it that she wasn't ready for? What secrets were still being kept from her? Did Emrys know? And why did Akira, of all people, know more than she did?

The Droden princess lowered her voice, the words incomprehensible to Sayra once again. Desperate to hear more, she moved from her crouch, only to move in the same direction as Sylven. They bumped into each other, but unlike Sayra, Sylven wasn't able to keep steady before catching himself against the hedge with a soft rustle of leaves.

"Did you hear that?" Akira whispered, her voice sharp with suspicion.

Thinking quick, Sayra muttered, *"Aura."* She was careful to use the dark archetype of majik, the kind that summoned elements. She focused the spell on a wind affinity.

A gentle breeze picked up through the gardens, moving leaves and branches alike. Sayra and Sylven didn't breathe, but she could see Sylven tensing, ready to spring into action if need be. The silence stretched into eternity, broken only by the soft chirping of crickets and the sounds of her summoned wind.

Vander said at last, "It seems to have been the wind. Let's be off. We shouldn't dawdle in one place too long anyway."

Footsteps sounded as they moved away, fading into the distance. Only when she was sure they were gone did she stand, her legs shaky with relief and adrenaline.

It wouldn't have been the first time she made a mistake if her spellcasting went wrong. Sayra had access to both light and dark archetypes of majik. When she focused her majik leaning toward light, she could summon majik associated with the elements, such as healing for a water affinity spell. With dark archetypes, that water spell could easily turn into a blade of water. Other Arcanists didn't have that problem since they were limited to light or dark.

She almost set fire to Emrys's room once when she had only meant to warm it up with a light archetype spell.

"What in the name of the Goddess was that about?" Sylven asked, facing her in the near darkness.

"I don't know," she said. "But I believe my mother may have answers. As much as I hate saying it, this is bigger than my history with her." A grim, resentful knot twisted in her stomach.

Vander referred to her mother as the informant, a title for those who weren't sworn to secrecy to know her by. Akira must not know *everything* then, meaning Sayra should be able to piece together what it all meant if she arranged another meeting with Arene von Lykken.

Sylven agreed with a silent nod, the two of them returning to the hallway. Sayra dusted off the crepe folds of the exposed front of her gown, suddenly very aware of how frazzled she must have appeared. "I only hope Emrys doesn't hold back whatever it is they know," she said, Sylven scowling beside her as he moved to straighten his maroon vest.

"I suppose I, too, must speak with Emrys," Sylven grumbled. "Though I would be overjoyed for answers, I would like to think he wouldn't withhold anything with such importance."

Sayra was about to agree, but then the doorway opened to the Valkyrie's dormitory, and a dark face appeared in full armor.

"Sayra. I've been looking for you," Nes said cooly, her icy eyes trained on Sylven and the dirt collected at the hem of his trousers. Then at the dirt on Sayra's heels and a stray leaf that clung to Sayra's cloak.

"We were, um, at a dinner," Sylven stumbled out.

Why was he so flustered?

"Kenji and Akira wanted to dine with us," Sayra explained in a hushed tone as Nes stopped beside her. "I'll have to fill you in later."

An Arcanist at the end of the hall wore the ivory robes of a monk, going from lighting fixture to fixture, using majik to renew the spells.

"I'll be off." Sylven bowed his head before turning with haste.

"Goodnight, Sylven," Sayra drawled, bemused as he muttered a goodnight in response before sequestering himself in the Arcanist's dormitory.

"I'll run late if I don't head straight for my patrol, but I'd like to hear about it tomorrow morning." Nes hesitated, her face twisting with regret. "I'm sorry about last night, Sayra. I shouldn't have mentioned your brother."

Sayra waved it away. "It's fine. I know you never would bring him up intentionally. It's already forgotten." When Nes still didn't move, she added, "I'll talk with you more tomorrow, okay?"

"Okay."

They separated, Sayra tugging off her heels when she reached her room at last.

Flicking a match, she set fire to the oil candles lining her wall. While she was troubled over what she had overheard, Sayra was thankful for the conversation she had with Sylven. It had been months of ups and downs, and they finally had reached some sort of mutual understanding. Feeling lighter than she had in a long time, Sayra placed a disk into the music player Sylven gifted her, humming a melody every Faendan knew by heart as she readied for sleep.

CHAPTER TEN

EMRYS

The echoes of shuffling feet and murmured conversations filled the air in the dome as Emrys gathered his belongings at the end of the combat lecture. He caught sight of Sylven making his way toward him, a determined set to his jaw. But before Sylven could reach him, a commotion erupted in the hallway outside. The usual post-class chatter gave way to excited whispers and hurried footsteps.

Emrys immediately joined the fray, watching as a first-year Arcanist gathered everyone's attention.

"Did you hear?" the boy exclaimed, his voice carrying over the mass of navy uniforms. "A Thapulan emissary is here!"

His blood ran cold.

"They're requesting the Goddess's blessing," another student added, his voice tinged with awe and apprehension.

Emrys's mind raced, piecing together the implications of the unexpected development. Thapula, the distant country across the sea, had long been a subject of circulating rumors and vague threats. The forces and technology the Thapulans wielded were vastly superior. While Emrys worked diligently with Ken—one of many in his private employ—to begin their own advances, they would never compare to those of the enormous empire. With their population untouched by daemonkind, they held no disadvantages. Not when men there had never been hunted by the Horde. Unless Thapulans engaged directly with daemons, they wouldn't have to bear the fear an Arcanist would. Daemons only attacked those with majik or those who posed a threat to them.

But Emrys knew Thapulans wanted majik. Specifically, he knew they were out to acquire the means to use majik at any cost. Who wouldn't be allured by the prospect of the arcane arts, to wield the majikal force and acquire power beyond what people thought possible? Humanity's greed would be their downfall.

He thought he had another month before they would send an emissary to fish out the Holy Family's blessing for majik. Apparently not.

"Emrys!" Sylven's voice called out behind him. "We need to talk about—"

"Not now." Squeezing his eyes shut for a moment, Emrys sent a quick prayer to the Goddess for her aid. "I apologize for the bluntness, but I need to investigate this further before we may talk." He opened his eyes, turning to face Sylven.

Sylven's thick brows furrowed, a mix of frustration and understanding crossing his face. "Let me help," he said.

For a moment, Emrys hesitated. His secrets pressed down on him, urging caution. But despite their current spat, he knew they were thicker than blood. If there was anyone other than his parents and Sayra he could trust, it was Sylven. And with current events progressing as they had been, Emrys could use the help.

"All right," he conceded. "One wrong move, though, and we could jeopardize everything. I must seek out this emissary's whereabouts."

Sylven nodded, relief washing over his tanned features. "I've got your back," he promised.

Together, they slipped away from the crowded hallways, taking a lesser-traversed path toward the Holy Family's council chambers. He spotted the oligarchs of Zendiya in an alcove, Nikolay's green eyes briefly flicking to his. Emrys returned a quick nod of intention and kept walking. The air grew cold as they descended a servant's entrance into the cathedral, dodging a nun oblivious to their hiding spot behind a corner.

"There's a hidden passage," Emrys whispered, running his hand along a plain wall. "It leads to an observation alcove above the chambers. We can watch from there without being seen."

His fingers found a slight indentation, barely noticeable unless someone knew what to feel for. With a soft click, a section of the wall swung inward, presenting a narrow staircase winding upward. They ascended in silence; the only sound was their muffled footsteps and the distant murmur of voices growing louder. At the top, Emrys pressed his back against the marble wall, careful not to disturb the navy and gold tapestry dangling between him, the small alcove, and the chamber below. He gestured for Sylven to take the other side of the tapestry, and they both peeked through the thin line between it and the wall.

The council chamber lay beneath them, a majestic expanse adorned with vaulted gold-etched ceilings. Intricate mosaics, depicting vivid historical scenes, adorned the walls. The air was filled with the faint scent of freshly polished marble and rose incense. Angelic statues, expertly carved, stood sentinel along the perimeter, their presence instilling a sense of being watched and judged.

Both the Zefares and council were already comfortably seated in a crescent of exquisite wooden chairs, their ivory velvet lining providing a soft and luxurious touch. The flickering of candlelight danced across their serious expressions, casting shadows on the ornate walls of the chamber. The room fell into a hushed silence, broken only by the occasional rustle of robes and the distant echo of a church bell.

Emrys marked Catara Zefare's platinum trademark bun and ivory armor sitting beside the Grand Priest. Her cousin, Jax, rubbed his shaved face at her left, appearing perturbed. To the Grand Priest's right sat his wife, ever so dainty and meek in her robes of ivory.

And there, standing before them, was the Thapulan emissary.

The emissary was unlike anyone Emrys had ever seen, over seven feet tall and lithe, with skin the color of burnished bronze. His clothing was comprised of elegant layers showcasing intricate designs.

"Honored members of the Holy Family," the emissary began, his voice melodious yet carrying an undercurrent of steel. "I come bearing a request from the Emperor of Thapula."

Emrys and Sylven exchanged a glance, both thinking the same thing. Whatever was about to unfold in that room could change the course of history.

As the emissary continued to speak, laying out his request for the Goddess's blessing, Emrys felt dread grasp at his chest. He knew, with a certainty that bordered on premonition, it was only the beginning. He held his breath, his eyes darting between the onlookers. Their faces were impassive, but he could see the subtle signs of unease—a tightened jaw here, a clenched fist there.

"I plead on behalf of my peoples' case," the emissary continued, his eyes flicking between the council members. "For if we do not receive help, we fear that our country may fall against our own foes. On behalf of Thapula, I beg for your aid. In exchange, my emperor has seen it fit to share designs of our superior machinery to help industrialize your land. This collaboration could prove of benefit to all peoples, should you decide to work with us."

Emrys racked his brain for any scrap of knowledge that could corroborate the emissary's case. Had he heard of Thapula having enemies? Through his sparse overseas connections, he had only been fed knowledge of Thapula's desire for more power—thus, their desire to obtain majik by any means necessary. Their continent was close to the size of all the countries in Emrys's continent of the Goddess's land. For them to have an enemy...

What would the mightiest continent in their world fear? Was it a rouse to gain sympathy?

The Grand Priest rose, his robes rustling. Catara's father emanated an air of immense authority and spiritual power, his presence commanding both respect and reverence. His piercing hazel eyes reflected a lifetime of wisdom and unwavering determination. The sharpness and refinement of his features mirrored Catara's own. As he stood there in his ceremonial robes, the same runic gold as Catara's armor adorned him, symbolizing his elevated status within the religious order. The silver strands of his hair and the faint lines etched onto his face hinted at the passing of time, though he was well into his fifties. When he spoke, his voice was measured and calm, but Emrys could detect the underlying strain.

"Esteemed emissary of Thapula," he began, "we have heard your request, and we understand the gravity of your situation. However, I'm afraid we cannot simply grant the Goddess's blessing as you ask."

The emissary's eyes narrowed, a shade of something—anger? disappointment?—crossing his face before it smoothed back into diplomatic neutrality. "May I ask why?" he asked. "I have come long and far to carry this request as my emperor wishes to learn of your faith."

The Grand Priest spread his hands in a gesture of apology. "The Goddess's blessing is not ours to give or withhold. It is bestowed by Her divine will alone and to those who are followers of the faith. We are merely Her humble servants, and to my knowledge, Her faith has been isolated to the confines of this land."

"Surely," the emissary pressed, "there must be some way to encourage Her favor to those foreign and willing to learn? Our empire has much to offer in return. You wouldn't condemn hundreds of thousands of people for the sin of gluttony?"

A murmur ran through the assembled council members. Emrys saw several exchanging glances, and he knew they were offended by the accusation of feeding only themselves with the ability to wield majik.

Another council member spoke up, her voice gentle but firm. "I'm afraid it's not that simple. The Goddess's blessing is a sacred gift, not a commodity to be bartered or traded."

The emissary's posture stiffened almost imperceptibly. "I see," he said, his tone cooler. "And if we were to... seek this blessing through other means?"

The threat, though veiled, was unmistakable. Emrys saw Sylven tense up across from him.

The Grand Priest's face hardened. "I would strongly advise against any such action," he said, all pretense of diplomacy falling away. "The Goddess's consequences would be severe. Perhaps if your empire were to instill the faith throughout its foundation first and establish it as the predominant one, then we may reconsider."

The emissary bowed, a gesture that seemed more mocking than respectful. "Thank you for your time," he said. "I will, of course, relay your response to my emperor. I'm sure he will find it most interesting."

As the emissary turned to leave, Emrys caught a glimpse of something in his eyes—a cold, calculating look that validated his worst fears. The situation was far from over.

The doors closed behind the emissary with a resounding thud, leaving the council chamber in stunned silence. Emrys and Sylven exchanged a look of grim understanding. Emrys's mind raced, piecing together the complex chessboard that was forming before them. Thapula's emissary was like a bold knight, making an unexpected leap into their territory. The Holy Family, with their steadfast refusal, stood as immovable rooks, guarding their corners of the board.

As the council members below dispersed, the Grand Priest retreating to a more recluse setting with his immediate family members, Emrys motioned for Sylven to follow him back down the hidden staircase. They had much to discuss and even more to prepare for.

⚬✦⚬

The heavy oak door of Emrys's room closed behind them with a soft thud, muffling the distant chatter of students in the hallway. The familiar scent of old books and a sandalwood candle enveloped them as Emrys laid his bookbag down beside his mahogany desk. He ran a hand through his dark hair, his mind still racing from the confrontation with the Thapulan emissary. But as he turned to face Sylven, he knew there was an even more pressing matter at hand. He spelled his room for privacy without further delay.

"All right. What's going on?"

Sylven dropped his bookbag beside the bookcase, stress lines wrinkling his face. "I don't even know where to begin. What does Thapula have to do with any of this? Between them, Vander, Akira, and Kenji..." He ran his hands behind his neck and started pacing between the door and Emrys's darkly accented bed.

Emrys watched Sylven, his own unease growing with each of his friend's steps. He took a deep breath, knowing the time for secrets had passed. "Have you ever heard of Ophelia Majik Co.?" He moved to his desk, opening a hidden compartment underneath it and pulling out a small leather-bound book.

Sylven's eyes locked onto Emrys with a mix of curiosity and apprehension. "The artifact shop in Tern? What does that have to do with anything?"

"It's more than just a shop," Emrys explained, his fingers tracing the embossed cover of the book. "It's a network. A group of people dedicated to uncovering the truth about the Holy Family and their control over majik."

Sylven's eyes widened, and he stopped beside Emrys's table. "You're part of this group?"

Emrys nodded, sitting down in his plush ebony chair. "I founded it. We've been investigating the Holy Family for years, trying to uncover their secrets, their true motivations. I take it Sayra had time to explain our coming venture into Tern to meet with my mother?" At Sylven's sound of confirmation, he continued, "Then, so long as you join us, I'll arrange for introductions. They are the sole reason I know as much as I do regarding Thapula."

"I'm all in, Rys," Sylven said, a hint of exasperation in his tone. "I'm tired of secrets. I'm *tired* of the distance between us all."

As am I, Emrys thought. Unfortunately, secrets were the only thing keeping them all alive. He opened the book across his spotless desk, revealing pages of coded notes and diagrams. "Then you should know that Thapula intends to acquire majik by any means. They are preparing for war as we speak. Today was their first step, meaning the rest isn't terribly far off."

Sylven peered at the book, confusion written in his eyes.

Emrys turned a page, and a map with strange markings was displayed. "And now that Thapula has entered the game, they're not just after the Goddess's blessing, Sylven. I fear they're after the source of majik itself."

"They somehow know that majik isn't a Goddess-given gift?"

"Possibly."

Realization slackened Sylven's mouth. "If they find out about you and Sayra having parts of the relic imbued into your bones..."

Emrys closed the book, looking Sylven square in the face. "That's why we need to act now. We need to expose the truth about the Holy Family, stop Thapula, and find a way to end the threat of the Horde once and for all."

A dry laugh escaped from Sylven, his head shaking in disbelief. "That's all, huh? Vander is scheming some sort of plan against you. Sayra and I followed him and Akira last night after our dinner with Kenji. Oh, by the way, Kenji offered me a position in his court. As a daemon hunter. His own personal *sicarius*. When I said no, he threatened me by saying I'd regret it." Sylven began pacing again. "Anyway, when Sayra and I followed Akira and Vander, they were whispering some plan of theirs involving Sayra."

Emrys stood immediately, his blood pounding in his ears. "What did he say?"

"Something about Sayra being the key in their plan and that time was limited. However, Vander disagreed and said they couldn't rush it even though Kenji was growing impatient." Sylven turned, snapping his finger in the air with a mocking expression. "Oh! I couldn't forget the part where Vander said, 'I worry about the extent of knowledge my family's informant may know and what she'll share with Sayra. The Valkyrie isn't ready. Not yet. Not until we figure out how to use it.'"

It.

Anger curled in Emrys's chest, and his fingers whitened into balls at his sides. The audacity of his brother to concoct his own plans in defiance of his family, and with Kenji and Akira no less, infuriated him. And for his brother to care so little for Sayra that he viewed her as a tool...

A darkness crept into his mind, beckoning traitorous thoughts with an evil persuasion. It pled for him to storm Vander's room and burn him alive. To simply burn the whole monastery while he was at it. Wouldn't that solve most of his problems? It was enticing to think of the flames engulfing Va—

Stop it, Emrys demanded of himself, repressing the influence of *nefas* majik. Use it once, and it would haunt an Arcanist for life if they escaped its grasp. If he were to fall to it again, there would be no telling if he'd ever regain his mind before it went mad entirely.

"Please tell me you know nothing of this," Sylven said, his defeated voice drawing Emrys's attention.

"No." Emrys's voice sounded strangled to his own ears. "No, I didn't."

For a moment, he was silent. Sylven studied him, searching for any sign of deception, but Emrys held his gaze steadily. "What do we do then?"

"I'll look into it. For now, please take care when interacting with any of that lot. I cannot fathom what Kenji and Akira would contribute to any plan of theirs." And the fact that Kenji offered a place in his court to Sylven... and, by default, Sayra as well. Emrys wasn't oblivious. He knew Kenji was the possessive sort. He knew the man was displeased his engagement had been cut off despite what the Droden emperor promised him. There weren't many outside of his immediate court who held the pedigree the von Lykkens did.

That, at least, made sense. Though a dark trundle of jealousy ticked his jaw, the thought of Kenji trying to get Sayra back...

Sylven sat on the edge of Emrys's bed, his hands flattening on his downy black comforter. "You really like her, don't you?"

Emrys felt his heart constrict at Sylven's words, all the anger and jealousy sinking low. He turned away, unable to meet his friend's gaze. The truth hung heavy between them, unspoken but undeniable. "It doesn't matter," Emrys said, his voice just above a whisper. "However I feel, it can't interfere with our mission. With Sayra's path. There's too much at stake, and I won't ask any more from her. How could I when everyone wants something? There's only so much anyone can give before there's nothing left."

Sylven sat in silence, his eyes burning holes in Emrys's back. Finally, he spoke. "But your feelings already have interfered, haven't they? That's why you've been pushing her away and she you."

Emrys distractedly hid the book back in the hidden compartment, feeling his choices pressing down on him. "I had to," he said, remembering the way Sayra looked at him just yesterday. The softness in her beautiful jade eyes as they searched his for a pause longer than appropriate and the lingering edge of longing that reciprocated that of his own. The warmth of her face when his hand tucked her silky-smooth hair behind her ear weeks ago. "For her sake. For all our sakes."

Turning to face Sylven, he cleared his throat. "I can't be a distraction when she has to focus on keeping herself safe and training with majik. Besides..."

Memories of the time he felt her lips on his own surfaced. His fear of losing her and the need to do something overcame all sense of rationality, compelling him into that last-ditch effort. For a handful of seconds, he lost himself in that sweeping gesture, and his very soul lifted sky-high when she returned it, knowing that on a fundamental level, Sayra wanted him too.

But...

But. The devastation she experienced afterward hit him harder than he cared to admit. Sayra was horrified at what she had done with *nefas* majik, but also that she had kissed him. More than perhaps anyone, Sayra was dedicated to being a faithful Valkyrie, her sole responsibility to protect Sylven. Valkyries were honor bound to remain ardent to that cause, and to deter from it and have a relationship... it wasn't entirely frowned upon, but for Sayra, it was akin to an act of dishonor.

It didn't matter that Emrys could barely breathe when he was close to her, nor that he couldn't focus in their shared lectures when his whole world seemed to revolve around her every move. Her every look. Goddess, she had stolen his heart with that fierce determination, sharp wit, and unparalleled beauty that any art in the world couldn't capture.

Emrys had lost his heart to her long ago. What he would give to live in a normal world and court her without any boundaries driving them apart.

Sylven stood, approaching Emrys slowly. "Who am I, or any other, to stand in the way of any semblance of happiness you can have?" he said with a sad understanding. Something like defeat lowered his shoulders. "It sounds like such things will be far and fleeting for us all until we can do the impossible and overthrow all that threatens us."

A surge of gratitude dampened the aching loneliness, but it mixed with a sharp pang of guilt. "Sylven, I'm sorry. For everything. For lying, for pushing you away. I thought I was protecting you and her, but—"

"You were hurting us both," Sylven finished for him. He placed a hand on Emrys's shoulder. "I understand now and apologize for my own shortsightedness and selfish tendencies. Neither of us was in the right, but perhaps myself even more. And I want you to know, if there's a chance for you and Sayra, even in the midst of all this chaos, I think you should take it."

Emrys frowned at his brother in all but blood. "But your feelings on the matter were strong. I don't say all of this to try and convince you to be okay with it."

A rueful smile crossed Sylven's face. "My feelings aren't important right now. What's important is that we stand together, that we support each other. And if that means supporting you and Sayra, then that's what I'll do."

A lump formed in Emrys's throat. "Sylven, I... thank you. But I can't. Not yet. Not while there's so much at stake."

"Then we focus on the mission. On protecting Sayra, on uncovering Vander and Akira's plans, and on stopping Thapula. But Emrys..." He stepped back and waited until his friend met his gaze. "Don't close your heart off completely. When this is all over, if we make it through, promise me you'll give yourself a chance at happiness."

The start of a smile pulled at Emrys's mouth. "I promise."

Vander, Kenji, and Akira, Emrys mused, were playing as bishops, moving diagonally through the shadows with their secret plans. And Sayra... Sayra was the enigmatic queen, potentially the most powerful piece on the board yet unaware of her significance. As for himself and Sylven, Emrys couldn't help but feel like they were pawns, trying to navigate a game where the rules seemed to shift with every move. But pawns, he reminded himself, had the potential to become something more if they played their moves right.

Despite all that continued to stack against them, Emrys stood straighter than he had in a while.

CHAPTER ELEVEN

SAYRA

Sayra ducked low, narrowly avoiding a swipe of Breane's sword by mere inches. The afternoon sun warmed the Valkyrie training arena, stealing the chill from the polished marble columns surrounding the dirt pit. Sayra's muscles burned with exertion as she circled her opponent, her *spyd* a reassuring weight in her hand. The chain whip coiled around her arm, its daggered end sharper than any blade.

Breane's blonde braid whipped under her helmet, brown eyes sharp and focused as she pulled out of her strike with a twirling motion. She narrowly avoided the return jab of Sayra's weapon, backpedaling several steps as Sayra danced around her chain, catching several feet of it around her knee and altering the trajectory midair. It whistled across the space where Breane had stood a blink of an eye before.

Sweat beaded across Sayra's brow, the armor clad over her body making it seem hotter than the spring sun already did far above. She reigned in her chain with precise movements, her dancer's grace coming into play.

"Again?" Breane called out, her voice light.

Sayra acknowledged her suggestion with a wild grin, and in an instant, they were in motion. Steel against steel clashed in the arena as

Sayra's newly gifted dagger darted out between blows, and Breane's sword grazed the steel links of Sayra's *spyd*.

As they exchanged blows, Breane's voice carried over the sound of their combat. "I heard there was some excitement on the wall the other night," she said casually, deflecting a strike from Sayra's chain. "Apparently, the daemon acted aberrantly and shifted focus *away* from an Arcanist toward a Valkyrie. You wouldn't happen to know anything about that, would you?"

For a moment, Sayra's rhythm faltered, her mind flashing back to the daemon attack. She recovered fast, but not before Breane had pressed her advantage, forcing Sayra to leap back. "Just rumors," she grunted, launching a counterattack. "You know how people like to talk."

Breane nodded, parrying Sayra's strike. "True enough. Still, it's odd how often you seem to be around when strange things happen."

The implication in Breane's words made Sayra's skin prickle. She redoubled her efforts, and her *spyd* became a blur of motion. "Just bad luck, I guess," she said through gritted teeth.

"Or good luck," Breane countered, her sword meeting Sayra's chain in a shower of sparks. "Depending on how you look at it. You always seem to come out on top, don't you?"

Sayra's jaw clenched. She didn't like where the conversation was going. With a flick of her wrist, she sent the *spyd's* chain wrapping around Breane's blade. For a moment, they were locked in a contest of strength.

"What are you getting at, Breane?" Sayra asked, her voice low and wary.

Breane's eyes glinted with curiosity. "I'm just wondering if there's more to you than meets the eye, Sayra. You're not like other Valkyries, are you?"

Ice ran in Sayra's veins. How much did Breane suspect? How much had Vander told her? She wrenched her *spyd* back, breaking the deadlock and sending them both stumbling.

"I don't know what you mean," Sayra said, her heart pounding. "I'm just trying to do my job, like everyone else."

Breane opened her mouth to respond, but Sayra didn't give her the chance. With a fierce cry, she launched into a flurry of attacks, and her *spyd* became an extension of her will. Breane was forced on the defensive, sword a blur as she fended off the onslaught.

In the back of her mind, Sayra knew she was overreacting, and her sudden aggression might have been suspicious. But she couldn't help it. The fear of discovery, the burden of her secrets, it all came pouring out in a torrent of steel and fury in the adrenaline haze. With a well-timed sweep of her chain, Sayra sent Breane's sword flying. The blonde Valkyrie hit the ground hard, the point of Sayra's dagger at her throat.

They stayed frozen like that, both panting heavily. Then, slowly, a smile spread across Breane's face. "Impressive," she said, a note of respect in her voice. "You're full of surprises, Sayra."

She withdrew her weapon, offering a hand to help Breane up. As she pulled the other Valkyrie to her feet, she couldn't shake the feeling she'd just been tested. And she wasn't sure if she passed or failed. As they made their way out of the arena, Sayra's mind whirled with questions. What did Breane know? What was Vander planning, and did it have something to do with Akira and Kenji? And how much longer could she keep her secrets safe?

Her *spyd* and dagger at her hip felt heavier than ever, but not nearly as much as her stomach did when her eyes found a roguish face smirking at her beside a column.

Vander.

Sayra was far too frazzled to attempt any sort of banter, choosing instead to take the long way back to her dormitory. She edged around a few other Valkyries in the training grounds, her muscles aching from the intense sparring session with Breane. The marble corridors of the monastery echoed with her footsteps, the air growing cooler as night approached. She couldn't shake the feeling of unease that had settled over her during the training, Breane's probing questions still ringing in her ears.

As she entered her small room, Sayra's eyes were immediately drawn to the worn leather journal sitting on her desk. Her mother's journal. It had been there for weeks, untouched, a constant reminder of the secrets and burdens she carried. With a sigh, she pushed the thought aside and headed for the washroom.

The cool water was a blessing on her skin as she showered, washing away the sweat and grime of the day. But it did little to cleanse her mind of the worries that plagued her. As she dried off and dressed in fresh black fitted garments, her gaze kept drifting back to the journal.

Sayra knew she should be preparing for her night patrol on the monastery wall. It was her duty, after all. But something about the quiet of her room made the journal seem more enticing than ever. And the questions... they kept stacking up. With a mix of anticipation and dread, she sat down at her desk and reached for the leather-bound book. The cover was soft and worn beneath her fingers, indicating years of use. Sayra steeled herself for whatever revelations lay within and opened it to the first page. The neat, flowing script of her mother greeted her eyes.

I, Arene von Lykken, set these words to paper with a heavy heart and a troubled mind, for I have learned a truth so terrible, so world-shattering, I fear for the very future of our realm. My family, it seems, has been burdened with a grim destiny—to bring down a foe so powerful, so deeply entrenched in the fabric of our world, the very thought of opposing them seems like madness.

And yet, oppose them we must. For if we do not, the balance of our world will be forever lost, plunging us all into an age of darkness from which we may never recover.

I write these words not knowing if I will live to see our mission through, not knowing if my children will be forced to bear this burden in my stead. But I pray to the Goddess that somehow, someway, we will find the strength to face what lies ahead.

For now, I can only record what I have learned in the hope that it may guide those who come after me. May the Goddess grant us the wisdom and courage to face the trials that lie ahead.

Sayra's hands trembled as she read the words, her mother's voice seeming to echo in her mind. But to see it laid out so blatantly, to feel that destiny pressing down on her... it was almost too much to bear. Somewhere along the line, her chosen destiny was ruined by one out of her control.

She flipped to the next page, her eyes devouring the words.

The Holy Family, those who we have revered and obeyed for generations, are not who they seem. Their power, their very existence, is built on a foundation of lies and evil majik. They do not protect us from the Horde—they create it. They do not safeguard the balance of majik—they corrupt it for their own ends.

I have seen things in the depths of Saint Highburn Monastery that haunt my dreams. Failed Valkyrie candidates, twisted and warped by forbidden rituals. Arcanists driven mad by the power they are forced to channel. And at the heart of it all, relics of unimaginable power—the source of all majik and the key to the Holy Family's dominion over our world.

But there is hope. If I reveal their true intentions and actions, then we as a continent could reverse the damage dealt to us. And I believe that if we can steal their relics, if we can unlock their true power, we may have a chance to set things right.

Sayra's mind reeled with the implications of what she was reading. She imagined learning it all for the first time, finding it nearly impossible, and yet... it explained so much. The secrecy, the strict control over who could use majik, the ruthless elimination of any who opposed them.

She read on, her heart pounding.

I have made contact with others who share my suspicions, who have glimpsed the truth behind the Holy Family's facade. We are few, and we must move in secret, but we are determined. We will delve into the furthest reaches of the continent to find more pieces of truth, we will uncover the full extent of the Holy Family's crimes, and we will bring them to justice.

But the path ahead is fraught with danger. The Holy Family's reach is long, and their agents are everywhere. We must be cautious, we must be clever, and above all, we must be prepared to sacrifice everything for the sake of our cause.

To my children, if you are reading this, know I love you more than life itself. Know that everything I have done, everything I will do, is to secure a better future for you. And know that if the burden of this fight falls on you, you are stronger than you know. You are the hope of our world, the light that will pierce the darkness that threatens to engulf us all.

Tears stung Sayra's eyes as she read her mother's words. The love, the fear, the determination—it was all there, laid bare on the page. She could almost see her mother as she wrote those words, her face set in grim determination, her hand steady even as her heart trembled. Sayra's breath caught in her throat. She reread the passage a second and third time, hardly daring to believe what she was seeing.

The next pages appeared darker and fresher, as if they had been written after the journal was completed. She was about to read on when a knock at her door startled her back to the present.

"Sayra?" Kimimari's voice called from the other side. "Are you ready? Our patrol starts in ten minutes."

Sayra cursed under her breath. She had lost track of time, absorbed in the pages of her mother's journal. "Coming!" she called back, hastily closing the book and tucking it into a drawer. Beside it was a tiny notebook filled with majik words she'd been studying and practicing with to an absurd degree.

She threw on her armor, dashing toward the wall with Kimimari to compensate for her tardiness. Nuns gave them looks of surprise to see their mad dash, but Sayra would be damned if she gave the Holy Family *any* cause for distrust. Another supervising Valkyrie waved them to their post when they arrived just in the nick of time.

The night air was crisp and cool as Sayra and Kimimari made their way along the northern wall of Saint Highburn Monastery. Their Valkyrie armor clinked quietly, and the steady rhythm of their footsteps echoed off the stone.

Sayra's mind was still reeling from what she had read in her mother's journal, but she forced herself to focus on the present. The wall was their second line of defense against the Horde, and distraction could be deadly. She cast her gaze out over the darkened landscape, searching for any sign of movement, any hint of danger.

Beside her, Kimimari was a silent, steadfast presence. The taller Valkyrie moved with fluid grace, her dark eyes constantly scanning their surroundings. They had patrolled together often enough that they had developed a comfortable rhythm, each instinctively covering the other's blind spots.

Sayra glanced at her companion, noticing the distant look in Kimimari's eyes. "What are you thinking about?" she asked, breaking the silence.

Kimimari startled as if pulled from a deep reverie. "Oh, it's nothing really," she said, a small smile tugging at her lips. "I was just thinking about a new origami design I want to try."

"Origami?" Sayra's eyebrows rose in surprise. "I didn't know you were into that."

Her companion's smile widened beneath her helm, and her black bun peeked out when she crooked her neck. "It's a hobby I picked up a few years ago. There's something calming about folding paper into intricate shapes. It helps me unwind. I neglected it while we were acolytes, but now that we have free time..." She shrugged her wide shoulders.

"That sounds lovely," Sayra said, intrigued. "What kind of designs do you make?"

"All sorts," Kimimari replied, her obsidian eyes lighting up with enthusiasm. "Animals, flowers, geometric shapes. Lately, I've been working on a series of miniature Valkyrie figures. It's challenging but rewarding."

Sayra found herself smiling at her friend's passion. "I'd love to see them sometime."

"Really?" She looked pleased. "I'd be happy to show you. Maybe I could even teach you a few simple folds."

They walked in silence for a few moments before Kimimari spoke again, her voice softer. "You know, sometimes I dream about opening a little shop when I retire. Selling my origami creations, maybe alongside some books and pressed flowers."

Sayra turned to her, surprised by the revelation. "Really? Well, then. I'd absolutely have to be your first customer."

Kimimari half-heartedly flicked a hand at her hip, a hint of sadness creeping into her expression. "It's just a dream." In her unspoken words, the truth clung to them. Many Valkyries died in their line of work, and there was no guarantee they could ever retire. "Being a Valkyrie is important. It's what I need to do. But sometimes, I can't help but wonder what a quieter life might be like."

Sayra felt a pang of guilt. How much did she really know about her friend's hopes and dreams? She knew Kimimari chose a Valkyrie career path to escape poverty and send money back to her adoptive family. Even if none of them cared for her. "Kim, I... I'm sorry. I feel like I haven't been a very good friend lately. I should have known about this."

Kimimari's eyes met hers, a mix of understanding and concern in their depths. "It's all right, Sayra. We've all been busy. But can I be honest with you?"

Sayra nodded, bracing herself.

"I've been worried about you. And Nes," she said, her gloved hand resting on the pommel of her sword. "You both seem so distant lately. Like you're carrying some heavy secret. I miss how things used to be. All of us were together, and there were no barriers between us."

Sayra's heart clenched. She hated keeping secrets from her friends, hated the distance that had grown between them. But how could she possibly explain everything that was happening?

"Kim, I..." she began, struggling to find the right words. "You're right. There is a lot going on that I can't really explain right now. But I promise, when I can, I'll tell you everything."

Kimimari studied her for a long time before nodding slowly. "All right. Just know that I'm here. Whatever's going on, whatever burdens you're carrying, you don't have to face them alone."

Sayra's eyes burned, everything swelling and threatening to throw her overboard. But slowly, she reigned all that in, knowing it was not the time or place to risk it. "Thank you, Kim. That means more than you know."

They were about halfway through their patrol route when Sayra felt it—a faint, insidious chill that crept up her spine and settled in the pit of her stomach. She froze, her hand instinctively going to the hilt of her *spyd*.

"Kimimari," she whispered, her voice tight. "Do you feel that?"

Kimimari nodded, her face grim. "Daemon," she confirmed, her own hand moving to her sword. "But faint. Like it's far away."

Sayra nodded, her eyes straining to pierce the darkness beyond the wall. The fear majik of the Horde was unmistakable, a primal terror that could paralyze the unprepared. But what she felt was just an echo, a whisper of that fear. It was unsettling in its subtlety.

"There," Kimimari breathed, pointing toward the distant shore of the glittering lake.

Sayra followed her gaze. At the very edge of her vision was a shape. It was too far to make out details, but the wrongness of its silhouette was unmistakable. A daemon stood motionless at the distant bank's edge. Where the wards lay.

"It's just watching," Sayra said, her grip tightening on her weapon. "Why isn't it attacking?"

Kimimari shook her head. "I don't know. I've never seen one act like this before."

They stood frozen, watching the distant figure. The fear majik pulsed gently, like a heartbeat, but never intensified. The daemon made no move to approach, seemingly content to stand and observe.

And then, as if things weren't strange enough, a second shape emerged from the tree line to join the first.

"*Fy faen,*" Sayra swore in her native tongue. "There's two of them now."

Kimimari's sharp intake of breath was the only indication of her shock. "We need to alert the others," she said, her voice tight with controlled fear. "This isn't normal daemon behavior."

Sayra nodded, but before she could respond, she caught movement out of the corner of her eye. Turning, she saw two familiar figures approaching along the wall—Lynn and Netta in their armor.

"Sayra! Kimimari!" Lynn called out as they drew closer, her usually cheerful voice tinged with worry. "Do you feel that? We were just about to sound the alarm."

"We feel it," Sayra confirmed, gesturing toward the lake. "Look."

The four Valkyries stood in a line, their eyes fixed on the distant shapes by the water. The daemons remained motionless, their presence a silent challenge to everything the young warriors thought they knew about the Horde.

"What are they doing?" Netta said, her usual bravado noticeably absent. "Why aren't they attacking?"

"I don't know," Sayra said, her mind racing. "But I don't like it. It feels deliberate." *Like they're sending a message.*

Lynn shivered visibly, her gloved hand seeking out Sayra's for comfort. "What kind of message?"

Sayra squeezed her friend's hand, wishing she had a reassuring answer. But truth be told, she was as unsettled as the rest of them. The behavior was unprecedented, and in her growing experience, unprecedented usually meant dangerous.

"We need to report this," Kimimari said, her voice steady despite the tightness in her posture.

Sayra nodded, but a part of her hesitated. After what happened on the wall last time, and the rumors circulating of how the daemon sought her over the Arcanist, she worried about what was to come.

"Netta," she said, making a quick decision. "Go find Sanctus Catara. Tell them what we've seen. The rest of us will stay here and keep watch."

Netta's beady eyes glared at her from the slit of her helmet, her hatred of Sayra remembered. "Don't boss me around." With a last glance at the distant daemons, she made a noise of annoyance. "I'm only going to find Sanctus Catara because I'd rather not be around you three altogether." She took off at a sprint along the wall, her footsteps fading quickly into the night.

Auburn streaks glinted in Lynn's braid as she frowned at Netta's back. "She is so rude always."

A snort escaped from Kimimari as she unclenched her fists. Sayra was far too tense to engage in any further conversation, waiting for the other foot to drop. The remaining three Valkyries turned their attention back to the lake, watching in tense silence. The fear majik continued to pulse gently, a constant reminder of the unnatural presence at the edge of their majik boundary protecting the monastery grounds.

"Do you think..." Lynn began hesitantly, her voice quiet. She had been striving more than usual to perfect the language of the common tongue, which grew noticeable when she spoke slowly. "Do you think they can see us? The way we can see them?"

It was a chilling thought, and one that had already occurred to Sayra. The idea that the daemons might be studying them, learning about their defenses and patterns, was deeply unsettling. "I don't know," she admitted. "But we have to assume they can. We can't underestimate them." After all, Emrys and his network proved to her the daemons were changing. Some were far too intelligent, and others became more aberrant of the typical behaviors.

Kimimari nodded in agreement. "They've never shown this level of intelligence before. At least, not that I've heard of. It's always been mindless aggression, attack on sight."

The minutes stretched on, feeling like hours. The daemons remained motionless, their silent vigil an unspoken threat. Sayra wondered what they were waiting for and what signal or event would spur them into action.

When Netta returned, accompanied by a grim-faced Sanctus Catara, Sayra's hands had grown clammy.

"Report," Catara commanded as soon as she reached them, her hazel eyes already fixed on the distant shoreline.

Sayra stepped forward, bowing along with Lynn and Kimimari. "Two daemons, Sanctus Catara. They appeared approximately thirty minutes ago. They've made no aggressive moves. Just stood there."

Catara's eyes narrowed as she studied the scene. "Unprecedented," she murmured, almost to herself. Then, louder, "Have they shown any indication of violence?"

"No, Sanctus Catara," Kimimari replied. "They've been completely still the entire time."

Catara was silent, her sun-kissed face unreadable. When she spoke again, her voice was tight. "This changes things. If the Horde is evolving, becoming more strategic, we may be facing a threat greater than we ever imagined."

Sayra felt a chill that had nothing to do with the night air. She thought of her mother's journal and the terrible secrets hidden within its pages. Was this part of it? Were these daemons somehow connected to the Holy Family's machinations?

"What do we do, Sanctus Catara?" Lynn asked, her voice small.

Catara's gaze swept over the four young Valkyries, her expression softening slightly. "For now, we watch. We learn. And we prepare. Double the patrols. Increase training. If the Horde is changing its tactics, we must be ready to change ours."

She turned back to the lake, her posture rigid with resolve. "Whatever comes, we will face it. We are Valkyries, guardians of this realm. And we will not falter."

The words landed for the others. Sayra could see it in their straightened backs and the sharper edges of their eyes. But for Sayra, she faked the response, something in her mind whispering it was just the beginning.

⸺⬥⬦⬥⸺

The first hints of dawn were starting to lighten the eastern sky as Sayra stumbled back to her room. As she shed her Valkyrie armor, piece by piece clanking to the floor, she felt the exhaustion settle deep into her bones. The eagle of Sylven's family crest flashed over her chest piece, the armor's unique color between ivory and gold glinting between thin weaving vines of obsidian. She managed to change into her sleeping clothes before collapsing onto her bed, her eyes already heavy with fatigue.

She fell to sleep within a heartbeat, pulled into a realm of swirling shadows and half-formed shapes. In her dream, Sayra stood in a vast, misty plain. The ground beneath her feet was insubstantial, more like smoke than solid earth. Ghostly figures drifted by all around her, their features indistinct and ever-changing.

She tried to call out, but no sound escaped her lips. The ghostly figures seemed to take no notice of her, floating by as if she wasn't even there.

And then, cutting through the eerie silence, a voice echoed across the plain. It was neither male nor female, young nor old, but a sense of urgency made Sayra's spectral heart race.

"Find the spell," the voice said, seeming to come from everywhere and nowhere at once. "Find the spell against the Horde's fear before it's too late."

Sayra tried to respond to ask what spell and where she should look, but no sound came from her mouth. The ghostly figures around her began to move faster, swirling in a dizzying dance.

"The fear will consume all," the voice continued, growing more insistent.

The mist began to thicken, obscuring the ghostly figures. Sayra felt a sense of panic rising within her. She needed to know more, needed to understand.

"Where?" she managed to croak out, her dream voice a whisper. "Where do I look?"

"Hidden pages within..." The voice seemed to be fading, growing distant as the mist closed in. She couldn't decipher any other words.

Sayra tried to run toward the voice, but her feet wouldn't move. The mist swirled around her, thicker and thicker, until she could see nothing but gray. And then, with a gasp, she bolted upright in her bed, her heart pounding and her nightclothes damp with sweat. For a moment, she sat there, trying to catch her breath and make sense of the dream. It had felt so real, so vivid. The urgency of the mysterious voice still echoed in her mind.

"The journal," she said to herself, her eyes darting to the drawer where she had stashed her mother's leather-bound book. "The hidden pages..."

Despite her exhaustion, Sayra felt a surge of adrenaline coursing through her veins. She swung her legs over the side of the bed, wincing as her sore muscles protested the movement. Sayra walked across the cold floor to her desk. Her hands pulled open the drawer and retrieved the journal.

As she held the worn leather tome, Sayra couldn't shake the feeling she was on the verge of something important. The dream, the warning... it all felt too significant to ignore. "Hidden pages," she said, turning the book over in her hands. "What hidden pages?"

She flipped through the journal, her eyes briefly scanning each sheet of paper with renewed intensity. But everything was visible, nothing clueing her in to anything hidden. She waved the book by its spine, and nothing remarkable came of it. Feeling silly, Sayra replaced the journal in its hiding spot, leaning over her desk and pawing at her tired eyes. It was a simple dream, after all. There'd been too much stress on her as of late, and she reasoned she needed sleep.

Tucking herself back into bed, Sayra tried to relax back into its grasp, but lingering unease pooled in her mind.

Chapter Twelve

SYLVEN

The carriage rattled Sylven along the dirt road in the afternoon, its rhythmic clatter punctuated by the steady clip-clop of horses' hooves. He and Sayra sat on one side, facing Emrys and Nessika on the other. They left Saint Highburn Monastery for the city of Tern to meet with the queen of Acacea. Emrys fidgeted with the cuff of his forest-green frock coat, his dark eyes fixed on Sayra as she pored over the worn leather journal in her lap. Beside him, Nessika sat ramrod straight in her armor, her eyes constantly scanning their surroundings, ever vigilant. Across from them, Sylven leaned back in his seat, his hazel eyes flicking between Sayra and the passing sunlit landscape outside the window.

Ahead of them, in a separate carriage, rode Vander and Breane.

Sayra's voice, low and intense, filled the small space as she read from the journal. "'I found my mother's journals hidden in a false bottom of her old trunk after my firstborn's birth. The secrets contained within changed everything I thought I knew about our family.'" She paused, her fingers tracing the faded ink on the page before her. "'This I must not ruminate long here for, as everything necessary will be passed in accordance with my bloodline's wishes. Even after learning of a destiny grander than anything I could ever dream of, it would never have prepared me to see the world fulfilling it around me.'"

The others leaned in, drawn by the gravity in her voice. Sayra turned the page, and Sylven clasped his hands over his black trousers, the edges of his cream vest askew.

"'Today, I witnessed something that has shaken me to my very core,'" Sayra read, her voice taking on the cadence of her mother's written words. "'The Grand Priest, the man I am sworn to protect, the supposed embodiment of the Goddess's will on earth, committed an act so heinous, so utterly at odds with everything we are taught to believe, that I can scarcely bring myself to put it to paper.'"

Sylven felt a chill run down his spine. He glanced at Emrys, noting how the prince's jaw clenched, his hands balled into fists on his knees.

Sayra's hand tightened around the journal. "'It took well over a decade of exceeding expectations and remaining faithful to the Holy Family to witness the true meaning of depravity. In the depths of the monastery, in chambers I never knew existed, I saw him perform a ritual. A young Valkyrie candidate, no more than fifteen, was strapped to an altar. The Grand Priest... he used some kind of dark majik, drawing it out of an artifact I've never seen before. The girl's screams... I'll never forget them as long as I live. Her body twisted, contorted, as the majik poured into her. And then she changed.'"

Sylven felt his stomach lurch. Across from him, he heard Nessika's sharp intake of breath.

"'When it was over,'" Sayra read, her voice shaking, "'what lay on that altar was no longer human. It was a daemon. The Grand Priest had transformed her, corrupted her very essence. And he smiled, Goddess help me, he smiled as if he'd accomplished some great feat.'"Nessika's face wrinkled.

"'This was not an isolated incident. Over the next few months, I witnessed more of these transformations. Failed Valkyrie candidates, Arcanists who asked too many questions, even common folk who had the misfortune to discover something they shouldn't have. All of them twisted and warped into the very monsters we're sworn to protect the world against. And that, *that*, was a kindness in comparison to the worst yet in store.'" Sayra's voice grew stronger as she continued, "'I knew I had to do something, to stop this madness somehow. But I was alone, surrounded by those who either didn't know or didn't care about the atrocities being committed. And then I discovered I was with child.'"

Sylven saw Emrys stiffen, his eyes locked on Sayra with an intensity that was almost painful to witness.

"'I couldn't stay,'" Sayra read, her voice filled with a mix of admiration and sorrow for her mother's plight. "'I couldn't bring a child into this world of secrets and corruption. So, I concocted a plan to distance myself and keep my family safe. I ran. To the only person I thought I could trust. A distant relative's husband, a man with connections outside the Holy Family's sphere of influence.'"

Sayra paused, her eyes scanning ahead. When she spoke again, her voice was filled with wonder. "This is where it all changed. Listen to this," she said, looking up at them.

"'Through my relative's husband, I was introduced to a woman who would change the course of my life. Queen Evangelina of Acacea. She, too, was with child, and in her, I found not just an ally but a kindred spirit. She had long harbored suspicions about the Holy Family, and my testimony confirmed her worst fears.'"

Sylven watched as Emrys leaned forward, his eyes wide. It was his mother they were talking about, his family's involvement in a conspiracy that spanned generations.

Sayra read, "'Evangelina and I spent long hours discussing what could be done. We knew we couldn't confront the Holy Family directly. They were too powerful, too entrenched. But perhaps... perhaps we could plant the seeds of their downfall in the very next generation.'"

Sylven had a feeling he knew where the story was going.

"'It was Evangelina who first suggested using the relic once we realized it began to decay outside of the monastery grounds,'" Sayra read, a whisp of her blonde hair falling to cusp her cheek. "'We had all heard whispers of its power, of its ability to grant or enhance majik abilities. Once, we believed it to be the Goddess who gifted it, but now we realize it was this very relic. We concocted a bold, daring, and idiotic plan, but only managed to steal away two out of the four pieces. For some reason or another, the integrity began to decay at a rate that alarmed us. We had no time to figure out why and became desperate. Desperation gives birth to grand ideas, some transcending what we previously thought was possible. If we could use it on our unborn children, give them powers beyond what the Holy Family could control or understand...'"

Sylven looked at Emrys and saw the way he tucked his emotions behind a cool demeanor. Everyone thought the Goddess had bestowed an extra gift to the younger prince of Acacea, one that allowed him to sense the use of majik, whereas it was once an unheard-of affinity.

"'The risk was great,'" Sayra continued reading, "'but the potential reward was greater still. We made a pact, Evangelina and me. We would use the relic on our children, imbue them with the power to one day challenge the Holy Family. And we would do everything in our power to prepare them for the fight that lay ahead. So, we tested it on her youngest son after birth and then my daughter. Some may have laughed at our hubris, but it worked. For us to bear this responsibility was one thing, but to have to pass this incomprehensive burden on to infants... May the

Goddess deliver us forgiveness for our greatest sins once our souls pass through the void.'"

As Sayra's voice trailed off, a heavy silence fell over the carriage.

Sylven looked at his friends, taking in their reactions. Emrys sat rigid. Nessika's hand had moved to the armrest, her knuckles white. And Sayra... Sayra looked half-present and half-lost in her mind.

Sylven found himself speaking, his voice sounding strange to his own ears. "What does this mean for us?"

Sayra looked up from the journal, and her green eyes met his. "It means we have a responsibility," she said, her voice steady despite the tremor in her hands. "Our mothers, they sacrificed everything to give us this chance. We have to see it through, and I must speak with mine once more. I need to know what she meant about my family's secrets. Anything that could help, we must learn."

As the carriage rolled through the ornate gates of Tern, Sylven saw a shift in the atmosphere. The bustling city streets seemed to pause, a ripple of recognition and reverence spreading through the crowd as they caught sight of the royal crest emblazoned on the carriage door. Sylven watched, a mixture of apprehension and discomfort settling in him as people stopped in their tracks, bowing deeply as they passed. He glanced at Rys, noting the practiced ease with which his friend acknowledged the crowd's deference with a regal nod.

Nessika was on high alert, watching with the eyes of an eagle for any potential threat.

"I'll never get used to this," Sylven muttered under his breath, earning a small understanding smile from Sayra. However, he noted her eyes immediately went back to studying Rys the moment no one was looking.

Now that he knew what to look for, it was abundantly obvious. When Sayra smiled, Rys's eyes always widened just so, as if they had just witnessed the grandest work of art. When Rys glanced away, Sayra admired the cut of his frock coat and the regal features of his face. Her tone softened when speaking to him, and his face shifted whenever he would look her way.

A wistful twinge ate at his stomach.

As they approached the city center, a contingent of royal guards fell into formation around their carriage, their polished armor gleaming in the afternoon sun. The clatter of hooves on cobblestone echoed off the tall, elegant buildings that lined the streets, an area of prosperity and importance. When they came to a stop in front of a grand, ivy-covered building that Sylven recognized as one of the royal family's private residences, a flurry of activity erupted around them. Stable hands rushed to attend to the horses, while attendants materialized to assist them from the carriage.

Sylven felt distinctly out of place as he stepped onto the street, acutely aware of the many eyes upon them. An attendant bowed low before him. "Lord Astor," the man said reverently, "it is an honor to welcome you to Tern." Then he turned to address the princes as they climbed from their respective carriages. "Prince Emrys and Prince Vander, it is my pleasure to greet you both. Please allow me to escort you and your companions inside."

Sylven nodded, still unused to such a formal address after being at Saint Highburn Monastery for so long. He fell into step beside Emrys as they were led through an intricately carved wooden door and into a cool, dimly lit foyer.

"This way, Your Highnesses, my lords and ladies," their guide said, leading them down a long hallway adorned with tapestries and portraits of stern-faced ancestors.

As they approached a set of heavy double doors at the end of the hall, Sylven felt a surge of nervous anticipation. They were about to meet the queen, Emrys's mother, the woman who had set so much of things in motion.

The heavy oak doors swung open noiselessly, as if guided by an invisible hand, displaying a study adorned with exquisite taste. Towering windows immediately caught his eye, and the shelves decorated with meticulously crafted leather-bound books and intriguing artifacts followed suit. A massive fireplace dominated one wall, its hearth cold in the spring heat. Overhead, an intricate crystal chandelier glittered.

At the center of the room stood a large ornate desk, its surface covered in maps and documents. Behind it, an enigmatic figure stood, captivating all who beheld her. With a crown of Emrys's dark tresses, her piercing gaze seemed to penetrate the very depths of one's soul—Queen Evangelina.

Sylven's first impression was of fragility. The queen was slight of build, her once-dark hair now streaked with silver. Her face bore the lines of age and worry, and there was a tiny tremor in her hands as she moved around the desk. But as she drew closer, her gown of deep-sapphire silk brushing against the floor, Sylven saw the steel beneath the frail exterior. Her eyes, just like Emrys's, were sharp and alert, missing nothing as they swept over the assembled group.

"Welcome, my dears," Queen Evangelina said, her voice warm but carrying an undercurrent of authority that commanded attention. An elegant crown of silver was tucked in her wavy hair above a necklace of white gold, set with a large deep-blue sapphire that matched her gown perfectly. "I'm so glad you've all arrived safely."

She embraced Emrys first with flowing sleeves, her love for her son evident in the way she held him close for a moment before releasing him. Then she turned to Vander, her smile tightening almost imperceptibly as she kissed his cheek.

"Mother," Vander said, his tone respectful but cool. "You're looking well."

"Thank you, Vander," she replied, before turning her attention to the others.

Her gaze fell on Sayra, and her expression softened. "And you must be Sayra von Lykken," she said, stepping forward to take Sayra's hands in her own. "I've so looked forward to meeting you, my dear. You have your mother's eyes."

Sylven watched as Sayra's composure faltered for a moment, clearly caught off guard by the queen's warmth and the mention of her mother.

"Thank you, Your Majesty," Sayra managed, dipping into a curtsy. "It's an honor to meet you."

Queen Evangelina smiled with mischief in her gray eyes. "Please, when we're in private like this, call me Evangelina. We're all friends here, united in a common cause."

She turned to Sylven and Nessika, acknowledging them with a nod. "Lord Astor, Valkyrie Nessika, thank you both for your dedication and loyalty. Your roles in what's to come cannot be overstated."

Her gaze fell on Breane. "And Valkyrie Breane. Before you take your leave with the guard, I trust you've been keeping my boy in line?"

Breane bowed deeply. "I do my best, Your Majesty," she replied, amusement in her voice.

Queen Evangelina chuckled. "I'm sure you do."

Breane left the room to assume a guard position, leaving the rest of them to their privacy.

Folding his arms, Vander raised a brow at his mother. "Nessika will be joining us?"

The unspoken words lingered. He thought Nessika shouldn't be included if his Valkyrie wasn't.

"Indeed. Emrys has conveyed in our correspondence Sayra's wish to include her Valkyrie compatriot. I will honor it." The queen gestured to a seating area near the fireplace, where plush armchairs and sofas were arranged in a semicircle. "Please, let's all sit. We have much to discuss, and I'm afraid time is not on our side."

As they moved to take their seats, Sylven couldn't help but notice the way the queen leaned ever so on Emrys's arm, the only outward sign of any physical weakness.

Once they were all seated, Queen Evangelina adjusted her flowing skirt and looked at each of them in turn, her expression growing serious. "First, I want to thank you all for coming. What we're about to embark on is dangerous, make no mistake. But it's also necessary. The fate of our kingdom, perhaps of the entire world, hangs in the balance."

She paused, her gaze lingering on Sayra. "Sayra, I know you must have many questions. About your mother. About your role in all of this. I promise you all will be explained. But first..." She glanced at the ornate clock on the mantelpiece. "We're waiting on one more person to join us."

Sylven studied the others, noting how Vander barely seemed to contain his impatience and the protective stance Nessika had taken near Sayra.

The heavy oak door of the study creaked open, drawing all eyes to the figure that stepped through. Arene von Lykken entered the room, her posture dignified. Her blonde hair, so similar to Sayra's, was pulled back in a simple braid under her hood, and she wore a modest gray traveling cloak that seemed at odds with the opulent surroundings.

Sylven watched as Sayra's body tensed, her eyes locking onto her mother. A lifetime of unspoken words and their last encounter hung between them. In a moment that was so personal, Sylven felt every bit an intruder.

Queen Evangelina broke the tense silence. "Arene, my dear friend. I'm so glad you could join us."

Arene nodded, her eyes briefly meeting the queen's before returning to Sayra. "Your Majesty," she said softly, taking a hesitant step toward her daughter. "Sayra..."

Sayra stood, her armored figure striking against the backlighting. Sylven could feel the lingering hurt and anger from their last meeting but also a flicker of something new—understanding and perhaps even the beginnings of forgiveness—leaking through their mental bond. Her block had slipped, a sign of her inner shock at the situation.

"Mother," Sayra said, her voice steady but laden with meaning.

For a moment, neither moved. Then, with a deep breath, Sayra closed the distance between them. Emrys tensed where he sat, appearing as if he may launch upward at any second.

Sylven hoped the encounter wouldn't be a repeat of the last.

Chapter Thirteen

SYLVEN

Sylven barely breathed as Sayra drew nearer to Arene.

"I've had time to think," she said, her voice low enough Sylven had to strain to hear. "To read your journal, to understand... and I can't say I agree with everything you did, but I think I understand why you did it."

Arene's eyes welled with tears. "Oh, Sayra," she breathed. "I never meant to cause you so much pain. Everything I did—"

"I know," Sayra interrupted gently. "You were trying to protect me. And now we need to protect each other. To fight this battle together." With those words, Sayra stepped forward and embraced her mother.

Arene held her tightly, years of separation and longing pouring out in that single gesture.

Sylven's chest tightened at the grief that pulled at Arene's eyes and the gratitude that welled within them. He felt a lump form in his throat as he watched the reunion. Glancing around the room, he saw the impact on the others as well. Emrys wore a small, satisfied smile, while Nessika loosened her shoulders. Even Vander seemed moved, though he quickly schooled his features back into neutrality.

Queen Evangelina stood, her face joyful and determined. "This is a moment I've hoped to witness for many years. But it's only the beginning. Now, we must prepare for the fight ahead."

As Sayra and Arene separated, wiping tears from their eyes, the queen gestured for everyone to retake their seats. "Arene, please join us. I believe formal introductions are in order."

Arene nodded, composing herself as she took a seat next to Sayra. Sylven couldn't help but notice how she unconsciously leaned toward her mother, as if making up for years of lost closeness.

Queen Evangelina began the introductions. "Arene, you of course know my sons, Emrys and Vander."

The princes nodded, Emrys with warmth, Vander with cool politeness.

"And this is Lady Nessika, Emrys's Valkyrie," the queen continued.

Nessika bowed her head respectfully, her posture still alert and protective.

"And, of course, Lord Sylven Astor, Sayra's Arcanist."

Sylven felt a jolt as the queen's piercing gaze fell on him. He bowed, suddenly very aware of his position in the gathering of royalty and legend. Before, it all felt like he was a second thought, but he truly was a part of it all now. Something greater.

"It's an honor to meet you all, some once again," Arene said, her voice gaining strength. "I've heard so much about each of you from Evangelina's reports. Your dedication to our cause gives me hope for the future we're fighting for."

Sayra straightened in her seat. "Mother, perhaps you could tell us more about what you've been doing all these years. Your journal only covered so much."

Arene nodded, her eyes sweeping to the queen. At Evangelina's encouragement, she began to speak.

"After I left," she said, choosing her words carefully, "I dedicated myself to uncovering as much as I could about the Holy Family's true nature and their plans. I stayed put for many years, acting the part of a loyal Valkyrie. After we stole the relic pieces, though, that was no longer an option. I faked my death with much help from Evangelina, and from there, I traveled across the continent, following whispers and rumors, piecing together fragments of ancient lore."

She leaned forward, her voice dropping as if sharing a great secret. "What I found... it's more terrible and more hopeful than we could have imagined."

He glanced at Emrys, seeing his own unease mirrored on his friend's face.

"There's a sanctuary beneath the monastery," Arene continued. "Ancient beyond reckoning. It's the true source of all majik in our world. The Holy Family found it centuries ago, and they've been using it to maintain their grip on power ever since."

Queen Evangelina folded her hands. "Tell them, Arene. They need to know everything if we're to have any hope of success."

Arene's gaze swept across the room before settling on Sayra. "The Holy Family's power, their control over majik, it all stems from the ancient relic within the sanctuary as a whole. The four pieces we know of are part of something far greater. Something that dates back to the origins of the Goddess herself."

A collective gasp went through the room.

"What do you mean by the origins of the Goddess?" Emrys asked, his voice tight.

Arene's face turned to him. "There are stories, legends so old they've been all but forgotten. They speak of a time before the Goddess, when majik flowed freely through the world. But with that power came great destruction. Wars that reshaped continents, creatures of nightmares that roamed unchecked. The relic as a whole was created to contain that power, to bring balance to the world. But over time, it was broken."

"And the Holy Family found the pieces," Sayra said, crossing her armored arms with a faint clinking noise.

Arene nodded. "Their bloodline spent generations studying them, using their power to establish their dominion over majik."

Sylven's mind was racing. "But if this relic is so powerful, why haven't they used it to completely dominate the world? Why maintain this facade of religious authority and nearly wipe out most of the male population in the process?"

"Because they can't control it fully. Not yet. The relic's power is too great, too volatile. They need a way to harness it safely. And as we've discovered, the relic pieces cannot withstand being moved from their cradle under Saint Highburn Monastery for one reason or another." Queen Evangelina frowned, her feet shifting as she tucked them further back.

"Which is where you two come in," Arene said, looking at Emrys and Sayra. "By infusing you with the relic's power as infants, we hoped to create vessels that could withstand its full force."

For a second, Vander paled. He regained his composure, but his face warred with his shock. "What do you mean 'you two'? I was under the distinct impression only Sayra had a piece of the relic within her."

Regret clouded the queen's delicate features. "As you both know, my sons, there is much we must withhold for the greater good. As Emrys now knows, we tested a small piece of one relic on him first to ensure it could be done before infusing the whole of the second piece into Sayra."

Something dark grew in Vander's eyes, his posture stiffening. "I see."

Sylven watched as Vander's reaction unfolded. The revelation clearly caught him off guard, and Sylven couldn't help but wonder how the new information might affect the dynamics between the brothers and their plans moving forward.

Sensing the tension, the queen's gaze lingered on her eldest son. "Vander, I know this must come as a surprise. We never meant to—"

"To what, Mother?" Vander interrupted, his voice tight with controlled fury. "To exclude me? To deem me unworthy of this grand destiny you've planned?"

Emrys held out a palm. "Brother, it's not like that. We didn't know—"

"Didn't we?" Vander snapped, rising to his feet. His fists were clenched at his sides, and Sylven could see the struggle for control playing out across his features. "I've always known there was something different about you, Emrys. Something that sets you apart. And now I know why."

The room fell silent. Sylven glanced at Sayra, seeing his own unease reflected in her eyes. The family drama was threatening to derail their entire meeting, and they couldn't afford such distractions with so much at stake.

Queen Evangelina stood, her regal bearing seeming to fill the room despite her small stature. "Vander, please. This was never about worthiness. It was about protecting you, about ensuring the survival of our line if the worst should happen. You are the crown prince, the future of our kingdom. We couldn't risk—"

"Couldn't risk what?" Vander demanded, his voice rising. "Couldn't risk me having the power to truly lead? To make a difference?"

Stepping forward, Arene's voice was calm but firm. "Prince Vander, please understand. The power of the relic is not a gift. It's a burden. A dangerous, potentially deadly burden. We had no way of knowing if the infusion would even work, let alone what the long-term effects might be."

Vander's gaze snapped to Arene, his eyes narrowing. "And yet you were willing to risk it on my brother and your daughter?" His voice dripped with disdain. "How noble of you."

Eyes narrowing, Sayra's focus honed in on Vander. Sylven could see the hurt and anger radiating from him, and he sympathized despite his misgivings about the crown prince. For someone to learn they had been kept in the dark about such a monumental secret, to feel as though they had been deemed less worthy than their younger sibling... it was a bitter pill to swallow.

Emrys stood, moving to stand beside his brother. "Vander," he said, placing a hand on his shoulder, "this changes nothing between us. You are still my brother, still the future king. The relic's power doesn't define us."

For a moment, Vander seemed to waver, the anger in his eyes warring with uncertainty. But then he shrugged off Emrys's hand, his expression hardening once more. "Doesn't it?" he asked bitterly. "It seems to me that it defines everything. Our futures. Our destinies. The very fate of our kingdom."

His mother stepped forward, her eyes shining with unshed tears. "My son," the queen said, her voice thick. "I have made many mistakes in my life, but loving you, believing in you, was never one of them. You are stronger than you know, with or without the relic's power."

Vander held his mother's gaze for a moment, a storm of emotions playing across his face. His shoulders sagged. "I need some air," he said, his voice strained. "Excuse me."

With that, he turned and strode from the room, the heavy door slamming shut behind him.

In the wake of Vander's departure, a heavy silence fell over the room. Sylven could see the toll the confrontation had taken on everyone. Queen Evangelina looked older, more fragile than ever, while Emrys's face tightened. Sayra and Nessika exchanged worried glances, clearly unsure of how the new development might affect their plans.

With a heavy heart, Queen Evangelina turned to address the group. "Vander will need time to process this information. In the meantime, we must press on."

Arene nodded, picking up where she had left off. "As I was saying, the Holy Family's control over the relic is incomplete. They've been searching for a way to fully harness its power for generations. And now, they're closer than ever to achieving that goal."

"How?" Sayra asked.

Arene's face grew grim. "During my last days serving them, they had discovered an ancient ritual, one that would allow them to merge the relic pieces and channel their full power. But it requires a sacrifice. A powerful sacrifice."

Sylven swallowed. "What kind of sacrifice?" he asked, though he feared he already knew the answer.

"A life," Arene said with a heaviness. "Not just any life, as they've failed the many attempts they've tried, but one I believe to be infused with the relic's power. They need either Emrys or Sayra. Possibly both. To date, we do not think they have pieced this together. They are under the impression that the relics are missing, or they were destroyed along with my attempts to smuggle them out."

The room fell silent as the revelation settled over them. Sylven glanced at Emrys and Sayra, seeing the shock and horror on their faces. He felt a surge of protectiveness toward them both, his friends who had been thrust into this dangerous game through no fault of their own.

Queen Evangelina spoke up, her voice steady despite the gravity of the situation. "This is why we've brought you all together. We need to stop the Holy Family before they can complete this ritual. But more than that, we need to find a way to destroy the remaining relic pieces for good, to ensure this power can never be misused again. With any luck, we may also close the rifts spilling the Horde into our world using Sayra's relic."

"What did you mean by the origins of the Goddess?" Nessika spoke up, a gloved hand tucking back her straight, shoulder-length hair behind her ear.

"The legends speak of a time before the Goddess, when majik was wild and uncontrolled. They say that the Goddess herself was born from this chaos, a being of pure majik who sought to bring order to the world," Arene said, her gait off from the false leg as she moved to sit beside Sayra once more.

Queen Evangelina nodded, adding, "According to these ancient tales, the Goddess created the relic. We don't know for what ends or what means she accomplished this feat."

Tapping his fingers on the back of his hand, Emrys asked, "How have you come by this knowledge?"

"There's a language beyond our understanding written around each relic, one as old as the Goddess herself, if I were to assume," Arene said, lowering her chin. "While we weren't able to decipher it, I was able to make another connection to what knowledge I gleaned from the Holy Family. Ley lines run throughout the entire continent, and while we haven't charted them extensively, we know the direction of major lines and conjunction points, especially ones localized to frequent travel routes. While I've been gone, I've spent the majority of my time on the southern continent, exploring these patterns, and I've discovered something revolutionary."

A part of Sylven dreaded what was to come. How much more could they learn without crumbling? Vander hadn't lasted long, and from the stressed appearances of Nessika, Sayra, and Emrys, none of them were far behind. Their whole world was being turned upside down at once, and the very distinct possibility of the Goddess's origins being so different than what they were taught...

He swallowed. Hard.

"At a major ley line conjunction, I found more of those ancient symbols. The exact ones on the relic pieces." Arene's mouth twisted into a bitter smile. "Ruins of a temple dotted the earth nearby, and as I investigated, I was ambushed."

A soft intake of breath sounded as Sayra stared wide-eyed at her mother. Emrys's brow knitted together in concern. Sylven and Nessika listened with rapt attention as the queen's empathetic expression changed into one of thinly veiled sorrow.

"The local populace wasn't so kind to intruders, especially within their sacred grounds. It took time, but I convinced them I was no friend of the Holy Family, and I sought only the truth. Eventually, they believed me and took me in. I listened to their own truths and opened my ears to their stories of old."

Jerking back, Emrys's gaze sharpened with understanding. "The Southern Democracy of Highlands." His tone was incredulous, as if he berated himself for not seeing it all along.

"The enemy of your enemy is your friend," Nessika murmured to herself.

A proud glint crossed the queen's gray eyes.

"Yes. The Holy Family seeks to have them destroyed for this very reason. They harbor old folktales that would carry any of them to the noose if told within holy grounds. I learned what I could from them, taking that knowledge and returning here with it."

Sylven listened intently as Arene continued her explanation, his mind racing to process the implications of what she was saying. He glanced around at the ornate tapestries adorning the walls, their intricate designs suddenly seeming to hide secrets of their own.

"What exactly did you learn from them?" Sayra asked, shifting in her seat, the leather creaking softly beneath her.

Arene's face grew solemn, the lines around her eyes deepening. "They spoke of a time when the world was in chaos, torn apart by unchecked majik. They believe that the Goddess—or rather, the being that would become our Goddess—was born from that chaos, a manifestation of majik itself. But she wasn't alone."

Another collective intake of breath swept through the room. Sylven felt his heart rate quicken. He gripped the arms of his chair, anchoring himself.

"According to their legends," Arene continued, "there were others. Beings of immense power, neither good nor evil, but forces of nature unto themselves. The Goddess sought to bring order to the chaos, to protect the mortal races from the destructive potential of uncontrolled majik. But the others had different ideas."

Queen Evangelina picked up the thread. "The stories speak of a great war, a conflict that reshaped the very face of our world. In the end, the

Goddess emerged victorious but at a terrible cost. To remove the power of her defeated foes and save the world, she created the relic."

"But if that's true," Nessika said, "then destroying the relic could undo the Goddess's work. Perhaps she intended for a different outcome."

"Indeed. It would destroy majik entirely. But we have no other choice at the current rate. Time has erased any forthcoming truth that may have come from her intentions. The Goddess brought us thousands of years of peacetime, but alas, humankind can never be content with the balance given to them. We must destroy the remaining relics and close the rifts before we further corrupt any lingering trace of her."

A world without majik... without daemons... Sylven's chest ached at the thought of losing his ability to connect with the ley lines, but was it not worth a shot to save humanity?

Chapter Fourteen

SAYRA

Dinner was about to be served, everyone save Sayra and Arene leaving the chamber. Sayra watched as the others filed out of the room, leaving her alone with her mother for the first time in years. Arene stood by the window, her silhouette framed by the fading light of day.

"There's more, isn't there?" Sayra asked, breaking the silence. "Something you didn't want to say in front of the others."

Arene turned, her eyes meeting Sayra's. There was a deep sadness there, tinged with a fierce determination. "You've always been perceptive," she said with a small smile. "Yes, there is more. Something I've only recently discovered, and something that concerns you directly."

Sayra felt her heart rate quicken. "What is it?"

Arene's weathered face grew close, her silver-streaked hair gleaming as she gripped Sayra's metal-clad shoulders. Sayra could feel the urgency in her mother's touch, see the worry etched in the lines around her eyes.

"The relic piece within you is not just a source of power. It's a key. A key to unlocking something far greater and more dangerous than we ever imagined," Arene said, her voice low and intense.

"What do you mean?" Sayra asked, matching her mother's volume.

Arene's gaze darted around the dimly lit chamber before returning to Sayra's face. "Our destiny is tied up in secrets. There's so much I wish I could explain, but we lack both time and privacy." A chill ran down Sayra's spine as her mother continued, "Everything you need to know rests in a false bottom of your trunk in Faenda, at our family home. Old majik is at work here, Sayra. Something grander than I could have ever envisioned."

The stone walls seemed to press in around them as Sayra struggled to process the revelation. The musty scent of ancient tomes filled her nostrils, grounding her in the present moment. "But, Mother, I don't understand. What more could there possibly be?"

"The symbols I found at the ley line conjunction, and the people there, spoke of a destiny originating from a time before humanity was born. Older than life itself and woven into our bloodline. A chosen one who would wield the power of the relic to either save our world or destroy it." Her grip tightened, her eyes boring into Sayra's. "With everything coming to a head much quicker than I anticipated, I don't think there will be another generation before this destiny must be fulfilled. I believe that chosen one is you."

Footsteps sounded outside the closed door, and a frantic edge overtook Arene's face. "Sayra, you must swear to me not to share that information with anyone else. This destiny, we only have one shot at fulfilling it. Even the slightest of missteps will cause us to fail, and our bloodline has forewarned us of the consequences should the wrong ears overhear. You must go home and look within the false bottom. Our family's journals are hidden there. Do not share them with any other until you've read them or else you put us both in grave danger, along with your friends." Her voice picked up in intensity and pace. "We have a year for our plan to be enacted. There is time, but we must be careful. Keep reading through the journal I've given you. Do you understand?"

There were a million protests rising to the tip of her tongue. Why couldn't she share with a trusted few? Why couldn't Arene simply give her a summary of what was written in these journals? What did she mean by old majik? And what destiny could be greater than to end the Holy Family and close the rifts?

"Yes. I swear I will do what you say," Sayra breathed as the doors opened.

Vander's face was wary, and he searched theirs as if to decipher what had just been said. Sayra felt her mother's hands fall away as Vander held the door open. She straightened her spine, forcing her face into neutrality.

"I hope I'm not interrupting," he said, his voice smooth as silk. Gone were his anger and frustration, replaced by his normal smirk and assessing gaze. "We have dinner waiting, and we'll not eat without you both present."

Sayra followed her mother and Vander out of the room. The opulent dinner passed in a blur of polite conversation and forced smiles, Sayra's thoughts far from the present. As the night wore on, she counted the minutes until she could escape the suffocating atmosphere of false pleasantries and hidden agendas.

As the moon climbed high in the sky, she felt a familiar tingling at the edge of her consciousness. Sylven's clear and urgent voice echoed through their mental link.

It's time. Meet us in the east courtyard in five minutes.

Sayra's heart quickened. The cool night air was a welcome relief as she made her way to the rendezvous point. Slinking out of the manor through Emrys's recommended route proved rather easy and uneventful. She moved silently, her Valkyrie training allowing her to blend seamlessly with the darkness.

"And that makes four." Sylven's low voice greeted her as she rounded a corner. He stood with Nessika and Emrys, all dressed in dark clothing that melted into the night.

Emrys nodded, his eyes scanning their surroundings. "We need to move quickly. The night patrol will be making their rounds soon."

As they slipped out of the manor grounds and into the sleeping town beyond, Sayra was weary of it all. The sneaking. The secrets. The impossible layers that kept piling up higher and higher, threatening to topple and crush her beneath.

The streets were nearly deserted, only the occasional stray cat or late-night reveler crossing their path. Sayra's hand rested on the hilt of her knife under her cloak, ready for any potential danger. Cobblestone buildings piled around her as they wove through the maze of shady alleyways, the occasional oil lantern dotting the way. Tavern signs creaked in the shallow breeze as it blew through, whistling all the while a merry tune contradicting their alert cadence. They rounded a corner, and two evocatively dressed women looped around a man's arms as they giggled by a bustling tavern. A woman sang a brawly song inside, words that made Sayra blush echoing from patrons keeping pace.

They arrived at an unassuming building tucked away in a quiet corner of the town. A weathered sign bearing the name "Ophelia Majik Co." swung gently in the night breeze of the artifact shop.

"This is it," Emrys murmured, approaching the door. He knocked in a specific pattern, the sound echoing in the stillness of the night.

For a moment, nothing happened. Then, with a soft click, the door swung open. Inside was a dimly lit interior and a man who wore a permanent tilt to his mouth.

Kent greeted them with a cheeky grin, his muddy eyes sparkling with mischief. "Well, well, look what the cat dragged in! Come on in, you sneaky bunch. We don't want any nosy neighbors getting an eyeful, do we?"

He ushered them inside with exaggerated gestures, keeping up a running commentary. "Watch your step there, Your Highness. Wouldn't want you to trip and scuff those royal boots. And you, Miss Valkyrie, try not to knock over my priceless artifacts with that impressive knife-shaped thing on your hip, eh?" He danced around one of his many display tables, where intricate trinkets were craftily showcased on fine fabrics and platforms.

Sayra couldn't help but smile at Kent's antics as he led them behind the merchant's desk. He pulled a lever disguised as an old candlestick, revealing a hidden staircase behind a hulking shelf of financial documents and folders. They removed their hoods, Sylven and Nessika looking distrustfully at the stairwell.

"Down you go into the secret lair," Kent stage-whispered. "Don't worry, I had the evil-alchemist decor removed last week. Now it's all cozy and rebellion-chic."

As they descended the stairs, the playful atmosphere gave way to a more serious mood. The basement opened up into a well-lit war room, maps and documents covering every available surface. Cassandra and Ty were already there, their faces grave as they looked up from a pile of papers. Contrasting upbeat music spun from a nearby box, drowning out their faint footsteps as the five of them moved from the stairwell.

An in-depth map with elevated landmarks was spread across a back rectangular table, every country on their continent noted along with those surrounding them across vast oceans. Portraits of the Holy Family and others Sayra still didn't recognize hung across the wall above it, descriptions and notes pinned beneath each.

Sayra's mouth smirked at the tiny devil horns drawn over the Grand Priest's face. Now it all made that much more sense.

On the short wall to her immediate right of the doorway, a heavily inked map of their continent, emphasis around the monastery, dangled. Shelves of tomes and notebooks bound with labels covered the last free wall, the space almost the exact same as the last time she was there with Emrys. A lavender scent rose from the incense beside the music player.

Electric-blue eyes grew huge with outrage. "Kent, now there are *two* Valkyries?" Cassandra's voice rose to a shrill level. "*And* another man?"

Sayra tensed at Cassandra's outburst.

Kent held up his hands in a placating gesture, his usual grin replaced by a more serious expression. "Now, now, Cass. Let's not jump to conclusions. These ladies and gents are on our side."

Ty stepped forward, his imposing figure seeming to fill the small space. "Cass," he said, his deep voice firm, "we discussed this. They're part of the plan now."

Emrys moved to stand beside Sylven and Nessika, his presence a silent show of support. "I can vouch for their loyalty," he said, his voice carrying royal authority. "They're crucial to our mission."

Cassandra's eyes narrowed, flicking between Sayra and Nessika. The upbeat music created a backdrop contrasting the standoff.

Finally, Cassandra's shoulders slumped, her black curls spilling across her lavish lilac gown and somewhat exposed bosom. "Fine," she said, her voice clipped. "But if this goes south, it's on your heads." She pointed a pale hand at Emrys and Kent. Then, at the high-cheekboned thief. "You too, Ty."

Kent clapped his hands together, his lady-swooning grin returning. "Excellent! Now that we've got the obligatory trust issues out of the way, shall we get down to business?"

He gestured toward the map-covered table. "We've got some juicy intel that I think you'll all find very interesting. And possibly terrifying. But mostly interesting!"

As they gathered around the table, Sayra exchanged a quick glance with Sylven. His face was impassive, but through their link, she could feel his unease. It surprised her that he'd let his barrier down intentionally, but she reciprocated the gesture. In response to her reassurance, he lowered his chin a hair. Whatever they were about to learn, it was clear their already complicated mission was about to become even more dangerous.

Ty began unrolling a fresh map over the existing one, his large hands careful with the delicate parchment. "We've uncovered some disturbing patterns in Horde activity," he said, his voice grave. "And it's not just here. Reports are coming in from across the continent."

Emrys stepped forward, the flickering candlelight casting shadows across the panes of his handsome face. His dark eyes swept the room, commanding attention without a word. The soft clink of his formal attire, a deep-navy frock coat with silver embroidery, punctuated the silence as he moved.

"Before we proceed," he began, his rich voice filling the cramped space, "allow me to properly introduce our new allies." He gestured toward Nessika and Sylven, who stood slightly apart from the group.

Maps rustled softly in a draft from somewhere unseen, and the lavender incense smoke curled lazily around their feet.

"This is Valkyrie Nessika," Emrys said, nodding toward the tall, striking Valkyrie. "She's not only my contracted Valkyrie but one of our most trusted confidants. Her skills in combat and strategy are unparalleled."

Nessika inclined her head, her piercing ice-blue gaze sweeping the room with a mix of caution and curiosity etched across her tawny skin. Her hand rested casually on the hilt of her sword, poking from the confines of her black cloak, the gesture both reassuring and subtly threatening.

Emrys turned to Sylven, whose tanned face still remained impassive. "And this is Lord Sylven Astor," he continued. "Sayra's contracted Arcanist and heir to the Astor duchy." Sylven's gaze scanned the room analytically. His fingers twitched at his sides as if itching to reach for the piles of intelligence at their beck and call. "His arcane knowledge and analytical mind have already proven invaluable to our cause."

At last, Emrys turned to Sayra, and a million words were expressed in his eyes as Sayra met his sight. "And Sayra needs no introduction, yet I will give it. Without her, our cause would be hopeless, and my purpose here meaningless."

A flush warmed her body, and it took every ounce of self-control to fight away the rising blush and meet his eyes evenly.

Kent's cheeky grin widened, his teeth gleaming white against his well-trimmed scruff. He spread his arms wide, nearly knocking over a precariously balanced stack of books. "I'm Kent, a regular citizen who deals with shady business and rusty artifacts. Welcome to our little rebel clubhouse, newcomers!" he exclaimed, his voice echoing off the stone walls. "Don't worry, we only sacrifice the occasional goat to the chaos gods on Tuesdays."

Leave it to Kent to ease tension. Sayra exhaled through her nose.

Cassandra, leaning against a cluttered desk, rolled her eyes dramatically. Her slender frame was tense, but some of the hostility seemed to have drained from her posture. Her eyes lowered to the floor, however, and something flitted through them. Ty, a mountain of a man whose head nearly brushed the low ceiling, merely nodded in acknowledgment.

Emrys's expression grew somber, the playful atmosphere dissipating like mist in the afternoon. "Now that we're all acquainted," he said, his tone grave, "perhaps we should address the matter at hand." He turned to Ty, whose massive hands rested on the map-covered table. "You mentioned disturbing patterns in Horde activity?"

Ty's fingers traced lines on the map only he seemed to see. His furrowed brow highlighted concern. "The Horde's behavior has shifted," he rumbled, his deep voice reverberating in the cramped space. "We've been tracking unusual patterns, particularly around Tern."

Cassandra stepped forward, her lithe frame weaving between stacks of books and scattered parchments. She pointed to a cluster of red marks on the map. "These aren't just random attacks anymore. They're organized. Purposeful."

Kent leaned against a bookshelf, his usual grin replaced by an uncharacteristically serious expression. "And that's not even the worst part," he added, running a hand through his disheveled hair. "We've had reports of daemons wandering south toward the monastery."

Nessika nodded. "I can confirm that," she added, glancing at Sayra. "My daemon encounters have more than doubled in the past month."

Goosebumps rose along Sayra's arms. She stepped closer to the table, the scent of old parchment and ink filling her nostrils. "I've seen it too," she said, her voice steady despite the unease churning in her stomach. "On my patrols. There's been an increase in daemon activity near the walls. Just recently, two of them sat outside the wards to watch. Not attack. Not move. Just *watch*."

The room fell silent. Sylven shifted beside her, his presence a comforting warmth in the cool basement air.

Emrys paced the length of the table, his boots echoing on the stone floor. His brow furrowed in concentration, fingers absently tracing the embroidery on his coat sleeve. "This can't be coincidence," he murmured, more to himself than the group.

Ty pointed to another area on the map, his calloused finger resting on a spot just south of the monastery. "We've had reports of daemons gathering here," he said, his voice grave. "From there, however, we've lost the trail of where they go in the mountain range."

Sayra could feel Sylven's unease through their mental link, mirroring her own growing apprehension.

Kent pushed off from the bookshelf, sending a small cloud of dust into the air. "So, the million-gold question is," he said, his voice cutting through the heavy silence, "what in the name of all that's holy—or unholy, I suppose—are they waiting for?"

The question hung in the air unanswered. Sayra's mind raced, her mother's warnings about destiny and ancient powers echoing in her thoughts. As she looked around at the grim faces of her companions, she couldn't shake the feeling they were standing on the precipice of something monumental—and potentially catastrophic.

Emrys paused in his pacing, his shoulders tense beneath the fine fabric of his cloak. He turned to face the group, his dark eyes shadowed with concern. "There's more," he said, his voice low and measured. "A Thapulan emissary visited the monastery recently."

Beside Sayra, Nessika stiffened, her armor creaking with the sudden movement. The room seemed to grow smaller, the walls pressing in as Emrys's words settled over them.

"Thapula?" Cassandra whispered, her eyes wide with disbelief. "But it's too early."

Emrys nodded grimly. "The emissary came with a request. They seek the Goddess's blessing."

A collective gasp echoed through the basement. Kent let out a low whistle. Ty's massive hands clenched into fists on the table, causing the maps to crinkle beneath them.

Sayra could feel the cool stone wall against her back as she leaned against it for support. "During the last meeting, you mentioned they wanted majik and would try to conquer our lands to gain it. You expected this. Granted, not this soon. Am I recalling this correctly?"

"Yes."

Nessika shook her head. "This can't be a coincidence," she said, her eyes narrowing. "First the Horde's strange behavior, and now Thapula's sudden interest. Are you certain they will employ violent methods to acquire majik?"

The soft rustle of Sylven's clothing seemed unnaturally loud in the tense silence. "It's true," he confirmed, his voice steady. "I was there with Emrys when the emissary made the request."

All eyes turned to Sylven, the air thick with unasked questions. He met their gazes unflinchingly, his posture straight and confident despite the gravity of the situation.

"The Holy Family denied the request," Sylven continued, his hands tucking into his trouser pockets. "But the emissary had something unsettling about him. It felt like a threat, even if it wasn't stated outright."

Emrys nodded, his expression grim. "Indeed. The implication was clear. If we wouldn't grant them the blessing willingly, they would seek alternative methods."

The basement fell silent save for the soft crackle of candlewicks and the distant, muffled sounds of Cassandra's heel scuffing back and forth across the floor. The lavender incense had burned out completely, leaving behind a faint, acrid scent that seemed to underscore the ominous nature of their discussion.

Kent broke the silence, his usual jovial tone subdued. "Well, folks," he said, running a hand through his disheveled hair, "I think it's safe to say we're in deeper waters than we realized. And there might be a kraken or two lurking about."

With a sigh, Emrys gestured to the table. "Let's all sit, shall we?"

They all gravitated toward the large scarred oak table at the center of the room. The scraping of chair legs against the stone floor echoed as they took their seats, each lost in their own thoughts about the implications of Thapula's interest and the Horde's unusual behavior.

Emrys lowered himself into a high-backed chair at the head, his regal bearing evident even in the underground war room. His dark eyes scanned the faces around him, assessing and calculating. Despite the late hour and the gravity of the situation, he remained poised, his fingers laced together on the table before him. To Emrys's right, Sylven settled into his seat with a quiet grace that belied his inner turmoil. His sight darted between the maps on the table and the concerned faces of his companions. Though his tanned face remained impassive, the slight furrow of his brow betrayed his deep concentration.

Sayra took the seat to Emrys's left, the wood creaking as she sat. Pulling her wheat-blonde braid forward, she leaned back into the chair as Nes took the seat beside her.

Nessika's tall frame somehow managed to look both relaxed and battle-ready. Across from Sayra and Nessika, Cassandra perched on the edge of her chair with a distrustful grimace. Her slender fingers drummed a nervous rhythm on the table's surface. Kent sprawled in his chair next to Cassandra, his usual carefree demeanor subdued by the gravity of the situation. His fingers absently toyed with a small gadget pulled from one of his many pockets, the quiet clicking providing a counterpoint to the tense silence.

At the far end of the table, opposite Emrys, Ty's large frame dwarfed his chair. His dark eyes honed in on Cassandra's tapping manicured fingers, a deep frown growing.

As they settled, the conversation began in earnest, their voices low and urgent. They discussed the implications of Thapula's request for the Goddess's blessing, debating the timeline in which the empire may become an immediate issue. For the time being, they pushed back the matter for the next meeting. The discussion then turned to the Horde's strange behavior. Sayra and Nessika shared more details about their patrol observations, describing the increased daemon activity and the unsettling way the creatures seemed to gather rather than attack. The others listened intently, connecting their reports to the broader patterns they had observed across the continent.

As the night wore on, they delved into the possible connections between Thapula's sudden interest and the Horde's unusual actions. Could there be a link? Was some greater power at play, manipulating both human nations and daemonic forces for an as-yet-unknown purpose?

The conversation inevitably led to discussions of strategy and preparation. They debated the best ways to gather more information, weighing the risks of sending more spies to Thapula against the need for concrete intelligence. Especially after the emissary from Thapula divulged a secret enemy. One even Kent couldn't grasp knowledge on, which stumped them all. Ever so crafty, Kent gave a brief update on the status of remarkable events, from the stability of Faenda's recent upheaval to the Zendiya Oligarchy's installation of a new cathedral on behalf of the Holy Family.

Throughout it all, Emrys guided the discussion with the skill of a seasoned diplomat, ensuring all voices were heard and all possibilities considered. But as the first rays of dawn neared the early morning, they knew their time was running out to return unnoticed. The cool air nipped at their faces as they made their way through the quiet streets of Tern. Most of the town's inhabitants were still nestled in their beds, leaving the cobblestone paths eerily empty.

Emrys led the way, his dark cloak billowing in the gentle breeze. Sylven walked beside him, hazel eyes alert and scanning their surroundings. Nessika and Sayra brought up the rear, their hoods pulled low over their faces. As they turned down a narrow alley, a figure stumbled out from behind a stack of crates. It was a woman, her face hidden beneath a tattered hood. She swayed unsteadily, reaching out toward them with trembling hands.

Something felt wrong about the situation.

"Please," she whimpered, her voice cracking. "Help me."

Emrys stepped forward, his hand outstretched toward the distressed woman. Compassion softened his features, even as wariness entered his companions' faces.

"It's all right," Emrys said, his voice gentle and reassuring. "We're here to help."

But as he drew closer, Sayra felt a chill raise bumps on her arms. Something wasn't right. The woman's movements were too jerky, too unnatural. And then, for just a moment, the hood slipped, and Sayra caught a glimpse of the woman's face.

Horror gutted her at the sight.

"Get back!" Sayra shouted, her hand flying to the dagger at her hip. But it was too late.

The woman's head snapped up, showing a visage that was the stuff of nightmares. Half of her face was human, with wide, terrified eyes and trembling lips. But the other half... twisted, mottled flesh merged seamlessly with daemonic features. A glowing red eye pulsed in a socket surrounded by scales, and jagged teeth protruded from a distorted jaw.

Time seemed to slow as the creature lunged at Emrys, its human hand morphing into razor-sharp claws mid-strike. Emrys, caught off guard by the sudden transformation, barely had time to throw up a hasty majikal barrier. The creature's claws raked across the shimmering shield, sending sparks of energy flying.

But the barrier wasn't enough. With inhuman strength, the daemon woman shattered Emrys's defense, her claws finding purchase in his shoulder. Blood blossomed across his cloak as he was thrown into the wall, an audible crack as his head bashed against it, landing him in a heap beside the monstrosity.

Chapter Fifteen

SYLVEN

Sylven watched in horror as the seemingly helpless woman transformed before their eyes, her form twisting into a nightmarish fusion of human and daemon. One moment, Rys was reaching out to help; the next, he was crying out in pain as the creature's claws tore into his shoulder.

In that instant, chaos erupted.

Nessika was the first to react, her sword singing through the air as she threw herself between Emrys and the creature. The blade connected with the daemon-woman's arm, drawing an otherworldly shriek from its twisted mouth. But instead of recoiling, the creature seemed to grow more frenzied, its attacks becoming wilder and more unpredictable.

"Emrys!" Sylven shouted, his voice nearly drowned out by the daemon-woman's inhuman shriek.

Time seemed to slow as Sylven's training kicked in. His mouth moved to form majik spells. But before he could complete them, Sayra and Nessika both blocked his view. Gritting his teeth, Sylven knew he would only get in the way if he cast majik.

The two Valkyries moved with fluid grace, years of training evident in every motion. Nessika's sword flashed out, while Sayra brandished her dagger with deadly intent. They flanked the creature, forcing it back and away from Emrys.

Sylven used the moment of respite to rush to Rys's side. The prince's face was ashen, his breathing labored as he clutched his wounded shoulder. "I'm all right," Rys grunted, though the growing bloodstain on his coat belied his words.

"Like hell you are," Sylven muttered, slipping an arm around Rys to support him. He could feel the warm stickiness of blood seeping through the fabric of his friend's coat. "We need to get you away from it."

But retreat wasn't an option. They could double back, but there was no way Sylven would leave Sayra and Nessika to fight alone.

A clash of steel on claw drew Sylven's attention back to the fight. Nessika had engaged the creature directly, her sword a blur of motion as she parried and struck. Sayra darted in and out, her dagger seeking any opening in the daemon's defense.

But even with their combined skill, the Valkyries were struggling. The daemon-woman moved with unnatural speed and strength, better and faster than their Valkyrie gifts could keep up with, its attacks growing more frenzied with each passing second. Sylven could see fatigue beginning to show in Sayra and Nessika's movements.

Somehow managing a dozen feet, Emrys's body began stumbling. Sylven cursed, gently lowering Emrys to the ground. He tore off his own cloak, bunching it up and pressing it hard against the wound. Emrys hissed in pain, his body going rigid.

"Stay with me, Emrys," Sylven grunted, his voice tight with fear. "Don't you dare die on me, you royal pain in the arse."

It concerned him more than anything when Emrys didn't respond, the back of his cloaked head limply resting against the alley wall.

Behind him, the sounds of battle intensified. Sylven wanted desperately to turn and help, but he knew if he let up pressure for even a moment, Emrys's life could slip away.

Nessika's sword sang through the air, clashing against the daemon-woman's claws with a sound like screeching metal. The creature moved with unnatural speed, its attacks coming from impossible angles. Nessika was hard-pressed to keep up, her blade a constant blur of motion as she parried and countered.

Sayra darted in and out of the fray, her dagger seeking any opening in the daemon's defense. But the creature's skin seemed to ripple and shift, wounds closing almost as quickly as they were inflicted.

"This isn't working!" Sayra shouted, narrowly dodging a swipe that would have taken her head off. "We need a new plan!"

Nessika grunted in agreement, but they had no time to strategize. The daemon-woman pressed its advantage, its attacks growing more frenzied with each passing second. Its human features were all but gone now, replaced by a visage of pure daemonic fury.

Sylven's mind raced as he tried to think of a solution. He could feel Emrys's life ebbing away beneath his hands. The prince's breathing had grown shallow, his skin clammy and cold to the touch.

"Come on, come on," Sylven muttered, desperately racking his brain for a solution, anything that might help. But his panic made it hard to focus, the arcane words slipping away like smoke in his head.

A cry of pain snapped his attention back to the fight. Nessika staggered back, blood streaming from a deep gash across her arm. Her sword went flying to the ground as she clutched her injured limb.

The metal skidded several feet from where Sylven knelt. Useless.

The daemon-woman howled in triumph, advancing on the wounded Valkyrie. Sayra threw herself between them, her dagger a silver blur as she fought to keep the creature at bay. The daemon-woman seemed to sense their desperation. It let out a bone-chilling laugh, a sound horribly human and utterly inhuman at the same time. Then, with a speed that defied belief, it attacked.

Sylven threw up a hasty shield spell in front of Sayra, but the creature's claws tore through it like paper. With only a dagger to protect herself, Sayra didn't have time to block the second set of claws tearing through her thigh. He heard Sayra cry out and Nessika's grunt of pain as she regained her footing.

As he kept pressure on Rys's wound, Sylven realized with a sinking heart that they were outmatched. The creature, the impossible fusion of human and daemon, was beyond anything they had trained for.

The Valkyries redoubled their efforts. Sayra was panting heavily, her movements becoming desperate as she tried to fend off the relentless attacks.

Sylven's mind continued to race, searching for a solution. They couldn't keep things up much longer. Soon, the commotion would draw attention from the townspeople, and then they'd have an entirely new set of problems to deal with. They'd want to know how it got there, how it was made, and whether there were more. None of which he had answers for. They didn't need widespread fear to cause an uprising when it could be an isolated incident. Regardless, they needed more information before acting further.

It all happened so fast.

A tail reached out from the woman's cloak as she spun faster than the eye could trail. It whipped across Sayra and Nessika's legs, tumbling them both to the ground.

The daemon-woman advanced toward Sylven without hesitation, its twisted face split in a grotesque grin of triumph. Sylven stood his ground, knowing he was the only thing standing between the monster and his injured friend. He held his hands against Rys's soaked shoulder, preparing to cast another spell, even if there wasn't much he could do.

Time slowed for a second as his eyes met Sayra's behind the monstrosity. Sylven could see the raw fear in her face, for she could never get to him in time. Not before he would die, and Rys with him. But she braced herself upward, her dagger poised and ready, and with a single look, they knew exactly what to do.

Sayra lunged forward in a precise, powerful stroke just as the daemon-woman's claws made a final reach for Sylven and Rys.

"*Commutatio!*" Sylven cried out, all his majik focused on the one spell.

In a flash, Sayra's body appeared where Nessika's sword once lay, her lunging body stabbing the razor-sharp tip of her dagger directly into the daemon's heart. The daemon-woman folded around the blade, a gasp gurgling from its throat.

Sayra's face was vicious as she tore through the abomination, black blood splattering across her face. Together, the two collapsed into the ground, the daemon dead beneath Sayra. The Valkyrie jerked her elbow back, bracing her hand against the dead daemon's shoulder as metal squelched out of its carcass. Across from her, Nessika got to her feet and picked up her sword, now right beside her boots.

Both were worse for wear, their cloaks in tatters and bloodied cuts crisscrossed on their limbs. But Rys...

Snapping back to the prince, Sylven's stomach plummeted at Rys's ashen face, lolled to the side.

Blood covered Sylven's hands, the cloak soaked. "Rys? *Rys?*" Sylven got out, his voice growing desperate. He turned to call out to Sayra, but she was already kneeling beside him with a panicked face.

"Move the cloak, Sylven," she ordered, her hands reaching forward as she prepared to spell cast.

Behind her, Nessika's face was terrified, her breaths coming in shallow gasps. The sword clattered to the ground, both of her hands clasping together as she began feverishly praying to the Goddess.

Carefully, Sylven pulled back the material with shaking hands, revealing a shredded cloak masking deep scores in Rys's right shoulder. Without delay, Sayra removed what fabric she could from the wound. What Sylven saw made bile rise in the back of his throat.

His heart pounded in his ears as he stared at Emrys's wound, the severity of it fully exposed. The prince's flesh was torn and ragged, deep gashes showing glimpses of bone beneath. An artery was nicked between the mess of sinew. Blood continued to seep from the wound, each pulse weaker than the last.

The alley closed in around them, and the warmth of Emrys's blood on Sylven's hands made his stomach churn. Sayra's hands hovered over the wound, her face pinching as she began to weave healing majik. "*Sana*," she whispered. Her loose strands of wheat-blonde hair, matted with sweat and blood, fell across her face as she worked. Despite her own injuries, her focus never wavered. Sylven could see the strain in her eyes, the desperate hope her powers would be enough as her hands hovered just above Rys's shoulder.

Sylven felt utterly helpless. His own majik, helpful in battle, seemed useless now. He watched Sayra work, willing her to succeed and pleading silently for the Goddess's mercy. Memories of his time with Rys flashed through his mind—their first meeting, countless hours of study and training, shared laughter and sorrows. The thought of losing him was unbearable.

"Come on, Rys," Sylven whispered, his voice hoarse. "You can't leave us like this. We need you." His crimson fingers curled into the fabric of his coat.

Sayra's brow furrowed in concentration, beads of sweat forming on her forehead as she poured more energy into her healing spell. Her mouth moved as she whispered the majik into being. The air around them seemed to thicken from the arcane arts, a faint glow emanating from her hands. But Emrys remained still, his chest rising with shallow breaths.

Time seemed to stretch endlessly as Sayra worked. The sounds of the waking town grew louder around them.

"*Sana*," Sayra said again between gritted teeth, a prayer in its own right as she layered healing spell after healing spell.

Nessika's prayers had devolved into quiet anguish, her composure cracking under the weight of their circumstances. Sylven felt his own eyes burning with unshed tears. He had always seen Rys as invincible, a pillar of strength and determination. To see him teetering on the edge of death shook Sylven to his core.

"Please," Sylven murmured, not sure if he was addressing Sayra, the Goddess, or Rys himself. "Please don't die."

Then, not believing his own eyes, Sylven watched as the majik worked. Beneath Sayra's glowing hands, Rys's torn flesh began to knit together, the deep gashes slowly closing. It was as if time itself was reversing, undoing the damage wrought by the daemon-woman's claws.

"It's working," Sylven breathed. He was afraid to speak too loudly, as if the slightest disturbance might break the spell.

Sayra's face had beads of sweat rolling down her temples. Her hands trembled with the effort of maintaining the healing majik, but her determination never wavered. The soft golden glow emanating from her palms seemed to pulse in time with Emrys's heartbeat, growing stronger with each passing moment.

Nessika crept closer, her ice-blue eyes wide with hope and fear.

As the wound continued to close, color began to return to Rys's face. His ashen pallor gave way to a healthier hue, and his breathing deepened. Sylven felt a surge of hope so powerful it was almost painful.

"Goddess above," Nessika said, her gloved hand covering her mouth.

Suddenly, Rys's eyes fluttered open. They were unfocused at first, clouded with confusion and lingering pain. But as his gaze settled on Sayra, recognition dawned.

"Sayra?" Rys's voice was hoarse, scarcely audible. He blinked and looked over to his friend. "Syl...?"

A choked laugh escaped Sylven's throat, relief washing over him in waves. "Yeah, it's me," he said, blinking back tears. "Welcome back, you royal idiot."

Beside him, Sayra pursed her mouth to keep it from warbling. She kept one hand over his shoulder but moved her second just over his head, where a gash bled at the corner of his hairline. It slowly knitted together under her touch, leaving behind only a faint pink line. Her eyes never left his face, drinking in every sign of life and recovery.

"Easy," she murmured as Rys tried to sit up. "You've lost a lot of blood. Take it slow."

Rys grimaced but complied, easing back down with Sylven's support. His dark eyes, slowly clearing up, flicked between Sayra and Sylven. "The daemon..." he began, his voice rough.

"Dead," Nessika supplied, her own relief evident in her voice. "Sayra and Sylven took care of it."

A ghost of a smile touched Rys's lips. "Of course they did," he said, his gaze lingering on Sayra with pride and admiration.

Sylven watched as Sayra's eyes flickered, then lowered to a small scratch on the back of Emrys's hand. Just as her hands reached the area, Rys stopped her with his own.

"That's enough," Rys said softly, his fingers gently wrapping around Sayra's wrist. "You've done more than enough already. Save your strength for yourself and Nessika. Both of your wounds need attention more than my minor scrapes."

Sayra hesitated, her eyes meeting Rys's with a mix of concern and reluctance. For a moment, the two of them seemed lost in their own world, communicating without words. Sylven felt a pang in his chest, a complex thing he couldn't quite name. But she nodded in acquiescence, lending him a hand to stand.

As Rys rose unsteadily to his feet, Sayra suddenly threw her arms around him, pulling him into a fierce embrace. The action seemed to surprise them both, but Emrys wrapped his arms around her in return.

Sylven watched as Rys closed his eyes, lowering his head to rest beside Sayra's. The prince's shoulders seemed to sag. Rys's arms tightened around Sayra, his fingers digging into the fabric of her cloak as if he were afraid she might disappear. She pressed her forehead against his chest, her face twisting in a saddening expression. Rys's other hand moved to cradle the back of Sayra's head, his fingers tangling in her blonde hair. Sayra's shoulders shook with a single silent sob, her composure breaking after the ordeal.

But she quickly reigned it in, and Sylven had to look away from the moment. Nessika picked up her sword with her good arm, her gaze heavy. Swallowing hard, Sylven balled up his cloak in his fist, working to steady his own nerves after it all.

A hand patted his back, pulling his attention to Nessika. She nodded at him, conveying so much in that gesture.

She saw it, too, then.

A bittersweet smile tilted her full mouth, and she began assessing the extent of her injuries. "You did well," she said, as much praise as she'd ever lavish on him.

Sylven shook his head. "You more than me."

At that moment, the first rays of dawn broke into the alleyway, a brilliant gold shining on Rys and Sayra. Rys pulled back, his gray eyes searching Sayra's face. His thumb gently brushed away a tear from her cheek, leaving a smear of blood in its wake. The tenderness of the gesture pulled at Sylven's heartstrings. At the small part of him that wished things were different.

I'll be happy for them, no matter how I feel for her, he thought, beginning to turn away.

But far behind them, Sylven saw a cloaked figure observing them from the shadows at the end of the alleyway.

"Nessika," Sylven warned, his body going tense.

Following his line of sight, the Valkyrie furrowed her brows at the figure.

Everything around him froze.

Chapter Sixteen

EMRYS

In that fleeting, precious instant, Emrys wished he could freeze time itself. He knew moments were but that, a blip in the grand scope of their lives. Yet selfishly, desperately, he yearned to live in that exact sliver of eternity. With Sayra enveloped in his embrace, her arms clinging to him as if he were her last anchor in a storm-tossed sea, Emrys felt his defenses crumble like sandcastles before the tide. A wave of gratitude for her, for all of them, filled his chest until he thought it might burst. And when her shoulders shook, he held her even tighter, silently promising he would always be her rock.

The scent of her hair, tinged with sweat and the metallic tang of blood, filled his nostrils. He could feel the rapid beat of her heart against his chest, a tangible reminder of how close they had come to losing everything. The warmth of her body against his seemed to chase away the lingering chill of his near-death experience.

In that moment, Emrys allowed himself to acknowledge the depth of his feelings for Sayra. It was more than he'd ever allowed himself to feel for any other. He had always been far too guarded. It was something profound and terrifying in its intensity. Something that, in any other circumstance, he might have retreated from out of duty or fear.

But there, in the aftermath of their brush with death, those barriers seemed insignificant. He tightened his arms around her, pouring all the words he couldn't say into that embrace.

When the sob abated, Emrys pulled back and wiped a sole tear away, his thumb gentle against her cheek. Their eyes locked, and for a moment, the world around them faded away. The chaos of the alley, the looming dangers, and even their companions receded into the background. Emrys was lost in the depths of Sayra's green eyes. His heart raced, and he felt an overwhelming urge to close the small distance between them, to express with actions what he couldn't with words.

But reality intruded, harsh and insistent.

Nessika tore past them down the alleyway, and he turned in the nick of time to see a shadowy figure sprint around a corner far away.

I'm going to assess the situation, Nessika thought to him through their *anima* link.

Be careful, he said back. And though he was loath to, Emrys let Sayra pull away. He watched as Nessika disappeared around the corner, his heart racing with renewed anxiety.

The stench of blood and something otherworldly hung about them. Sayra set to healing her major wounds, worry etched into her face as her eyes kept peeking back to where Nessika had disappeared.

"We need to move," Emrys said, his voice low and urgent. "We can't be found here with this." He gestured to the daemon-woman's corpse. The sight of the twisted body made him narrow his eyes. They had come close to disaster, and unknown dangers still lurked in the shadows.

Nessika reappeared at the mouth of the alley, shaking her head. "Lost them," she said, frustration evident in her voice. "Whoever it was, they're fast. And they know these streets better than we do."

Sayra's bloodied brow furrowed with concern. "Could it have been another daemon? Or someone working with them?"

Emrys shook his head, wincing at the movement. "We can't afford to speculate right now. We need to get somewhere safe and regroup." He paused, weighing their options. "We have to tell the queen."

The others exchanged wary glances. Sylven was the first to voice their shared concern. "And how do we explain why we were out here in the first place? We can't exactly tell her about Ophelia Majik Co., I'm assuming."

Emrys's mind raced, trying to formulate a plausible story. "We could say we were following up on a lead about unusual daemon activity. It's not entirely untrue, and it would explain our presence in the town at this hour."

Nessika nodded slowly. "It could work. But we'd need to be careful with the details. One slip and the whole story could unravel."

"It's a risk we have to take," Emrys said firmly. "My mother needs to know what we're up against."

The group fell into a tense silence, each contemplating the gravity of their situation. Sayra spoke up. "Whatever we decide, we need to do it quickly. We can't stay here much longer."

Emrys nodded, straightening up despite the lingering pain. "All right. Let's move. We'll finalize our story on the way back to the manor and pray to the Goddess my mother believes us."

With that, they began the delicate task of moving the daemon-woman's body, folding it within Sylven's cloak. Sayra healed up a majority of the cuts she and Nessika sustained from the daemon, leaving Sayra noticeably tired by the time they began the tedious trek back with the body. As Emrys helped, his mind whirled with possibilities and fears. He couldn't shake the feeling they were standing on the precipice of something enormous.

How was the daemon-woman made? How did she get inside Tern? And who was it that spied on them?

—◦✛◦—

Returning was a tedious affair. The morning sun streamed through the tall windows of Queen Evangelina's study, casting long shadows across the ornate carpets. Emrys stood near the fireplace, his body tense despite his efforts to appear calm. The events of the night weighed heavily upon him, from their clandestine meeting at Ophelia Majik Co. to their harrowing encounter with the daemon-woman.

They had managed to relay their fabricated story to his mother, Arene, and Vander after cleaning up from the ordeal. The tale had been met with a mixture of concern and skepticism, but the revelation of the human-daemon hybrid quickly overshadowed any doubts about their nocturnal excursion. As the initial shock of their report wore off, Emrys's mother sat behind her massive oak desk, her fingers steepled in front of her face as she processed the information. Vander leaned against a bookshelf, his usual smirk replaced by a thoughtful frown. Breane stood at attention outside of their enclosed space, preventing anyone from intruding on their conversation.

Arene paced in front of the windows, her silver-streaked blonde hair catching the sunlight with each turn. Her green eyes, so like Sayra's, were narrowed in concentration. Sylven, Sayra, and Nessika sat in plush chairs, their exhaustion evident on their faces.

Queen Evangelina was the first to break the heavy silence. "A human-daemon hybrid," she said, her voice shaken. "In all our years of fighting the Horde, we've never encountered anything like this. What could it mean?"

Stepping forward, Emrys saw all eyes upon him. "It means the game has changed," he said, his voice steady despite the churning in his stomach. "If this isn't a one-time occurrence, our entire understanding of the threat we face is obsolete."

Vander leaned away from the bookshelf, his dark eyes glinting with concern. "But how is it even possible? The very nature of daemons should make such a fusion impossible."

"Unless," Arene interjected, her pacing coming to an abrupt halt, "the Holy Family found a way to manipulate the very essence of both human and daemon and combine them in a dangerous, sustainable way. A feat that would require knowledge and power beyond anything we've seen before. It could explain the person spying on your encounter with the hybrid. Perhaps it was a test of sorts."

"Maybe so." A chair creaked as Sylven leaned back. "Could the creation of the hybrid be connected to the relics? We know they have the power to grant or enhance majikal abilities. Could they also be used by the Holy Family to merge different forms of life?"

Cold seeped into Emrys's bones. If the relics were indeed capable of such a thing, the potential for misuse was staggering.

Standing, the queen's silk gown rustled as she moved around her desk. "Whatever the cause, this development changes everything. Our plans... our strategies... all of it must be reevaluated in light of this new threat."

"Agreed," Vander said, his usual cockiness replaced by a grim determination. "But we need more information. We can't make any moves until we understand exactly what we're dealing with."

Sayra spoke up for the first time since entering the study, and her voice was strong despite the weariness evident in her posture. "We should start by examining the remains we brought back. Perhaps there are clues in its physiology that could help us understand how this fusion was achieved." Even as she said it, the disgust in her voice was obvious.

As the discussion continued, Emrys found his gaze drawn to Arene. She had resumed her pacing, her brow furrowed in thought. Suddenly, she stopped, fixing Emrys with a piercing stare.

"There's still one thing that bothers me," she said, her voice cutting through the ongoing conversation. "Why didn't you inform the queen or myself of your plans before leaving? Do you have any idea how dangerous that was?"

The room fell silent once more, all eyes turning to Emrys. One wrong word could unravel their entire deception, and he wasn't ready to share his connections yet. An instinct told him to hold that secret fast.

"The influence was fleeting for both Sayra and I," Emrys said, meeting Arene's gaze steadily. "We couldn't understand what sort of majik it was, but an instinct pulled us toward it with urgency. We could feel it growing further away, but we didn't want to cause unjust alarm where none was initially warranted. None of us expected this development, for a daemon hybrid was unprecedented."

"I believe the relic influences more than just our majik," Sayra said quietly, a faraway look in her eyes. "It compels us, in a manner of speaking, to actions or thoughts that are beyond our understanding."

At that, Emrys glanced at his mother. Queen Evangelina's mouth frowned, and her gray eyes held a sorrow Emrys knew to be regret. Even though their actions had been for the greater good, he understood his mother didn't want the burden to weigh on them. It was the sole reason he couldn't find even a spark of anger toward her for withholding the truth from him, not when he would have done the very same thing she was condemning herself for.

"And I believe Sayra to be right." Emrys adjusted his stance, dipping his head in her direction before stealing a look at her mother.

Arene held his gaze for a moment, and Emrys felt as if she could see right through him. She nodded at last, though her expression remained troubled. "In the future, you will inform at least one of us before undertaking such a risky venture. Is that clear?"

"Absolutely," Emrys replied, relief washing over him. He glanced at his companions, seeing similar expressions on their faces.

Queen Evangelina stepped forward, placing a hand on Emrys's shoulder. "Arene is right," she said, her voice warm but firm. "We can't afford to take unnecessary risks. We need to trust each other implicitly if we're to have any hope of success."

Emrys nodded, feeling a pang of guilt at the deception they were perpetrating. But he pushed the feeling aside, focusing on the task at hand. "So, what's our next move?" he asked, looking around at the assembled group.

"I'll assist with the daemon-hybrid's examination," Arene offered, her earlier suspicion seemingly set aside in the face of their new challenge. "My experience with both human and daemon physiology could prove useful."

Queen Evangelina nodded her approval. "Good. While you work on that, I'll reach out to our forces throughout the kingdom. If this hybrid is part of a larger pattern, we need to know about it and be prepared for what may come."

"And what about us, Your Majesty?" Nessika asked, gesturing to the rest of them. "How may we help?"

"Returning to Saint Highburn Monastery is your best course of action," the queen replied. "Be cautious, and act as normal as possible in the meantime. We don't want to alert the Holy Family to our suspicions.

If they're behind this abomination, we can't risk tipping our hand too soon."

As the group continued to discuss their plans, Emrys half listened. They were venturing into unknown territory with the abnormal Horde patterns and hybrids. And all the while, they were balancing on a knife's edge of secrets and lies. It didn't sit quite right with him. And so, when everyone broke once more for breakfast, Emrys moved to speak with the queen.

As the others began to file out of the study, Emrys caught his mother's eye. "Mother, might I have a word in private?"

Queen Evangelina nodded, her brow furrowing at the seriousness in her son's tone. But before she could respond, Vander's voice cut through the room.

"A private word, brother?" he asked, his tone light and smirk crooked. "Surely whatever you have to say to Mother can be shared with me as well. We are all in this together, after all."

Emrys felt a flicker of frustration, quickly masked. He studied his brother's face, trying to gauge his intentions. Vander's expression was open, almost earnest, but something in his eyes gave him pause. For a moment, he considered sharing what he knew of Ophelia Majik Co.'s latest developments. But as he opened his mouth to speak, a sudden, inexplicable unease washed over him. It was as if a cold hand had gripped his heart, warning him to be cautious.

"Of course, Vander," Emrys said, forcing a smile. "You're right."

Vander thumbed the upturned end of his nose, seeming pleased at Emrys's words. As the last of the others left the room, closing the heavy oak door behind them, Emrys faced his mother and brother. Queen Evangelina settled back into her chair, her eyes moving between her sons with curiosity.

"What's troubling you, Emrys?" she asked gently.

Emrys took a deep breath, his mind racing. The truth he had intended to share—about Ophelia Majik Co. and about their true reasons for being out that night—suddenly felt dangerous, exposed. Instead, he spun a new tale, one that felt safer but left a bitter taste in his mouth.

"I'm worried about Sayra," he said, the lie coming easier than he would have liked. "Her powers are growing slowly, and I fear she may be struggling to advance fast enough to combat this new daemon development. Especially after the *nefas* majik incident. She's had difficulties with managing it. Perhaps there might be something in the royal archives that could help. Some ancient text on maximizing training majikal abilities."

Vander's eyebrows rose, a trace of something crossing his face before it settled back into neutral curiosity. "Interesting," he mused. "I wouldn't have thought her abilities were causing such concern."

Queen Evangelina leaned forward, her face etched with worry. "This is serious, Emrys. If Sayra's powers are becoming unstable, it could jeopardize everything we've worked for."

Emrys nodded, feeling a pang of guilt at the concern in his mother's voice. "I don't think it's reached that point yet," he reassured her quickly. "But I'd rather be prepared."

As his mother and brother began to discuss possible resources and strategies, Emrys felt the deception settle heavily on his shoulders. He had come there intending to share the truth, to seek guidance. Instead, he wove a new web of lies, even as his mother thanked him for sharing his concerns and expressed her extreme relief he was okay.

But as he caught Vander's eye across the room, noting the calculating look that clung there for just a moment, Emrys couldn't shake the feeling he had made the right choice. Something was off, though he couldn't quite put his finger on what.

For the time being, he would play along and keep his secrets close, hoping when the time came to share the truth, it wouldn't be too late.

Chapter Seventeen

SYLVEN

The carriage jostled along the winding road, its rhythmic swaying almost hypnotic. Sylven gazed out the window, watching the lush countryside roll by in a blur of greens and golds. The events of the past few days weighed heavily on his mind, a tangled mess of secrets, lies, and horrifying revelations. Sayra, Nessika, and Rys slumbered, their faces relaxed in the grip of exhaustion. Sylven envied their ability to find rest. His own mind buzzed with unanswered questions and nagging doubts, making sleep an elusive luxury.

Sayra's head had moved to rest on Rys's shoulder during her sleep, her wheat-blonde braid spilling across his chest. Even in sleep, Rys's arm curved protectively around her from the top of the plush cushions. It looked casual enough that one could have explained it as a lapse while being unaware, but Sylven knew it was only a matter of time before the two came to terms with it. He couldn't stare at them for more than a heartbeat.

Nessika, ever the vigilant Valkyrie, had somehow managed to fall asleep sitting up, her hand never straying far from the hilt of her sword beside him. The sight almost made Sylven smile.

Almost.

As the carriage hit a particularly rough patch of road, Sylven's gaze was drawn to the window once more. The royal entourage stretched before and behind them—a procession of carriages and mounted guards, their polished armor gleaming in the afternoon sun. It was an impressive sight, one that would no doubt draw attention when they arrived at Saint Highburn Monastery.

Sylven's stomach twisted at the thought. How were they supposed to act normal after everything they'd experienced? The human-daemon hybrid, the web of lies they'd spun for the queen, and the growing strain within their group all felt like a powder keg waiting to explode. Hours passed, marked only by the changing landscape and the steady clip-clop of horses' hooves. As the familiar spires of Saint Highburn Monastery appeared on the mountainous horizon, Sylven couldn't help thinking things would only get worse.

He reached out, gently shaking Rys awake. "We're almost there," he said softly, careful not to startle the others.

Rys blinked slowly, disorientation clouding his features for a moment before reality set in. He nodded, carefully extracting himself from Sayra without waking her. As he straightened his clothes, Sylven couldn't help but notice the way Rys's gaze lingered on Sayra's sleeping form, a softness in his eyes that spoke volumes.

"Should we wake them?" Sylven asked, gesturing to the still-slumbering Valkyries.

Rys shook his head. "Let them rest a bit longer. They've earned it."

The carriage rolled through the monastery gates, the sudden change in terrain rousing Nessika and Sayra. They woke with a start, hands instinctively reaching for weapons before realizing where they were.

"We're back?" Sayra asked, her voice still thick with sleep.

Sylven nodded. "Welcome home," he said, unable to keep a touch of irony from his voice.

Massive steel-reinforced gates with etchings of the Goddess on the front swung open as the gate guards recognized their entourage. As they passed through, the bustling marketplace came into view. Colorful awnings stretched over wooden stalls, creating a patchwork of vibrant hues against the monastery's austere stone walls. The air was thick with a cacophony of scents: fresh bread from the baker's stall, aromatic herbs and spices from traveling merchants, and the earthy smell of leather goods. Arcanists in fitted navy overcoats mingled with Valkyries in training leathers, browsing wares that ranged from mundane necessities to exotic trinkets. A bookseller's stall overflowed with tomes and scrolls, while nearby, an apothecary arranged vials of mysterious liquids. At the far end, a weaponsmith hammered away, the rhythmic clanging adding to the lively atmosphere.

As the small mountain grew in height, so did the monastery. Levels upon levels spanned the mountaintop between residential sectors, the academies, and the cathedral at the top. Snow dotted only the tallest of mountains in the distance. As their carriage came to a stop in the small marketplace near the entrance, Sylven saw a familiar face pushing through the gathering crowd. Waylen's boyish features were a mix of excitement and concern beneath his mop of blond hair as he approached.

"There you are!" he called out as they disembarked. "I was beginning to think you'd all run off to join a traveling performing crew or something."

Amidst everything, Sylven had entirely forgotten about Waylen. He felt a genuine smile tug at his lips. Waylen's easygoing nature was a balm to his frayed nerves. "Missed us that much, did you?" he quipped back.

Waylen's grin faltered as he took in their haggard appearance. "What happened to you lot? You look like you've been through hell and back."

Sylven exchanged a quick glance with the others. "It's been an eventful trip," he said carefully.

Waylen's eyebrows shot up, sensing there was more to the story. But before he could press further, Rys stepped in, seamlessly slipping into the situation before they drew more attention.

"Waylen, my friend," he said, clapping him on the shoulder. "I'm afraid we can't chat long. There's much to be done, and I'm sure the monastery staff is eager to debrief us on our absence."

Waylen nodded, though Sylven could see the questions burning in his eyes. "Of course, of course. But later, yeah? You two owe me a proper explanation over a drink or two."

"That we do," Sylven agreed, more than an ounce of guilt making him mentally swear he would do better. It didn't escape him that he was now in the very predicament Rys had been for years... and how embittered Sylven had become when finding out.

As they made their way through the crowded marketplace, Sylven saw dozens of curious stares directed his way. Students and staff alike whispered and pointed, no doubt wondering about the reason for their grand return. He squared his shoulders, forcing his face into a mask of calm indifference.

⟶◦❖◦⟵

The Arcanist common room was empty on the late weekend night. Sylven sank into one of the plush beige couches beside the warm hearth, feeling the tension in his muscles unwind. Across from him, Rys and Waylen were engaged in a quiet discussion about their latest assignments from their respective professors. Elegant banners bearing the crest of the

Holy Family hung along the walls. The light from the fireplace danced across the mosaic windows, casting ever-changing patterns on the plush navy carpet beneath their feet.

"I still can't wrap my head around the intricacies of elemental affinities." Waylen sighed, running a hand through his tousled hair. "How can fire and water possibly work together in a single mesh spell?"

Rys drummed his fingers on the armrest, his eyes alight with academic fervor. "It's all about balance," he explained. "Think of it like cooking. Too much of one ingredient can ruin the dish, but the right combination creates something extraordinary."

Sylven nodded, grateful for the mundane nature of their conversation. It was a welcome distraction from the secrets he carried. "The trick is in the timing," he added. "You have to introduce each element at precisely the right moment, with the perfect aligning of intentions between Arcanists."

Waylen's good-natured face scrunched up in concentration. "Right. Timing. Got it." He suddenly brightened, reaching into his bag. "Oh, I almost forgot! I brought something to help us unwind a bit."

With a flourish, he produced a bottle of red wine. "From my family's vineyards," he said proudly. "Thought we could use a little celebration after your grand return."

Rys raised an eyebrow, a smile tugging at his lips. "How very thoughtful of you, Waylen. Though I hope you're not planning on making a habit of smuggling wine into the dormitory."

Waylen grinned as he poured three generous glasses he'd smuggled in his bookbag. "What the monks and nuns don't know won't hurt them, right?"

As the night wore on and the wine flowed freely, Sylven relaxed despite his best efforts to stay alert. The warmth of the fire, the soft cushions of the couch, and the familiar camaraderie of his friends all conspired to lull him into a false sense of security. It was too much like old times, all the hours the three of them spent talking and studying. When the bottle was nearly empty and their voices had grown soft with the lateness of the hour, Waylen dropped a piece of information that cut through Sylven's wine-induced haze.

"You know," he said, "it's the strangest thing. Vander's been asking a lot of questions about my family's port lately. All sorts of stuff about our business dealings, shipping routes, that kind of thing."

Sylven watched as the rise and fall of Rys's chest ceased for a handful of seconds, though the prince's face remained carefully neutral. "Oh?" Rys said, his tone casual. "That is interesting. Any idea why?"

Waylen shrugged, oblivious. "No clue. Said something about wanting to learn more about the kingdom's commerce. Seemed pretty keen on it, though."

As Waylen launched into a detailed explanation of his family's wine export business, Sylven caught Emrys's eye. They shared a look of mutual concern, both realizing Vander's interest might be far from innocent curiosity.

The comfortable warmth of the common room suddenly felt stifling.

Two Arcanists, fourth years by the look of their badges, passed by the couch. Their eyes lingered on the empty wine bottle, and Sylven felt a flash of paranoia.

Emrys rose to his feet, his princely composure intact despite the late hour and the wine. "I believe it's time we retired for the night," he announced, his tone brooking no argument. "We have early classes tomorrow, after all."

The cool stone of the dormitory hallway felt solid beneath Sylven's unsteady feet as they made their way up to their rooms. The oil lanterns lining the stairwell cast dancing shadows on the walls, creating an almost dizzying effect. In his room, Sylven stripped off his uniform, the fabric rough against his fingertips. The shower's hot water was a blessing, washing away the remnants of the day and clearing his head somewhat. Steam filled the small bathroom, fogging the mirror and leaving beads of moisture on every surface.

He toweled off and pulled on a soft cotton shirt and loose pants. The rich aroma of wine still lingered on his breath. Sylven could taste the sweetness on his tongue and feel the pleasant warmth spreading through his limbs.

Collapsing onto his bed, he stared up at the ceiling. The wine had loosened something in his mind, a question that had been nagging at him for months bubbling to the surface.

Before he could think better of it, Sylven reached out through his mental link with Sayra. The connection felt hazy, tinged with the effects of the alcohol.

Sayra? he projected, his mental voice slightly slurred even in his head. *Are you awake?*

There was a moment of silence then a groggy response. *Sylven? What is it? Is something wrong?*

No, no, he reassured her quickly. *I just... I wanted to ask you something. That day, months ago, when we were at my family's manor. My mother pulled you aside and whispered something to you as we were leaving. What was it? It's been driving me crazy.*

The silence that followed seemed to stretch for an eternity. Sylven could hear his own heartbeat, feel the softness of his pillow beneath his head, and smell the faint remnants of soap the nuns had washed his linens with.

Finally, Sayra's voice came through, hesitant but clear. *Have you been drinking?*

Sylven felt a flash of irritation, quickly followed by shame. *I'm fine,* he insisted, even as his eyelids grew heavy. *I just want to know. Please. It's been eating at me for months.*

There was a long pause, and Sylven could almost feel Sayra's internal struggle through their link. When she spoke, her voice was soft, filled with a warmth he rarely heard directed at him.

Your mother pulled me aside that day because she was worried about you, Sylven. She told me to keep you safe, to protect you at all costs. Sayra's voice caught. *She made me promise that I wouldn't die on you. That I would always be there to watch your back.*

Sylven felt a lump form in his throat. His mother's concern. Sayra's promise. It all suddenly felt so overwhelming. *I didn't know,* he managed to get out.

She loves you, Sylven, Sayra continued, her voice gentle. *And she trusts me to keep you safe. I won't let either of you down.*

Sylven could feel tears pricking at the corners of his eyes. The wine had stripped away his usual defenses, leaving him raw and vulnerable. *But why didn't she tell me herself?*

I think, Sayra said slowly, *she wanted to make sure you had someone watching out for you without feeling smothered. Your mother knows how independent you are and how much you want to prove yourself. She's a sharp woman, perhaps not the most kind, but she is loving. She just shows it in a roundabout way.*

A soft chuckle escaped Sylven's lips, despite the tightening in his chest. *That does sound like her.*

Sylven. Sayra's voice grew serious. *I want you to know that I take that promise seriously. Not just because your mother asked me to, but because...*

well, because I care about you. We may not always see eye to eye, but you're my Arcanist, and I'll always have your back.

The sincerity in her voice touched something deep within Sylven. A warmth spread through him that had nothing to do with the wine. *Sayra, I... thank you. I'm sorry for all the times I've been difficult. I do appreciate you, you know. Even if I'm not always good at showing it.*

He could almost feel Sayra's smile through their link. *I know, Sylven. And for what it's worth, I'm glad we're in this together. Whatever comes our way, we'll face it as a team.*

Sylven felt his eyelids growing heavier, the conversation and the late hour taking their toll. *Sayra?* he murmured on the edge of sleep.

Yes?

I heard you that time when you brought me to the infirmary, after I knocked myself unconscious. And I've been wanting to say this for a long time. It's just I'm not good at this sort of thing. But—Ah, Goddess, help me. Sylven rubbed his forehead, wincing at himself. *I'm glad it's you. My Valkyrie, I mean. I wouldn't want anyone else. You're one of the few good people left I can call honorable and worthy. I admire your resolve despite how much of a prick I've been. I'll always have your back as well.*

He had to stop himself before he said something he couldn't take back... about her being a woman he grew to regard in different ways.

As he drifted off to sleep, Sylven thought he heard Sayra's voice, soft and fond. *Sleep well, Sylven. I'll be here when you wake up.*

For the first time in months, Sylven fell into a deep, peaceful sleep, secrets and fears temporarily lifted from his shoulders.

Chapter Eighteen

SAYRA

The early morning light filtered through Sayra's window. She sat cross-legged on her bed, and her mother's worn leather journal was open in her lap. Her fingers turned the pages, eyes scanning the familiar handwriting.

After faking my death, I journeyed south, following the patterns of ley lines. But nothing could have prepared me for what I found.

Sayra's breath caught as she read on, the world around her fading away as she became immersed in her mother's words.

The rift loomed before me, a monstrous tear in the very fabric of reality. It was as if the earth itself had been violently ripped apart, leaving a gaping wound that stretched for miles. The chasm must have been impossibly deep, its bottom lost in swirling, inky darkness that seemed to writhe and pulse with malevolent life.

Even from a mile away, I could feel its presence—a weight pressing down on my chest, making each breath a struggle. The air shimmered with a crimson aura, pulsing like a sickly heartbeat. Bolts of crimson lightning occasionally arced across the rift, illuminating the twisted, nightmarish shapes that lurked just beyond the veil of our world.

The fear majik emanating from it was unlike anything I'd ever encountered. Primal, overwhelming, all-consuming. It clawed at my mind, threatening to drive me mad with terror. Every instinct screamed at me to run, to flee as far as I could, but I forced myself to stay, to observe.

The edges of the rift were jagged and raw, as if the very stone had been torn asunder by some unimaginable force. The ground around it was blighted and dead, not a single blade of grass or living creature for miles. The silence was oppressive, broken only by an occasional low, ominous rumble from the depths of the chasm. It was as if all hope, all light, and all goodness had been sucked away, leaving only a yawning pit of despair. The very air tasted of ash and decay, and I could feel the corruption seeping into my bones the longer I stayed.

This, I knew without a doubt, was the source of our world's torment. The birthplace of the Horde. A wound in reality that bled chaos and destruction into our world. I wanted to turn away, to shut my eyes and pretend I had never seen such horror. But I knew I couldn't. This was why I had come, why I had left everything behind. I had to understand, had to find a way to stop it. No matter the cost.

To imagine, though, that there are two of these on our continent. To imagine the burden of these rests on the shoulders of a young girl. I will do everything in my power to lessen what I can.

With a heavy heart, Sayra rose from her bed, her legs unsteady beneath her. As she began to prepare for the day ahead, her mind was overwhelmed with all she had learned from Arene and the queen of Acacea. From her mother's journal. And there was much more to learn as well. As she left her room, Sayra didn't notice the unmarked box collecting dust sitting on the floor beside her dresser, forgotten in the consuming haze that became her life.

⸺◈⸺

As Sayra approached the arena's massive wood-carved door for their joint combat class, Sylven nudged her with his elbow. She turned to face him, her wheat braid swinging across her lower back and black training uniform.

"So, von Lykken, ready to dazzle everyone with your graceful flailing?"

Sayra snorted, raising an eyebrow at him. "Flailing? Please. I think you're confusing me with your spellcasting, *Astor*. I've seen more coordinated movements from a drunken goat." Ahead, she spotted Nessika speaking quietly with Emrys amidst the crowd of people entering the dome.

"Ah, but have you seen how effective drunken-goat style is?" Sylven retorted, a mischievous glint in his hazel eyes. "It's all about the element of surprise. They never see it coming."

"Neither do your allies," Sayra shot back, her lips twitching with amusement. "I'm still recovering from that fireball that singed my eyebrows last week because you positioned yourself poorly."

They passed through the doors, and the enormous training space opened before them. Dust motes floated in the air.

Sylven waved a hand dismissively. "Details, details. Besides, I thought it rather improved your look. Gave you a certain *smoldering* quality."

Sayra groaned at the pun, shoving him playfully. "That was terrible, even for you. Keep that up, and I might just let the next daemon we face eat you."

"You wound me, truly." Sylven clutched his chest in mock pain. "And here I thought we were developing such a beautiful friendship."

"Beautiful like a carriage wreck maybe," Sayra said, but there was no real heat in her words.

As they continued through the arena, both sobered. Sayra glanced at Sylven, a small smile playing on her lips. "Try not to embarrass me too much in there, okay?"

Sylven grinned back. "Wouldn't dream of it. That's your job, after all."

Snorting, Sayra folded her arms and waited with the Valkyries as the Arcanists made their way to the locker rooms to change into appropriate training attire. Akira and Kenji hadn't spared them a glance since that dinner between them, though his threat still hung around. For the time being, she chose to focus on more pressing matters than his childish tantrums. As the men left, Sayra was glad to see Sylven and Emrys clapping each other on the back, speaking in a friendly manner with a shorter boyish-faced Arcanist—Waylen, if she recalled correctly.

Lynn's boot absently traced patterns on the smooth stone floor, her usual cheerful demeanor subdued. "Do you miss home?" she asked suddenly, her voice soft and wistful.

Sayra and Nessika exchanged surprised glances.

"Sometimes," Sayra admitted, thinking of Faenda's lush forests and the few good memories of when her family was whole. "Why do you ask?"

Lynn sighed, her freckled face etched with a melancholy that seemed out of place on her usually bright features. "It is silly, I know of it. We train to be Valkyries, defenders of the realm. But sometimes..." She trailed off, looking embarrassed and twiddling with the magenta ribbon in her short auburn braid.

"It's not silly," Nessika said. "Go on."

Lynn chewed on her lower lip for a second. "Sometimes I dream of my mother's garden. Herbs drying in the kitchen, soil between fingers.

Last night, I awoke sad because I could not remember the exact shade of blue of the forget-me-nots that grew by the home."

Sayra felt a pang in her chest, recognizing the ache of homesickness in her friend's words. Neither of them had been back in years.

"I love this. I do," Lynn continued, her voice growing stronger. "I love training and learning to protect others. But there is days when I can trade it all for one more quiet evening helping my father in his workshop or listening to my mother's endless chatter about the village gossip." She looked up, her brown eyes shimmering. "For both, is it wrong to want?"

Sayra reached out, squeezing Lynn's hand. "Of course not. It's what makes you human, Lynn. It's what makes you a good Valkyrie."

Nessika nodded in agreement. "Our connections to home and the people we love—they're what we're fighting to protect. Never be ashamed of that."

Lynn managed a watery smile. "Thanks. I just... I worry sometimes that I'm not cut out for this. That I'm too soft. Too sentimental."

"Nonsense," Sayra said firmly. "Your kindness and your ability to see the beauty in small things—that's your strength."

Lynn's smile grew more genuine. "You really think so?"

"We know so," Nessika affirmed.

As the locker room doors began to open, signaling the return of the Arcanists, Lynn straightened her shoulders, pawing at her eyes quickly.

They approached the middle of the arena, and Sayra caught sight of Emrys. The prince's dark hair was neatly combed, his posture regal even in training gear. His gaze started turning toward her, and she quickly glanced away.

"Okay," Lynn said, her voice gaining its usual cheer, though Sayra could hear the depth of emotion behind it. "No moping. Let's go show these Arcanists what we're made of."

"That's our girl." Sayra grinned, relieved to see the melancholy leave Lynn's demeanor.

But when Catara arrived in black training leathers, Sayra's relief was short-lived. Catara strode into the center of the arena with a dozen people in her wake. The instructor's piercing gaze swept over the assembled students, assessing them with the keen eye of a seasoned warrior.

"Today," Catara announced, her voice echoing in the vast space, "we have a special training session. I've invited some of our upperclassmen to join us." She gestured to a group of older students entering the room, their confident strides and a year's additional experience marking them as more practiced fighters.

The upperclassmen formed a half-moon around them, and a grinning face caught her attention. Vander's gray eyes winked at Sayra, and his gait was noticeably confident as he whispered something to a stone-faced Arcanist beside him. At his left, Breane's eyes assessed the room, falling last on Sayra. She nodded once in greeting.

Waylen and Jayde stood nearby, the former bouncing on the balls of his feet with nervous energy while Jayde rolled her eyes at his antics.

As Catara began pairing them off, Sayra felt a flutter of anticipation in her stomach. But when the instructor's eyes landed on her and Sylven, an unexpected name left her lips.

"Valkyrie Sayra, Arcanist Sylven, you'll be facing Arcanist Vander and Valkyrie Breane."

Sayra's head snapped up, meeting Vander's dark gaze across the arena. The crown prince's usual smirk was in place, but there was something cold in his eyes that had her furrowing her brows.

"Oh joy," Sylven muttered under his breath. "His Royal Smugness himself."

"Careful," Sayra whispered back, her lips hardly moving. "He might hear you and demand we polish his boots as punishment."

Sylven snickered, but his eyes tightened just so.

Vander and Breane approached, the latter's blonde braid swinging with each step. "Little brother's friends," Vander drawled, his voice dripping with false warmth. "How delightful."

"It'll be just like our normal sessions, Sayra," Breane said, her tone light as she stretched her arms across her chest.

Everyone moved to the side, giving them plenty of space to spar. Sayra stood shoulder to shoulder with Sylven as they faced Vander and Breane. The crown prince's dark eyes glittered with anticipation, an assured smirk playing on his lips.

"Begin." Catara stepped back.

Sayra struck first, launching forward with a quick jab aimed at Breane's solar plexus. Breane deflected the blow with her forearm, countering with a swift hook that Sayra managed to duck under. The rush of air above her head showed how close the punch had come. Not wasting a moment, Sayra spun, using her momentum to deliver a roundhouse kick. Breane blocked it with her shin, the impact sending a shockwave through both of them. They broke apart, watching each other warily.

Vander and Sylven circled each other, hands raised in fighting stances, eyes locked in fierce concentration. Vander struck first, lunging forward with a swift jab. Sylven's hands moved in a fluid arc, conjuring a shimmering translucent barrier that deflected the punch with a sizzle of energy. Words of majik whispered in the air.

Sayra could feel Sylven's support majik flowing through her, sharpening her reflexes and speed. She feinted left before striking right, her fist grazing Breane's cheek as the older Valkyrie leaned back just in time.

Breane retaliated with a flurry of strikes, her fists a blur of motion. Sayra's arms moved in tight, efficient patterns, blocking and deflecting each punch. The sound of their combat echoed through the arena, both Arcanists fighting beside them.

Retaliating swiftly, Sylven dropped low near Sayra, sweeping his leg toward Vander's ankles. The crown prince leaped, his ward flaring to life as a dome of swirling energy cushioned his landing. The clash of majik and physical force sent ripples through the room, the very air seeming to vibrate with power.

As they grappled, Breane managed to lock Sayra's arm, using her superior leverage to throw Sayra over her hip. Sayra hit the ground hard but rolled with the impact, springing back to her feet in one fluid motion. But before she could steady her feet, Breane's foot was mere inches from her shoulder. The shine of her black boot almost grazed Sayra, but Sylven's perfectly timed ward blocked it.

Sayra could have hugged the fool.

The two Valkyries danced across the arena floor, their movements a deadly ballet of strikes, blocks, and counterattacks. Sweat glistened on their skin, their breathing heavy but controlled.

The ley lines beneath them pulsed with energy, responding to the Arcanists' call.

Sweat beaded on the men's brows as they pushed their skills to the limit, neither willing to yield. Their wards flickered and reformed in rapid succession, a dazzling display of majik that left spectators in awe of their prowess and determination. Physical and arcane combat merged seamlessly, creating a spectacle of raw power and skill.

As the fight wore on, Sayra began to notice something was off. Her movements felt sluggish, as if she were fighting underwater. Each punch and kick required more effort than it should have, her limbs seeming to drag through the air. Then, a bizarre tingle stole energy from Sayra's limbs.

Breane noticed the change, her brow furrowing in confusion. But she didn't let up, capitalizing on Sayra's suddenly slowed reactions. Her fists found gaps in Sayra's defense that hadn't been there before, landing solid hits on her ribs and shoulders.

Something's wrong, Sayra told Sylven, her teeth gritting. *Someone else is using majik on me, and it's weighing me down.*

She could feel his understanding through their link, tinged with frustration.

Gritting her teeth, Sayra pushed through the strange resistance. She feinted again, following through with a spinning elbow strike that caught Breane by surprise. The older Valkyrie stumbled back, giving Sayra a moment to regroup. But the reprieve was short-lived. As Breane recovered, Sayra felt the oppressive force grow stronger. Her muscles strained as she blocked another of Breane's strikes, the impact jarring her arm.

In a desperate move, Sayra attempted a takedown, aiming to grapple Breane to the ground. For a moment, they were locked in a contest of strength, neither willing to yield. Sayra could feel her hidden majik stirring, responding to her desperation, and she fought to keep it contained.

With a sudden burst of strength, Breane broke free of Sayra's grip. The unexpected motion threw Sayra off balance. She stumbled, her foot catching on the uneven stone floor.

Breane seized the opportunity. Her fist flashed out, connecting solidly with Sayra's solar plexus. The impact drove the air from Sayra's lungs, sending her sprawling to the ground.

Then, her opponent charged Sylven's back.

Get up, get up, get up, Sayra told her uncooperative limbs. They felt like cement blocks, too heavy to move. To Sylven, she shouted, *Behind you!*

In the nick of time, Sylven summoned a barrier that managed to stave off Breane's attack.

But she didn't hold back, and Vander began viciously assaulting Sylven. The barrier around him started to crack, his loss seemingly imminent.

Anger flared in Sayra's chest, hot and bright. She pushed against the invisible force holding her back, feeling something inside her respond. Her majik, usually carefully hidden, stirred restlessly.

Sayra. Sylven's voice was tight with warning. *Don't.*

She knew he was right. They couldn't risk exposing her abilities. Not there, not then. But as Breane's fist came dangerously close to breaking Sylven's ward, Sayra felt her control slipping.

The ward shattered from Breane's kick. Without hesitation, Sayra summoned her energy to dispel the majik forcing her down. But there was nothing. Fear clutched Sayra's heart as she was helpless to do *anything*.

With a wide grin, Vander tucked his hands in his pockets as Breane's fist stopped an inch from Sylven's face, their victory won. But he wasn't staring Sylven down. No. Something brightened in his eyes as he offered a hand to Sayra, and the majik released her all at once.

As it would be in poor taste to reject it, Sayra allowed Vander to assist her up, and his eyes didn't leave hers for a second.

"Well fought, Valkyrie Sayra."

"And you, Arcanist Vander," Sayra said, working hard to keep her voice even.

Catara ordered the next match to take their place as they cleared the floor.

The excitement still lingered on Breane's face as she walked beside Sayra. She lightly patted her shoulder. "Are you all right?" the taller Valkyrie asked. "You seemed off at the end."

Forcing a smile, Sayra attempted to look nonchalant when she shrugged. "You're the better fighter. It was a great match."

As the next one commenced, Sayra pulled back from the group of Valkyries and Arcanists as they observed the remaining matches. She assessed her majik, finding it was normal once more. That well inside of her hummed with it, ready to be used.

What happened? Sylven asked her, a hazel eye peaking at her from the side of his tanned face.

Pressing her lips into a line, Sayra stared at the back of Vander's head. *I'm not sure. I tried to dispel the majik on me. I knew better than to try to use it on myself or you, but I couldn't use it at all. My majik was... gone. For at least a minute. It was as if I had a seal on it all over again.*

Concern radiated from Sylven as he grew quiet. He folded his arms, his muscles bunching under his navy long-sleeve shirt. *To my knowledge, no one can repress majik unless it's a direct seal on a person. But that requires physical contact and an extensive spell. As for the interfering majik, it could have been a wind or earth user. We'll have to speak with Emrys. It's one thing for someone to cheat but another entirely if someone or something can repress majik.*

Agreed.

Neither one of them said it, but Sayra knew they both suspected Vander's hand in the development. It was too convenient, too suspicious after what they had witnessed between Vander and Akira that night.

But what exactly was his intention?

Chapter Nineteen

SAYRA

Nuns were scurrying every which way as Sayra, Nes, and Lynn walked back to their dormitory. Saint Highburn Monastery's yearly *proelium* challenge would begin tomorrow, and there was much for the staff to prepare. Between them and the normal swarm of Arcanists and Valkyries, the three of them took the garden route to navigate through the grounds.

"This place is chaos," Lynn said, exhaling when they were in the quiet of the gardens at last.

After all that had gone down, the crowds were the least of Sayra's concerns, but she couldn't help but ask if Lynn had seen anything abnormal. "Speaking of chaos," she said, lowering her voice, "have you noticed anything strange lately? During patrols or training?"

Lynn's smile faded, her freckled face growing serious. "You mean besides the usual our-world-might-be-ending strangeness with daemons?" She bit her lip, hesitating before continuing. "I... I have been having dreams. Nightmares. About the Horde, but they're different. Organized. Intelligent."

Nes and Sayra exchanged concerned glances.

"And," Lynn added, her voice tiny, "I've been waking up with these strange symbols on my mind. They fade by morning, but—" She cut herself off. "It is silly."

Nes stepped over a fallen branch. "No, not at all, Lynn. What kind of symbols are they?"

Lynn's figure seemed to fold in on itself. "Every morning, I copy them in a notebook. I do not understand why. Feels... important somehow."

"Lynn," Nes said gently, "why didn't you tell us sooner?"

Sayra's heart skipped a beat. Between her strange dreams and everything else... was it a coincidence?

Lynn shrugged, her usual confidence wavering. "I thought I was crazy. Strange dreams? Symbols? It is like something out of the cheesy romance novels Kimimari pretends not to read."

Despite the gravity of the situation, Sayra couldn't help but smile at Lynn's ability to inject humor into even the darkest moments. "You're not crazy," Sayra assured her, squeezing her friend's hand. "And..." She hesitated, meeting Nes's gaze. She nodded at Sayra. "I'd like to see them if that's okay?"

Lynn nodded, visibly relaxing. "Of course. Thanks. For all the insanity in our lives, for you two to keep me sane, I am glad." Her brown eyes twinkled mischievously. "Well, sane as a Valkyrie can be."

"I have to check in for my patrol soon, but can we meet later this evening to go over this?" Nes asked, looking between them.

Lynn brightened, agreeing with a dimpled smile. "Gives me time to say hi with Casber."

They parted ways, and Sayra hastily closed the door to her room behind her. The late afternoon sun cast shadows across the sparse furnishings. She peeled off her sweat-soaked training gear, wincing as the fabric clung to fresh bruises. Within minutes, she had showered, dressed in a clean pair of training leathers, and re-braided her damp hair with a silver ribbon.

As she moved toward her dresser for a pair of boot socks, her foot caught on something. Glancing down, she noticed a small, unmarked box that had fallen to the side of the furniture. Frowning, Sayra vaguely remembered seeing it before but had been too preoccupied with recent events to investigate. Curiosity piqued, she bent down to retrieve it. The box was lightweight, wrapped in simple brown paper with no markings or address.

Sayra carefully unwrapped the package. The paper fell away to reveal a polished wooden box, its surface smooth and unmarred. With hesitating fingers, she lifted the lid.

Her breath caught in her throat.

Nestled inside, on a bed of soft velvet, lay a pair of the most beautiful gauntlets she had ever seen. The leather was a rich, deep brown, supple and clearly of the highest quality. Intricate patterns were etched into the surface. Gold accents glinted like stars against the dark leather. Emerald gemstones lined the back of the hand in varying sizes, each cut of the highest caliber stone.

But it was more than just their beauty that struck her. As Sayra lifted one from the box, she could feel her power thrumming. They were Arcanist gauntlets, designed to amplify and focus majik. And yet they were clearly made for her hands, smaller and more delicate than the standard issue.

A folded piece of paper fluttered to the floor as she examined the gauntlets. Setting them carefully back in the box, Sayra retrieved the note, her heart racing as she recognized the elegant handwriting.

Dearest Sayra,

Happy birthday. I hope these gauntlets serve you well in the challenges ahead. They're specially crafted to work with your unique abilities. A perfect fit for someone as extraordinary as you.

May they keep you safe when I cannot be by your side.

Always yours,

Emrys

Sayra read the note twice more, her fingers tracing the letters. The words "dearest" and "always yours" seemed to leap off the page, igniting a warmth in her heart that spread throughout her body. Her fingers hovered over his signature, the ink curling to form those last three words bolder than any others. Emotions warred within her—gratitude, affection, and a twinge of guilt for having forgotten about the gift for so long. She remembered the small box by her door on that chaotic day, just before everything had gone sideways. With reverent care, Sayra slipped the gauntlets onto her hands. They fit perfectly, as if molded to her very skin. For a moment, she closed her eyes, reveling in the sensation.

It was as if she were blind the entirety of her life, but the moment the metal pressed against her skin, everything sharpened into focus. Sayra could sense the abundance of ley lines with stark clarity throughout the monastery, and her breath whooshed in amazement. From her studies, she collected valuable information on how to differentiate each. Fire, for instance, had an unusual warmth the moment her majik searched for it beneath her feet. Water was mellow and chilled and the wind cool and whispering. Earth was solid and strong and unrelenting.

Sayra flexed her fingers.

Unbidden, memories of their time together flooded her mind. The intense training sessions where Emrys's hands would gently correct her form, lingering just a moment too long. The late-night conversations where they'd shared their fears and dreams, huddled close while studying in his room. The way his eyes would seek her out in a crowded space, a silent connection amidst the chaos.

Her heart pounded as she allowed herself, for the first time, to truly acknowledge the depth of her feelings for Emrys. It was more than admiration for his skills and more than gratitude for his guidance. It was something profound, something that both thrilled and terrified her.

Before she could talk herself out of it, Sayra was on her feet, hastily pulling on her boots. She replaced the gauntlets inside the box, leaving them on her dresser. She had to see Emrys. She had to thank him properly for the gift. And she had to say... well... she didn't know what yet.

Sayra's footsteps echoed off the marble walls as she made her way to his quarters. But when she arrived at his door, her soft knock was met with silence. Disappointment washed over her. Where could he be?

Then it hit her. The library. Emrys had a routine of visiting the vast repository of knowledge on specific days and times, and it was one of those times. With renewed determination, she set off toward the heart of the monastery.

Intricate mosaics depicting scenes from the Holy Family's history adorned the marble walls. As she passed by, Sayra nodded politely to a group of nuns, their ivory habits bobbing by as they hurried, deep in conversation. A pair of young Arcanists huddled near a window, their heads bent over a thick tome, whispering excitedly about some discovered spell.

Near the grand staircase, Sayra spotted Monk Ibski. His weathered face creased in concentration as he lectured a small group of first-year students. His voice carried, filled with passion, as he explained the intricacies of elemental affinities.

The library doors loomed before her, intricately carved wood inlaid with gold. As she pushed them open, the familiar scent of old parchment and leather-bound books stacked within the three levels the library boasted enveloped her. The cavernous space was filled with towering bookshelves and crystalline chandeliers glowing with majik lighting above. Sayra's eyes swept over the rows of circular mahogany tables, most occupied by students bent over their studies. She walked around the perimeter, finding a corner tucked away from prying eyes.

And then she saw him.

Emrys sat alone at a table near the back, surrounded by stacks of ancient tomes. His dark hair fell across his forehead as he bent over a particularly large volume, his brow furrowed in concentration. His strong jawline and the curve of his lips caught her eyes. As if sensing her presence, Emrys looked up and her eyes rose. The moment their gazes connected, his expression shifted from surprise to concern. He must have seen something in her face—the mix of nervousness and anticipation she couldn't quite hide.

"Sayra?" he said, rising from his seat. "What's wrong?" His voice was low and urgent, filled with worry. In two quick strides, he was in front of her, his black cloak flaring around him in his haste.

Something *was* wrong because Sayra couldn't fight it any longer.

As her lips met Emrys's, all thoughts of caution and hesitation melted away. His mouth was soft and warm, and she could feel the steady beat of his heart against her chest. His arms slid around her waist, pulling her closer, deepening the kiss. She could feel his passion mirrored in her own, igniting a wildfire inside of her that threatened to consume them both.

For a moment, she forgot about everything else—the monastery, her studies, even the danger that lurked just beyond the walls. All that mattered was this moment, this connection, and this man who held her so tightly in his arms.

And it felt so right.

When they parted, they were both breathless. Emrys's dark eyes bore into hers, filled with desire and something more—something she hadn't allowed herself to hope for.

"Sayra," he whispered, his voice hoarse. "Are you sure?"

She smiled up at him, her cheeks flushed with embarrassment and excitement. "Yes," she admitted, tracing her fingers along his jawline and the faint stubble there. "I don't regret what happened between us."

He chuckled at hearing the words he had once spoken to her. It felt so long ago. He pressed a gentle kiss to her forehead. "I was drawn to you before I even knew why. Now, I have more than a thousand reasons why you leave me breathless."

They stood there in silence, Sayra's heart in her throat. Her mouth curved up, and her eyes lined with silver. Emrys leaned in and kissed her once more. It was deeper, filled with months of unspoken feelings and longing.

This time, she knew there would be no going back.

When she leaned out of it, Sayra was loath to remove her arms from the fabric of his coat. Emrys rested his forehead against hers, a smile playing on his lips.

"I've wanted to do that for so long," he murmured.

"Me too," she said, her cheeks flushing, braving the words before her courage left her. "Thank you, Emrys, for the birthday present. It's perfect. I've only just opened it, and I would have sooner had I known it was from you. I'm sorry it took so long."

Emrys pulled back, and she saw the amusement tugging at his expression. "If I would have known opening your gift would have led to this, I would have insisted you do it much sooner."

A laugh escaped her before she could help it.

His mouth curved further. "I'm glad you like them."

"Love them," Sayra corrected, feeling lighter than she had in months.

"Even better." His hands trailed down her arms.

There were a million things Sayra knew she should share. Between Lynn's recent confession, the fight with Vander and Breane, and a sinking suspicion her dreams were more important than she originally thought...

But for once Sayra wanted to be selfish. She wanted to bask in the moment, for she felt in her bones it wouldn't be this good for long.

Sayra? a voice in her head said.

Her face drooped at the unease in his voice. *What's wrong?*

Seeing her reaction, Emrys straightened. "Is it Sylven?"

Vander and Akira are meeting again. I just saw her sneak up to Vander's room. She may have seen me as she turned into his room. I couldn't duck behind the corner fast enough, Sylven said, his voice apologetic.

"Yes," Sayra said to Emrys. "Akira is meeting in Vander's room as we speak."

Their joy evaporated like mist in the morning sun. She bit her lower lip, and her mind struggled to put together the many pieces of their puzzle.

Emrys's posture changed instantly, his shoulders squaring as he shifted to strategist mode. His dark-gray eyes, which had been soft with affection, sharpened with focus. A sudden tautness locked his jaw.

"We need to move," he said, his voice low and urgent. He glanced around the library, ensuring no one was within earshot.

Sayra nodded, her blonde braid swaying with the movement. She propped a hand on her hip, mentally preparing herself for whatever lay ahead. "What's our plan?"

Emrys ran a hand through his raven hair. The golden accents on his navy uniform caught the light as he moved. "We need to get closer, try to overhear what they're discussing. If we can't, then it may be time to confront him." He gathered his belongings with haste.

As they made their way out of the library, a group of Arcanists passed by. Their footsteps echoed on the polished marble floors, the sound barely audible over the pounding of Sayra's heart.

Sylven, Sayra communicated through their link, *we're on our way. Keep watch, but don't take any risks.*

Understood, came Sylven's terse reply.

As they approached the Arcanist dormitories, the corridor grew busier from students and Valkyries alike leaving for dinner, forcing them to walk closer together. Sayra could feel the heat radiating from Emrys's body, their hands grazing occasionally. They climbed up to the second floor in the Arcanist dormitory. Rounding a corner, they spotted Sylven leaning against the floor's common room wall, his hazel eyes alert and focused on Vander's door further down. His usually impeccable appearance was disheveled, his walnut locks out of place on his head.

Sylven greeted them with a quick nod. As they inched closer to Vander's door, fragments of conversation began to filter through the thick wood.

"Can't keep waiting, Vander." Akira's voice, sultry and persuasive, reached Sayra's ears. "We need to act soon."

Vander's reply was muffled, but his tone sounded uncertain. Sayra strained to hear more, her breath catching as Akira spoke again.

"Don't you see?" Her voice dropped lower, a hint of vulnerability creeping in. "I'm risking everything for this. For *us.*"

Sayra's eyes widened, meeting Emrys's shocked gaze. She could feel Sylven's surprise through their link.

"I know, I know." Vander's voice came in clearer, tinged with frustration and something else. Longing? "But the timing still isn't right. Akira, you know I love you more than anything. But you must have patience."

"Patience?" Akira scoffed, her voice rising. "While your brother and that Valkyrie girl get everything they want?"

There was a moment of silence followed by the sound of footsteps. Sayra held her breath, afraid they'd been discovered. But the footsteps faded, replaced by Akira's voice, soft and cajoling.

"Trust me, Vander. With my influence in Droden and your position here, we could have it all. Power, prestige, and each other. The Holy Family will be brought to their knees, and we'll be free to share our relationship with the world. It will be an era of peacetime like no other, a true unity between our countries."

Sayra's stomach churned. This was all about their secret *fling*? She glanced at Emrys, seeing his jaw clench in anger.

"You're right." Vander's voice was resolved. "We'll do it your way. But we need to be careful. If anyone suspects…"

"They won't," Akira purred. "I'll make sure of it. You're mine, Vander, and I'm yours. Soon they will all know it. The others can worry about the trivial details."

The sound of rustling fabric reached them, followed by a soft moan that made Sayra's cheeks burn. She looked away, catching Sylven's equally embarrassed expression.

We should go, Sylven's voice sounded in her head.

Sayra nodded, tapping Emrys's arm. As they began to retreat, an Arcanist rounded the corner of the stairwell, giving them a curious stare before walking down the hall. They followed Emrys's lead into his room, Sayra erecting a spell for privacy the moment his door closed.

Emrys's room was warmly lit, the soft glow of majik lamps brightening when they entered. Sitting at his table, Sayra leaned back into the ebony chair. Sylven leaned against the desk, his arms crossed over his chest, while Emrys paced the length of his burgundy rug, his brow furrowed in concentration.

"All right," Emrys said, breaking the tense silence. "Putting aside Vander's personal relationship problems for the moment, let's go over everything we know to see if we can make sense of this."

Sayra nodded, her jade eyes meeting Sylven's. "Lynn's been having dreams," she began. "Nightmares about the Horde, but they're different. Organized. Intelligent. And she's been waking up recalling strange symbols."

Sylven's eyebrows shot up. "Symbols? What kind?"

"She's been copying them into a notebook," Sayra explained. "Says they feel important somehow."

Emrys stopped pacing, his stance intense. "We need to see those symbols. They could be significant."

Sylven cleared his throat. "There's more. During our sparring match with Vander and Breane, something interfered with Sayra's majik."

Emrys's gaze snapped to Sayra. "What do you mean?"

She shifted uncomfortably. "It was like my majik was repressed. I couldn't access it at all." She shrugged helplessly, not comprehending it but explaining every detail.

"That shouldn't be possible," Emrys muttered, resuming his pacing. "And the timing with Vander and Breane as your opponents after what we've learned..."

"There's something else," Sayra added, her voice soft. "I've been having dreams too. A voice keeps telling me to find a spell that protects against the Horde's fear majik."

The room fell silent. Sylven pushed off from the desk, his hazel eyes wide. "A spell against fear majik? That could change everything."

Emrys nodded, his expression grave. "If such a spell exists, it could turn the tide in our fight against the general Horde, even if the hybrids don't wield it."

"But how do we find it?" Sylven asked. "And what does it have to do with Lynn's dreams or the interference in our match?"

Sayra stood, her hands clenched at her sides as she looked up at them. "I don't know, but I can't shake the feeling that it's all connected somehow. These pieces are part of a larger puzzle."

Emrys stopped in front of her, his eyes searching hers. "You're right. There's more at play here than we can see. We need to gather everyone and pool our knowledge."

Surprise flitted across Sayra's face. "I didn't think you'd be willing."

Silent and careful, Emrys removed his cloak with a practiced movement, draping it over his dark comforter. His efforts were slow, wrapped in deep contemplation. At last, he said, "We have no other choice. If you and Lynn are both having dreams, with much more at play here, I think the Goddess is trying to tell us something. It may be that we have to widen our circle to discover what she's trying to tell us."

Sylven nodded in agreement. "Nessika, Kimimari, Lynn... even Waylen. They might have pieces we're missing."

Pressing her lips together, Sayra watched the toe of her boot tap on the rug. If anyone had asked her months ago if she believed in the Goddess, her answer would have been a resounding no. But her mother believed. There was more and more evidence of a higher power coming into her awareness, and the dreams felt so lifelike. None of that could be happenstance.

There was only one explanation, and it was that of a higher power guiding them for a greater purpose. The strings of fate had pulled them all together, weaving them into a pattern that was only now beginning to take shape.

A shiver tingled her spine at the thought.

Emrys took a deep breath, pulling Sayra's attention to him as he squared his shoulders. "All right. We'll arrange a meeting. Somewhere private. We need to lay all our cards on the table."

As they began to plan, Sayra couldn't shake the feeling they were on the cusp of something colossal. The pieces were there, scattered and obscure, but she could sense the discovery was right at their fingertips.

She only hoped it wouldn't yank the rug from under them.

Chapter Twenty

EMRYS

Emrys stood before Vander's door, his hand poised to knock. The corridor was quiet, most students still lingering in the dining hall. He had left dinner early to hunt down Vander, and soon, he would meet with Sayra, Sylven, and the others. He prepared himself for the confrontation ahead. His knuckles rapped sharply against the polished wood.

"Enter," Vander's voice called from within, amusement coloring his tone.

Emrys pushed the door open, stepping into his brother's room. The space was opulent, even by royal standards. Rich tapestries adorned the walls, depicting scenes of ancient battles and mythical beasts. A large, four-poster bed dominated one side of the room, its sheets of the finest Acacean silk. The air was thick with vanilla incense, curling tendrils of smoke rising from an ornate burner on Vander's desk.

Vander himself lounged in a high-backed chair, a crystal glass of amber liquid dangling from his fingers. His shirt was partially unbuttoned, teasing a glimpse of his toned chest. A roguish smile played on his lips as he regarded Emrys.

"Little brother," Vander drawled, taking a sip from his glass. "To what do I owe the pleasure?"

Emrys's jaw clenched, but he forced his voice to remain steady. "We need to talk about what happened during combat class."

Vander's eyebrow arched, his smile widening. "Ah, yes. Quite the spectacle, wasn't it? Your little Valkyrie put up quite a fight."

"Cut the act, Vander," Emrys snapped, his patience wearing thin. "Something happened to Sayra's majik during that match. I want to know what you did."

Vander chuckled, setting his glass down on a nearby table with a soft clink. He stood, stretching languidly like a cat. "My, my. Such accusations. What makes you think I had anything to do with it?"

Emrys watched as Vander sauntered over to the window, his movements fluid and controlled. A mischievous glint appeared in his eyes.

"Because it shouldn't be possible," Emrys pressed. "Repressing someone's majik without direct contact? That's unheard of."

Vander turned, leaning against the windowsill with casual grace. "Perhaps your Sayra isn't as powerful as you thought. Or maybe," he paused, a sly grin spreading across his face, "she was simply outmatched."

Emrys felt his temper flare, but he forced it down. Losing control wouldn't get him the answers he needed. Instead, he changed tack.

"You know, it's interesting," Emrys said, his voice deceptively calm. "When you found out about Sayra and me, about the relic, you seemed rather upset."

For a fraction of a second, Vander's composure slipped before his nonchalant mask slid back into place. "Upset?" He scoffed, running a hand through his dark hair. "Merely surprised, dear brother. It's not every day one learns of such unique circumstances."

Emrys stepped closer, his eyes never leaving Vander's face. "No, it was more than that. You were jealous. Angry, even. Why is that, Vander? What does it matter to you?"

His smile faltered for a moment, but he quickly recovered. Vander moved to his wardrobe, idly adjusting the collar of a hanging shirt. "You're reading too much into things, Emrys. Always so serious."

"Am I?" Emrys pressed, following Vander's movements. "Then explain to me why you've been meeting with Akira in secret. What are you planning?"

Vander couldn't hide his surprise. His hand froze on the wardrobe door, his body tensing visibly. When he turned back to Emrys, his eyes were cold, all pretense of amusement gone. "You've been spying on me," he said, his voice low and dangerous.

Emrys stood his ground, meeting Vander's gaze unflinchingly. "I've been protecting our family. Our kingdom. Something you seem to have forgotten about."

For a moment, the brothers stared at each other. Then, unexpectedly, Vander laughed. It was a harsh sound, devoid of humor.

"Oh, Emrys," he said, shaking his head. "Always the dutiful son, the perfect prince. Did it ever occur to you that maybe, just maybe, I have Acacea's best interests at heart too?"

Frowning, Emrys was caught off guard. "What do you mean?"

Vander moved closer, his eyes burning with an intensity Emrys had never seen before. "You think you're the only one who can save our kingdom? That you and your precious Sayra are the keys to some grand destiny?"

He reached out, gripping Emrys's shoulder tightly. "Wake up, little brother. The world is changing, and we need to change with it. Sometimes, that means making difficult choices. Even if you happen to forget when the little Valkyrie distracts you with sweet words and passionate kisses."

Emrys shrugged off Vander's hand. "It seems I'm not the only one spying on the other."

"Indeed," Vander drawled. He stepped back, and his usual smirk returned. "Do what you must. Enjoy whatever fleeting romance you want with that girl. In the end, I'll be the one to save our kingdom. *I* am the crowned prince, in case you've forgotten."

Rage curled Emrys's fists, and a sinking feeling nearly had him hurling them at Vander's face. It all made sense. The way Vander had been acting the past few months, how he had Breane poking around on his behalf, and his current alliance with Akira of all people. His jealousy of Emrys and habit of appearing in the right places at the right times...

"You were behind the dormitory fire."

Pocketing a hand, Vander took care to pick up his vice with the other, swirling the alcohol within. He stared at it, contemplating. "You have a tendency to be too clever for your own good."

His rage exploded, cracking Emrys's mask and releasing a snarl beneath. Lunging forward, he grabbed the fabric of Vander's shirt, pulling him to his face. Amber liquid sloshed from his glass, spilling drops down his hand and onto the black and gold rug beneath them.

"How could you?!" Emrys roared, everything inside of him restraining his other fist from flying. "You almost *killed* her and other Valkyries! That majik you had cast on her room was forbidden. You sacrificed an Arcanist's *life* for that."

A sneer crossed Vander's face as he beheld the wasted alcohol. "Now, now. Look what you've done."

"I swear to the Goddess, Vander, if you hurt her—"

The crowned prince snapped. He threw the glass to the ground, the fine work shattering into dozens of pieces. "You'll what?!" he shouted back, his face leaning into the space between them. "You. Have. No. Power!"

For a second, that malicious majik crept into his thoughts, cooing to him to burn Vander where he stood. The man deserved it for having caused a needless death and for almost killing Sayra. After all, Vander posed a credible threat to everything they had planned. But Emrys forced that *nefas* influence down, down, down.

"Do our parents know?"

A raging fire burned in Vander's gray eyes. "No, and they will not know until my plan unfurls and surpasses that of yours. And you will say *nothing to anyone.*"

Slowly, oh so slowly, Emrys shook his head. "You are not my king yet, Vander."

Faster than Emrys could blink, Vander gripped his navy vest, pulling Emrys inches from his own face. "You forget yourself. You and Sylven both will be my vassals one day. Whether she's still contracted to Sylven or has romantic ties to you, she, too, will be within my kingdom. What actions you take now will dictate what kind of future the three of you have, *if* there will be any future at all."

The threat made Emrys release Vander's shirt, but only just. As king, Vander could have the ability to sentence their very deaths if he wished. After hearing what he was capable of, extremes further than Emrys would have previously imagined, he knew the promise his brother made wasn't empty. Even if his brother had done something atrocious, even if he proved to be a threat himself, Emrys wouldn't risk Sylven and Sayra. Not when there had to be other options.

And so, Emrys lowered his hands to his side and lifted his chin, biding his time. "I sure hope you know what you're doing, Vander."

Pushing Emrys back, Vander turned in disgust as his brother regained his balance. "Get out."

Complying, Emrys slammed the door behind him and stormed down the hallway. He strode through the dimly lit corridors of the cursed monastery, his footsteps echoing off the cold stone walls. He couldn't help but feel as if the walls themselves were closing in. His fists clenched and unclenched at his sides, his mind reeling from the confrontation.

As he approached the empty classroom where the others waited, he paused to compose himself. He ran a hand through his hair, trying to calm the storm of anger and fear that raged within him. Vander's revelations and threats pressed down on him like a physical force. How could he tell them about Vander's involvement in the dormitory fire? About the threats against them all? The knowledge sat like lead in his stomach, and he knew he had to come to a decision fast on what to share.

It was too soon to fully entrust everything to Waylen, Kimimari, and Lynn. There was a sound reason his parents were strict regarding what information to share with them and what they may impart to others. The more people who knew, the more of a liability they presented. Especially when living under the roof of the very enemy they sought to destroy. He would give them pieces in exchange for any they may trade with him, but for now, Emrys wasn't willing to chance the risks.

Pushing open the heavy wooden door, Emrys stepped into the classroom. A thin translucent barrier wrapped around him, sending a tingle of majik through his skin. Sayra had already spelled the place for privacy. Desks had been pushed to the sides, forming a makeshift circle in the center where they sat, their faces painted with concern and anticipation.

Sayra looked up as he entered, her jade eyes immediately locking onto his. She must have sensed his distress, for she half rose from her seat, her brow furrowing with worry. Beside her, Nessika's hand rested on the hilt of her sword, ever vigilant in her armor. Sylven leaned against a desk, his navy-clad arms crossed, while Waylen fidgeted nervously with the sleeve of his cloak. Lynn and Kimimari sat close together, their black-clad shoulders touching in a silent show of support.

He closed the door behind him, the soft click seeming to echo in the expectant silence. As Emrys moved to join the circle, his mind settled on what to say. "For those who haven't been thus far included, I have news," he said, his voice steady despite the turmoil within. "And I'm afraid it's worse than you could have ever imagined."

Brown eyes widened on Lynn's freckled face, and Waylen nervously continued fidgeting with his cloak.

"Before we begin," Emrys said, his voice low and measured, "I need to know what each of you has experienced recently. Anything out of the ordinary, no matter how insignificant it might seem."

Lynn rubbed her arms, her voice just above a whisper. "I have been having dreams. Strange symbols fade by morning, but..." She hesitated, glancing at Sayra, who nodded encouragingly. "Sayra says they might be important."

Kimimari nodded, her usually stoic expression tinged with concern. "The Horde's presence around the monastery has become more coordinated. It's as if they're being directed by some greater intelligence."

Waylen cleared his throat, his fingers stilling on his cloak. "I've noticed..." His mouth closed, and his face grew sheepish, as if he were chiding himself.

"Anything helps, Waylen." Sylven's tone was reassuring. "Trust me, there's nothing you could say that would be stranger than things we've discovered."

Swallowing hard, Waylen settled back into his chair. "I've noticed that I've been pulled toward the cathedral more often than not."

Near him, Sayra went still.

"It beckons me in a strange way, and when I attend mass, the urge only grows stronger, as if I need to get closer somehow." Waylen laughed at himself, rubbing the back of his neck.

"I've had a similar experience," Sayra said, frowning at her hands. "It's like an instinct keeps drawing my attention to it, though I've never followed it. My dreams of late have been asking me to find a spell that combats the Horde's fear majik and to look for hidden pages."

Emrys absorbed this information, his mind racing to connect the pieces. He turned to Sylven and Nessika, silently prompting them to share.

Nessika's hand tightened on her sword hilt. "And I've observed the same as Kimimari."

Sylven's jaw clenched. "There's been interference. During training, Sayra's majik was suppressed. It shouldn't be possible."

Emrys nodded, his expression grave. "What you've all experienced is connected. The Holy Family, the Horde, the very nature of majik itself—it's all changing. And we're at the epicenter of it."

"What do you mean, Sayra's majik?" Lynn asked, her expression puzzled.

Sayra stood up and moved beside Emrys. She looked at each of her friends and Waylen in turn. Her palm rose in front of her. "*Sphera.*" A ball of bright fire formed over her hand, the flickering flames highlighting the shock on the newcomers' faces.

"Oh my Goddess," Kimimari whispered as Lynn gasped.

Waylen's jaw dropped.

Then Sayra told them everything she knew from the day she accidentally used majik to their recent visit to Tern. Throughout it all, Lynn's eyes grew watery, and Kimimari remained stoic, her hands clasped into a fist before her. Waylen kept glancing at him to confirm what Sayra said was true, and Emrys would nod every so often.

Horror and disgust writhed across their faces when Sayra detailed the daemonic, corrupt trials the Holy Family conducted under their very feet. She detailed the Horde encounter where she used *nefas* majik and the hybrid daemon that found them. But she carefully danced around the details of Ophelia Majik Co., glossing over any specifics with a summary sentence that Emrys had allies in Tern they spoke with.

For which he was thankful. He didn't want to expose their location or identities yet.

"The Holy Family..." Waylen hunched over his knees, clasping his hands in front of his mouth.

"Control," Emrys said grimly. "Fearmongering. They've been manipulating us all, keeping us dependent on them for protection against a threat they themselves created."

Sniffing, Lynn's mouth warbled as she stood to give Sayra an enormous hug. "I am sorry."

Blinking hard, Sayra returned the hug fiercely. "No, Lynn. I'm sorry for not telling you guys sooner."

"It's not your fault." Kimimari's voice was steady. "None of this is. You can't blame yourself for something done to you. Now that you do know, what comes next will fall on your shoulders. But it isn't a burden for you alone. We are all in this, no matter what. This is our cadre being threatened." Her obsidian eyes marked each of them in turn, finally resting on Emrys. "We aren't four strong anymore. There are seven of us, and what we can accomplish together—"

A smirk lifted Nessika's face beside her. "Is endless," she finished.

Confidence had Waylen lifting his head, and his face warmed at the flame-tattooed Valkyrie.

Emrys paused, weighing his next words carefully. "There are forces at work here that we don't fully understand. Some within these very walls who would see us fail." His eyes met Sayra's, a silent apology for the secrets he still had to keep.

Her brows pinched as Lynn returned to her seat, pawing at her face.

"We need to be vigilant," Emrys continued. "Trust no one outside this room. And above all, we must protect each other. The trials ahead will test us in ways we can't imagine." He looked at each of them in turn, his voice firm. "We'll expose the truth next year, but it won't be easy. We'll face dangers from all sides. Are you prepared for what that means?"

Sayra glanced up at him, folding her arms and dipping her chin. Sylven straightened, his eyes hardening with resolve. A corner of Nessika's mouth quirked up.

Lynn and Kimimari exchanged a look before nodding solemnly. Waylen still had a nervous tap in his foot but met Emrys's steady gaze.

"We're with you," Sayra said, her voice strong and clear as the others chimed in with similar words. "Whatever comes, we will face it."

Emrys felt a surge of gratitude and determination. As he looked at their resolute faces, he knew that despite the darkness ahead, there was hope. Even if his brother sought to undermine their plans and hybrid daemons were appearing, they wouldn't be alone.

"Then let's begin," Emrys said, his voice filled with quiet authority. "We have much to discuss, and time is not on our side."

Chapter Twenty-One

SYLVEN

Chewing on his lip, Sylven digested everything they had learned thus far. "Perhaps we should start with something tangible." He glanced at Lynn as the auburn-haired Valkyrie sat cross-legged on her chair. "Lynn brought her notebook with the symbols appearing in her dreams. We could take a look and see if anything comes of it."

Lynn nodded, reaching into her satchel to retrieve a worn, leather-bound notebook. She placed it on the floor at the midpoint of their circle, and everyone leaned in to get a better look.

As Lynn opened the book, Sylven's eyes widened at the intricate symbols scrawled across the pages. They were unlike anything he'd seen before—swirling lines and angular shapes that seemed to dance across the paper.

"These are remarkable," Rys murmured, his brow furrowed in concentration.

Propping an arm on her thigh, Kimimari's eyes scanned the pages intently. Her jaw slackened. "I've seen these before," she said, her voice just above a whisper.

All eyes turned to her.

"Where?" Sayra asked eagerly.

Kimimari shook her head, frustration evident on her face. "I can't remember exactly. It was a long time ago in Droden. Maybe in an old book? But they look familiar."

Sylven felt a mix of excitement and disappointment. A lead but a dead end for the time being. He turned to Sayra. "What about your dream? The one about needing a spell to combat the Horde's fear majik?"

Sayra nodded, and her eyes were distant as she recalled the reverie. "It was urgent. Like a warning. The voice said we needed to find this spell before it was too late."

"Could these symbols be related to that spell?" Waylen asked, gesturing to Lynn's notebook.

"It's possible," Rys said thoughtfully. "If Kimimari has seen them before, they might be part of an ancient language. One that could contain powerful, forgotten majik."

Tapping her chin, Sayra said, "It could be that the hidden pages my dream referred to are Lynn's pages of symbols. Maybe that's our lead for discovering the spell."

Sylven felt a surge of resolve. "Then that's where we start. We need to research ancient languages and look for any mention of spells against fear majik. And we need to figure out why Lynn and Sayra are having these dreams."

A troubled edge tightened Rys's face. "I'm not entirely certain that's necessary for finding a counterspell to the Horde's fear majik."

"What do you mean?" Sayra asked, tucking a stray strand of hair behind her ear. A few more lingered around her face, but they were too short to be tucked into her braid.

The prince stared at the far wall, and Sylven could practically see the mechanisms of his mind whirling. A loud whooping noise caught their attention just outside their door, and for a moment, they all froze. If their instructors caught them in there, there would be questions, and the last thing they wanted was to draw unnecessary attention. But when a group of boys laughed hysterically and kept walking, his hackles lowered.

"As you, Sayra, and I know, she can cast majik without the incantation. Verbal or mental," Rys said to Sylven. "Twice now, she has cast spells without being aware of the wording beyond what she intended. Once, she cast a spell to slow Netta in her acolyte trials. A second time, she cast a spell that pushed away another Arcanist's majik in the dormitory fire." Turning, Rys looked toward Sayra. "We don't fully understand what you are capable of majik-wise, but I do think that would be within the realm of possibility if we explored it further."

For a moment, Sayra contemplated his words. Her eyes were haunted by those memories.

Sylven thought it over. Rys had a valid point. Not only did Sayra replicate something Sylven hadn't achieved in over a decade of majik work, but she did it twice. First with a spell he could perform with a majik incantation only, then again with a spell he'd never heard of. She only needed the intention behind her spellcasting to perform the majik.

"Maybe," Sayra said, staring at the floor. "Both of those times, I was in a situation that felt out of my control, and the majik sort of took over. It wasn't intentional, but I can try to replicate it. But if it's possible for me to form a spell against fear, then what are the dreams Lynn and I are having about?"

"Possibly something that we aren't aware we need a solution to yet." Emrys sighed. "There's a much bigger picture we can't fully visualize, and I think it's wise if we explore two paths at once."

Waylen's body perked up in his chair. "One is the cathedral?"

Nodding, Rys allowed a small smile to curl his mouth.

"And the other is me practicing majik without incantations to find a counterspell," Sayra guessed, stealing a glance at Rys's second nod of confirmation.

Clasping his hands behind his back, Rys strode into the focus of their circle, eyeing Kimimari first. "We won't have any opportunity to explore Droden to find where you've first seen these symbols, but I have a hunch that Arene may recognize them."

A soft inhalation near Sylven caught his attention.

Sayra's head jerked up, and her gaze switched between the prince and the tall Valkyrie. "The same symbols my mother found down south. The ones that have to do with the truth of the Goddess." Energy had lifted her words to a positive note.

Ahhhhh. Sylven allowed an excited grin to spread across his face. "Arene's the next piece of the puzzle we need, then. She may know what these mean or where to go next." He pointed at Lynn's notebook. "And if we memorize the general look of those symbols, we may even stumble across them in the cathedral. If both Sayra and Waylen are urged to check. It may need to be them, specifically, who can find them."

"Precisely," Rys agreed, turning to his left to meet his gaze. His mouth curved up.

"But what about the Horde?" Nessika asked, her fingernails tapping on her metal plates.

Lynn's face was drenched in worry and anxiousness, and Kimimari placed a hand on her shoulder. The smaller Valkyrie gave Kimimari an unconvincing smile.

Turning right, Rys's face grew pensive. "Their abnormal behavior concerns me, but until we have further leads, only time will tell. I could speculate different possibilities, but often our fears are worse than what lies ahead. For now, we'll just have to monitor their progress."

"All right then," Sayra said, scanning their faces. "We have a plan."

There were many loose ends, and while that would usually stress Sylven more than he'd accept, this was different. They had possible avenues to venture for solutions, and more than ever, they were on the same page. Everyone he cared about in the monastery knew the truth. More than ever, the Goddess had shown her hand. To give them such clear signs and directions, well, it gave him hope they were on the right path.

Chapter Twenty-Two

SAYRA

The afternoon sun beat down on the moderately sized colosseum of Saint Highburn Monastery, its warm rays glinting off the polished marble and granite that formed the impressive structure. Sayra squinted against the glare as she and Sylven made their way through the bustling crowds of Arcanists, Valkyries, staff, and visitors to find their seats. The air was thick with excitement and anticipation, the low hum of conversation punctuated by occasional cheers and gasps from the ongoing matches.

While not as grand as those found in the capital cities, the colosseum was still a sight to behold. Its circular shape rose three tiers high, with seating for several thousand spectators. Intricate carvings adorned the outer walls, depicting angels and legendary Arcanists and Valkyries of the past. Majik-powered lamps were interspersed throughout the structure, ready to illuminate the arena as the day wore on into evening. In the colosseum's center, the arena was a marvel of engineering and majik. The ground was covered in a mixture of sand and finely crushed stone, providing secure footing for the competitors. Shimmering wards encircled the fighting area, designed to contain stray spells.

Sayra and Sylven found their seats in the second tier, which offered a clear view of the matches below. The hard stone benches were a far cry from the comfortable chairs of the monastery's lecture halls, but Sayra hardly noticed the discomfort. Her attention was focused entirely on the spectacle before her.

Sylven sat beside her, looking uncharacteristically relaxed in his casual attire. He wore a finely tailored vest of deep burgundy over a crisp white shirt, the sleeves rolled up to his elbows to combat the unusual spring heat. His dark trousers were neatly pressed, and his usually messy hair had been tamed into a more presentable style. The overall effect was striking, and Sayra couldn't help but notice the appreciative glances he was receiving from some of the female spectators.

For her part, Sayra had opted for practical comfort over style. She wore her standard training outfit: form-fitting black leggings and a sleeveless tunic of soft, breathable fabric. Her blonde hair was pulled back in its usual tight braid, a silver ribbon woven through it. As they settled into their seats, Sayra's mind wandered to the meeting of the previous day. The revelations and plans they had discussed weighed heavily on her, a constant undercurrent to her thoughts. The notebook filled with mysterious symbols, the pull toward the cathedral, Kimimari's vague recognition of them, and her own dream about a spell to combat the Horde's fear majik—it all formed a complex web she wondered at.

Her eyes drifted to the arena below, where two pairs of *anima* were engaged in fierce combat for the *proelium's* first round. One Arcanist, a tall man with fiery red hair, was weaving intricate patterns in the air, summoning gusts of wind that buffeted his opponents. His Valkyrie partner, a stocky woman with a shaved head, used the wind to enhance her own attacks, her sword strikes coming faster and harder than should have been possible.

Their opponents, a lanky Arcanist specializing in earth majik and his nimble Valkyrie partner, were holding their own. The ground beneath their feet shifted and rippled, disrupting the wind Arcanist's footing, while the Valkyrie darted in and out with lightning-fast strikes.

Sayra watched intently, her trained eye picking up on subtle techniques and strategies. She couldn't help but imagine herself and Sylven down there, facing off against other pairs. Would they be able to work together as seamlessly as these teams? Despite their recent improvements, there was still a distance between their skills and a lack of the innate trust and experience that the best *anima* pairs possessed.

It would take time before they could be proficient enough to compete next year.

"Impressive, isn't it?" Sylven's voice broke through her reverie. "The way they anticipate each other's moves and how the Arcanists and Valkyries complement each other's strengths."

Sayra nodded, her eyes still fixed on the match. "It is. I wonder how long they've been training together to achieve that level of synchronization."

As she spoke, the earth Arcanist below managed to trap the wind Arcanist's foot in a sudden outcrop of stone. In the split second of distraction, the earth Valkyrie closed in, her blade stopping mere inches from her opponent's throat. The crowd erupted in cheers as the match was called.

Admiration and determination straightened Sayra's spine. She and Sylven had a long way to go to reach that level of teamwork, but watching these matches and studying the techniques on display—it was all valuable experience. As the next pair of *anima* took their positions in the arena, Sylven's voice spoke through their mental link.

There's something you should know.

She turned, catching his eye. His face was taut with concern, but those around them were practically vibrating with excitement at the next match about to start before them. *What is it?* she asked.

Below, the contest began. An Arcanist with close-cropped silver hair thrust his hands forward, sending a wave of earth surging toward his opponents. His Valkyrie partner, a lithe woman with a wickedly curved blade, used the momentary distraction to close the distance.

It's about Emrys and Vander, Sylven continued. *Last night, before our meeting, Emrys confronted Vander.*

Sayra's breath caught in her throat. *What happened?*

In the arena, the opposing *anima* pair reacted with practiced precision. The Arcanist, a man with light-brown hair, countered the earth wave with a blast of vicious fire. His Valkyrie, built like a mountain, met the attacking woman head-on, their blades clashing in a shower of sparks.

Emrys discovered... Sylven paused, and Sayra could feel his hesitation even through their mental link. *Vander was behind the dormitory fire.*

The world seemed to tilt on its axis. Sayra gripped the edge of her seat, and her knuckles turned white. Around her, the crowd cheered as the fire Arcanist unleashed a spectacular display of majik, but she barely noticed.

That's not all, Sylven continued grimly. *Vander threatened Emrys if he shared this with anyone or got in the way of his plans. Said that as future king, he could control our fates, including yours.*

The implications of the revelation crashed over Sayra like a tidal wave. She thought of Vander's smug smirks and calculated moves. How long had he been working against them? And to what end?

In the arena, the battle reached a fever pitch. The earth Arcanist had created a fortress of stone, while his Valkyrie darted in and out, harrying their opponents. The fire Arcanist's attacks grew more frenzied, and his flames licked at the stone defenses but failed to breach them.

Does anyone else know? Sayra asked, her fingers gripping even tighter.

No, Sylven replied. *Emrys didn't want to risk telling everyone at the meeting. He's worried about how far Vander's influence might reach if he learns of Rys sharing this information and any consequences that may befall us as a result.*

Sayra nodded slightly, understanding the need for caution.

The crowd's roar snapped her attention back to the match. The mountain of a Valkyrie had breached the stone fortress, her massive broadsword reducing a section to rubble. But it was a trap. The earth Arcanist's partner burst from the debris, her blade flashing as she struck.

What do we do? Sayra asked, the question encompassing far more than just Vander's betrayal.

Sylven's mental voice was resigned. *We trust no one outside our inner circle. Rys was very clear he wanted us not to utter a word or act suspicious around Vander and Breane. He's concocting some sort of plan but wanted us to know to be on the lookout for anything Vander may be up to.*

I don't like it, but I understand, she thought, a grim edge to her words.

Agreement resonated in their link.

As Sayra's focus returned to the current match, a familiar voice cut through the crowd's cheers, drawing her attention.

"Sayra, Sylven, what a pleasant surprise."

Turning, Sayra saw Kenji and Akira approaching, their attire a striking blend of Droden and traditional styles. Kenji wore a finely crafted haori of emerald silk over a black nagagi, the ensemble completed by a charcoal hakama. Intricate golden embroidery adorned the haori's edges. Beside him, Akira was resplendent in a form-fitting kimono of midnight blue, decorated with a subtle swan pattern. Her dark hair was elegantly pinned up with ornate kanzashi.

Sylven went rigid. "Kenji, Akira," he said, inclining his head in mock respect.

Kenji's eyes lingered on Sayra, a hint of hunger in their depths that made her skin crawl. "Would you mind terribly if we join you? The view from here seems excellent."

Sayra nodded, summoning her most charming smile. "Of course, Kenji. We'd be honored."

As Kenji and Akira settled beside them, Sayra couldn't help but notice how Kenji positioned himself closer to her than strictly necessary. The warmth of his body so near brought back memories of that dinner, of his hand squeezing hers too tightly as he kissed it goodbye.

Below, a new match was beginning. A reedy Arcanist faced off against one with eyes like chips of ice. Their Valkyrie partners circled each other warily, blades at the ready.

"Quite the spectacle," Kenji remarked, his upturned eyes on the arena. "Though I must say, I'm more interested in how you two have been faring. Have you given any more thought to my offer, Sylven? The end of the semester nears."

Sayra felt Sylven's stress spike through their link. His voice, however, remained steady. "Your offer was most generous, Your Highness. I've been giving it careful consideration."

Kenji nodded, a satisfied smile playing on his lips. "I'm pleased to hear it. A position as a *sicarius* in the Droden court would be a prestigious start to your career. And of course," he added, his gaze sliding to Sayra, "we would ensure that both you and your Valkyrie were well taken care of."

In the arena, the lanky Arcanist unleashed a whirlpool of water. His opponent countered with a wall of ice that cracked under the force.

Sayra compelled herself to maintain her composed exterior, even as her stomach churned. "Your thoughtfulness is appreciated, Prince Kenji. It's a weighty decision, one that requires careful deliberation."

Akira's head tilted forward, and her voice was as smooth as honey when she spoke. "Indeed, it is. But think of the opportunities. The connections you could make, and the experiences you could gain. Droden's court is unparalleled in its influence and resources. We could, perhaps, move any family members or friends into our guest ward and make our castle a more welcoming home for you both."

As she spoke, her eyes flickered to Sylven, a coy smile playing on her lips. Sayra remembered how Akira had flirted shamelessly with him during dinner, her low-cut dress and suggestive comments grating. She must not have been overtly loyal to Vander with such behavior.

Sylven nodded slowly, his face a mask of polite interest. "You make compelling points. We will certainly give it thorough consideration."

To Sayra, Sylven thought, *Do you think we could push them into the fighting pit and be done with this conversation?*

Alas, Sylven. Likely not.

And to believe I once thought you were the bane of my existence...

Really? Her eyes glared at him for a split second from the corner of her vision.

A smirk lifted Sylven's face. *Really?* he mocked back in a higher pitch.

The urge to stick her tongue out was overwhelming.

The crowd erupted in cheers as the ice Arcanist's defenses crumbled, his Valkyrie partner dodging a cresting wave of water.

Kenji's attention was momentarily drawn to the arena. "Impressive," he murmured. "Though I imagine you two could put on quite a show yourselves. I've heard whispers of your growing prowess. Your coordination during the combat lecture was remarkable."

Sayra felt uneasy at the insinuation they would be participating in the competition next year. While it was true, they hadn't shared that fact with many. Had he heard something from Akira? What exactly did Akira learn from Vander?

"You're too kind," she replied, her tone modest. "We still have much to learn."

"Humility is admirable," Kenji said, his eyes lingering on Sayra. "But don't underestimate yourselves. I have a keen eye for talent."

The match below reached its climax, the water Arcanist's Valkyrie disarming her opponent with a dazzling display of swordplay. As the crowd roared its approval, Kenji leaned closer to Sayra, his breath warm on her ear.

"I've missed our private conversations, Sayra," he murmured, his voice low enough that only she could hear. "Perhaps we could arrange some time to catch up. For old times' sake."

She felt her heart rate spike, remembering bruises hidden beneath her long sleeves and his crushing grip aching her bones. She forced herself to remain calm, her smile never wavering. "I'm flattered, Kenji, but I'm afraid my duties keep me quite busy these days."

Kenji's eyes narrowed, but his smile remained in place. "Of course. Duty is paramount. But surely you can spare a moment for an old friend?"

Before Sayra could respond, Sylven's voice cut in, his tone carefully respectful but with an undercurrent of steel. "I'm sure we can find time in our schedule for a proper meeting. Perhaps with Emrys present and other Arcanists from each country. I know we're always eager to foster good relations between our lands."

Kenji's smile tightened almost imperceptibly. "Of course. How... prudent of you, Sylven."

As another match began below, Akira deftly steered the conversation to lighter topics such as the latest fashions in Droden and the upcoming social season. But Sayra remained on edge, acutely aware of Kenji's proximity and the glances he kept throwing her way.

Through it all, she maintained her charming facade, laughing at the right moments, offering just enough engagement to be polite without encouraging anything further. She could feel Sylven's steady presence through their link. As the sun began to dip lower in the sky, painting the colosseum in hues of gold and crimson, Kenji and Akira rose to leave.

"We've enjoyed your company immensely," Kenji said, his expression warm but his eyes devoid of sincerity. "Do think about my offer, Sylven. I believe it could be mutually beneficial, though it will soon expire." As he spoke, his gaze lingered on Sayra. "And Sayra," Kenji added, reaching for her hand. "With the end-of-the-year ball coming up, I do hope you spare me a dance. I just know you will be the center of attention." He raised her hand to his lips, pressing a kiss that lasted a fraction too long to be proper.

Sayra felt Sylven's surge of anger through their link, quickly suppressed but unmistakable. As the Droden royals departed, she felt the tension slowly seep from her body. She and Sylven exchanged a look, both aware of the precarious game they were playing.

Are you all right? Sylven asked, concern evident in his tone.

Sayra lowered her chin, her eyes turning back to the arena as the *proelium* wrapped up. *I'm fine. But we need to be careful. Kenji's not going to give up easily.*

Agreed. A few seconds passed as they rose and followed the crowd out of the colosseum. *I had forgotten about the graduation ball,* Sylven mused, adjusting his sleeves beside her. *Yet another thing to dread.*

She knew little about it beyond its purpose as a celebratory event for Arcanists, Valkyries, family members and friends of those who attended the Arcanist Academy, and select staff members. From what she had gathered, there would be a grand feast following the ball that mostly encompassed chatting or standing guard, and then preparations for summer's departure.

And that was in a matter of weeks.

Their time to find answers at Saint Highburn was becoming *very* limited.

Chapter Twenty-Three

SAYRA

The next morning, the sun shone brightly across the cathedral courtyard as Sayra, Sylven, and Waylen stood at the base of the imposing structure. Sayra's eyes traced the massive sharp spires that lanced across the roof. Holy guards patrolled along the slim pathways, their silhouettes visible against the clear blue sky as they made their rounds every five minutes.

Sayra steeled herself for what lay ahead. Her blonde braid swung gently as she turned to her companions. Sylven stood tall and alert, his eyes scanning their surroundings with practiced vigilance. The gentle breeze tousled his walnut-brown hair. Beside him, Waylen fidgeted with the sleeve of his robe, his usually cheerful face etched with anxiety.

"Are you sure about this?" Waylen whispered.

Sayra nodded, and her face grew serious. "We need answers, Waylen. And if the Goddess is really calling to us, this is where we'll find them."

They began their ascent up the hundred grand steps leading to the cathedral's entrance. Each step felt significant, as if they were climbing toward something momentous. The cream-and-black-layered marble exterior gleamed in the morning light, only the faintest trace of dust scattered in occasional patches. As they climbed, Sayra's gaze was drawn to the statues of saints tucked away in spaced-out alcoves. She wondered about them. Were they all members of the Holy Family, or did the figures predate the Goddess's origins?

Circular columns sprouted from the ground, reaching up to merge with the building. A network of vined arches connected each, creating a sense of organic flow that contrasted beautifully with the sharp lines of the spires above. The effect was both awe-inspiring and intimidating, as if the very structure was a physical manifestation of the Goddess's power.

"Stairs are the bane of my existence," Sylven grumbled beside her, a deep frown crinkling his face.

A single brow rose. "I thought I was?"

Sylven made a noncommittal noise, waving his hand dismissively.

Sayra smirked at the tinge of amusement lingering from their link, peeking out of the corner of her eye to check on Waylen as they neared the top. His pale cheeks were blushed from the exertion and his breathing labored.

They reached the top of the stairs. Before them stood the mighty bronze-formed doors, their surfaces adorned with intricate inscriptions written in the common tongue. Vine-shaped irons locked the doors in place, their craftsmanship as much a work of art as a security measure. Above the doors, a diamond-shaped stained-glass window depicted the Goddess in all her glory. Sayra felt a shiver run down her spine as the Goddess's serene face seemed to gaze down at them, as if aware of their presence and purpose.

The familiar tug pulled at her mind, urging her to enter the cathedral.

With a shared glance, they pushed open the heavy doors and stepped inside. The moment they crossed the threshold, the sounds of the outside world faded away, replaced by a hushed reverence. Incense wafted through the vast space, an aromatic mixture of frankincense and myrrh that clouded Sayra's senses.

"Do you feel anything?" Sylven asked, his voice low and cautious.

Sayra closed her eyes, trying to focus on the strange pull she'd been experiencing. It was faint, like a whisper on the edge of hearing, but undeniably present. "It's here and stronger than before," she murmured. "But I can't pinpoint where."

Waylen nodded, his face starting to return to a normal color. "I feel it, too. It's almost like a song. Calling us deeper."

They moved through the holy space, their footsteps echoing in the cavernous interior. Rows upon rows of wooden pews stretched out before them, each carefully carved with symbols of faith. Sayra ran her hand along the smooth surface of a pew, marveling at the craftsmanship and the countless prayers that must have been whispered there over the years. As they wandered, Sayra's gaze was drawn to the intricate tapestries that adorned the walls. Each one depicted a scene from holy scripture, brought to life in vibrant threads and shimmering gold accents. She paused before a particularly striking image of the Goddess bestowing her blessing upon the first Arcanists and Valkyries.

"Who knew lies could be so beautiful," Sayra said quietly, her finger tracing the bottom of the rough fabric.

Sylven stepped up beside her. "It will pale in comparison to the truth. Of that, I'm certain."

They moved on, passing alcoves housing statues of saints and holy figures. Each one seemed to watch them as they passed. The pull she felt grew stronger with each step, guiding them deeper into the heart of the cathedral. Massive stone pillars rose from the floor to the vaulted ceiling high above, their surfaces adorned with intricate carvings of vines and holy symbols. Sayra craned her neck to look up, marveling at the architectural feat. The ceiling itself was a work of art, covered in frescoes depicting the creation of the world and the Goddess's role in shaping it.

As they approached the front of the cathedral, the ancient statue of the Goddess loomed before them. Carved from pure white marble, it depicted a woman of ethereal beauty, and her arms were outstretched in a gesture of benediction. Waves of thick hair tumbled from her head, misshapen in places from time's wear. At her feet, the Grand Priest's ornate perch stood empty.

"It's strongest here," Waylen said, his voice tinged with awe. "Right behind the perch."

Sayra nodded, feeling the pull like a physical force. She circled the perch, her eyes scanning every inch of the area. It was a marvel of craftsmanship, made of polished wood inlaid with gold and precious stones. But no matter how closely she looked, she could see nothing out of the ordinary. No hidden compartments, no secret symbols, and nothing to explain the strange calling they felt.

"I don't understand," she said, frustration creeping into her voice. "It has to be here. We can both feel it."

Sylven joined them, and his brow furrowed in concentration. His fingers traced the perch, searching for any hidden mechanism. "Maybe it's not something we can see," he suggested. "Could it be hidden by majik?"

Sayra closed her eyes again, reaching out with her other senses. She could feel the majik in the air, the ancient power that permeated the very stones of the cathedral from the ley lines below. It thrummed through her, a constant reminder of the forces at work around them. But try as she might, she couldn't detect anything unusual.

"I can't find anything," she admitted, opening her eyes with a sigh. "Whatever's calling us, it's beyond my ability to sense."

Waylen looked crestfallen, his demeanor dimmed by disappointment. "So what do we do now? We can't exactly start tearing apart the Grand Priest's perch looking for clues."

Sylven shook his head, his hand running behind his neck. "No, we can't. But at least we know for certain that there's something here. Something important enough for the Goddess herself to call you both to it."

Sayra nodded slowly, her mind racing with possibilities. She turned to look up at the statue of the Goddess, searching the serene marble face for any hint of guidance. The statue's eyes seemed to meet hers, and for a moment, Sayra felt a connection to something greater than herself, a trace of the divine that left her breathless.

"We'll have to find another way. Maybe in the library or…" She trailed off as the sound of approaching footsteps echoed through the cathedral.

Sylven tensed, his hand moving instinctively to where his left gauntlet would be if he were wearing it. Waylen's eyes widened in panic, darting between his companions and the source of the sound.

"We need to go," Sylven hissed. "Now."

They hurried away from the altar, trying to look casual as they returned to the entrance. Sayra's heart pounded in her chest.

"A moment of your time, if you please."

The words cut through the air like a knife, freezing them in their tracks. Slowly, they turned, and dread settled in the pit of her stomach. At the perch stood Catara and Jax Zefare, their imposing figures walking toward them. Catara's platinum hair was pulled back into her trademark severe bun, her hazel eyes sharp and assessing as they swept over the trio. Beside her, Jax's freshly shaven face was set in a neutral expression, but there was a tenseness in his hands that belied his typically smug demeanor.

"Sanctus Catara, Sanctus Jax," Sylven said, his voice steady despite the nervous energy radiating from him. "How may we be of service?"

The Holy Family members passed the pews with measured grace, their movements fluid and controlled. As they drew closer, Sayra could feel their scrutiny.

"We hoped to catch you," Catara said, her voice smooth but with an underlying edge. "We wanted to congratulate you, Sayra and Sylven, on your performances in your combat class. You two create a formidable pair."

Jax nodded, his eyes scanning their faces. "Indeed. Your skills have improved remarkably since the beginning of the year. Particularly yours, Valkyrie Sayra."

Sayra inclined her head, careful to keep her expression neutral. "Thank you, Sanctus Jax. We've been training hard."

"Clearly. I hope to see you both participate in the *proelium* next year. I have an instinct you'll be a contender for first place," Catara said, a hint of a smile playing on her lips. "We couldn't help but notice your excursion to Tern last weekend. I trust it was well received?"

Sylven stepped forward, his posture relaxed but his eyes alert. "It was, Sanctus Catara. Queen Evangelina had business there, and it was our honor to pay our respects."

Catara and Jax exchanged a look, a silent communication passing between them. When Catara spoke again, her voice was deceptively casual. "I see. And did you encounter any difficulties during your travels?"

Sayra felt her heart rate increase but kept her voice level. "Nothing out of the ordinary, Sanctus Catara. The journey was smooth, and the city guards were most accommodating."

"How fortunate," Jax said, his tanned skin crinkling and his eyes sharp. "No unusual daemon activity? No unexpected encounters?"

Beside her, Sylven shook his head. His face outfitted polite confusion. "Not that I recall, Sanctus Jax. Is there something specific you're concerned about?"

Placing a hand on her hip, Catara's stance relaxed a hair. "Mere curiosity. We like to stay informed about any potential threats to our students' safety." She paused, her gaze sweeping over them once more. "And speaking of students, we saw the pair of you conversing with Prince Kenji and Princess Akira during the *proelium*. They have seemed quite interested in your company of late."

Apparently, the dinner they had requested didn't go unnoticed. While royalty of any country may request the formal dining hall for diplomatic reasons, it had to be approved by the Holy Family. They wanted to harvest good relations between the countries, after all. Sayra didn't think it would be remarkable to them in any sort of way, but for it to come up so late in the semester...

Sayra felt a chill run down her spine, but she managed a small smile. "They were very gracious. Prince Kenji was particularly interested in our training methods here at Saint Highburn after seeing our progress in the combat lecture."

"I'm sure he was," Jax murmured, his tone unreadable. "And did he happen to mention anything about Droden's plans for next year's *Grand Proelium*?"

Waylen's brown eyes were like saucers as he shifted from foot to foot. Annoyance had Sayra picking at a nail before she stopped herself. The Arcanist was acting suspiciously, which only validated Emrys's instinct to keep what Vander revealed secret. It appeared there was merit to being careful with such things. She didn't think Waylen would hold under much pressure.

Sylven shook his head, his voice steady despite the nervous energy radiating from their link. "Not in any detail, Sanctus Jax. They seemed more interested in our personal experiences here at the monastery."

"I see. And did you find their questions probing in any way? Perhaps touching on subjects beyond the usual pleasantries?"

Like your questions? Sayra wanted to say. What were they looking for?

"Not that I noticed, Sanctus Catara. Is there something we should be aware of regarding our interactions with foreign dignitaries?" Sylven asked.

Jax let out a short laugh. "Always the diplomat, Arcanist Sylven. No, nothing specific. We merely like to ensure that our students are prepared for such interactions."

"Of course," Sayra said, her tone respectful but with an underlying current of steel. "We're always mindful of our duty to represent Saint Highburn with honor."

"I'm glad to hear it." Catara shifted her gaze to Sayra, a softening in her expression that Sayra hadn't expected. "Valkyrie Sayra, might I have a word with you in private?"

She felt her heart skip a beat, but she managed to keep her voice steady. "Of course, Sanctus Catara."

Catara turned to Jax. "Perhaps you could discuss the finer points of today's sermon with Arcanist Waylen and Arcanist Sylven while we chat?"

Jax nodded, his eyes curious but not unkind as he gestured for Sylven and Waylen to follow him a short distance away.

Catara led her to a small alcove near the cathedral steps, partially hidden from view by a statue of a saint. When she turned to face Sayra, the concern in her intense eyes made Sayra's pulse quicken.

"Sayra," Catara began, her voice lowered, "I hope you know that you can always come to me if you're experiencing anything unusual."

Blinking, Sayra was caught off guard by the almost maternal tone in her voice. "Unusual, Sanctus Catara?"

Her eyes searched Sayra's face as if looking for something hidden beneath the surface. "Yes, unusual. Dreams of the Goddess speaking with you perhaps. Or feelings of being drawn to certain places or objects. Anything that feels different."

Sayra's mind raced, weighing the risks of honesty against the danger of being caught in a lie. She decided on a partial truth. "I have been feeling a heightened sense of the Goddess's presence lately. Especially here in the cathedral."

Catara's sight grew sharp. "I see," she said softly. "And have you heard anything?"

She thought of the pull she'd felt in the cathedral, the whispered urgings that had led her there. "No. We paid our respects to the Goddess today, but I've not heard anything unusual."

Catara nodded, her expression understanding. "Sayra, I want you to know that what you're experiencing... it's not unheard of. The Goddess speaks to some of us in ways that others might not understand." She placed a hand on Sayra's shoulder. The gesture was surprisingly gentle. "But these are dangerous times. The Horde has been behaving strangely, and we must be vigilant against all threats—even those that might seem to come from within."

"What do you mean, Sanctus Catara?"

Her voice dropped even lower. "I mean that not everything that whispers to us in the dark is the voice of the Goddess. Sometimes, other forces try to deceive us and lead us astray. Take heed of what you know to be true, and be cautious about what else might try to twist our doctrine."

What did *that* mean?

"I've noticed you've been present at the focal point of many bizarre circumstances of late between the zealots setting the dormitory on fire and the Horde's unusual new patterns near the walls. I've often wondered if the Goddess has placed you, specifically, in such places for a reason. Finding you here today at such timing only strengthened my curiosity." She squeezed Sayra's shoulder gently. "I want you to promise me something, Sayra. If you experience anything else—any visions, any calls, any unexplainable urges—you'll come to me immediately. Can you do that?"

Sayra nodded, her throat tight. "Of course, Sanctus Catara."

Stepping back, Catara's demeanor shifted back to its usual authoritative stance. "Good. Now, let's rejoin the others."

As she and Jax bid them farewell and returned to the back hallways of the cathedral, Sayra, Sylven, and Waylen remained rooted to the spot.

Once they were out of sight, Waylen let out a shaky breath. "By the Goddess, that was intense."

Sylven's jaw was clenched tight, his eyes still fixed on the cathedral doors. "They suspect something. We need to be more careful."

"And we need to warn Emrys. If they're asking about Tern and our interactions with Kenji and Akira, who knows what else they might be investigating."

As they passed through the doors, she couldn't shake the feeling they had been on the verge of something momentous before the interruption. The descent down the hundred steps felt faster than their climb up, urgency speeding their steps. As they reached the bottom, Sayra paused to look back at the cathedral towering above them. Its spires reached toward the heavens.

"We'll come back," she promised, more to herself than to the others. "Whatever the Goddess is trying to show us, we'll find it."

Chapter Twenty-Four

SYLVEN

The cushioned chair under him creaked as Sylven rested an elbow on Rys's desk, concentrating on the small wooden cube in his palm. Gemstones glinted around the back of his hands, the leather gauntlets cool against his skin. He could feel the ley lines pulsing beneath his feet, the raw energy of the earth waiting to be tapped. With a deep breath, he focused his will, channeling the majik through his body and into the cube.

"*Oriri,*" he said, willing the cube to lift.

And lift it did.

His eyes tracked its progress as the wood rotated above his hand, gently winding between his fingers as he splayed them.

Boring.

"*Oriri.*" This time, he focused on the chair and desk beneath him, a corner of his mouth crooking up when they lifted an inch off the ground in unison. The drain on his strength was minimal. With his gauntlets and being next to ley lines, it didn't take much to perform the majik.

A soft gasp from across the room broke his concentration. He released his hold on the majik, everything returning to the ground as gravity reclaimed the three objects. His eyes snapped to see Sayra, her hand extended, a blue-tinged flame dancing above her fingers. The firelight played across her features, highlighting the determined set of her jaw and the intensity in her jade eyes.

"Sorry," she said, noticing Sylven's gaze. "I didn't mean to disturb you."

Shrugging, Sylven placed the cube down. "It's easy majik that I've practiced for weeks. Nothing new."

Rys pushed off from the table across from Sylven, moving to stand beside Sayra. "That was impressive. You're getting better at controlling it without incantations."

Sylven watched as Rys's hand hovered near Sayra's, not quite touching but close enough that the flame between them cast their shadows as one on the wall. Clearing his throat, Sylven stood, stretching his cramped muscles. "It's incredible how quickly you're progressing," he said, moving to the window. Outside, the Valkyrie dormitory across the way was silhouetted against the darkening sky.

The fire fluttered out of existence as Sayra turned toward him. "I could say the same about you. Two months ago, you weren't able to levitate objects."

Rys said to Sayra, his voice soft but intense, "Try to create something more complex than a flame. But remember, no incantations. Let the majik flow naturally, guided by your will alone."

She nodded and closed her eyes. For a moment, nothing happened. Then, slowly, the air around her began to shimmer and coalesce.

Sylven watched in awe as tiny specks of light began to swirl around Sayra, like fireflies dancing in the twilight. They spun faster and faster, their glow intensifying until they merged into a single radiant form. A miniature tree of light stood in the room, its branches swaying in an unfelt breeze, leaves shimmering with an inner luminescence. It was beautiful, ethereal, and utterly impossible.

So much like the woman who summoned them...

"That's extraordinary," Rys said, examining the tree with an awed expression.

Sayra opened her eyes, blinking at what she saw. The tree pulsed in response to her surprise, its light flickering like a candle in the wind.

"I wasn't trying to make anything specific," she said, her voice filled with wonder. "I just thought about life, about growth and light, and this is what appeared."

Rys moved closer, his hand hovering near the glowing tree but not quite touching it. "This is pure creation majik," he said in amazement. "The kind of thing that hasn't ever been seen. Arcanists have only formed realistic illusions, but nothing with the elements of light or shadow. Sayra, do you have any idea how significant this is?"

Sylven watched as Rys and Sayra stood on either side of the shimmering tree, their faces bathed in its soft radiance. The air between them seemed to hum with a connection beyond mentor and student, beyond even friends. A pang of something—not only jealousy but a deep, aching awareness of his own limitations—shot through Sylven's chest. He looked down at the wooden cube on the desk, remembering how proud he'd been of his achievement just moments ago. It seemed paltry compared to what Sayra had done. To what Rys and Sayra would accomplish together.

How much aid could he truly bring to the table in their efforts against the Holy Family? He was a normal Arcanist restricted by a single archetype and element of majik. He didn't have a kingdom at his disposal, nor majik that could perform anything the mind could conceive.

"We should document this," Sylven said, breaking the spell that seemed to have fallen over the room. "If it's as rare as you say, Emrys, we need to record every detail."

Rys blinked as if coming out of a trance. "You're right," he said, moving to his desk to retrieve a journal and pen. "Sayra, can you maintain it while I notate this?"

Sayra nodded, her eyes never leaving the glowing tree. Her own gauntlets enhanced her connection to the ley lines and relic within her.

Even after they discussed Kenji's chat at the *proelium*, Catara and Jax's discovery of them at the cathedral, and Vander's efforts, Sayra and Rys were nearly unfazed, as if it were all to be expected. It rolled easily off their shoulders, and they summed up the solution as "staying the course." He couldn't think of anything better, but it felt like they were biding their time until the next bad thing happened to them. Rys had sent off a coded message to his mother and Arene, asking about the strange symbols in Lynn's dream and replicating them as best as possible. Until the end of the semester, all they could do was dig a hole in their trench and weather what was to come.

Patience was not Sylven's forte.

He'd keep practicing his majik, casting and fighting with Sayra, but...

He wasn't contributing anywhere else. Waylen and Lynn both had more to go on than he did. Nessika had witnessed the Horde activity on the wall and could report back. Hell, even Kimimari had a lead to explore whenever she returned to Droden.

Which left him useless.

As the days dragged on, Sylven went through the motions, a sense of melancholy settling over him like a heavy cloak. The routine of classes, training, and meals blurred together, each day indistinguishable from the last.

During their private training sessions with Rys, Sylven watched as Sayra excelled, her grasp of theoretical concepts growing as rapidly as her practical skills. She answered questions with a quiet confidence that hadn't been there before, earning approving nods from Rys and Waylen whenever he stopped by. Sylven, meanwhile, felt as though he was treading water, neither advancing nor falling behind. Sayra's progress astounded him. She manipulated elements without incantations, creating intricate patterns of light, shadow, fire, water, earth, and wind that danced across Rys's room. Sylven pushed himself harder, determined not to fall too far behind. He managed to levitate heavier objects, even altering their density for brief periods, but it felt hollow compared to Sayra's achievements.

Rys's absence in classes became a constant, nagging worry. The prince's usual seat in their shared lectures remained empty, and Sylven caught Sayra glancing at it more than once, concern crossing her face. When Sylven asked about Rys's whereabouts, Sayra merely shrugged, her expression carefully neutral.

"Royal duties, I suppose," she said, but Sylven could sense the uncertainty in her voice.

He had a sinking suspicion Rys had enacted yet another plan of his, declining to loop him or Sayra in for one reason or another. After the last four months, Sylven had learned to trust Rys's judgement, for better or worse. There was always a calculated reason why he didn't share specific details, but it still weighed on Sylven that he wouldn't let him in.

The quiet that settled over the monastery was eerie. No more surprise visits from Kenji or Akira. No suspicious glances from Catara or Jax. Even Vander seemed to have retreated into the background. It was as if they were all holding their breath, waiting for the other shoe to drop. In the late evenings, Sylven was alone in his room, staring at the wooden cube on his desk. He'd levitate it absently, and his mind would wander to darker places. What if he wasn't cut out for this? What if, when the moment came, he couldn't protect Sayra or help Rys? The doubts gnawed at him, growing louder in the silence of his room.

As the next week drew to a close, Sylven felt a restless energy building within him. Something had to give. There were only two weeks left in the academy year, and then the five-month semester would close. His family was eager to see him, sending a letter weekly. Even his mother deigned to write, asking how Sayra was treating him and how prepared he was for finals. His siblings, Lina and Regen, both chimed in, saying how proud of him they were. Regen demanded additional tips on his majik, and Lina was extra curious about what flowers Sayra liked most so she could pick some when they visited next.

His father was ecstatic that he'd attended the *proelium*. He went on and on about how they found a private tutor who could train him and Sayra that summer to help them prepare for the coming year's event. And damn it all, it made Sylven's throat clench.

His family truly cared for him. They were *proud* of him.

That night, he spent at least an hour thinking of the best response to mail back.

He sat at his desk, the soft glow of the majik lamp casting long shadows across his room. His eyes were fixed on the small wooden cube before him, watching it hover a few inches above the polished surface. With a sigh, he let it drop, the soft thud echoing in the quiet space.

A sharp knock at his door startled him from his brooding. Frowning, he rose and crossed the room, wondering who would be visiting at that hour. When he opened the door, he was surprised to find Nessika standing there, her usually calm demeanor replaced by an air of urgency. Her serious expression sent a jolt of concern through him.

Before he could ask any questions, she spoke in a hushed, urgent tone. "Sylven, you need to dress formally. Now." Her eyes darted down the hallway as if checking for eavesdroppers.

It was then he realized how she was dressed.

Her curvy, athletic frame was accentuated by a form-fitting black dress that fell just below her knees, a departure from her usual Valkyrie attire. The dress's high collar and long sleeves gave her an air of elegance. Her dark skin seemed to glow in the soft light of the corridor, contrasting beautifully with her straight shoulder-length hair. She had swept it to one side, and a delicate gold earring dropped from her ear. Her ice-blue eyes, usually sharp and vigilant, held a hint of anxiousness she struggled to conceal. A thin gold chain adorned her neck, disappearing beneath the collar of her dress, and she wore simple but elegant black heels that clicked softly on the stone floor as she shuffled in place.

"What? Why?" Sylven asked, confusion evident in his voice.

Nessika's jaw tightened. "There's been an alarming development. Foreign dignitaries are here, and we need to meet with them immediately before they depart. I can't say more here. Just hurry."

From Thapula? It had to be.

The urgency in her voice spurred Sylven into action. He nodded quickly and retreated into his room, leaving the door closed behind him. With swift, practiced movements, he changed into his formal attire. He donned a crisp white shirt, fastening the buttons with slightly trembling fingers. Over that, he pulled on a finely tailored vest of deep burgundy. The vest was adorned with intricate gold embroidery along the edges, a gift from his parents he reserved for special occasions.

Next came the jacket, a perfectly fitted piece in a rich dark brown that complemented the vest. Its collar was high and stiff, lending an air of formality and importance. He fastened the gleaming brass buttons, each one bearing the crest of his family. Then, he pulled on a pair of pressed black trousers, their crisp lines adding to the overall polished appearance. He slipped his feet into leather boots, their shine reflecting the room around him.

Finally, he adjusted a silk cravat at his throat, its gold color tying the entire ensemble together. Running a hand through his hair in an attempt to tame it, Sylven took a breath and stepped back out into the hallway where Nessika waited.

Her eyebrows raised at his appearance, and those icy eyes blinked in surprise before her serious expression returned. "Good. Now, follow me," she said, turning on her heel and setting off down the corridor at a brisk pace.

Sylven's brow furrowed. "What's going on? Is something wrong?"

Nessika shook her head, placing a finger to her lips. "No questions. Just follow me."

He followed, his mind racing with possibilities. Had something happened to Sayra? To Rys? He reached out to Sayra through their link, but was met with a firm block.

They wound their way through the monastery's corridors, passing tapestries and statues he barely registered in his worried state. Other students they passed gave them curious glances, but Nessika's determined stride kept anyone from approaching.

As they neared the formal dining hall, Sylven's confusion deepened. Why were they heading there? The last time he'd been in that room was for that tense dinner with Kenji and Akira. The memory made his stomach churn.

Nessika paused before the ornate double doors, turning to face Sylven. "Ready?" she asked, her hand on the door handle.

Before Sylven could respond, she pushed the door open and roughly nudged him inside with a maniacal grin.

"SURPRISE!"

The shout nearly knocked Sylven off his feet. He blinked, momentarily stunned by the sight before him. The formal dining hall had been transformed. Gone was the austere, imposing atmosphere, replaced by one of warmth and celebration. Colorful banners hung from the vaulted ceiling. The long dining table had been pushed to one side, laden with an array of dishes that made Sylven's mouth water instantly.

But it was the people that truly took his breath away. There, gathered in the room, were all his friends. Sayra stood at the forefront, a wide smile on her face. She wore a flowing dress of deep green that complemented her eyes, her blonde hair falling in loose waves around her shoulders from a high ponytail. A silver pendant hung from her neck. A dove, if he recalled right, and a black ribbon caught the light as it dangled from her hair tie. Beside her, Rys grinned, looking more relaxed than Sylven had seen him in weeks. The prince was dressed in a finely tailored graphite jacket, gold buttons gleaming.

Waylen bounced on his toes. His usual robes had been replaced by a smart waistcoat in a warm brown. Lynn stood next to him, resplendent in a pale-blue gown that swirled around her ankles, her auburn curls and matching *slør* piled elegantly atop her head. Tiny flower pins stuck out from her hair. On her other side, Casber's brown hair and eyes matched the shade of his own vest. His arm wrapped around Lynn's waist, and his mouth curved adoringly at her joy. Kimimari, for once without her ever-present armor, wore a sleek black jumpsuit that accentuated her broad athletic frame.

"What is this?" Sylven managed to stammer, his eyes wide with disbelief.

Sayra stepped forward, taking his hand and pulling him farther into the room. "It's your birthday, you idiot," she said, her voice warm with affection. "Did you really think we'd forget?"

In truth, Sylven had forgotten himself. With everything that had been happening, the date had completely slipped his mind. He felt a rush of warmth in his chest, touched by the effort his friends had gone to.

"I don't know what to say," he admitted, a smile breaking through his surprise.

Rys clapped him on the shoulder. "You don't have to say anything. Just enjoy it. Goddess knows we could all use a night off from everything."

As if on cue, music began to play from a music box beside the grand table, a lively tune that immediately had Lynn pulling Nessika and Casber onto an impromptu dance floor. Kimimari made a beeline for the food table, while Waylen trailed behind to have what looked like a serious conversation.

Sylven was steered toward a plush armchair that certainly hadn't been part of the dining hall's usual decor. As he sank into it, Sayra perched on the arm, while Emrys dragged over another chair to sit opposite them.

"How did you manage all this?" Sylven asked, gesturing to the transformed room.

Sayra's eyes twinkled mischievously. "Let's just say we called in a few favors. And may have been disappearing often to keep the preparations hidden."

Rys gave him a sly smile. "Turns out, when you're a prince, people are quite willing to bend the rules for you. Even in a place as strict as Saint Highburn."

Sylven shook his head in amazement. "I can't believe you went to all this trouble. Especially with everything else going on."

"That's exactly why we did it," Sayra said, her voice softening. "You've been different lately. Distant. We wanted to remind you that you're not alone in this."

Across from them, Lynn laughed as Nessika whirled her, the tall Valkyrie's blue eyes catching his. Sylven's smile grew a hair wider.

Casber swooped Lynn into his arms at the end of the whirl, his face splitting into a wild grin as she leaned on him.

Rys sat forward, his expression serious despite the festive atmosphere. "Sylven, I know you've been feeling out of place. Like you're not contributing enough. But you couldn't be more wrong."

Sylven felt a lump form in his throat. Had he been that transparent?

"And you're our friend. You matter to us," Sayra added. "Don't ever forget that."

Before Sylven could respond, Lynn appeared, slightly out of breath from dancing. "Come on, you three! You cannot sit talking all tonight. There is cake for eating and games to be played!"

"You can't sit around talking all night," Nessika corrected from behind, amusement glittering in her eyes. "There's cake to eat and games to play."

Huffing, Lynn wrinkled her face at the taller Valkyrie, but it didn't last long before her joy broke through.

With a laugh, Sayra pulled Sylven to his feet. "She's right. This is a party, after all. Time to celebrate!"

As the night wore on, Sylven found himself truly relaxing for the first time in weeks. He sampled dishes from the laden table, each one more delicious than the last. He joined in games of skill and chance, laughing at Waylen's exaggerated frustration when he lost and cheering Kimimari's victories.

At one point, he was in a corner with Nessika, watching as Sayra attempted to teach Rys a traditional Faendan dance. The prince, usually so graceful, was endearingly slow to learn as he tried to follow the intricate steps.

"It's good to see them like this," Nessika said. A warmness brightened her eyes. "Carefree. Happy."

Sylven nodded, a warm feeling settling in his chest as he watched his friends. "It is. I almost forgot what it was like to just be normal for a while."

"We'll have more moments like this once all of this is over. That's what we're fighting for, isn't it?" Nessika asked, side-eyeing him with a meaningful look.

"Yeah," Sylven said, his resolve strengthening. "Yeah, it is."

Her face wavered, and she swallowed down a regretful expression. "I think I've been wrong about a few things. I thought everything was so black and white for the past several years. Over these last few months, I've seen and heard so much that it's changed my entire perception of what my obligations are to the world. I've been harsh." Her blue eyes traced Sayra as Rys whirled her into a spin. "To Sayra. To you."

Sylven blinked, surprise drawing his full attention to the woman beside him.

"I apologize for my rudeness in the past. It was unfounded and immature how much I judged Sayra for finding something good within all this bad. Even Lynn and Casber. To look at them now..." A small laugh escaped her, her eyes bright as she glanced at the couple so clearly in love. "I think we shouldn't hesitate to grab whatever moments of happiness we can. So, I've decided I won't fight it anymore."

A mischievous look crept across her face. "Which is why I'm not afraid to say that you look especially dashing tonight, Lord Astor."

Sylven felt his face flush, a mix of surprise and flattery warming his cheeks. He cleared his throat, suddenly aware of how close they were. "I... thank you, Nessika. You look quite stunning yourself." And she was. He was aware of it the moment he opened the door earlier and saw what she was wearing. Nessika was every bit a portrait of sensuality and elegance.

Her smile widened, a playful glint in her ice-blue eyes. "Perhaps we could share a dance?"

Sylven nodded, a grin tugging at his lips. "I'd like that," he said, more confident than he ever felt around a woman.

As if on cue, the music shifted to a slower, more intimate melody. Nessika held out her hand, and Sylven took it, allowing her to lead him to the middle of the makeshift dance floor. They faced each other, a moment of hesitation passing between them before Sylven placed his hand on her waist, feeling the warmth of her body through the fabric of her dress. Nessika's hand came to rest on his shoulder, her touch light but unmistakably present. As they began to move, Sylven was struck by how perfectly they fit together. Their steps were synchronized, bodies swaying in harmony with the music and each other.

The room seemed to fade away, leaving just the two of them in their own private world. Sylven was captivated by Nessika's eyes, their icy-blue depths holding a warmth he'd never noticed before. Her perfume, a delicate blend of jasmine and vanilla, enveloped him. As they turned, Sylven caught a glimpse of Sayra watching them as she taught Rys another of her dances. For a fleeting moment, he felt a twinge of guilt, but when his Valkyrie's face split into a cheeky grin, her eye winking at him, his own mouth curled.

Nessika leaned in closer, her breath warm against his ear as she whispered, "You're full of surprises, Sylven Astor."

He smiled, tightening his hold on her waist. "So are you, Nessika Onai."

As the night began to wind down, Sylven was back in the plush armchair, a plate of cake balanced on his knee. Sayra and Emrys had rejoined him, both flushed from dancing and laughter.

One by one, he opened the gifts from his friends, each one touching him deeply. From rare books on advanced majik theory, a hand-knitted scarf in his favorite colors, and a finely crafted dagger to a beautifully bound journal with his initials embossed on the cover, it all made him smile warmly.

"Thank you," Sylven said, his voice thick. "All of you. This means more than I can say."

Sayra lifted a bite of cake in salute. "Who knew the great Sylven Astor could be rendered speechless?" she teased, a playful smirk dancing on her lips.

Sylven raised an eyebrow, and his composure returned. "I'm not speechless. I'm simply choosing my words carefully. A concept you might want to consider, von Lykken."

"Oh?" Sayra leaned forward, her eyes sparkling with mischief. "And here I thought you were just overwhelmed by my incredible gift-giving skills."

"Ah yes, because nothing says 'incredible gift' like an empty journal," Sylven retorted, unable to keep the smile from his face.

Sayra gasped in mock offense. "Empty? I'll have you know I filled the first page with a detailed drawing of your grumpy face."

"How thoughtful," Sylven deadpanned. "I'm sure it will come in handy when I need to practice my disapproving glares."

"Well, you certainly need the practice," Sayra quipped, her grin widening.

Their banter continued, and the familiar rhythm of their friendly jabs was comforting. As they laughed together, Sylven felt a warmth in his chest that had nothing to do with the cake or the wine and everything to do with the realization of how much these people truly meant to him. The wooden cube in his room seemed a distant memory. There, among his friends, Sylven didn't feel useless or out of place.

As the last of the floating lights dimmed, signaling the end of the celebration, Sylven made a silent vow. He would treasure the night and fight with everything he had to ensure they all had many more like it in the future. Tomorrow, they would return to their studies, their training, and their secret plans. But tonight, they were just a group of friends, celebrating life and each other.

His eyes met Nessika's admiring ones as they prepared to leave.

There were many great times ahead with everyone and, perhaps, something deeper with Nessika he hadn't allowed himself to think of before. The thought of what may come next and the possibilities they all had... that, Sylven realized, was the greatest gift of all.

CHAPTER TWENTY-FIVE

SYLVEN

The Arcanist dining hall buzzed with activity as Sylven and Waylen made their way to their usual spot. It was packed with navy-clad Arcanists of every year, gossiping about their breaks and upcoming classes. Six tables ran along its length, each representing a year's class of Arcanists. The hall was thick with the aroma of roasted meats and freshly baked bread, mingling with the excitement of students chatting about the final rounds of the *proelium*.

Sylven and Waylen settled at the fourth-year table, their plates laden with steaming food. Every table of students teemed with activity except for the sixth. Most students graduated in their fifth year. Only those who wanted an extra year for a major specialization were willing to stay the additional time. Hence, the table was about a fourth full.

Sylven was eager to reach that year. The classes were much smaller and more focused, and the opportunity to excel in majik was unparalleled for those seeking a career in it.

"So," Waylen said, spearing a piece of potato with his fork, "have you given any thought to your summer plans? It's not too far off."

Sylven nodded, his mind briefly flashing to the secret plans brewing beneath the surface. "I'll be heading back to the estate for a while, I think. Father's been hinting at some 'important discussions' we need to have."

Waylen grimaced sympathetically. "Sounds thrilling. Any idea what they might be about?"

"Probably the usual." Sylven shrugged, trying to keep his tone casual. "My future, the family legacy, why I haven't proposed to a suitable young lady yet…"

Waylen chuckled. "Well, you could always tell him about your thrilling dance with Nessika at your birthday party. That might keep him entertained for a while."

A small curve appeared at the corners of Sylven's mouth. "Very funny. What about you? Any exciting plans?"

"Actually, yes." Waylen's eyes lit up. "My father's been adamant to teach me the various aspects of running the Rothlander duchy. I'm looking forward to transitioning into the family business."

Drinking from his glass, Sylven lifted his brow. He placed the water back on the table and said, "That's fantastic, Waylen. You'll have to let me live vicariously through your experiences. I intend to escape that responsibility for a while longer."

They talked throughout the meal, watching as people came and went during the dining hours. Sayra's stress reached through their mental link, and he knew she was back to devising a way to counter the Horde's fear majik. He got the distinct impression she felt as if the world's fate rested on her shoulders. An understandable feeling, considering she was the sole person with the aptitude to do so. But as they rose to leave the hall, a curse slipped through Sylven's lips. The fourth-year student across from him shot a disapproving glower his way. Not that he paid the man any mind.

Tomorrow morning, he had a full paper due on the politically charged incident of the Yendenkin Violation. In that instance, a dark majik user injured a thief with excessive force rather than attempting to gently restrain the intruder. Personally, Sylven couldn't care less about the implications, but he had to write from the perspective of supporting the Arcanist's actions.

He hadn't even brought pen to paper on the topic yet.

Saying his goodbyes to Waylen, Sylven pinched the bridge of his nose, wishing that was all it took to remove the stress headache he felt coming on.

Entering his dormitory, Sylven pocketed his hands into his trousers, a lightly wrinkled white long sleeve crinkling at his wrists. He knew Rys would have already completed his own paper and debated going to ask him for help. His hand hesitated before touching Rys's door, jumping back and stretching forward again. Groaning in frustration, Sylven began pacing to either side, only breaking stride when a smug figure strode toward him.

"Sylven, my loyal subject," Vander greeted, his face as self-satisfied as ever. "Are you searching for my little brother as well?"

Rather than answering, Sylven jutted a fist out to rap on Rys's door. "Quite so." He forced the words out, knowing he had no standing to outright ignore the crowned prince. Within seconds, Sylven spotted Rys's tousled onyx locks in his periphery.

Rys assessed the people outside his door, his hand tensing on the doorframe.

"Rys, it seems both your brother and I wish to speak with you," Sylven said. He had a sneaking suspicion Vander was up to no good sinking into his bones.

Rys gestured into his room. His black sleeves were rolled to his biceps on the abnormally warm evening. Vander shot Sylven a wink as he entered, unusually chipper for the time of day. Typically, most of his painted-on charm and charisma melted as the day wore on, unless a special occasion was afoot.

Before Rys had even closed the door to his pristine room, Vander began *tsking*. "Young people these days are simply too malleable to manipulation," he lamented.

This was it. Vander had enacted the next phase of his own damned plan.

"What did you do, Vander?" Rys growled, his knuckles whitening on the doorknob. He gave Sylven a purposeful look, and Sylven immediately interpreted it with clarity.

Sayra? he asked through their link.

Yes, your grumpiness? she mockingly responded.

Inhaling, Sylven pressed onward. *Where are you? We believe Vander may have done something.*

The crowned prince became a picture of innocence. "Me? Nothing."

I'm with Kimimari in her room practicing majik. What gave you that idea?

"Well," Vander retracted, analyzing his nails. "I have it on good authority there may or may not have been a small something slipped into a bottle of wine for two lovebirds during their lakeside picnic this afternoon. I, perchance, may have also inspired this most lovely date with a painting and emotional tale."

It felt as if Sylven had been sucker punched. He knew *exactly* what Vander referred to.

The picture of Cliffside Lake hanging on Lynn's wall flashed through Sylven's mind. Horror iced his veins, and his mind grew frantic as he replied to Sayra. *Is Lynn in her room?*

Give me a minute.

"Why?" Rys seethed, his face paling at the scheme that must have been in the works for months.

"It's rather late, is it not? Shall we retire for the evening and hope nothing ill befalls those two incapacitated lovers?" Vander theatrically pondered, brushing his rounded and stubbled jaw with a hand.

She's not here. What's going on?

Cursing, Sylven ran his fingers through his disarrayed strands, looking to Rys for guidance on how best to handle his brother. *Come to Rys's room immediately. Gear up. Bring Kimimari and Nessika.*

Sayra's reply was decisive, not wasting a moment. *On it.*

"Where are they?" Rys demanded in a dangerous tone, striding forward until he was face-to-face with Vander, their height nearly identical if it weren't for the extra centimeter Rys had.

"Come now, your lack of tact is nearly offensive, *little* brother," Vander chided, looking down from his raised chin. "They aren't even our people. Who cares if they die?"

Sylven's temper flared, and his fist flung forward before he could think better of it. Vander's eyes widened at the movement, almost as if it were inconceivable anyone would lay a finger on him. Connecting firmly with the prince's jaw, Sylven watched with no small amount of satisfaction as the prince's body collided with Rys's desk. A handful of papers scattered to the floor as Vander's arm shot out to catch himself.

Rys's mouth twitched before becoming a firm line. "Vander, I will not ask again. Where are they?"

A speckle of blood showed on Vander's lower lip as he rose, and a grand thing happened. Piece by piece, Sylven watched as the deranged man's façade crumbled in front of them. It started with an eyelid twitching rapidly, then it progressed to a violent shaking in Vander's fingers. His face shifted into varying states of ire, but his eyes...

Sylven had never seen them murderous before.

His hand throbbed where it had contacted Vander's cheekbone, but the pain felt good.

"I assure you, Sylven, you shall rue your actions tonight. I *will* ensure that much," Vander spit out, swaying lightly as he steadied himself.

"You aren't the king *yet*, Vander." Rys's face wrinkled as he stared the crowned prince down.

The door flung open with force, Sayra bursting in with her friends in tow. Her wild eyes spotted Vander, and her face was positively wrathful as she strode with purpose. Sylven made no move to interfere, nor Rys for that matter. Vander had crossed the line, damned the consequences for his actions. It was time he faced repercussions.

"Ah, the ever-beautiful Sayra," Vander said, his mask replaced with a suggestive smile. It twitched the moment she grabbed his collar and drew him close.

"Where," Sayra quietly demanded, the power behind her singular word leaving no room for silly jests or further wordplay. The promise of violence hung heavy in her piercing eyes, and Vander's smile slipped.

"The eastern end of the lake. A small clearing where the lake meets the jutting boulder."

Dropping him, Sayra turned tail and bolted out, the two other Valkyries hot on her heels.

"Put on your best performance, if I may so request!" Vander called out, his face pale as he gathered himself.

Rys turned to grab his gauntlets, slipping them into his pockets. Without sparing a second, Sylven darted for his room and snagged his own. With a nod between them, Sylven and Rys moved to catch up with the Valkyries. Five people sprinting down the corridors naturally garnered attention, especially when one was the dark prince himself. If looks could kill, Sayra's would have massacred dozens by the time she slowed, turning into a garden near the training arena.

As they approached the monastery's side gates, Sylven felt a prickle of anxiety. The imposing iron-wrought barrier loomed before them, two Valkyries standing guard at the lake entrance with stern expressions.

"Remember," Rys whispered, his breath barely audible, "act casual. We're just out for a late-night stroll."

Sylven nodded, trying to school his features into something resembling nonchalance.

As they neared, one of the Valkyries stepped forward, her hand resting casually on the hilt of her sword. "It's getting late for a walk, isn't it?" she said, her tone pointed.

Rys flashed his most charming smile, the one that had won over countless nobles and dignitaries. "Indeed, it is, but the night is just beginning. I could use some fresh air. The lake is particularly stunning under the full moon."

The second Valkyrie frowned, her eyes scanning their group. "It's not safe to be out after dark. The Horde—"

"We're well aware of the risks," Nessika cut in smoothly. "But surely five of us, including three Valkyries, can handle a short walk within the warded lake grounds."

Sylven held his breath, watching as the guards exchanged a look. The moment stretched, tension building like a coiled spring.

Finally, the first Valkyrie nodded. "Very well. But don't stay out too long. And keep your eyes peeled."

As the gates creaked open, Sylven felt a wave of relief wash over him. They filed through, maintaining their facade of casualness until they were out of sight. Once clear of the guards' watchful eyes, they broke into a run, their pretense abandoned. Sylven's heart raced, not just from the exertion but from the possible repercussions if Catara and Jax caught them. Already, the two cousins distrusted their group. Going out for late-night strolls around the lake wasn't normal, not when few people rarely did so during the day. The last thing Sylven and the others needed was to pile on more suspicious acts, but Vander had left them no choice.

The moon hung low and complete in the sky, casting an eerie glow over the landscape. Shadows danced between the trees, their branches reaching out like gnarled fingers in the darkness. Sylven's eyes darted constantly, searching for any sign of movement, any hint of danger lurking in the gloom.

Ahead of him, Sayra's golden braid whipped back and forth as she ran, her movements fluid and purposeful. Her resolve was palpable, radiating off her in waves that seemed to push them all forward. Nessika and Kimimari flanked her, their faces set in grim masks of concentration. Their weapons all clinked against their armor. To his right, Rys kept pace, his dark eyes focused intently on the path ahead. The prince's usual composure had given way to raw urgency, and his face was tense.

The path began to slope downward, leading them toward the shoreline. The lake came into view, its surface a mirror of obsidian reflecting the starry sky above. In the distance, Sylven could make out the jutting boulder Vander had mentioned, a dark silhouette against the shimmering water.

As they neared the water's edge, the sound of their footfalls changed from the soft thud of packed earth to the crunch of pebbles and sand. Sayra was grinding her jaw as her eyes searched wide, the boulder Vander spoke of just twenty feet ahead. Sylven glanced over his shoulder at the towering monastery's wall, a torch flickering by as the guard patrolled the perimeter in the distance.

That's when Sylven felt it, that familiar dread and irrational fear. Rys shared a grim expression, his eyes full of concern at their predicament.

Two Arcanists and one powerhouse of a relic split between two humans all stood near the wards at nighttime. Naturally, the temptation for any Horde would be overwhelming, their majik a beacon in the night.

And all within the eyesight of the monastery guards.

Chapter Twenty-Six

SAYRA

"Nes, Kimimari," Sayra said, slowing to a jog as she scanned the small alcove in the forest. "Fall to my four and eight. I'll stay at twelve. Emrys, Sylven." Her eyes practically glowed in the showering moonlight, her gaze leaving no room for questions. "Stay in the center at all costs."

Nodding, Sylven edged toward the middle of the formation behind her. Sayra moved to a crouch, creeping around the last bush before reaching the open space. Sylven's knees creaked as he snuck behind her, eyeing the two dark shapes splayed against the grass ahead.

"There!" Kimimari's voice cut through the night, and her arm stretched toward the small clearing just beyond the boulder.

"That must be Lynn and Casber," Emrys whispered, his eyes snapping to the trees across the clearing. "Sayra, do you sense what I do?"

She exhaled, and her slight chin lowered a hair. "There are many daemons, just beyond the confines and held at bay by the wards. I can't fathom..." Her voice trailed off, her lips pursing. "I can't fathom what he has to gain by this. It's too obvious. There's something wrong about this."

Nes searched the clearing. "There's a trap here, isn't there?"

Sayra felt that slight thread pulling her and Emrys together, the connection of their relic pieces. Twisting her head, she saw his dark brows knit, concern lingering in his gray eyes.

"Without a doubt," Emrys said, anger underlying his words.

Sayra's heart pounded in her chest as she shifted behind the thick bushes at the side of the clearing, her eyes fixing again on the motionless forms of Lynn and Casber. Fear clogged her throat. The night air was thick with an unnatural stillness. No crickets chirped. No nocturnal creatures stirred. It was as if the entire world was holding its breath, waiting for the horror to unfold.

Sayra's skin prickled with goosebumps, a chill running down her spine that had nothing to do with the cool night air. She could sense it—the oppressive, malevolent presence of the Horde lurking just beyond the wards. The invisible barrier that had protected them for so long suddenly felt paper-thin, a fragile illusion of safety. Swallowing hard, she withdrew her gauntlets from her black pants. The normal relish she felt at the enhanced majikal connection was dimmed by the situation, but a part of her soul soared despite it.

Sylven shifted beside her, his tanned face pale. "We need to get them out of here," he said, gesturing toward Lynn and Casber.

"Wait," Emrys hissed, his hand shooting out to grip Sylven's arm. "Look."

On the far side of the clearing, beyond the jutting boulder and the placid surface of the lake, Sayra's eyes caught the moving shadows. At first, they were indistinct, wavering forms that could have been tricks of the light. But as Sayra watched, her heart racing, the shadows coalesced into solid shapes.

Daemons.

They emerged from the tree line like a nightmare given form, their grotesque bodies silhouetted against the starry sky. Sayra counted one, two, three... four in total. Each was different, a horrific amalgamation of twisted limbs, razor-sharp claws, and gaping maws filled with needlelike teeth.

The largest, a hulking beast that easily stood twice Sayra's height, paused at the edge of the trees. Its misshapen head swiveled, glowing red eyes scanning the area. For a heart-stopping moment, Sayra was certain it had spotted them. But its gaze passed over their hiding spot, focusing instead on the prone forms in the clearing.

"The wards," Kimimari breathed, her voice trembling. "They'll hold, right?"

As if in answer to her question, the lead daemon took a step forward. Sayra tensed, expecting to see it repelled by the invisible barrier. Instead, it passed through unimpeded, as if the wards didn't exist at all.

The world seemed to tilt on its axis. Sayra felt a wave of dizziness wash over her, her mind struggling to comprehend what she was seeing. It was impossible. The wards had stood for decades upon decades, an impenetrable defense against the Horde. And yet...

"No," Rys whispered, his voice tight with disbelief and horror. "This can't be happening."

But it was. One by one, the daemons crossed the boundary, their grotesque forms becoming sharper as they entered the moonlit clearing. Sayra could see them in horrifying detail—the way their muscles rippled beneath mottled, leathery skin, the gleam of saliva on their razor-sharp fangs, and the evil intelligence burning in their eyes.

And then the fear hit.

It was like nothing Sayra had ever experienced before. The muted hum of the fear majik suddenly exploded into a deafening roar, crashing over them like a tidal wave. Sayra gasped, her lungs burning as if all the air had been sucked from them. Beside her, she heard Sylven retch, his body convulsing as he fought against the overwhelming terror.

Sayra's vision swam, dark spots dancing at the edges. She tried to move, to reach for her weapon, to do anything, but her body wouldn't respond. It was as if her limbs were encased in lead, heavy and useless.

Through the haze of horror, she saw the daemons advancing on Lynn and Casber. The largest one, its massive form blocking out the moonlight, reached down with clawed hands the size of dinner plates. Sayra wanted to scream, to warn them, to do anything to stop what was about to happen. But the sound died in her throat, choked by the paralyzing grip of the fear majik.

"Sayra." Emrys grunted, his eyes wide with meaning.

It all clicked at once.

The Goddess had been warning her to find a defense against fear majik for this very reason. For months, Sayra had been told. And for what? She was a fish floundering on land, gasping for something she didn't have.

"We have to... we have to do something." Nessika gasped, her words slurred as if she were drunk. But even as she spoke, Sayra saw her body slumping to the ground.

No, no, no.

She tried to focus inward, summoning her intention and majik into an enormous well.

Repel the fear, she demanded of her majik.

But nothing happened.

The daemons were so close Sayra could smell them—a nauseating mix of rotting flesh and sulfur that made her stomach heave. She watched in helpless horror as one of the smaller daemons, a spindly creature with too many limbs, scuttled near Lynn's unconscious form.

"No," Sayra managed to croak out. She tried to push herself up, to fight against the crushing weight of the fear, but her body betrayed her. She fell forward, her gloved hands pressing into the damp earth. The scent of soil filled her nostrils, grounding her for a moment in reality.

Pooling more of her majik, Sayra began drawing simultaneously from the ley lines beneath the earth. She pleaded with her majik to cancel out the Horde's fear.

Yet nothing happened.

Through tear-blurred eyes, she saw Emrys attempting to stand. The prince's face twisted with determination and terror, sweat beading on his forehead as he fought against the invisible force holding him down. For a moment, it seemed he might succeed. He managed to get one knee under him, his hand reaching for the majik gauntlet at his wrist. But then the largest daemon turned, its baleful gaze locking onto Rys. The fear majik intensified, if such a thing were possible. Sayra felt it like a physical blow, driving the air from her lungs. Rys collapsed, his body twitching as his neck strained from the force.

The world seemed to narrow, tunnel vision setting in as Sayra's consciousness began to fade. She could still see the clearing, but it was as if she were watching from a great distance. She saw the daemons circling Lynn and Casber, their intentions clear in the hungry gleam of their eyes. She saw Nes, her face pressed into the ground, her body shaking with silent sobs as the fear overcame years of training. She saw Kimimari, her eyes wide and unseeing, frozen in a rictus of terror.

And then, as if things couldn't get any worse, she heard it. A sound that cut through the paralyzing fright, sending a fresh wave of horror through her body. It was Lynn's voice, weak and confused but unmistakable.

"Wha... what is happening?"

Sayra wanted to scream, to warn her friend, but no sound would come. She could only watch, helpless and horrified, as Lynn's eyes fluttered open. For a moment, there was only confusion there. Then Lynn's gaze focused on the monstrous form looming over her, and Sayra saw the exact moment when comprehension dawned.

Lynn's scream pierced the night, a sound of pure, primal terror that seemed to go on forever. It was joined a moment later by Casber's panicked shouts as he, too, regained consciousness only to find himself surrounded by nightmares made flesh.

Majik flowed uselessly through Sayra, refusing to acquiesce to her demands of it.

The daemons reacted to the sounds with renewed hunger, their movements becoming more frenzied. Sayra saw claws reaching and jaws opening wide. She squeezed her eyes shut, unable to bear witness to what was about to happen. But even with them closed, she couldn't escape. The sounds—Lynn's screams, Casber's desperate pleas, and the wet, tearing noises that followed—burned themselves into her mind, a horror she knew she would never forget.

Sayra pulled more majik from the ley lines, even as her internal stores of majik crawled through her limbs. She forced her eyes to open through the tears, and her hands curled into the damp dirt.

"I love you, Lynn," Casber cried out, his voice shaking with the force of his sobs. "I—"

His voice was suddenly silenced.

"CASBER!" Lynn's cry cut Sayra deeper than any sword ever had.

A sinister laughter echoed from the daemons as one pounced on Lynn.

Goddess, help us! Sayra prayed, a sob escaping her mouth as her soul reached for a greater power.

In a flash, the ley lines erupted beneath Sayra, the majik bending to the force of her will and expanding around her skin. Her hands dug into the earth, fingers curling around roots and stones. She pushed herself up, fighting against the invisible force that sought to keep her down. Her arms shook with the effort, muscles straining, but she refused to give in.

"Sayra?" Sylven's voice was weak, confused. She could feel his shock through their bond as he witnessed her defiance of the fear majik.

She didn't respond, couldn't spare the concentration. All her focus was on the task at hand. Inch by agonizing inch, Sayra rose to her knees, then to her feet. The world tilted and spun around her, but she remained standing.

The daemons turned, their glowing eyes fixing on her with spiteful interest. The largest one, the hulking beast that had led the pack, let out a bone-chilling roar. The fear majik intensified, battering against Sayra's defenses like a hurricane.

But Sayra stood firm. She reached out with her spell, feeling it spread from her body in waves. It clashed with the fear majik, light against dark, hope against despair. For a moment, the two forces seemed evenly matched, neither giving ground.

Then Sayra thought of Lynn and Casber, of their still forms lying in the clearing. She thought of Sylven and Emrys and her other friends, paralyzed and helpless. She thought of everyone in the monastery, blissfully unaware of the danger that had breached their defenses.

With a cry that was part rage and part determination, Sayra pushed harder. Her majik surged outward in a blinding flash of light, shattering the oppressive grip of the fear majik like glass.

The effect was immediate and dramatic. The daemons reeled back, shrieking in pain and confusion. Sayra's friends gasped as if coming up for air after being underwater, the paralyzing fear releasing its hold on them.

"You did it," Rys said, his voice filled with awe as he struggled to his feet.

Sayra didn't answer. Her focus was entirely on the daemons, her majik coalescing around her in the faintest shimmering aura. She took a step forward, then another, emerging from the bushes into the moonlit clearing.

"Get away from them," she growled, her voice carrying a power she'd never felt before.

The daemons hesitated, caught between their hunger and this new threat. Their leader snarled, taking a menacing step toward Sayra.

"*Hell Summoner*," it hissed with a humanlike lisp. "*Wait your turn.*"

Sayra sensed her cadre preparing to fight beside her. Far away from them, along the walls of Saint Highburn Monastery, she didn't spot a single lantern alight around the walls. Almost as if they were unmanned intentionally.

And in front of her were two lifeless bodies.

Chapter Twenty-Seven

SYLVEN

Sylven's eyes burned as he beheld the blood-spattered mess the Horde had left of Lynn and Casber. His knuckles whitened. Every fiber of his being wanted to yell at the skies and demand how anyone could be so cruel as to kill the two kindest people he'd ever met. He wanted to beat Vander to a pulp for what he did, for the futures he crushed in his reckless plan.

But...

He tore his gaze from the frozen Horde just across the clearing and said to Sayra, "You can't use majik. Not when someone may see. It's not worth blowing our plan. Let us take them on."

"Not if I only use fire," Sayra countered, her stubborn, tear-streaked face directed at him. "They'll see any evidence as Emrys's fire. Even wind is fine so long as I don't destroy anything with it. This is not up for debate. Your lives are on the line. I will not hesitate."

Nessika waved a hand at them, gathering their attention. Her eyes had dimmed, the blue darker than Sylven had ever seen. "How long do we have until your spell gives out?"

The moment the fear was repulsed, Sylven could breathe again. It was a miracle, a feat never performed by anyone before. But the problem with great spells was maintaining them. While spells placed on people or objects staked down with runes could last lengthy periods of time, it all depended on the force of the majik acting against it. The Horde compelled such immense power in their fear spell, continuously outputting it in a large vicinity, that any spell an Arcanist could summon would drain them of energy until they gave out, only lasting as long as one's strength.

Their lives would fully depend on Sayra's majikal stamina and the cumulation of nearly five months of training. A fraction of what any partially trained Arcanist wielded.

"Then we entrust our lives to you, Sayra," Rys said quietly, receiving a nod in response.

"How long do we have?" Nes asked.

"Long enough," Sayra promised, her fists clenched around her *spyd*. She quickly detailed a plan, all of them unsure how long the Horde would stand by. "Be swift. Be strong. Return alive. Please. You all are my world now." Her heavy gaze settled on each of them in turn.

When she met Sylven's, he dipped his chin at her and allowed his block on their link to lower. She felt his sorrow and anger at the injustice of it all but also his support and the care he had for her and the others. She blinked hard and inhaled deeply.

Her form darted forward first.

Nothing happened when they entered the flat space, Sylven reconsidering whether the Horde would move at all. Sayra slid next to Lynn's bloodied body, glass and wicker material strewn across a checkered blanket. Kimimari hauled Casber's remains in her arms, turning to retreat with Sayra in the lead. Sylven's stomach churned at the grisly chunk missing from Casber's throat, the fatal wound mocking a grin at him.

Sayra and Kimimari sprinted back to them. Bone-chilling laughter began cackling from the daemons, pulling Sylven's attention to a ring of fire Rys summoned around them.

Four of the most fearsome daemons from the darkest pits of hell charged. With thick, poison-oozing rear legs and membrane-bound arms ending in a singular-protruding four-foot spike, the daemons could cross vast distances and soar to cut off any hope of escape. Thornlike projectiles covered a vast expanse of their elongated necks, fangs gleaming with slimy saliva hanging below their decayed maws, the stench emanating causing him to gag. Three eyes crested their heads, one behind the skull and two orifices used as ears. From Rys's notes, these daemon types were the fiercest of the lot, known for their deadly precision and brute strength as twenty-foot monstrosities.

Only a handful of *anima* pairs could ever hope to survive a single one.

"*Tempestas,*" Rys shouted, buying time for them to seek cover, according to Sayra's plan. A grand storm of fire whipped around the Horde, the crimson and tangerine hues engulfing the daemons in a hellish light.

"*Ventus,*" Sylven summoned, his majik meshing with Rys's and speeding up the magnitude of the firestorm.

The creatures screeched, their joint cries sure to garner the attention of the monastery's guard.

It disturbed Sylven when he realized they weren't cries of pain, however. They were howling in glee.

Not a single one slowed.

Sylven poured more into his spell, only hindering them a fraction. The fire worked, but the daemons proved immune to the pain, laughing at their ludicrous efforts. Flakes of blackened skin drifted on the superheated air, a grisly snow that spoke of the daemons' unnatural resilience. The smell was horrendous to his nose.

Beside him, Rys stood like an avenging god. With a gesture that seemed to split the very air, he commanded the flames to new heights. The inferno responded to his will, surging upward in a column of fire that reached for the stars. The conflagration roared, drowning out all other sounds, a furious beast given form by Rys's majik.

His gauntlets pulsed with power, intricate runes glowing white-hot as they channeled unimaginable energies. The firelight danced across his features, casting deep shadows that made him look otherworldly. But it was his eyes that drew attention—those fathomless dark orbs reflected the flames, turning them into portals to some infernal realm. In that moment, Rys looked less like a prince and more like an elemental force of nature, terrible and captivating in his fury.

The daemons advanced through the hellscape, their forms wavering in the heat haze, appearing more like nightmarish apparitions than physical beings. And still, they came on, relentless in their hunger, undeterred by the display of majik arrayed against them.

Sayra moved with fluid grace, her hands a blur as she raised them skyward. The gauntlets on her wrists flared to life, pulsing with an otherworldly energy that made the air crackle. "*Murus!*" Her voice rang out, clear and commanding, and the very fabric of reality seemed to ripple in response.

At the same time, Rys and Sylven recalled their majik, paving the way for the next step in their plan.

In an instant, a wall of wind materialized before them, so dense it was visible. The air howled and churned, forming an impenetrable barrier that stretched across the entire alcove. Sylven could feel the raw power emanating from it, and his eyes went wide.

The timing was exquisite and not a heartbeat too soon.

Four monstrous daemons slammed into the wind wall with bone-jarring force. Their unearthly shrieks of fury pierced the night as they found themselves denied their prey. Claws raked uselessly against the barrier, leaving trails of sizzling energy in their wake.

From the corner of his eye, Sylven saw Nessika and Kimimari racing back, their faces grim with determination. Behind them, partially hidden by the underbrush, lay the still forms of Lynn and Casber.

Without hesitation, Sylven thrust his arm forward. "*Celeritas,*" he said, his voice resonating with power.

The effect was instantaneous and breathtaking. Nessika and Kimimari's forms blurred, their movements accelerating to a speed that defied human perception. They became living weapons, streaks of deadly precision as they engaged the outermost daemons on either side of Sayra's barrier.

Sayra raised her other hand. With a gesture that seemed to bend the very air to her will, she encased the two central daemons in a separate vortex of howling wind, effectively cutting them off from their brethren. The display of control was awe-inspiring, but Sylven could see the toll it was taking on her. A bead of sweat traced a glistening path down Sayra's forehead, her eyes fluttering with the strain of maintaining such complex spells. Her fingers trembled almost imperceptibly, but in the face of such overwhelming odds, even the slightest weakness could prove lethal.

"Steady," Rys's voice cut through the chaos. His eyes, dark and knowing, were fixed on Sayra, noting every sign of her growing fatigue. His tone carried both encouragement and warning. They were walking a razor's edge, and one misstep could spell doom for them all.

Sylven's chest heaved with exertion, his lungs burning as he summoned the dredges of his strength. With a snarl, he thrust his hands skyward, fingers splayed wide. "*Descensus!*" The word tore from his throat, raw and powerful.

The air around the outermost daemons suddenly condensed, forming a visible distortion that pulsed with contained energy. In a heartbeat, it exploded downward, a localized gravity that slammed into the creatures with devastating force. The impact was thunderous, driving the monstrosities into the earth with such violence the ground itself seemed to shudder.

Seizing the moment, Nessika and Kimimari darted in, their forms still blurred by Sylven's enhancement spell. Their blades were deadly arcs of silver cutting through the night.

"*Vi!*" Sayra's voice rang out, strained but unwavering. A surge of golden energy erupted from her outstretched hands, enveloping the Valkyries. The air crackled with power as her majik infused their strikes with supernatural strength.

Time seemed to slow as the empowered blades descended. For a fraction of a second, Sylven could see every detail with crystal clarity—the determination etched on the Valkyries' faces, the unholy light in the daemons' eyes, and the way the air seemed to part before the enchanted swords.

Then, with a sound like thunder, the blades struck home. They pierced the daemons' hides as if they were paper, driving deep into the monstrous bodies. Each creature possessed two hearts, a cruel redundancy that had spelled doom for many hunters in the past.

But not tonight.

A geyser of viscous black blood erupted from the wounds. The liquid hissed and steamed where it touched the ground, leaving scorched patches in the earth. The daemons' death throes were mercifully brief, their unearthly shrieks cutting off abruptly as both hearts were simultaneously destroyed.

As the massive bodies slumped to the ground, an eerie silence fell over the battlefield. Sylven allowed himself a moment of grim satisfaction, but he knew the fight was far from over. Two down, but more remained.

The two lingering daemons, their eyes blazing with unholy fury, suddenly surged against Sayra's wind barrier with renewed vigor. The wall of air rippled and distorted under the onslaught, Sayra's face contorting with the effort to maintain it.

But it wasn't enough.

With a sonic boom, the daemons burst through, chunks of compressed air exploding outward in a devastating shockwave. Sayra and the others stumbled back, momentarily stunned by the backlash of her broken spell. Sylven's legs braced against it, weathering the wind as it flew by.

"Nessika! Kimimari!" Rys shouted, his voice cutting through the chaos. He summoned a wall of blue-tinted flame at the nearest daemon that lunged at him.

The Valkyries needed no further prompting. They moved as one, a perfectly synchronized unit honed by years of training and shared hardship. Nessika darted left, her sword a silver blur, while Kimimari flanked right, her blade singing as it cut through the air. Stepping back, Sayra's body heaved from exertion, a majikal toll taking more than physical effort ever could.

Yet, she held the fear at bay and continued to strengthen the Valkyries' efforts.

Sylven gritted his teeth, pouring every ounce of his remaining strength into maintaining the spell. Sweat beaded on his brow, his vision blurring at the edges, but he refused to let up. The Valkyries' lives depended on the supernatural speed his majik granted them.

The battle that unfolded before him was nothing short of awe-inspiring. Nessika and Kimimari moved with a grace that defied human limitations, their enhanced speed turning them into living weapons. They wove around the daemons in an intricate dance of death, blades flashing in perfect harmony.

When one Valkyrie attacked high, the other struck low. As Nessika parried a vicious swipe from a daemon's claws, Kimimari was there in an instant, exploiting the opening. They communicated without words, a series of subtle glances and minute gestures allowing them to coordinate their assault with uncanny precision.

The daemons, for all their terrifying power, found themselves hard-pressed to counter the display of perfectly synchronized combat. Claws that should have eviscerated found only empty air as the Valkyries twirled away at the last second. Whenever either one was exposed, Sayra darted in with her *spyd*, nimbly flying in at the perfect moment to counter a strike and defend her sisters. Fangs gnashed uselessly, always a heartbeat too slow to catch their nimble prey.

Yet for all their skill and speed, the Valkyries couldn't land a decisive blow. The daemons' hides seemed to shrug off glancing strikes, and their unnatural reflexes allowed them to avoid the most dangerous thrusts. It was a stalemate of the most perilous kind, with neither side able to gain a clear advantage.

Sylven watched, his heart pounding, as Nessika executed a daring feint, drawing one daemon's attention while Kimimari attempted to flank it. For a moment, it seemed they might succeed in bringing the beast down. But at the last second, the daemon's third eye swiveled, catching the attack. With a speed that belied its massive bulk, it spun, forcing both Valkyries to retreat or be crushed.

The fight wore on, a deadly ballet of steel and claw, of human skill and monstrous power. Sylven could feel his majik reserves depleting rapidly, each second bringing them closer to the moment when the speed enhancement would falter. Beside him, Rys and Sayra stood ready, tense and alert, waiting for an opportunity to intervene without risking their comrades.

As the battle raged on, one thing became abundantly clear: it was a fight that would be decided by endurance as much as skill. The question that hung in the air, unspoken but felt by all, was chilling in its simplicity.

Who would tire first—the Valkyries, the Arcanists, or the daemons?

The answer, Sylven realized with growing dread, could mean the difference between survival and annihilation.

Then, all at once, both sides disengaged for a moment. A moment that gave them an opportunity.

"Once more, Sylven!" Sayra shouted.

"*Descensus!*" Sylven's voice thundered across the clearing. In an instant, the monstrous creatures were driven to their knees, pinned by an invisible, crushing force.

Sylven collapsed alongside them, his body betraying him as he sank to the ground, chest heaving with exertion. The spell had taken nearly everything he had left, but it had bought them a precious opportunity.

Nessika and Kimimari seized the moment without hesitation. Their movements were a blur, feet barely touching the ground as they surged forward, propelled by the lingering wisps of Sylven's wind majik. Sayra's earth-infused strength coursed through their limbs, turning each Valkyrie into a force of nature. As the Valkyries closed in, Rys withdrew his fiery assault. The flames died away, leaving behind a hellscape of scorched earth and acrid smoke. The remaining Horde writhed on the ground, struggling against Sylven's gravitational spell like insects pinned to a board.

But even in their weakened state, the daemons were lethal. A membrane-bound arm unfurled with nightmarish speed, its razor-sharp spike aimed unerringly at Kimimari's exposed throat. Time seemed to slow as the deadly appendage lashed out.

"*Duratus!*" Sayra's cry cut through the chaos. The air temperature plummeted as her ice majik took hold, frost crystallizing along the daemon's wing with audible cracks. The weight of the rapidly forming ice dragged the appendage down, mere inches from its target.

With a resounding crash, the frozen limb shattered against an invisible barrier—another of Sayra's spells, conjured in the nick of time to shield Kimimari. Shards of ice exploded outward, a deadly hail that peppered the battlefield.

Sylven watched in awe, his mind struggling to comprehend the sheer magnitude of Sayra's power. In a mere five months, she had mastered spells that took most Arcanists years to perfect. The diversity and control she displayed were nothing short of miraculous.

Kimimari, protected by Sayra's barrier, didn't miss a beat. She dropped low, her sword delivering two precise, devastating strikes. The daemon's twin hearts were pierced simultaneously, black ichor spraying from the wounds in a grisly fountain. Nessika, engaged with the second daemon, narrowly avoided a retaliatory swipe that would have torn her in half. She backpedaled swiftly, her face full of grim determination as she reassessed her approach.

Their momentary advantage was slipping away. Sylven could feel his gravitational spell weakening, his majik reserves all but depleted. The surviving daemon began to rise, shaking off the last vestiges of the spell.

Kimimari and Nessika circled warily, their movements perfectly synchronized as they sought a new opening.

As the daemon regained its footing, its baleful gaze promising a world of pain, Sylven knew he wouldn't be able to conjure another powerful spell. But he saw the shift in Sayra's countenance. Those impossibly bright jade eyes widened at what was behind him, a surge of fear knocking the breath from his lungs through their link. Her gaze locked onto him, and he saw a lifetime of emotions flash across her face in that fleeting moment.

"*Commutatio!*" she cried out.

The world lurched, reality seeming to fold in on itself. In the span of a heartbeat, Sylven found himself standing where Sayra had stood just a fraction of a second before. His mind reeled, struggling to comprehend the sudden shift in perspective. And then he saw it.

A monstrous spike, wickedly sharp, hovered mere feet from where Sayra kneeled in his place. Another daemon, having silently outflanked their formation, had been poised to strike a swift, fatal blow.

A blow meant for *him*.

Time seemed to slow to a crawl as the horrifying realization dawned on Sylven. Sayra had switched their positions, placing herself directly in the path of certain death. His death, stolen by his Valkyrie in an act of selfless sacrifice.

Just like his sister, Jess...

A tidal wave crashed over Sylven—fear, anguish, and a soul-deep terror that threatened to consume him. The thought of losing Sayra, of watching her die in his place, was more horrible than the thought of facing ten daemons at once. In that moment, he realized with crystal clarity how much she had come to mean to him and how integral she had become to his world.

Sayra was stout, her shoulders set with grisly fortitude. There was no hesitation in her stance, no regret in her eyes. She faced her impending death with the steadfast resolve of a true Valkyrie, ready to fulfill her sworn duty to protect him at any cost. Through their link, he could feel her exhaustion. She didn't have enough majik to spare but the one spell to save his life. But as Sylven watched, helpless and horrified, a bitter realization twisted in his gut. Sayra's life was worth so much more than his own—not just to him but to the entire world. She was the key to unraveling the daemons that plagued their land, the potential savior in the face of unimaginable threats. And there she was, prepared to throw it all away for him.

What was he, after all, but another Arcanist? Talented, perhaps, but ultimately replaceable in the grand scheme of things. The injustice of it all burned like acid in his veins.

In that eternal moment, as death reached for Sayra with greedy claws, Sylven saw not just the brave Valkyrie she had become but the layers of the person beneath. The friend, the confidante, the woman who had slowly but surely carved out a place in his heart. And he realized, with a clarity that was both beautiful and agonizing, he couldn't bear to live in a world without her.

Sylven wasted his years moaning and groaning at the excess, never giving enough time or consideration for others. He had been incredibly selfish with his time, never sparing it for family or friends. He looked down at other Arcanists and hated Sayra for simply devoting her life to another. And in the end, his own Valkyrie, the one who had shown him his folly in life and opened his eyes, was going to die for *him*. With Sayra's presence, Sylven realized he had finally moved on from his sister's death, and moved forward with a recovered soul. She had changed him, turning him into a person he liked.

Too late. He realized it all far too late.

And *that* was truly, all-consumingly unbearable.

A corner of his mouth quirked up at a new thought. It seemed he had found his purpose at last. While the others all had a role given to them by the Goddess, his was never clear—until then.

Sylven's life was meant to be given for Sayra's. For the person who made his life worth living again. He hardly had scraps left of his majik, but there was just enough for one last spell.

Beside him, Rys's eyes picked apart the scene before them. "No!" he cried out in horror, his features clearly outlining his despair.

Rising to his feet, Sylven's voice roared one last time, "*Commutatio*!" Every remaining dreg of majik he had was spent in that last swoop.

And just as he said it, an eight-inch-thick spike tore through his abdomen.

Chapter Twenty-Eight

SAYRA

Sayra was prepared to lay down her life in exchange for Sylven's. It was her duty, what she sweated, cried, and bled for the last four years. To be a guardian. To redeem herself by saving a life rather than ending it. While it may have been a tad overdramatic, Sayra meant those words to her mother under the grounds of Saint Highburn Monastery, always willing to make that ultimate sacrifice for those she cared about. When that daemon charged, she didn't hesitate to get Sylven out of harm's way.

One severely injured daemon and another fresh one would be no match for her comrades. She'd leave this world in their capable hands, ones that would invent a new way to bring down the Holy Family without her. Her only regret was the anguish that would be left in her wake, Sylven struggling to reconcile her loss so similar to his sister's. But he had Emrys and Nes, two people who wouldn't abandon him.

A part of her heart tugged when Emrys cried out for her. As the daemon's spike hurtled toward her, time seemed to slow for Sayra. In that fleeting moment, her thoughts turned to him. His handsome features flashed in her mind, along with the warmth of his rare smiles. She remembered their late-night training sessions and the thrill of discovering her powers under his patient guidance. The tender moments they'd shared, so brief yet so precious.

Regret washed over her. Why had she pushed him away for so long? In another life, perhaps they could have explored their connection further. She imagined a future forever out of reach—stolen moments in palace gardens, shared laughter over inside jokes, and the comfort of his arms around her after a long day. What she loved most about Emrys was his unwavering dedication, his quiet strength, and the way he saw her—truly saw her—when others looked past. He had believed in her abilities even when she doubted herself. As death approached, her heart ached with the bittersweetness of what could have been.

But that feeling was short-lived, the next word shattering her illusion completely.

"*Commutatio!*" Sylven roared behind her, Sayra lurching forward in preparation for what was to come.

Every fiber of her being screamed out when he flipped them once more, refusing to allow her to spare his life. Her foot hit the ground hard, her muscles bunching to propel her forward the moment the spike connected with his abdomen.

The world slowed to a nightmarish crawl as Sayra launched herself at Sylven in a desperate, futile attempt to save him. But she was too late. With horrifying clarity, she watched as the daemon's spike tore through Sylven's body, his face contorting in agony as the wickedly sharp point erupted from his back. Time stuttered as Sayra collided with his impaled form, her arms wrapping around him in a cruel mockery of an embrace. The daemon, irritated by her interference, swung its massive limb with terrifying force.

The movement sent them flying, Sylven's body sliding off the spike with a sickening, wet sound Sayra knew would haunt her dreams forever.

They hurtled through the air, a tangle of limbs and blood, toward the looming tree line.

With lightning-fast reflexes born of desperation, Sayra's hand found her *spyd*. She lashed out, the chain wrapping around a sturdy trunk, abruptly changing their trajectory. Gritting her teeth against the strain, Sayra clung to Sylven with every ounce of strength she possessed. They hit the ground hard, Sayra taking the brunt of the impact. She felt, rather than heard, the sharp crack of bone as at least one rib gave way in her chest. They skidded across the forest floor, a trail of broken undergrowth and blood in their wake, before slamming into a young pine tree.

As pain exploded across her chest, Sayra's world narrowed to a single, terrible focus: Sylven's limp form in her arms and the growing pool of crimson beneath them.

It didn't matter.

Nothing mattered except for the *dritt* of an Arcanist bleeding out across her chest. Struggling, Sayra propped her back against the tree, holding Sylven as carefully as she could manage.

The wound was catastrophic, a gaping chasm where Sylven's midsection should have been. Blood poured from the opening, staining Sayra's legs crimson as Sylven's entrails spilled out. His spine was completely severed, the damage so extensive that even the most skilled healers in all the lands would have been powerless to mend it.

Blood bubbled from Sylven's lips with each rapid, shallow breath. His eyes fluttered, struggling to focus as his life ebbed away with each passing second.

Sayra's vision blurred as hot tears streamed down her cheeks, her heart shattering into a million pieces. "*Sana,*" she choked out, desperately channeling every last scrap of majik she could muster.

The spell flickered weakly, knitting together a tiny patch of skin. It was woefully inadequate, a cruel joke in the face of such a devastating injury. Sayra's mind reeled with grief. Why hadn't she focused more on healing majik? Why couldn't she have started training years ago?

"*Sana,*" she tried again, her voice breaking. Another tiny area closed, but it was like trying to dam a river with a pebble. She could feel her other spells faltering in the distance, leaving Nes and the others exposed, but she couldn't bring herself to focus anywhere but on Sylven.

"*Sana,*" Sayra whispered, pouring her heart and soul into the word. Her majik reserves were all but depleted, her body trembling with exhaustion.

Sylven's eyes fluttered open, unfocused on her face. At that moment, everything she was losing crashed down upon her. Not just an Arcanist, not just her charge, but a friend, a confidant, a man who had become an irreplaceable part of her world.

As Sylven's life slipped away in her arms, Sayra felt a piece of herself dying with him.

It's okay, Sayra, he thought to her. Even his mental voice was strained and weak.

Those words... those damned words.

A racking sob shook her chest. Pain, so much pain, overcame her thoughts. It was happening all over again. First her brother and now a man who had become more like one to her than any other. When would people stop dying in her arms? Why couldn't it have been *her*?

"*Sana.*"

A brush of his fingers against hers, a thought passing between them. *You being here is enough.*

"*Sana.*"

No, no, no, no, no. It wasn't. She owed him more than this ending.

"Sana."

I'm grateful the Goddess made you my Valkyrie. You'll save this forsaken world.

"Sana."

Goodbye, Sayra. Thank you... for making my life meaningful once again.

Sayra cried in earnest. Their relationship had been built on antagonism, Sayra constantly needling him with teasing remarks. But beneath the surface, those moments had been precious to her. She saw through Sylven's moody Arcanist facade, recognizing a kindred spirit who carried the same deep-seated grief, turning it inward as she once had. Over time, she'd caught glimpses of the real Sylven—the barely concealed smiles he'd try to hide by turning away, the laughs hastily disguised as coughs and blamed on changing seasons or imaginary dust. She'd joked about him being a softie, but in her heart, she'd meant every word.

Sylven cared fiercely for those close to him, even as he punished himself for the shortcomings of other Arcanists. He deserved so much more—a long life filled with genuine friendships and family in a world where the Horde was nothing more than a scary bedtime story.

As Sayra cradled his broken body, she mourned not just for him but for all the moments they'd never share, all the walls they'd never break down together, and all the words unsaid. The unfairness of it all dug into her gut like a sword. All because she failed to protect him in those final moments.

What good was a Valkyrie who let their Arcanist die?

Sayra's forehead pressed against his cold one, and all movement from his chest ebbed. Her body shuddered with sobs. She didn't care about the thundering of the approaching daemon, about the cruel, remorseless laughter choking out of its throat. Her only thought was of the dead man she had grown close to in her arms, her tears trailing down his lifeless cheekbones.

Sayra reached out with her mind one last time, searching for their link to no avail. There was no recognition on the other side, no emotions swirling or responding to her own. Her mind was empty and entirely her own. Still, she couldn't—wouldn't—stop searching. Sylven had to be there.

He had to.

He had to.

Then, there was a flooding source, something smooth deep into the far reaches of her consciousness. It wasn't a person but a living, writhing force far beyond that of the human form.

It was the relic unlocking a new depth of her majik.

Without hesitation, Sayra claimed all of it. Pulling greedily, she stole the majik from the earth, pushing every ounce of it into one wish, one word.

"Sana."

A warm droplet fell from Sayra's nose, mingling with the crimson pool beneath her. The cost was steep, but before her eyes, a miracle unfolded. Sinew and bone knitted together, reforming Sylven's shattered abdomen. In the span of a heartbeat, his body was whole again. The bloodied shirt was the only evidence of his grievous injury.

But the victory was hollow. No breath stirred in Sylven's lungs, and his body remained still with the unmistakable quietude of death.

"No," Sayra whispered, her fragile hope crumbling to dust. The majik had mended his body, but Sylven's spirit had already fled beyond its reach.

Sayra's neck bent, and her forehead touched Sylven's one last time. The daemon loomed nearby, seeming to revel in her anguish as she cradled her fallen Arcanist, her shoulders shaking with pitchy sobs. She was unable to tear herself away from Sylven's lifeless form. Leaving him felt like a betrayal of everything she stood for, everything they had shared. In that moment, surrounded by death and the lingering threat of the Horde, Sayra felt more alone than she ever had before.

Why couldn't it have been her?

A guttural voice raised her head, the daemon baring its fangs. "*Hell summoner.*" It laughed. The words were chewed and spat out with a throaty bellow, nearly reminiscent of the sound of metal scraping against its likeness, the noise making her teeth grit in pain. "*You're next.*"

Majik surged from the earth, flooding Sayra's body with raw, untamed power. It coursed through her veins, setting every nerve alight, its rhythm a mocking counterpoint to her shattered heart. For a moment, the temptation to surrender to the overwhelming force, to let it consume her and end her suffering, was nearly irresistible. But a whisper of reason cut through her despair. Others still depended on her; she couldn't abandon them to face the nightmare alone. The daemon wouldn't stop with her death, and who knew when help would finally arrive from the monastery?

But everyone in the monastery, all the people who thought they were safe behind wards that no longer worked, they, too, were at risk. The Horde was coming, and they could do nothing to stop it.

With a blood-soaked hand and a soul heavy with grief, Sayra channeled all her pain, rage, and anguish into a single primal cry:

"*Secare!*"

The wind answered her call, a blade of pure destruction more powerful than anything she ever could have conjured on her own. As the daemon finally tired of its cruel game and leaped for the kill, the spell met its charge head-on. In a heartbeat, the monstrous form was cleaved in two, its dying screech cut short as it crumpled to the ground.

Black ichor seeped into the grass. But as Sayra watched the creature's death throes, she felt no triumph, only a hollow emptiness where her heart used to be.

A deep bitterness caused her lips to tremble.

If only Sayra had known how to source majik using the relic earlier, she could have single-handedly taken down the Horde without placing her friends in mortal danger. Without Casber, Lynn, and Sylven...

The thought was too much to bear.

Sayra needed to check on the others. She knew what her duty demanded of her. The last daemon should have been an easy kill for the three of them, and with this one down, falling into the call of sleep became more and more tempting the longer she held the link with the relic. The tingling intensified, a strange blur edging into her field of vision. Soon, her ears numbed to the call of her name, the voice distinctly reminding her of *him*.

Just for a few more seconds, she'd stay there with Sylven. She was unwilling to leave him and struggled even harder to think of saying goodbye. And so, Sayra closed her eyes, her back slumping onto the thin trunk. Her head sagged when she retracted her mind from the relic's influence, her torso slipping without permission toward the ground. There she lay next to her fallen friend, and between the two of them, only one of their hearts still beat. The other forever lost to the hands of the Horde.

Chapter Twenty-Nine

SAYRA

Dreams of her memories surfaced through the murkiness of Sayra's mind, snatches of childhood images playing along the timeline of her years. She remembered the sweet, cherished days spent trimming roses during the spring with her mother, relishing the divine scents rising from each. Sayra sneezed half the time afterward, but the scents were too enticing to prevent her from sampling each stunning flower. Those days, she enjoyed the summer dresses and learning the premise of what encapsulated a lady. Her mother had taught her well until she supposedly died.

Then, it became daggers and sparring, honing her trade to a deadly edge with her instructors. Sayra pawned the idea for dance and the *spyd* to her father to elevate her social standing to become an excellent candidate for marriage. Without delay, he enrolled her in the prestigious Academy of Dance with the legendary instructor of the school himself, Gorm Schaefer.

When her brother passed, Sayra no longer had anyone to protect her against her father's whims, and he immediately sought to bind her into a marriage contract. The application to the Valkyrie Academy was her saving grace; the friends she had and those she met along the way gave her a sense of belonging. But her tentative life was uprooted the moment majik entered.

All that floated in her mind now were the haunting images of Kimimari's near death in the dormitory fire, the sound of pleas and desperate attempts for the others in the hall to flee echoing through her skull. Of the inky *nefas* fire that nearly turned Emrys to ash when she fell into the majik's grasp, and the first time she let Sylven down all those months ago when they encountered their first daemon together.

That name.

Sylven.

It brought her to her knees, the recent memories replaying in a blood-stained shade, over and over until Sayra couldn't handle it anymore, covering her ears against the scream and her eyes from the scene. No matter what she did, the sound reached her, and she saw the gaping hole in his abdomen. That light that faded from his hazel eyes, glazed with pain and fear.

Sayra's snapped open, her lungs expanding with a gulp of air. She was back in her room, tucked into her bed with any trace of the previous night cleaned away. Her ribs felt healed under her gray pajamas, as if the staff had healed her in her sleep and returned her to the dormitory. Rain pattered against her window, the sky outside laden with stormy clouds. Trees swayed from the wind, a faint howling noise from her room.

"Sayra?" Lynn's head rose from her desk, and her face was a picture of concern.

The one life she saved after they rushed toward Lynn and Casber's bodies. When she and Kimimari assessed them back in the tree line, Sylven and Emrys fending off the Horde, Sayra found Lynn still breathing. She layered healing spell after spell, beyond relieved Lynn had only been knocked out by the daemon.

But Casber... Sylven...

Using her sheet to dab the wetness from her face, Sayra grunted as she hauled herself up, her chest aching where something remained broken inside. Her gray pajamas, wrinkled from tossing and turning, hung loosely on her frame. "You're okay?" Sayra asked. Her voice lacked feeling, the words not sounding like her own.

She reached for that mental link with Sylven, finding nothing in return.

"Alive." Lynn tried for a smile, but her big brown eyes watered above dark circles on her face. Switching to their native tongue, she said, "*I'm so sorry for everything. If we hadn't fallen for Vander's tricks...*" Her voice thickened, face remorseful as she struggled with her words. "*None of this would have happened.*"

Sayra's throat tightened at the warble in Lynn's voice. "You couldn't have known, Lynn," she said. Her fingers gripped her comforter, her eyes sinking to the fabric bundled in her grasp. She was seeing without seeing, speaking without words, existing without purpose. "I'm sorry I couldn't have done more for Casber. I'm so sorry, Lynn. I keep letting down the people close to you. I'm sor—"

Sayra didn't know when the tears came, nor when her shoulders began to shake with heaving sobs. Only that her friend came over, wrapping a comforting arm around her shoulders in solidarity. Lynn was present without speaking, giving Sayra the time she required to gather herself. She tightened her hold on her friend, feeling Lynn's body shake with fresh sobs as well. Lynn had always been the sweetest among them, her naivety and kind heart a beacon in their often-dark world. To see her in such pain was almost unbearable.

"I should have been faster," Sayra murmured, her own voice raspy. "Stronger. If I had just—"

Lynn pulled back suddenly, her tear-stained face a mix of sorrow and determination. "*No, Sayra. Don't you dare blame yourself,*" she said, her usually soft voice surprisingly firm. "*You did everything you could. You... you saved me.*"

Sayra looked away, unable to meet Lynn's earnest gaze. "But Casber..."

"*Listen to me,*" Lynn insisted, grasping Sayra's hands in her own. Her touch was warm, grounding. "*My brother always said we were stronger together, remember? He wouldn't want us to fall apart now. And Casber...*" Her voice broke on the name, but she pressed on. "*Casber would hate to see us like this. He'd probably try to make some terrible joke to cheer us up.*"

Despite everything, Sayra felt a small smile tug at her lips. "He was awful at jokes."

Lynn let out a watery laugh. "*The worst. But he always tried, didn't he?*"

For a moment, they sat in silence, remembering. The room felt less oppressive.

"I don't know how to move forward from this," Sayra admitted, her voice small. "Everything's changed, Lynn. How do we go on?"

Lynn squeezed Sayra's hands. "*Together,*" she said simply. "*We go on together. We remember him, we honor him, and we keep fighting. Because that's what he would want.*"

Sayra looked at her friend, really looked at her. Despite the tear tracks on her cheeks and the sorrow in her eyes, there was a strength there Sayra hadn't noticed before. Lynn had always been the innocent one, the dreamer. But here she was, holding them together when Sayra felt like she was falling apart.

"When did you get so wise?" Sayra asked, managing a weak smile.

Lynn returned it, equally fragile but genuine. *"I learned from the best. You've always been there for me, Sayra. Let me be here for you now."*

Knocking sounded at the door. At first it was soft, as if the person hesitated, then it gradually became more pronounced. Lynn rose to answer it, taking her time as Sayra steadied her breathing.

"May I come in?" a low voice asked, Sayra not quite believing her ears.

Before she knew it, Sayra was striding across the floor and reaching for the door, pulling it when Lynn stepped back. Blinking, she couldn't comprehend what she saw. Brilliant hazel eyes took her in, that rim of gold around his pupils telling her it was him.

Sylven was staring at her.

"I have to say, you've definitely seen better days," Sylven said, leaning against the frame of her entryway in a simple maroon long-sleeve and black trousers. A tired edge dimmed his subtle, happy look, but his mouth still smiled despite it.

Sayra didn't know whether to cry or laugh, a mixture of both escaping her lips before she could help it. Without sparing another moment, she forced him into a tight hug, a sound of surprise escaping his mouth as he was yanked forward. If it hurt, he didn't say. Instead, he returned the embrace, his chin falling to her right shoulder.

"You're alive," she breathed, hoping and praying to the Goddess it wasn't a dream. She couldn't care less about Arcanists being forbidden in the Valkyrie dormitory at this moment.

Sylven didn't move, sensing she needed the reassurance. "You were fairly out of it when I came to, but yes. Solely because of you," he said, his chest rumbling from his words. "Thank you."

Then that hadn't been her hallucinating when she heard his voice before passing out.

Sayra could hear his heartbeat, could feel the breath drawn and released every few seconds, and she was entirely grateful for it.

"I have sorrow, Sayra," Lynn announced beside her, guilt lining her words. "I did not know you knew not."

"I thought—" Sayra's throat became thick, the words catching. Reluctantly, she pulled back, unable to tear her gaze from his face. The color had returned to his cheeks, blood cleaned from his strong jawline, eyes gazing at hers with an unusual expression that she couldn't discern. What was going on in his head?

Wait.

"Why can't I sense you anymore?" she asked.

Lynn and Sylven shared a glance, the former dismissing herself with the promise that she'd return later to check in on Sayra. The door shut behind Lynn, Sayra's concern mounting by the second.

A slight blush had crept into Sylven's low cheekbones at Lynn's knowing expression, his hand scratching the side of his neck before he spoke. "Our best guess is that you somehow fried the link with the amount of majik you wielded." Upon seeing her distraught expression, he hastily added, "It's been coming back though. I knew the moment you awoke."

Bunching her brows, Sayra folded her arms. "Then why have I not felt anything?"

Loosening a breath, Sylven grew serious. "Because I've blocked it since."

A surge of frustration welled in her, a past grievance needing to be spilled. "Why? Why go through the effort? And while we're at it, why would you pull that stunt out there? You scared the *dritt* out of me, Sylven!" Her voice pitched to a crescendo. "It is my duty to protect you out there. You were *dead*." Her voice cracked, her lips warbling. "All because you went against my decision. I thought we were past this. You cannot ever pull a stunt like that again!"

Sylven's facial muscles tensed, and his head shook slowly. "I can't promise that."

"Why?" Sayra challenged, a tinge of desperation emphasizing that one word. Her eyes held his fiercely. If it came to it, she'd knock him unconscious every time before a Horde encounter. It would prove troublesome but would guarantee his safety at the very least. Just not from his perpetual grumpiness.

A muscle feathered in his cheek, his nostrils flaring. "Must you make me say it?" he growled, obviously bothered by whatever was plaguing him.

"Say what?" Sayra asked, infuriated with the stubbornness of her Arcanist. Perhaps it was divine retribution for all the years she'd been the same to others. What a pain she was.

Sylven turned away, his shoulders a rigid line of frustration beneath his crumpled shirt. For a moment, Sayra thought he might leave, fleeing from the moment of vulnerability. In the silence, the sound of raindrops pounding against her window was deafening.

But then he stopped, his head bowing. Without turning, he said, "You are the most infuriating, loud-mouthed, impatient, and impulsive person I have ever met. You constantly push my buttons, my limits frequently surpassed by your display of constant antics."

"Charming. You forgot charming," Sayra dryly interjected, tilting her head at his back. Her unbraided hair spilled around her shoulders, the ends curling around her waist.

"Despite me being forced into this contract and having every intention to hate you every minute of it, my resolve slowly became worn down by your presence." Sylven's head rose, a deep breath expelled as he turned to face her again. "You became someone I considered important in my life. It took a long while for me to realize it all. To see you more than a bother I was stuck with. You've shown me what it is to endure even when the world can prove so miserable."

Sylven's eyes were soft in a way she'd never seen before, his coming words leaving her stunned.

"I lost my way after my sister died, but now I know where I am to go next. I know what I want with such stark clarity that it's painful I didn't realize it sooner. It took almost losing you for my vision to clear, for me to finally realize what has been standing beside me all these months."

Sayra felt cemented in place as Sylven's hand rose, as if of its own accord. But then, he seemed to realize it, stopping himself. It found his pocket instead, tucking into the fabric.

"To realize *who* was standing with me," Sylven said, his eyes flicking between her widened ones. "Someone I can't afford to lose. You saw through my walls, even when I tried my damnedest to keep you out."

He paused before continuing. "You're still infuriating, impulsive, and louder than anyone I've ever met. But you're also the strongest, most determined person I know. You make me want to be better, to be the person I've only wished I could be. I'd follow you anywhere, Sayra. Even into the depths of the Horde's territory. Because I know you'd find a way to come out on top, no matter what. For months, I've been trying to ignore these feelings. I knew they could never lead anywhere. But I can't keep pretending they don't exist. Not when you asked me why I valued your life over mine."

Sayra's face reddened from the bombardment of compliments, but her stomach rolled with guilt and unease. She was utterly speechless and shocked.

His voice deepened. "You could have the world if you wanted, yet you were going to sacrifice it all for me. I will never allow that to happen, Sayra, because more than anything, I want you to live. You must live because I care for you more than I can admit."

Sylven looked into her eyes as if he saw all her flaws and imperfections at once but was unfazed by all of them. Memories flashed through her mind—every argument, reluctant smile, and moment of unexpected kindness. How had she been so blind? All the while, her thoughts kept returning to Rys, to the connection they shared and the potential they had only begun to explore. Guilt and confusion warred within her as Sylven laid bare his feelings. She saw the pain in his face, the resignation, and it made her heart ache in ways she hadn't thought possible.

"Sylven, I..." Sayra began, but the words died on her lips. What could she say? That she was sorry? That she wished she had known sooner? That in another life things might have been different?

And then came the final blow. "Your heart belongs with Rys," Sylven said. "And I wish you both only the happiest of relationships."

"I never knew," she finally managed. She wrapped her arms around herself. "I never realized..."

Sylven's smile was sad, tinged with a bittersweet acceptance. "I didn't want you to know. I thought it would be easier that way."

The silence stretched between them, filled with unspoken words and missed opportunities. Sayra felt tears prick at her eyes.

"I'm sorry," she said, the words feeling woefully inadequate. "I wish..."

Sylven's gaze dropped to the floor for a moment before meeting Sayra's eyes again. The room felt smaller to her somehow.

"I had to tell you," he began, his voice quiet but steady. "It wasn't fair, to either of us, to keep it bottled up. But Sayra, I want you to understand something." He paused, choosing his words carefully. "I don't expect anything from you. Not now, not ever. This wasn't about trying to change things or come between you and Rys."

At the mention of Rys's name, Sayra felt a flutter in her heart. Sylven seemed to notice, a pain crossing his face before he smoothed it away.

"Rys is more than just my friend. He's my brother in all but blood," Sylven continued. "I would never do anything to jeopardize his happiness. Or yours. You two have something special, something real. I see the way you look at each other."

Sayra opened her mouth to speak, but Sylven held up a hand, silently asking her to let him finish.

"I needed to be honest with you to clear the air between us. But I also need you to know that I'm going to move past this. These feelings... they're mine to deal with, not yours to worry about."

He ran a hand through his hair, a gesture Sayra had seen countless times before but now seemed charged with new meaning. "I care about you, Sayra. More than I ever thought possible. But I care about Rys too. And I care about our friendship. All of us. I won't let my feelings get in the way of that."

Sylven's eyes took on a distant look, as if he were seeing something beyond the confines of the room. "Besides," he said, an almost shy smile playing at the corners of his mouth, "there's someone else. Someone I think I might have feelings for."

Sayra felt her eyebrows rise in surprise. "Someone else?" she asked, unable to keep the curiosity from her voice. A tinge of hope eased some of her guilt.

Sylven nodded, his cheeks coloring. "Yeah. It's still new. I'm not sure what it is yet. But there's something there, something that feels right." He looked back at Sayra, his expression earnest. "I'm telling you this because I want you to understand. My feelings for you are real, but they're not everything. I have a life beyond this. Beyond us. And I'm going to be okay."

A weight lifted from her shoulders, even as a new kind of sadness settled in her. "I'm glad," she said softly. "You deserve to be happy, Sylven."

He grinned, a genuine smile that reached his eyes. "So do you, Sayra. So does Rys. And that's what I want for both of you."

The silence between them was different then, less charged but no less meaningful. Sylven stepped back, creating a physical distance that mirrored the emotional one he was trying to establish.

"So," he said, his tone lighter, almost reminiscent of their old banter, "are we okay?"

Sayra took a good look at him. She saw the boy who had frustrated her to no end, the man who had become her friend and partner, and this new version of Sylven, vulnerable and strong all at once.

"Yeah," she said, surprised to find she meant it. "We're okay."

Sylven's expression shifted, the openness of moments ago replaced by a more familiar seriousness. He straightened, his posture becoming rigid as he glanced at the door before lowering his voice. "Sayra, there's something else we need to discuss. It's about the Zefares."

She felt her body tense instinctively, and she summoned a spell of privacy. "What about them?"

"They've been questioning everyone involved in the incident. Rys, Nessika, Kimimari, Lynn, and me. It's only a matter of time before they come to you."

Her heart grew heavy. "What did you tell them?"

"We stuck to the story we agreed upon," Sylven replied, his voice steady. "We were out for a walk by the lake when we stumbled upon Lynn and Casber. We tried to help, but the Horde somehow crossed the wards and attacked one by one. In the chaos, Casber…"

Sayra only nodded. Neither of them were able to say the word.

"We emphasized that it was a desperate situation and that we all did the best we could. We said nothing about Vander's hand in it or Lynn's wine being spiked."

A deep hatred rose in her at that. Vander deserved to be thrown to the snakes, but even as every fiber of her wanted him to face the consequences, she knew it would only jeopardize them all. Sayra nodded slowly, absorbing the information. "And they believed you?"

Sylven's jaw tightened. "I don't know. They seemed to accept it, but they're not easily fooled. They are on a warpath trying to figure out why there weren't any guards patrolling that section of the wall and how the Horde passed over the wards." He paused, making sure Sayra was following. "When they come to you, you need to be prepared. Stick to the story. Don't volunteer any information they don't explicitly ask for."

Sayra met his gaze, seeing the worry blanketing his features. "I understand. I won't let us down."

She paced the length of her small room, her bare feet padding against the cool wooden floor. She paused at the window, fingers absently tracing the sill as she gazed out at the monastery grounds bathed in dimmed afternoon light. The events of the night replayed in her mind, each memory bringing a fresh wave of anger and anxiety.

She turned back to face Sylven, who leaned against her desk. His appearance was disheveled, his hair mussed and his shirt wrinkled. Dark circles under his eyes betrayed his exhaustion, and her anger spiked.

"Has Emrys found Vander yet?" Sayra asked, her voice tight. She resumed her pacing, the soft swish of her pajama pants a counterpoint to the creaking floorboards beneath her feet.

Sylven shook his head. "No, not yet. Vander's always been good at disappearing when he wants to."

She stopped and turned to face Sylven with fire in her eyes. "How could he do this? Lynn could have died. Casber *did* because of him." Her voice cracked on the last word, and she swallowed hard against the lump in her throat. "I can't believe we allowed this to happen. That we let him get this far without catching on."

Sylven stood, taking a hesitant step toward her. "None of us saw this coming, Sayra. Not even Rys."

At the mention of Emrys, Sayra's heart clenched. The fabric of her pajamas did little to ward off the chill that seemed to emanate from within. "How's he taking all this?"

Sylven's expression darkened. "Hard. It's his brother, after all. I think he feels responsible, like he should have seen the signs. After visiting you earlier, he has devoted every waking second to finding Vander."

Sayra nodded, understanding the responsibility all too well. Her heart clenched at the thought of Emrys checking in on her. Even with everything going on, he prioritized her. She pushed off from the wall, moving to sit on the windowsill. The cool glass against her back sent a shiver down her spine, but she welcomed the sensation. It made her feel more alert, more present in such a surreal moment. The rain's patter intensified behind her.

"What do we do now?" she asked.

"We wait," Sylven said, his voice heavy with resignation. "We wait for Emrys to find Vander and prepare for whatever comes next. The Holy Family, Vander's next move, all of it."

Sayra closed her eyes, thinking. When she opened them again, she met Sylven's gaze with renewed determination.

Then, as if suddenly remembering something, his expression sobered further. "There's something else you should know," he said, his voice hesitant.

Sayra felt her heart skip a beat. "What is it?"

Resting his hands on his knees, Sylven said, "They're holding a vigil for Casber this evening. In the main courtyard."

The words hit Sayra like a physical blow. Her legs were suddenly weak. "A vigil," she repeated, the word tasting bitter on her tongue. It made it all so final, so real.

Sylven nodded, his eyes haunted by Casber's last moments. His brutal end. "I thought you should know."

Sayra sank onto her bed. The thought of facing everyone, of acknowledging Casber's death in such a public way, made her stomach churn. But she knew she had to be there for Lynn if nothing else. "What time?" she asked, her voice barely audible. "And where?"

Across the room, Sylven rose, making way for the door. "Just after dinner in the cathedral."

"Thank you, Sylven," she said, wringing her hands. "For everything."

He gave her a sad smile. "Always," he replied, the word carrying everything that had been said and everything that never would be.

With a final nod, Sylven turned and left the room, leaving Sayra alone with her thoughts and the looming shadow of all that had happened.

⸺⊷✦⊶⸺

Sayra twisted a black *slør* into Lynn's thick auburn hair. The burnished gold fabric of Lynn's tunic wrinkled as she folded her arms. The candles dotted throughout her friend's room were snuffed out, leaving a faint musky scent in lieu of the normal floral notes that hung about. Tying the braid off, Sayra's throat was tight as she watched her friend button the black collar of her formal uniform.

Lynn's eyes were red-rimmed, her usually vibrant face pale and drawn. Kimimari stood by the window, her own uniform immaculate, fingers absently tracing the black vines of lace that trailed down from her shoulders. Nes sat on the edge of the bed, polishing her already gleaming boots with methodical strokes, as if the repetitive motion could somehow keep her mind at bay.

Lynn nodded at nothing, her gaze distant. "I don't know if I can do this, Sayra," she murmured, her voice cracking. "How can I say good-bye?"

Both Kimimari and Nes stilled, words not coming easy to either of them.

Sayra felt her heart constrict. She gently cupped Lynn's face, forcing her friend to meet her eyes. "You can do this," she said firmly. "We're all here with you. You're not alone."

From across the room, Nes spoke up, her voice uncharacteristically gentle. "Casber would want you to be strong, Lynn. He always admired your resilience."

Kimimari moved from the window, placing a hand on Lynn's shoulder. "We'll be right beside you every step of the way."

Lynn took a shaky breath and adjusted the black cuffs of her sleeves, the thick fabric stark against her pale skin. "I just... I keep expecting him to walk through that door with that goofy smile of his."

A heavy silence fell over the room. Sayra felt her eyes burn with unshed tears, but she blinked them back. She had to be strong for Lynn's sake. "Let's get through this first. One thing at a time."

Nes stood, her boots gleaming. "We should probably head down soon," she said, her voice soft but firm. "The vigil will be starting soon."

As they made their final preparations, Sayra couldn't help but reflect on how different they all looked in their formal uniforms. The dark gold tunics, the intricate black lace, the polished boots—it all seemed a far cry from their usual training gear.

Lynn took one last look at her pressed black trousers, her fingers tracing the gold sigil on her cuff. "He always said I looked beautiful in this uniform," she said, her voice haunted.

Sayra stepped forward, wrapping an arm around Lynn's shoulders. "And he was right. You do."

As they filed out of the room, Sayra walked in unison with Lynn. Kimimari and Nes formed a protective flank around them, their small cadre silent as they wound through the monastery. At last, they crested the cathedral's stairway. Rain had dampened their clothes along the way, mocking tears down their faces. Their boots treaded over a navy carpet lining the aisle, absorbing much of the water their footprints left.

Myrrh and frankincense hung in the filled capacity, a sea of burnished gold, navy, and black accents across every pew. Every Arcanist, Valkyrie, and staff member who could attend were present. Some whispered quietly as Sayra's cadre walked past. Grief lined many of their faces, with shocked expressions on others.

That urge prodded Sayra's mind, nudging her toward the cathedral, though each of her feet were leaden. Fatigue pulled at her eyelids, and the exhaustion from using so much majik was still eating at her.

As they passed the alcoves housing statues of saints and holy figures, Sayra couldn't help but feel a twinge of resentment. Where was their so-called protection when Casber needed it most?

The ancient statue of the Goddess loomed before them as they approached the front of the cathedral. Her arms were outstretched in eternal benediction. At her feet, in front of the Grand Priest's ornate perch, a simple marble casket had been placed. Sayra felt her breath catch in her throat at the sight, and Lynn's breath hitched beside her.

We have spots reserved for you four in the front. Sylven's words echoed in her mind.

Thank you. Sayra lowered her voice when speaking to Lynn. "Almost there."

She spotted Sylven and Emrys in their academy uniforms with enough room for four beside them. The spot was close enough to see the casket but far enough back to avoid drawing attention. They filed in, Sayra sitting down with relief beside Emrys.

For a sweet moment, he reached for her hand, turning her attention to his stoic face. His eyes were alight with concern, only abating when she lowered her chin into a quick nod. *I'm fine*, she conveyed with a look. She made to pull back, but when his thumb grazed the back of hers, she felt a quick flush of warmth at the tiny, seemingly insignificant, gesture. She squeezed his hand in return.

A scuffle of motion caught her attention. Catara and Jax were near the front, the gold on their uniforms luminous. And there, lurking in the shadows near the end of a pew, was Vander. His face was impassive, but Sayra could see a glimmer of something in his eyes that made her blood boil. Beside him, Kenji and Akira spoke.

As the last of the attendees filed in, a hush fell over the gathering. The Grand Priest emerged from a side chamber, his robes rustling as he made his way to stand before the casket. His piercing hazel eyes scanned the crowd, meeting Sayra's for a moment and stilling. A strange premonition shook her at that moment, something forbearing that warned of danger. Then he turned, and it was over as quickly as it began. He raised his hands, and the vigil for Casber commenced.

A lump formed in Sayra's throat as the first prayers were intoned. She glanced at Lynn, seeing silent tears streaming down her friend's face. Without a word, Sayra moved closer, offering what little comfort she could in the moment of shared grief. The cathedral's vast space seemed to shrink, loss and sorrow pressing in from all sides. As the vigil continued, Sayra found her mind drifting, memories of Casber's laugh and kind smile flashing through her thoughts. She clenched her fists at her sides, a quiet determination building within her.

His loss would not be in vain. Whatever it took, whatever sacrifices had to be made, she would see justice done. For Casber, for Lynn, and for all of them.

Vander would pay for what he had done.

Chapter Thirty

SAYRA

As the service concluded, the somber crowd filtered out of the cathedral. Whispers and pointed looks their way had Sayra clenching her fists. She was certain they had heard some version of their daemon encounter by then. She stood rooted to the spot, watching as Lynn hovered by the casket. Lynn wanted privacy, and Sayra hung back with the others for some time. The air was thick with whispered conversations and muffled sobs, grief hanging over everyone like a shroud.

Sayra's eyes were drawn to the Grand Priest, who was speaking to his daughter and nephew. His ornate robes shuffled about him. As if sensing her gaze, he turned, his intense eyes locking on hers. With a subtle gesture, he beckoned her forward.

Sayra felt her heart drop to her stomach, a cold sweat breaking out across her skin. He was the man who had given her the cross on the nape of her neck, the mark that granted her Valkyrie abilities. At that time, his presence was a kind and comforting one. How wrong her perception had been. He was, perhaps, the evilest of them all, condoning and ordering the horrors beneath their feet. His presence filled her with dread. As she hesitated, torn between fleeing and obeying, she felt a gentle touch on her arm. Emrys stood beside her.

"Go," he said. "I'll be waiting here. If anything goes south, tell Sylven."

Behind him, Sylven lowered his chin. *We won't hesitate to move if they have discovered your majik.*

Swallowing hard, Sayra nodded. She turned and approached the Grand Priest, the man already moving for a door behind the massive columns supporting the cathedral. As she drew closer, she noticed Catara and Jax falling into step behind her. Their presence did little to ease her anxiety. The trio followed the Grand Priest through a small, concealed door near the altar, entering a narrow corridor that led to his private office.

The office was quite plain compared to the grandeur of the cathedral. It was a tiny circular room, every available surface covered in ancient tomes and scrolls. The walls were lined with dark wood shelves holding countless books. A massive desk dominated the center of the room, its surface cluttered with papers and strange artifacts that Sayra couldn't identify. The air was heavy with the scent of old parchment and something else, something metallic and vaguely unpleasant that made Sayra's skin crawl. As the Grand Priest moved behind his desk, Sayra felt that strange urge grow stronger. It was as if the Goddess herself was whispering in her ear, urging her to look closer to see what was hidden beneath the surface.

Everything okay so far? Sylven asked.

Yes.

"Valkyrie Sayra." The Grand Priest's voice cut through her thoughts, smooth and cultured. "First and foremost, you and your friends have my most sincere condolences. To lose an Arcanist on the Goddess Eveline's sacred grounds... it's an absolute tragedy. We will investigate how the Horde managed to overcome our wards and pray to the Goddess that we may avoid such a calamity in the future. I trust you're recovering well from the attack?" Worry lightened his words, but she knew it to be fake.

Sayra forced herself to meet his gaze, fighting to keep her expression neutral. "Yes, Your Holiness," she replied, proud her voice didn't waver. "I'm grateful for the strength the Goddess has granted me and the others."

The Grand Priest smiled, but she knew the mask he wore, and she could tell it was forced. "Indeed. And yet, I can't help but wonder about the events of that night. If you're willing, could you shed light on how the attack occurred? Anything you could share may be of great benefit."

Sayra felt her heart rate spike. She could sense Catara and Jax behind her, their presence a silent threat as they stared from where they stood. Fighting to keep her voice steady, she detailed exactly what Sylven had told her to share.

Jax had navigated himself to stand beside his uncle's desk, but Catara remained beside her. Almost... protectively? The Valkyrie's concern appeared genuine in her tanned features, and her hand twitched when Sayra described the last daemon as it entered the fray.

"Everything happened so quickly. I simply acted on instinct as best as possible," Sayra said, her voice just above a whisper. She didn't have to fake the pain or force the water to her eyes. Clearing her throat, she raised her gaze from the floor to Catara's burning expression. "The next thing I knew, I awoke in my room."

The Grand Priest stroked the graying hair on his chin, his eyes boring into hers. "You and the others have been through quite an ordeal. I can only thank Eveline that more of you didn't fall to the hands of the Horde when none of you should have lived from that awful experience. The Goddess has indeed had her hands on your path. Through a few trials, it would seem."

Sayra went as still as a statue, fearing they could see the way her palms grew clammy.

"I believe she has great plans for you. Though as to what they are, I wonder..." The Grand Priest trailed off, his hand stilling.

The statement sent a jolt of fear through her. Could he know about the Goddess's voice? About her hidden majik? Sayra forced herself to remain calm, even as her mind raced for a plausible answer.

A heavy sigh escaped the Grand Priest, and he relaxed his hands on his lap. "I suppose only time will tell. Have you been well otherwise? Any strange dreams or prompts from the Goddess that have influenced your presence at any of these recent events?"

The Horde attack on her when traveling to Astor manor, the dormitory fire, the daemons beside the lake... all of which they knew about.

"I've only had a nightmare last night, Your Holiness," she said, allowing a tremor to enter her voice. "Reliving the attack. But nothing unusual beyond that."

The Grand Priest studied her for a long moment, his expression pinching. Finally, he leaned back in his chair. "I see. Such trauma can have unpredictable effects. We'll be keeping a close eye on you, Sayra. For your own safety, of course. If we can be of any assistance or if you ever come across anything strange, please don't hesitate to request a meeting with me. Along with Eveline, I believe you are special to our cause."

First Catara and now her father. There was definitely something they knew that she didn't.

But as he spoke, Sayra's eyes were drawn to a strange symbol carved into the binding of a leather-bound book behind him. It seemed to pulse with an inner light, and that urge to look closer, to understand, grew even stronger. For that split second, she saw an etching of what looked like a chalice, but when the Grand Priest finished speaking, her eyes flicked back to him.

"Thank you, Your Holiness. I won't hesitate," she lied, bowing as was decorum.

She all but ran from there the moment Catara opened the door for her.

Sayra found Emrys and Sylven waiting by the pews. The cathedral was eerily empty, and the absence of Casber's casket reminded her of the situation's finality. Emrys stood tall, his posture rigid, but his dark eyes betrayed a flicker of concern as they met hers. Similar in height, Sylven's slightly broader frame relaxed a hair when he spotted her.

"Are you all right?" Emrys asked, his voice low and controlled. His face remained impassive, but Sayra could see the stress in his shoulders.

Sayra nodded, not trusting her voice just yet. Emrys studied her for a moment longer before giving a curt nod of his own. "Let's go," he said, turning for the cathedral doors.

As they stepped out into the cool evening air, Emrys kept pace beside her, his presence a silent comfort. They walked in silence for a few moments, the sound of their boots on the cobblestones echoing in the quiet courtyards between marble and stone buildings.

"They're burning Casber's remains now," Emrys said, his voice steady but tinged with a hint of sadness. "It's tradition for those who fall to the Horde in his country. They believe it prevents any lingering evil from taking hold."

"The others went with Lynn to be there for her." Sylven's voice lacked its usual depth, his hands pocketed as they walked.

Sayra wanted to say something, to express the grief and anger swirling inside her, but the words wouldn't come. Not when the ones she wanted to say most of all would condemn them if overheard by the wrong ears. It felt like an eternity ago when Emrys first warned her about secrecy when she confronted him about majik in her trials. Oh, how right he was to take such precautions.

As they made their way back to the dormitory, Sayra became acutely aware of the whispers and stares following them. Groups of Arcanists huddled together, their conversations dropping to hushed tones as Emrys, Sylven, and Sayra passed.

"Can't believe the wards failed..."

"Heard they took on a dozen Horde single-handedly..."

"Something's not right about it all..."

The snippets of conversation reached Sayra's ears, making her skin prickle with unease. She glanced at Emrys, wondering if he heard them too, but his face remained impassive, his stone-cold gaze fixed straight ahead.

A group of Valkyries scurried out of their path, eyes wide with awe and fear. Sayra caught one of them whispering, "That's her, the one who survived the attack."

Emrys must have sensed her discomfort because he subtly shifted closer, his arm brushing against hers as they walked. It eased her mind a bit. As they approached the dormitory, the whispers seemed to grow louder and more insistent. Countless eyes burned into her back, the air thick with unasked questions and wild speculation.

"Ignore them," Emrys murmured, his voice so low only she could hear. "They don't know anything."

Sayra nodded, grateful for his steadfast presence. Emrys paused as they reached the dormitory entrance, turning to face her. For a moment, his stoic facade cracked as he looked at her.

Coughing once, Sylven rubbed at the back of his neck. "I'll see you both later." He left but in the direction of the Arcanist training area.E mrys's eyes searched hers, a silent communication passing between them. Then he asked, "Can we speak? In my room?"

Sayra felt her heart skip a beat. Despite the seriousness of the day's events, the prospect of a moment alone with Emrys sent a flutter through her stomach. She nodded, not trusting her voice.

Together, they made their way through the Arcanist dormitory. The halls were quieter than usual, the somber mood of the vigil still lingering. A few students glanced their way, but Emrys's presence seemed to deter any further whispers or stares.

Emrys ushered her inside his room with a respectful distance between them, closing the door softly afterward. His room was as neat as always, with books stacked precisely on his desk and his bed made with military precision. But Sayra barely noticed those details. Her eyes were drawn to Emrys as he turned to face her, his carefully maintained composure finally slipping away.

In two swift strides, he crossed the room and pulled her into his arms. Sayra melted into his embrace, feeling the stress and fear of the day beginning to ebb away. She buried her face in his chest, inhaling the familiar scent of him—juniper, black pepper, vetiver, and something uniquely Emrys.

"I was so worried," he murmured into her hair, his arms tightening around her. "When the Grand Priest called you in…"

Sayra pulled back, looking up into his face. The concern in his dark eyes made her heart ache. "I'm okay," she assured him, reaching up to cup his cheek. The shape of his jawline always reminded her of chiseled marble, but his skin was warm beneath her palm. "Really."

Emrys leaned into her touch, his eyes closing briefly. When he opened them again, they were filled with a mix of tenderness and determination that took Sayra's breath away. Emrys's lips met hers with a hunger that surprised them both. The kiss was sweet yet desperate. Sayra's hands tangled in Emrys's dark hair, pulling him down closer as his arms tightened around her waist. For a moment, the world outside ceased to exist, their shared breath and racing heartbeats the only reality that mattered.

But all too soon, Emrys pulled away, his face contorting into an expression of self-loathing that made Sayra gasp. He stepped back, running a hand through his disheveled black hair, unable to meet her eyes.

"Emrys?" Sayra whispered, reaching out to him.

He shook his head, his voice rough when he finally spoke. "I should have known. About Vander. About all of it. Casber's death is on me."

"You couldn't have known what Vander was planning. It's not your fault."

Emrys turned away, his shoulders tense. "He's my brother, Sayra. I should have seen the signs. I should have stopped him."

The pain in his voice was palpable. Sayra stepped closer, gently placing a hand on his arm. "Emrys, look at me."

Slowly, he turned, his dark eyes filled with a torment Sayra couldn't fathom.

"And when you..." he began, his voice cracking. "When you almost sacrificed yourself for Sylven, I felt my world falling apart. I can't lose you, Sayra. I can't."

The raw vulnerability in his admission stunned her. Emrys, always so controlled, so composed, was laying his heart bare before her.

"I'm terrified," he continued, his deep voice quiet. "Terrified of losing you to this fight, to the Holy Family, to my own brother's machinations. I don't know if I'm strong enough to face that."

Emrys sank onto the edge of his bed, and his hands gripped the edge. Sayra moved to sit beside him on the downy comforter, gently resting her head on his shoulder. For a moment, they sat in silence, the sound of their breathing the only noise in the room. She could feel the stiffness in Emrys's body as he fought to regain his composure.

Sayra spoke, her voice soft but firm. "You won't lose me, Emrys. I'm right here, and I'm not going anywhere."

He turned his head, pressing a kiss to her hair. "I know," he murmured. "But the thought of it haunts me. Every time you're in danger, every time we face another threat, I'm afraid it'll be the last."

Sayra lifted her head, meeting his gaze. The vulnerability in his dark-lashed eyes made her heart ache. "I can't promise that nothing will happen," she said. "But I can promise that I'll fight with everything I have to stay by your side."

A ghost of a smile crossed Emrys's face. "And I by yours."

She reached out, taking his hand in hers. Their fingers intertwined. "You don't have to be strong all the time, you know," she said with gentleness. "It's okay to be afraid. It's okay to lean on me sometimes."

Emrys squeezed her hand, his thumb tracing gentle circles on her skin. "I'm not used to that," he admitted. "Being the prince, being an Arcanist... I've always had to be the strong one, the one with all the answers."

"But with me, you don't," Sayra said, her eyes looking up into his. "With me, you can just be Emrys."

He turned to face her fully. "How did I get so lucky?" he wondered aloud, his full lips curving into a smile she'd only seen him wear with her.

Sayra leaned into him. "I ask myself the same thing every day."

For a moment, they gazed at each other, the world outside fading away. Then, slowly, Emrys leaned in, his lips meeting hers in an achingly tender kiss. It was different from their earlier passion—this was a reaffirmation, a promise.

As they broke apart, Sayra lay beside Emrys on her side. They remained there, their fingers intertwined, staring up at the ceiling. The room was quiet, save for the soft sound of their breathing and the distant murmur of students in the hallway. Sayra felt the exhaustion of the day settling into her bones, but she couldn't bring herself to leave. She turned her head, studying Emrys's profile. The elegance of his nose, the long lashes that framed his eyelids... every feature was familiar and endlessly captivating. Even now, with their troubles evident in the slight furrow of his brow, he was breathtakingly handsome.

She admired the way his black hair fell across his forehead, resisting the urge to reach out and brush it back. Her eyes traced the line of his throat down to the collar of his shirt, where it lay open, showing his muscled skin. Sayra felt a warmth bloom in her chest, feelings of admiration and desire that never failed to surprise her with its intensity.

As the night deepened, Sayra reluctantly murmured, "It's getting late. I should probably go."

Emrys turned to face her, his eyes searching hers. "Stay. Just for tonight. I need to know you're here, that you're safe."

The request hung in the air between them, loaded with unspoken emotions. Sayra felt her resolve crumble. "I was already half asleep anyway," she said with a small smile.

Relief washed over Emrys's face. He pulled her closer, wrapping an arm around her waist. Sayra nestled into his embrace, her head tucked under his chin, their bodies fitting together perfectly. As sleep began to claim her, Sayra felt a profound sense of peace settle over her. There, in Emrys's arms, the troubles of the world seemed far away. The warmth of his body, the steady rhythm of his heartbeat, the familiar scent of him—it all combined to create a safe haven.

Emrys pressed a gentle kiss to the top of her head. "Goodnight, Sayra."

"Goodnight, Emrys," she whispered back, her eyes already drifting closed.

As they fell asleep, tangled together on Emrys's bed, the worries and fears that had plagued her throughout the day seemed to recede. And in the back of her mind, she felt her piece of the hallowed relic reach out to his, a thread all too similar to the link she had with Sylven. Their majik seemed to settle, too, as if preparing for sleep.

For that moment to have lasted longer, Sayra would have given anything.

Chapter Thirty-One

SYLVEN

The last few days had felt surreal to Sylven. Almost dying had that effect. He wouldn't have changed anything, even if he hadn't been saved by Sayra's majik. But when his lungs cried out for air after he thought he was dead, a weak gasp coming from them, his eyelids fluttered toward the collapsing Valkyrie next to him.

After the daemon threw him, Sylven thought something happened to Sayra in those seconds he was unconscious. It terrified him, but all the blood he found stemmed from him rather than her. It took Sylven far too long to regain his mobility, struggling to search her for any obvious injury. Their bond was practically nonexistent, his mind determining the worst for an awful minute before he thought to feel for a pulse. Her heartbeat was strong to his immense relief. Later, he would concern himself over the severing of their mental link.

He floundered to his feet, somehow not collapsing with Sayra in his arms. It was painstakingly slow going. While he was somehow entirely healed, he was beyond exhausted as he trudged through mild underbrush to find the others. Their voices drifted through the trees, frantically calling out to them. He managed a single shout, his breath already escaping him at the end of the syllable.

Fortunately, they all gathered without further incident. That last daemon they eliminated proved to be more of a challenge than anticipated. It mystified them to find one daemon sliced cleanly in half, but the easiest conclusion was that it had been Sayra's doing somehow, along with restoring his lower abdomen. It was inconceivable Sylven was still alive. Lynn had also stirred awake.

Then they learned of Vander's influence over the past couple of months, slowly gaining Casber's trust with honeyed lies and gifts, working his way through him first before meeting Lynn. In the end, Vander couldn't help but share his favorite place to woo women with Casber, surprising Lynn with the fine date and plenty of assurances of its safety.

It was utterly detestable.

When an alarm went up in the monastery, they didn't get long to ponder it. It was a whirlwind of questions and medical assessments. Then the vigil. Then...

"Is she okay?" Sylven asked, his footsteps quiet as he walked beside Nessika.

Black hair shifted around the Valkyrie's smooth face as her ice-blue eyes looked at him. *Really* looked at him. There was something lingering there that was somehow softer but more determined at the same time. The garden lighting reflected in the various puddles as they wove around them.

"No," she said bluntly, her thin brows lowering. "But she will be one day. Kimimari is staying with her tonight. We'll take shifts. Sayra is tomorrow, then me after." A heavy sigh. "She's being reassigned duties right now. There are a few contracts that have opened up recently, and the Holy Family is determining where her next duty will lay."

Sylven chewed on his tongue for a moment, his eyes wandering to the cloudy sky above. "Perhaps Rys can see if his family can hire her."

"If possible, that would be best," Nessika said quietly, her words heavy.

They walked in silence for a few moments, recent events hanging between them. Sylven was acutely aware of Nessika's presence beside him, the way her shoulder occasionally brushed against his as they navigated the winding path.

"How are you holding up?" Nessika asked suddenly, her voice soft with concern. "I know you're okay now, but when we saw you both... there was so much blood." Her voice dropped to a whisper, a haunted edge to her eyes.

Sylven turned to look at her, surprised by the intensity in her voice. Their eyes met, and for a moment, the world seemed to stand still. There was something in Nessika's gaze, a warmth and rawness that made his heart skip a beat.

"I'm all right," he assured her, his voice fainter than he intended. "Thanks to Sayra."

Nessika nodded, a small smile tugging at the corners of her mouth. "She's something else, isn't she? But don't sell yourself short, Sylven. You're pretty incredible, too. I saw what you did out there." She grasped his hand in hers, squeezed, then let go.

The simple gesture sent a jolt of electricity through Sylven. He wished she hadn't let go. He didn't know what to say to that, not when he knew in his bones Sayra had more to contribute to the fight than he did. They continued walking, a comfortable silence settling between them. Sylven felt a shift in the air, a new awareness of Nessika that both excited and terrified him.

"Whatever happens next," she said as they neared the end of the garden path, "we'll get through it."

As they parted ways at the dormitory entrance, Sylven lingered, reluctant to say goodnight. There was so much left unsaid between them, so many new feelings to explore. But now wasn't the time, not with grief and uncertainty hanging over them all.

"Goodnight, Nes," he said softly. "Thank you. For what you've said."

"Goodnight, Sylven," she replied, her smile warm and genuine. "Try to get some rest."

As he watched her disappear into the Valkyrie dormitory, he felt a glimmer of hope amidst the darkness. There was something more for him to fight for beyond the ultimate goal of bringing the Holy Family down.

Nessika.

Someone to move on from the past with. Someone who could offer him a future. He could have sworn he saw Jess smiling at him out of the corner of his eye, but when he turned, all he saw was an empty corridor.

⸺❖⸺

The remaining time at Saint Highburn Monastery seemed to blur together for Sylven. Security around the monastery had increased tenfold, pulling the Valkyries for double shifts when it came to patrols. The wards were monitored closely by Arcanists, and the whole situation was shadily swept under the rug.

With finals looming, he had become buried in books, his mind a whirlwind of arcane theories and historical facts. The library became his second home, old parchment and ink a constant companion. Sayra continued her secret majik practice, occasionally involving Sylven in her training sessions. Those moments, though exhausting, became exciting. They devised ways for Sylven to create new uses of his majik. Watching Sayra's power grow, feeling the raw energy of her new and untapped alchemy, reminded Sylven of the enormity of what they were involved in.

It only took them a matter of minutes to realize what she had accomplished that night against the Horde. She had previously expended all her body's majik whenever casting spells, which was a limiting factor for any Arcanist. But she wasn't like them. Using only the relic, she could summon a vast amount of majik without channeling her own energy. An important distinction since she had previously relied on her own body's power for spellcasting. A distinction she accidentally made to save his life.

Thank the Goddess.

So long as there were ley lines, they theorized, she could harness an unlimited pool of majik.

However, as the days passed, Sylven spent more and more time with Nessika. Their relationship blossomed in the quiet moments between his study sessions and her patrol duties. Stolen glances across classes, shared smiles during combat training, and late-night conversations in the gardens all served to ignite that spark between them.

Throughout it all, the mystery of the Grand Priest's office and the book with the chalice rune weighed heavily on their minds. They believed Sayra's dream about hidden pages was pushing them toward it. Sylven, Sayra, Emrys, Waylen, and Nessika spent countless hours strategizing, trying to devise a foolproof plan to gain access to the office undetected. They pored over the monastery's layout, studied the guards' patrol patterns, and even considered using majik to create a distraction. But in the end, the risk was too great. With the Holy Family's suspicions already focused on Sayra, any misstep could spell disaster for all of them. The frustration of being so close to potential answers, yet unable to act, was grating.

And Vander...

He was suspiciously absent. They rarely could catch sight of him before he slunk away, and Breane was with him every second. He knew they would try something otherwise.

As Sylven put down his quill after completing his final exam, a mix of relief and apprehension washed over him. The immediate pressure of academics had lifted, but the larger challenges looming on the horizon felt more real than ever.

He gathered his belongings, his mind already racing with thoughts of what came next: the journey to Acacea, the meeting with Emrys's parents, the continued search for answers... It seemed it would never end. He stepped out of the examination hall.

Tonight was the graduation ball, and tomorrow they would be leaving for Acacea.

CHAPTER THIRTY-TWO

SAYRA

Sayra stood before the full-length mirror in her bathroom, hardly recognizing the reflection staring back at her. The emerald gown she wore was a masterpiece of craftsmanship, its fabric shimmering like liquid jewels. The bodice hugged her curves perfectly, intricate beadwork sewn into it. The skirt flowed gracefully to the floor, a small train trailing behind her. Her hands smoothed over the delicate fabric as she turned, admiring the way the low back revealed just enough skin to be alluring without crossing into impropriety. The sleeves, made of sheer material and adorned with tiny emeralds, draped elegantly over her arms.

"You look stunning," Kimimari said from her perch on Sayra's bed. Unlike Sayra, she was dressed in her formal Valkyrie armor, polished to a mirror shine for the evening's guard duty.

Sayra smiled at her friend as she ducked around the corner. "Thank you. I feel a bit like I'm playing dress-up, to be honest. I can hardly believe I used to wear such things daily in Faenda."

She returned to the mirror, carefully applying the finishing touches to her makeup. A sweep of gold eyeshadow made her green eyes pop, while a touch of rouge added a healthy glow to her cheeks. Her lips were painted a soft pink, enhancing their natural color. With practiced hands,

Sayra began to style her hair into an elegant updo. Soft tendrils framed her face, while the rest was swept up into an intricate series of braids and twists, secured with jeweled pins that matched her dress. A thin gold ribbon tied its way in there.

A part of her was wistful at the process. She once cherished the variety of fabrics her dresses had and the way a different palate of make-up colors could entirely alter her look. But... that was all part of her past.

"Here, let me help with that," Kimimari offered, moving to assist with a particularly tricky section.

As they worked together, a comfortable silence fell between them. Sayra slipped on her heels, delicate strappy affairs in a shade of gold that complemented her dress perfectly. A pair of emerald drop earrings and a simple gold necklace completed the ensemble. However, she hesitated when spotting her silver dove necklace from her mother. She almost wore it, but it didn't match.

"I can't believe this is it," Sayra said, turning to face Kimimari. "Our last night at Saint Highburn before summer break."

Kimimari's usually stoic expression softened. "It's been quite a year, hasn't it?"

Sayra nodded, a lump forming in her throat. "I'm going to miss you, Kim. Promise you'll write?"

"Of course," Kimimari assured her, pulling Sayra into a careful hug, mindful of wrinkling her dress. "And you must tell me everything about Acacea. I expect a full report on the royal court gossip."

Sayra laughed, the sound tinged with a hint of sadness. "Deal. And you have to keep me updated on your new post with Ashar. I'm thankful you'll be here with Lynn."

The Holy Family elected to keep Lynn's contract within the monastery walls after the daemon breach. They wanted to reinforce their ranks more than ever to convince students and future prospects all would be safe once more.

Kimimari's eyes gleamed. "It will be a quiet summer, but Lynn and I will have each other in the meantime."

"Absolutely," Sayra said, squeezing her friend's hand.

A knock at the door interrupted their moment. "That'll be Nes," Sayra said, her heart fluttering with anticipation.

Kimimari grinned. "Go. Enjoy your night. And Sayra?" She paused at the door. "Be careful out there. Whatever you're getting into... just watch your back, okay?"

Sayra nodded, touched by her friend's concern. "I will. You too, Kim. Stay safe."

With one last hug, Kimimari slipped out, leaving Sayra alone with her thoughts.

As Sayra stepped into the hallway, she was greeted by the sight of Lynn and Nes. Lynn, dressed in her Valkyrie armor like Kimimari, offered a warm smile and a wave as she prepared for her patrol duty. Nes, on the other hand, was a vision in a deep sapphire gown that complemented her ice-blue eyes perfectly.

Nes's dress was a masterpiece of simplicity and elegance. The off-shoulder neckline accentuated her graceful neck, while the fitted bodice flowed into a skirt that moved like water with every step. Her dark hair was swept up in an intricate braid and adorned with small silver pins.

"You both look incredible," Lynn said, her eyes sparkling before growing distant. "Have fun tonight, and be safe."

Sayra pulled Lynn into a quick hug, conveying everything in that gesture. When she pulled back, she caught the way Lynn's eyes blinked hard as she shooed them away.

Sayra and Nes made their way toward the reception hall, and the excited chatter of other students echoed in the distance. The atmosphere was electric with anticipation for the evening ahead. Rounding a corner, they nearly collided with Sylven and Emrys. The moment seemed to freeze as Emrys caught sight of Sayra. His usually composed expression faltered, eyes widening as he took in her appearance. For once, the stoic prince seemed at a loss for words.

But so was she.

Emrys wore a beautifully tailored frock coat in a deep midnight blue. The coat fit him perfectly, accentuating his broad shoulders and trim waist. Golden buttons marched down the front, their surfaces polished. The high collar framed his jaw, giving him an air of regal authority. Beneath the coat, a crisp white shirt peeked out, its collar standing stiffly against his neck. A cravat in a shade of deep emerald, perfectly matching Sayra's gown, was tied intricately at his throat. The hint of color brought out the warmth in his dark eyes, which were currently wide with admiration as they took in Sayra's appearance.

His trousers were pressed, falling in a straight line to polished black boots that gleamed. Every detail of his outfit spoke of meticulous care and attention, from the golden cufflinks at his wrists to the subtle embroidery along the edges of his coat. Emrys's black hair was styled neatly. It made him look older and more serious, if that were possible.

Sylven, looking handsome himself in a perfectly tailored beige suit, glanced between Emrys and Sayra. "I think you broke him, Sayra," he quipped, a grin tugging at the corners of his mouth.

Emrys, recovering, cleared his throat. "Sayra, you look absolutely breathtaking," he managed, his voice lower and more intense than usual.

A blush crept up her cheeks, her heart fluttering at the naked admiration in his gaze. "Thank you," she said softly. "You're quite dashing yourself."

Sylven, still grinning, offered his arm to Nessika. "Shall we leave these two to their mutual admiration and head to the ball?" he asked, his tone light but his eyes soft as he looked at Nes.

She laughed a sound of pure joy. "We shall," she agreed, taking Sylven's arm. "Try not to be too late, you two," she added over her shoulder as they walked away.

Left alone, Sayra and Emrys stood for a moment, drinking in the sight of each other. Emrys, resplendent in his formal attire, looked every inch the prince he was. But it was the warmth in his dark eyes, the softening of his usually guarded expression, that truly took Sayra's breath away.

"Shall we?" Emrys asked, offering his arm with a smile that was reserved only for her.

We'll be keeping a close eye on you, Sayra. For your own safety, of course.

The Grand Priest's words haunted her, the insinuation that there was something more behind them raising the hair along the cross tattoo on the back of her neck. But being beside Emrys eased those worries. The restless nights she once had, and the endless cycle of nightmares, ceased to exist when she slept beside him.

She took his arm, promising herself to take it day by day.

"I haven't seen Sylven this happy in a long time," Emrys said, watching as his friend walked with Nes, arm in arm.

A corner of Sayra's mouth quirked up, recalling the admission Sylven had made to her.

There's someone else. Someone I think I might have feelings for.

Sayra's heart warmed at Nes's laugh and the way Sylven seemed to bask in the noise as they disappeared ahead. "I think it has been a long time coming."

Emrys and Sayra paused at the threshold of the reception hall, taking in the breathtaking sight before them. The grand space, normally impressive, had been transformed into a magical wonderland for the graduation ball.

The white-veined granite floors gleamed, polished to mirrorlike perfection. A plush burgundy carpet ran wide down the middle, creating a regal pathway leading to the celebration's heart. The room was alive with motion and color, a sea of formal attire mingling with the distinctive dresses of Valkyries and women and the coattails of Arcanists and men. Two sweeping staircases, their railings entwined with intricate wooden carvings resembling vines, curved gracefully upward to connect to the second floor.

At the center of the hall, rising majestically to create a third floor, stood an enormous dais. Upon it, an exceptionally skilled orchestra played, their melodies weaving through the air and filling the space with joyous music. The musicians were dressed in formal black and white. Crystal chandeliers, each a work of art in its own right, appeared to float from the arched ceiling. They cast a soothing, ethereal light over the gathering, their facets sparkling like countless stars.

Here and there, the more colorful attire of family members who had traveled for the occasion added splashes of vibrant hues to the mix. Staff members, dressed in their formal best, circulated with trays of refreshments. The air was filled with the soft clink of glasses, the murmur of conversation, and bursts of laughter. Near one of the staircases, Sayra spotted a group of her fellow Valkyries, their faces alight with excitement. On the other side of the room, a cluster of Arcanists engaged in animated discussion, their hands moving in the practiced gestures of those accustomed to wielding majik.

"It's beautiful," Sayra breathed, her eyes wide as she took in the scene.

Emrys nodded, his eyes not on the decor but on Sayra's face. "Shall we?" he asked, offering his arm once more.

As the excitement in the reception hall reached its peak, a hush fell over the crowd. Jax Zefare, clad in his formal Holy Family robes, ascended the steps to the central dais. His presence commanded attention, and all eyes turned to him as he raised his hands for silence.

"Esteemed graduates, honored students, and distinguished guests," Jax began, his voice carrying easily through the vast space. "It is my great pleasure to welcome you all to this evening's celebration."

Sayra felt Emrys's hand tighten on hers as they listened. Around them, a sea of faces looked up at Jax with anticipation. But her stomach sank low. Somewhere close, she could sense Sylven's distaste rippling through their link.

"To our graduates," Jax continued, his gaze sweeping across the room, "I offer my sincerest congratulations. You have proven yourselves worthy of the title you now bear—Arcanist. Your dedication, perseverance, and commitment to the protection of our realm are a testament to your character."

A swell of pride rippled through the crowd.

"And to those who have completed another year of study," Jax added, his tone warming, "I commend your hard work and growth. Each year brings new challenges, new lessons, and new opportunities for greatness. You have risen to meet them all with admirable determination."

Sayra snorted. *You could say that.*

"As you stand here tonight on the cusp of new beginnings, I urge you to remember the oaths you have taken, the bonds you have forged, and the sacred duty that now rests upon your shoulders." Jax's voice took on a more solemn tone. "The path ahead may not always be easy, but I have every confidence that you will face whatever challenges arise with courage and conviction."

Then Jax's expression lightened, his trademark lopsided smile crossing his face. "But tonight," he declared, his voice ringing with enthusiasm, "we celebrate your achievements! Let the music play, let laughter fill these halls, and let the dancing begin!"

With a grand gesture, Jax signaled to the orchestra. The first notes of a lively waltz floated about as applause erupted throughout the hall.

"By the power vested in me by the Holy Family," Jax proclaimed, "I hereby declare this graduation ball commenced!"

The floor before the dais quickly cleared, forming a large open space. Even after all that had transpired, more than a part of Sayra itched to join the dance.

Sensing this, Emrys turned to her, a questioning look in his eyes. "May I have this dance?" he asked, offering his hand with a bow.

Sayra felt a flutter of excitement in her stomach as she placed her hand in his. "It would be my pleasure," she replied, allowing him to lead her onto the dance floor.

A familiar thrill coursed through her veins. The orchestra's melody swelled around them, and with a graceful movement, they fell into step with the waltz.

Sayra's years of dance training took over, her body moving with fluid precision. She could feel the eyes of the other dancers on them, but her focus was entirely on Emrys. His hand on her waist was firm yet gentle, his touch sending sparks through the fabric of her gown. As they glided across the floor, Sayra decided to test Emrys's skill. She added a subtle complexity to her steps, challenging him to keep up. To her delight, he matched her move for move, his dark eyes glinting with amusement and determination.

"Trying to catch me off guard, are you?" he murmured, a rare smile playing at the corners of his mouth.

Sayra grinned back, feeling daring. "Perhaps. Think you can keep up?"

In response, Emrys executed a flawless turn, spinning Sayra out and drawing her back in with breathtaking precision. The move brought them closer together, their bodies nearly flush. Sayra's breath caught in her throat at the intensity in Emrys's gaze.

They moved together as if they'd been dancing for years, each anticipating the other's movements perfectly. Sayra could feel her heart pounding and not just from the exertion of the dance. As the music reached a crescendo, Emrys dipped Sayra low, supporting her weight effortlessly. Time seemed to stand still as they held the pose, their faces inches apart. Sayra was acutely aware of every point of contact between them, of the strength in Emrys's arms and the warmth of his breath on her cheek.

Then, just before he raised her back up, Emrys leaned in close. His lips brushed her ear as he whispered, his voice low and filled with emotion, "I've studied strategy all my life, but I never planned for you. You're a beautiful surprise that's changed everything."

Sayra's heart skipped a beat at Emrys's words. As he slowly raised her from the dip, their eyes locked, and she saw in his gaze a reflection of her own feelings. Ones that grew deeper than she could have ever imagined.

"You're right," Sayra murmured, her eyes sparkling with a mischievous edge. "You definitely should have had me open my birthday gift from you sooner."

A low chuckle sounded from Emrys, his eyes brimming with amusement. His hand tightened on her waist, drawing her closer as they continued to move with the music.

"I'll remember that for next year," he said.

As they twirled across the dance floor, Sayra became aware of the eyes upon them. Other couples had given them space, watching in awe as they moved with graceful precision. She caught glimpses of familiar faces—Sylven and Nessika, looking on with knowing smiles; Waylen stuffing his face with macarons; even Catara, her expression unreadable as she observed from afar.

But none of that mattered. In that moment, there was only Emrys, the music, and the connection between them that seemed to transcend the physical realm. Sayra could sense the pulse of his majik, intertwining with her own in a dance as intricate as the one their bodies performed. As the music began to wind down, Emrys guided them toward the edge of the dance floor. With a final elegant turn, he brought them to a stop, his hand lingering on her waist even as the last notes faded away.

"Sayra," he began, his voice low and intense, "I—"

But before he could finish, a commotion near the entrance to the hall caught their attention. Heads turned, conversations halted, and a hush fell over the crowd as two figures strode into the room, their presence commanding attention.

Sayra felt Emrys stiffen beside her, his hand dropping from her waist as he straightened to his full height. She followed his gaze, her own body tensing as she recognized the newcomers. Vander and Kenji had arrived, and with them, reality came crashing back down. The magical bubble of their dance shattered, leaving Sayra white knuckled. As Vander's eyes scanned the room, eventually landing on them with a calculated gleam, Sayra steeled herself.

The night of celebration was over.

As the crowd began to shift and mingle after Vander's arrival, Sayra felt a tap on her shoulder. She turned to find Kenji standing before her, his usual smug smile in place.

"Sayra, darling," he said with an exaggerated bow, "might I have the honor of this dance?"

She hesitated, glancing at Emrys. His face was a mask of carefully controlled neutrality, but she could see a dangerous glint to his onyx eyes. With a subtle nod from him, Sayra turned back to Kenji.

"Of course, Kenji," she replied, her voice cool and polite.

As he led her onto the dance floor, Sayra couldn't help but notice the satisfied gleam in his black eyes. His hand on her waist felt possessive, unlike Emrys's gentle touch. They began to move with the music, Kenji's steps precise and calculated.

"You look ravishing tonight, Sayra," he murmured, his eyes roaming over her in a way that made her skin crawl. "Green always was your color."

Sayra forced a smile. "Thank you. You're too kind."

As they twirled across the floor, Sayra became increasingly aware of Kenji's scrutiny. His eyes never left her face, as if he was searching for something. The satisfaction in his expression grew with each passing moment, setting Sayra's nerves on edge.

"I must say," Kenji continued, his voice low, "I'm rather pleased with how things have turned out. Wouldn't you agree?"

Sayra's brow furrowed. "I'm not sure I understand what you mean."

His smile widened, revealing teeth that were predatory. "Oh, I think you do. Or you will very soon."

As the music began to wind down, Kenji pulled Sayra closer. "Enjoy your last night at Saint Highburn, my darling. The coming year will be quite different."

Sayra stiffened, pulling back to look Kenji in the eye. "What are you talking about?"

Kenji's expression was one of mock innocence. "Oh, nothing you need to worry about. I'll be leaving early tomorrow, so I wanted to make sure we had this moment."

As the final notes of the song faded away, Kenji released Sayra with a flourish. "Until we meet again, Sayra. And we will meet again very soon."

With that, he melted into the crowd, leaving Sayra standing alone on the dance floor, her mind racing with the implications of his words. As she made her way back to Emrys, dodging dancing people, she couldn't shake the feeling Kenji's ominous warning and entrance with Vander were linked.

The joy and magic of the evening had vanished, replaced by a gnawing sense of dread.

Emrys turned from another Arcanist as Sayra approached, her face betraying her unease. "Is everything all right?" he asked quietly. Beside him, the Arcanist he was speaking to left to join others wearing the white color of Zendiya. Nikolay, with his pale blond hair and emerald eyes, gave her a spare glance before talking to the two other Arcanists beside him.

Strange, she thought. Seeing any of those three part ways in social gatherings was rare.

Sayra put her back to the marble wall, watching the ball unfold warily. "I'm not sure," she admitted, her voice low. "Kenji said something unsettling. And with Vander's arrival, I can't help but feel like something's brewing."

Emrys nodded, his dark eyes scanning the room. "We'll discuss it later," he murmured. "For now, let's try to get through the evening without raising suspicion."

They moved to the side of the dance floor, finding a spot where they could observe the room while maintaining a semblance of normalcy. Sylven and Nessika twirled past them, lost in their own world. Despite what happened, Sayra couldn't help but smile at the sight of her friends so happy.

"They look good together," she said, trying to lighten the mood.

Emrys hummed in agreement. "Indeed. It's nice to see Sylven finally letting his guard down."

How far those two had come.

As the night wore on, they mingled with others, laughed at jokes, and even shared another dance. But beneath the facade of celebration, both Sayra and Emrys remained vigilant, their senses attuned to any hint of danger or deceit. By the time the ball wrapped up, everyone dispersing for their quarters, Sayra was ready to crawl into bed and throw away her heels.

She did *not* miss how her feet ached after hours of wearing them.

Sayra sank onto her bed, her freshly cleaned hair leaving a cool trail on the back of her gray cotton pajamas. The ball had exhausted her, but her mind could not shake Kenji's ominous words.

She glanced at her desk, where her mother's journal was hidden. With a sigh, Sayra rose and retrieved the book, settling back onto her bed with it cradled in her lap.

For a moment, she simply stared at the cover, tracing the faded embossing with her fingertips. Then she opened it to the last entry she had read.

The familiar scrawl of her mother's handwriting greeted her.

This journal is nearly full, and I find myself at a crossroads. The cache is set up at [REDACTED]. Everything's in place. Weapons, supplies, and, most importantly, the family journals. Generations of von Lykken knowledge, all the truths the Holy Family wants buried. It's all there waiting.

My work isn't done. There's more out there, answers scattered across the world. I need to keep moving and searching. Ancient sites and forgotten lore are the keys to understanding the relics, and the Holy Family's power is out there somewhere. I have to find it.

[REDACTED] in Faenda will keep an eye on things and keep me informed. They're trustworthy. If I need to be reached, it'll be through them. I've done what I can to prepare the way. The rest is up to fate now. I'll keep writing, keep documenting everything I find. This journal's done its job. Time to start a new one.

The truth is out there. I won't stop until I find it.

Sayra closed the journal, tapping her fingers along the spine. She'd read the whole book over and over again, wishing for more. At some point in the coming year, she'd have to return home to find the rest of her family journals in the fake bottom of her trunk. Her mother had said they were still in her room. Her father, Bjørn, declared Sayra's room off-limits after she disgracefully fled from their modest manor.

Sayra wondered who Arene's contact was, circling around the idea of it being Lynn's mother. The two were friends once upon a time. More importantly, she felt like the hidden journals—

Her eyes went wide.

Journals... pages...

Sayra donned her cloak and slipped her aching feet into boots, still sore from the night of dancing in heels. She burst out of her room, the cool night air hitting her face as she raced down the corridor. Her footsteps echoed in the empty hallway, but she paid no heed to the noise.

As she rounded the corner to the Arcanist dormitory, she nearly collided with a startled student. Mumbling a hasty apology, Sayra pressed on, her mind whirling with possibilities. She reached Emrys's door. Without pausing to catch her breath, she knocked urgently, shifting from foot to foot as she waited for a response. The seconds felt like hours.

Emrys opened his door, clearly having just emerged from the shower. His dark hair was damp and tousled, droplets of water still clinging to the ends. He wore simple navy pajama pants and a loose white shirt that clung to his still-damp skin. His juniper, black pepper, and vetiver masculine cologne filled the air. For a moment, Sayra's train of thought derailed completely. She found herself acutely aware of Emrys's presence—the way the thin fabric of his shirt hinted at the lean muscles beneath, the strong set of his shoulders, the way his eyes, alert despite the late hour, focused intently on her.

She walked by him into the room, quickly spelling it for privacy. "Emrys, I've figured it out," she said, her eyes bright with excitement. "The dream, the whispers about hidden pages, it's talking about the other journals my mother left for me in the cache she mentioned."

Emrys blinked, his mind clearly working to catch up with Sayra's revelation. "You know where they are? I thought the location was redacted."

Sayra took a deep breath, forcing herself to organize her thoughts. "My mother's other journals. The ones she mentioned in her last entry. They're hidden in a false bottom of a trunk in my old room. That's what the dream was trying to tell me—we need to get those journals!"

Understanding dawned on Emrys's face, followed quickly by concern. "Are you certain? Making arrangements to visit Faenda might be feasible, but only if we know for sure what to look for."

Sayra's excitement dimmed as the practical challenges of their situation set in, but her determination remained unwavering. "I don't know completely," she admitted. "But this is important, Emrys, regardless. My mother made me swear to keep it secret when we met in Tern, and out of respect for her, I didn't share it earlier, but she told me to return home and read those journals as soon as possible. The Goddess's warning thus far has been proven founded. I think this is our next solid lead."

Emrys nodded slowly, his mind already working on potential solutions. "I understand. Let's speak to my parents and see what we can do to make this happen."

"Thank you, Emrys," she said softly. "For listening, for understanding. I don't know what I'd do without you in all of this."

Emrys smiled, a warm, genuine expression that made Sayra's heart skip a beat. The way his face opened up was utterly charming.

"It's the least I can do," he replied, his voice low and sincere.

In the quiet of the room, Sayra suddenly became acutely aware of their proximity and the intimacy of the moment. Her eyes met his, and an outpouring of affection washed over her.

"You know," she began, a corner of her mouth crooking up, "you looked incredible tonight at the ball. That frock coat, the way you carried yourself... you were every inch the prince." She paused, a full smile playing at her lips. "But this? Seeing you like this, relaxed and unguarded? It might be my favorite version of you yet."

Emrys's took a step toward her, closing the distance between them. She noticed the way his muscles flexed along his arms as they wrapped around her.

"I never thought I'd fall for anyone. I always believed my duty as a Valkyrie would be enough. But you..." She reached up, her hand running along his shoulder "I'm so thankful I fell for you. You've changed everything, and I wouldn't have it any other way."

The air seemed to crackle with unspoken desire. Emrys's hand came up to his cheek to cover hers, his touch warm and comforting.

"Sayra," he murmured, his gaze intense. "You've changed everything for me too. I never knew I could feel this way about anyone."

Slowly, giving her every chance to pull away, Emrys leaned in. Their lips met in a soft, tender kiss that quickly deepened, filled with all the passion they'd been holding back. Sayra's arms wound around Emrys's neck, pulling him closer. She could feel the warmth of his body, the strong beat of his heart thumping through his chest.

For the remaining hours of that last night at Saint Highburn Monastery, she didn't think once of the Holy Family or their odds of beating everything stacked against them.

Chapter Thirty-Three

EMRYS

The first rays of dawn were just beginning to paint the sky as Emrys made his way through the quiet corridors of Saint Highburn Monastery. His footsteps echoed off the stone walls, the sound amplified in the early morning stillness. Despite the hour, his mind was sharp, focused on one last task before their departure. He reached the library, its massive oak doors looming before him. Emrys slipped inside. The scent of old parchment and leather-bound books enveloped him as he navigated the towering shelves, making his way to the secluded alcove where he often received coded messages from his family.

His heart quickened as he approached the spot, hope and apprehension warring within him. But as he searched the usual hiding tome, he found nothing. No message, no update, and no reassurance from his parents. Emrys frowned, a sense of unease settling in his stomach. It was unusual for his family to maintain such prolonged silence, especially given the gravity of their situation. The last he'd heard, they were pursuing a lead on the daemon hybrid in Tern, a creature that could potentially upend everything they thought they knew about the Horde. They had promised to keep him informed, to share any new developments before their in-person meeting. Yet there he stood, empty-handed and increasingly concerned.

With a final sweep of the area, Emrys reluctantly accepted there would be no last-minute communication. He made his way out of the library, his mind churning with possibilities. Had something gone wrong? Were his parents unable to send a message safely? Or was there simply nothing new to report?

As he emerged into the courtyard from the small marketplace, bustling activity surrounded him. Despite the early hour, the monastery was alive with movement. Students lugged trunks and bags, calling out goodbyes to friends. Valkyries in polished armor stood at attention, their eyes scanning for any sign of threat. Arcanists hurried about, performing last-minute checks on their routes and inventory.

Emrys made his way to the main gate, where several carriages stood ready for departure. He spotted Sayra first, her braided golden hair and silver ribbon swaying behind her. She was deep in conversation with Nessika, both of them gesturing animatedly in their armor. Sylven leaned against the carriage nearby, his usual scowl softer as he watched Nessika.

"Rys!" Waylen's voice cut through the general clamor. His friend was waving from beside one of the carriages, a broad grin on his face. "Over here!"

As Emrys approached, he took in the scene before him. Their small group had gathered, an island of calm in the sea of activity. Sayra turned, her green eyes brightening as she caught sight of him. For a moment, the memory of their kiss the night before flashed through his mind, sending a warm thrill through his body.

"There you are," Sayra said, her tanned skin crinkled as she noted his unease. That thin line of a scar under her eyes shifted from the movement. "Everything all right?"

Emrys nodded, pushing aside his concerns for the moment. "Yes, just doing a final check," he said, his tone carefully neutral. He'd share his worries with her later when they had more privacy. "Have you been able to check on Lynn before we head out?"

Pain glossed over Sayra's eyes, and her fingers clutched at her sides. "Yes. She's hurting. I wish more than anything she could come with us."

Emrys's shoulders loosened a hair, regret and culpability clinging to him like a second skin. More than almost anything, he had hoped his family could secure her a contract, but as he hadn't heard back... It seemed the Holy Family was keeping her there in the meantime. Perhaps he could figure something out once he convened with his parents. He owed it to Lynn to get her out of there, especially after all that happened with Casber.

"We'll figure something out. I promise," he said quietly, willing it to be true.

Sayra's chin lifted just so, her face full of trust and compassion. A face he'd go to any length to keep that way, even if it meant going extraordinary distances.

"Well, we're all set here," Sylven said, his hazel eyes scanning the group. His burnt-orange vest shifted over his white long-sleeved shirt as he patted the carriage. "Shall we get this show on the road?"

They said their goodbyes to Waylen, who would be leaving the following day with Jayde to go to his home on the other side of Acacea. He promised to visit them as soon as possible, but he had familial affairs to see to first. As they began to load their belongings into the carriages, Emrys couldn't shake the feeling that something was amiss. His eyes flicked toward the second carriage loaded with Vander and Breane's belongings. Neither of them were present.

He helped Sayra into the carriage, their hands lingering together a moment longer than strictly necessary. As he climbed in after her, Emrys took one last look at Saint Highburn Monastery. The massive marble and stone structure loomed against the brightening sky, its spires reaching the heavens. For all its faults, for all the secrets and lies it held, it was a work of utter beauty. A host to unimaginable evils.

"Well now, little brother. I do thank you for kindly waiting for my arrival," Vander called out, a sideways grin revealing his rows of white teeth.

Emrys didn't spare him a moment's glance, slamming the heavy carriage door behind him. Nessika didn't ask before drawing the curtains closed, her own face wrathful at the sight of the crowned prince.

As the carriage lurched into motion, Emrys settled back into the cushions.

⸺⚭✦⚮⸺

The sun was dipping above them, casting long shadows across the cobblestone streets of Tern as their carriage rolled to a stop. Relief and anticipation settled in Emrys's chest. They had arrived at last, albeit with the knowledge their respite would be brief. Tomorrow would bring another early departure, but they had time to rest.

As they disembarked, Emrys couldn't help but notice the determined set of Sayra's jaw. Even after hours of travel, she was focused, her mind still whirling from hours of majik practice. The moment they were secluded, he knew she'd be back at it. As the Navarre staff bustled around them, replenishing supplies and preparing for the next day's journey, Emrys gravitated toward her. In a moment when no one was looking, he slipped his hand into hers, relishing the warmth of her skin against his.

Sayra's mouth curved just a bit, but her demeanor was casual since they tried not to act too forward around others. The remainder of the evening passed in a blur of majik practice and stolen glances. When they retired to their rooms in the Navarre estate, Emrys found sleep elusive, his mind too full of all he had to share with his parents in the coming days.

Dawn came all too soon, painting the sky in hues of pink and gold as they set out for Korith. The journey was long, but for once, it didn't feel tedious. The carriage was filled with easy conversation and occasional bursts of laughter.

Emrys marveled at the change. Gone was the tension that had once existed between Sylven, Nessika, and Sayra. In its place was a camaraderie that warmed Emrys's heart. Nessika, usually so reserved, was joining in, her sharp wit eliciting chuckles from all of them.

"I never thought I'd see the day when Sylven willingly left a book untouched," Nessika quipped at one point, gesturing to the forgotten tome in Sylven's luggage.

He rolled his eyes, but there was no real annoyance in the gesture. "Perhaps I have grown fond of the company I keep," Sylven retorted, his gaze softening as it landed on Nessika.

As they approached Korith, the landscape changed, giving way to the sprawling cityscape. The river that cut through the center of the city glimmered in the afternoon sun, a lifeline connecting Korith to the distant capital and, beyond that, the vast ocean separating them from Thapula.

The summer heat had the men rolling up their sleeves in the afternoon sun. Emrys envied the Valkyries and their seemingly inhuman tolerance for the temperature, their armor remaining firmly in place until they crossed the city limits.

Throughout the next day of travel, Sayra's resolve seemed inexhaustible. Despite hours of practice in the carriage and during their evenings, she wasn't able to master pulling majik only from ley lines. Over and over, her mind pulled from her own reserves. And while her reserves were vast, Sayra wanted to test the limits of her majik using only ley line sources. Emrys watched her with a mixture of admiration and curiosity, his mind working to understand the full extent of the relic's influence on her abilities.

"It's remarkable," he mused aloud as they left Korith behind. "The way your majik regenerates is unlike anything I've ever seen."

Sayra nodded, her brow furrowing in concentration. "It's strange," she admitted. "When I draw from myself, it takes much more out of me. But forgoing my own majik stores allows me to tap the endless supply of the lines below. It's not taxing on me like it is for other Arcanists."

As the journey wore on, they remained ever vigilant for the Horde. In a moment of what Emrys could only describe as shared madness, Sayra and Nessika decided to jog alongside the carriage, claiming a need for exercise. Emrys and Sylven exchanged amused glances, content to remain in the shade of the coach. As the women's laughter drifted in through the windows, Emrys relaxed into his seat.

The city of Mouver, where they'd meet with his mother and father, peaked over a grassy hill ahead. They all became visibly relieved at the sight, knowing it wouldn't be long until they reached their final destination. Sayra poked her head out the window, squinting her eyes at the distant blur.

"Nes, can you take a second to look at this? I'm not sure if I'm seeing correctly," Sayra said, swooping back into the carriage to switch spots with Nessika.

Half a minute later. "You're not seeing things," Nes confirmed grimly, twisting her head to look at Emrys. "The city is on fire."

"What?" Sylven shot forward, unable to spot it.

"You can't see the smoke without our vision," Sayra said, a finger tapping on the cross rune on the back of her neck. Valkyries had better senses in general.

Sylven's head swiveled toward Emrys. "What does this mean?" he asked.

Sayra and Nessika both looked at him, their faces drawn and hands gravitating toward their weapons.

Emrys's heart chilled, his instincts screaming something was terribly wrong. "Nothing good," he replied, his words heavy with apprehension. "We'll have to gain a better perspective when we near."

They lapsed into an uneasy silence, their shared dread pressing down on them like a physical force. As they drew closer, the true extent of the situation became horrifyingly clear. Thick plumes of smoke rose from the eastern part of the city, twisting and writhing against the sky like malevolent spirits. The entry gate stood wide open, a gaping maw leading into an ominous emptiness. There was no sign of movement, no hint of life—just an eerie, unnatural stillness that made Emrys's skin crawl.

His mind raced, grappling with the implications. His parents, the king and queen, were supposed to be there. The thought of what might have befallen them sent a surge of panic through his body, which he ruthlessly suppressed. He couldn't afford to lose control.

Sylven's face had gone pale, his eyes wide with horror. Emrys knew they were thinking the same thing—this was bad, possibly worse than anything they had encountered before. But they had no choice. Turning back would mean certain death, caught out in the open when night fell.

And the fate of the kingdom, perhaps of the entire world, hung in the balance.

With a shared look of grim determination, they prepared to face whatever horrors awaited them within the city walls. The majik-wielders put on their gauntlets, Sayra doubling down with her *spyd* as well as her own jeweled gloves.

Sayra and Nessika were already moving, their bodies tense with anticipation as they leaped from the carriage, weapons at the ready. Breane followed suit, the three Valkyries forming a protective line in front of the nervous drivers and the agitated horses. Despite their differences, Sayra and Nessika communicated with short words to Breane.

Emrys met Sylven's eyes one last time before they, too, disembarked. The sound of their feet hitting the ground seemed unnaturally loud in the oppressive silence that blanketed the area. Vander climbed out from his own carriage. His upturned nose was flared, and his gray eyes were wide as he followed behind them. As they made their way down the main road, Emrys felt his gorge rise. The devastation was beyond anything he had imagined. Abandoned carts littered the street around the gate, their contents spilling across the cobblestones. Here and there, dark stains marred the ground—blood, he realized with a sickening lurch of his stomach.

Their carriages remained behind, the road too cluttered for them to pass. Emrys found himself grateful for the distance it put between them and their only means of escape. Whatever had happened there, whatever they were about to face, at least their drivers would have a chance to flee if things went wrong. Emrys's hands tightened, his eyes darting from shadow to shadow, expecting at any moment to see movement, to face whatever force had brought such destruction. But there was nothing.

Just emptiness, devastation, and the growing certainty that something unspeakable had occurred there.

As they rounded a corner, the full extent of the carnage came into view. Emrys felt his breath catch in his throat, his mind struggling to process what he was seeing. In that moment, standing amidst the ruins of what should have been a thriving city, he realized they had stepped into a nightmare.

Guards that manned the gates had been slaughtered, grisly splotches of gore where they were drug into their final resting places. Carnage was scattered everywhere; buildings were obliterated, wood and stone littered the ground, and deep scores marred the stone pathway. Shattered glass spilled through windows. In one, a young lady no older than Sayra was splayed out. People of each gender and all ages were dead. Sayra checked the condition of a few in vain in the hope of finding a survivor.

There were none.

With each step deeper into the city, the wrongness of the situation intensified. There should have been sounds. People talking, animals moving, the general bustle of city life. Instead, there was nothing but the soft crunch of their footsteps and the ominous crackle of distant flames.

Sylven wiped his clammy brow beside Emrys, the scene surreal around them. Dried blood, rigid corpses, and destruction of unparalleled amounts extended in every direction. Nothing about the city made sense. The guards and positioning of the residents were all in places that indicated normal daily routines. They weren't all sheltering in place, which would have occurred in the event of a Horde attack, and not a single weapon had been drawn; yet the mass damage and markings in the stone indicated a daemonic presence. Was it the new Horde hybrid that did this? There weren't any traces of fear majik, so Emrys doubted any normal Horde lingered.

By his best estimates, the fallen hadn't been dead longer than half a day at most. Whatever killed them had to be nearby.

The city square lay ahead, several buildings smoking from a still-smoldering fire as they picked their way through the carnage. Then Emrys noticed something. It was like a switch had been flicked in his elder brother. Vander strode ahead, almost nonchalant about the destruction of his people. Something flashed in his eyes when his brother took the lead, hands in his trouser pockets and whistling a somber tune.

It completely unnerved Emrys, that pestering feeling telling him to run. That something terrible and far worse than the Horde ambush at the lake was about to occur.

And that Vander orchestrated it all.

Chapter Thirty-Four

SAYRA

A change in the wind's direction sent smoke wafting by Sayra, her nose wrinkling as they progressed into the middle of the city. Market stalls were completely obliterated, and the dead were dispersed about the cracked and broken cobblestone. Statues crumbled throughout the square, and sharp scores, almost clawlike in the way they raked across stone and wood, ruined beautiful architecture. The only sounds hailed from their echoed steps, the occasional crackle of fire eating away at the scant remnants of wood, and Vander's irritating whistle.

They circled the central podium of the market square, closing in as a tight-knit group as they happened upon a blocked road, an extraordinary number of lined carriages tossed and splintered, most with people still inhabiting them. Torn banners hung from rafters, gathered citizens brightly colored in various clothing styles lining the sides of the roadways, their bodies piled and strewn haphazardly.

Piled.

Sayra's brows knitted together.

Vander hastened his speed, forcing Sayra and the others to quicken behind him. The procession winded throughout the main road, appearing like a parade of sorts, with the breaks of performers piled between gaps of carriages. Even the horses died, indicating a death caused by anything but the Horde's hands. The visual information she gathered was a mess, and nothing made any reasonable sense about what could have caused the atrocity.

Sayra ground her teeth together, knowing it couldn't be long until they happened across the royal ensemble. She hoped with every fiber of her being she was completely wrong and Emrys's parents weren't among those counted dead.

But her gut told her it was only a matter of time before they discovered the bodies.

Sylven felt similarly through their link, their combined anxiety gnawing at her as they neared the end of the line. An elegant carriage remained intact—tattered but standing. Emrys broke through their ranks, rushing to where Vander inspected the carved wood barring the way into the cabin. He pushed his brother aside with a snarl, forcing the door open and frantically scanning the interior. Sayra rushed behind him, worried about his state of mind and sending one last prayer to the Goddess his parents weren't within.

Emrys froze, his eyes locking on a shadow on the bench within.

Sayra pulled close to him, her eyes marking two crowns on the velvet seats inside. Purposefully placed, drops of blood flecked each. Behind her, Vander's tune intensified, his feet carrying him further down the street, where the population of the deceased dwindled.

"Emrys." Sayra softly broke him from his trance, placing a hand on his shoulder.

Distraught, his head swiveled on its axis, his breaths coming faster. Sayra's heart twisted, knowing the immense pain he was tormented with upon seeing his parents' crowns and after witnessing his city snuffed by some unknown force. Sayra could only imagine what he was going through. Emrys, always a master of his every word and every movement, turned and reached for his brother.

Breane moved to intercept him, but Sayra's arm shot out, her *spyd* wrapping around the Valkyrie's torso as she yanked the blonde guardian off her feet. Nessika shot Sayra a knowing glance before rounding behind her Arcanist.

With one brutal movement, Emrys gripped Vander's neck and slammed him against a stone wall, his face vividly depicting the definition of ire. "What did you do?" he shouted, his body trembling.

Vander gasped, a self-satisfied grin splitting his reddening face. "I must say, I always amused myself with taking an estimate of what would bring you to snap. Whomever would have guessed it was two crowns in a broken shack of wood?"

Breane yanked forward, throwing Sayra off-kilter as she stumbled to reign in the Valkyrie. "Let me go, Sayra," she growled, her face more than a little peeved at the interference.

Fury coiled a dark snake inside of her, wringing very little desire out of her to help Breane. Sayra pretended to consider the Valkyrie's request for a moment. "Let me go, Sayra. *Please.*" She smiled a devilish thing.

"*Please*," Breane seethed, her face snarling.

"No, no. That simply won't do. You must repeat the entirety of the line all at once. It's far more harmonious that way." Sayra sighed, woefully shaking her head. She knew her wrath showed in her green eyes.

"Where are our parents?" Emrys asked, his voice laden with the promise of violence.

The angry Valkyrie repeated Sayra's exact phrase. Sayra just gave Breane a pouty look in response. "I think not."

Vander's Valkyrie then moved to fight in earnest.

"Stop, Breane!" Vander called out, halting her charge toward Sayra. "Let's lead them to my parents' place of residence." His words were breathy from the force against his throat.

Emrys released his brother, pushing him forward forcefully. "Show us. But Vander..." Emrys trailed off, his elder brother giving him a look that read: *Well? Get it out.* "If I find you have meddled in any part of this, I *will* kill you myself."

Sayra's arm lowered in distracted concern, this version of Emrys far crueler than any she'd seen before. He hated his brother. Sure. He would justifiably be in the right to hold any sort of hatred against his brother for Casber and Lynn's sake, much less this. *Helvete*, Sayra would make the same promise toward Vander if she were in Emrys's place and would support him if he did. But Emrys wasn't the sort to be rash and impulsive and act on anger in such a way.

But perhaps he had a darker side.

The air grew thick with dread as they approached the Navarre manor. She wrapped her weapon methodically, the familiar motions a poor distraction from the horror that surrounded them. Her eyes met Sylven's, and the grim set of his jaw only amplified the sick feeling in her stomach. Vander's mournful tune grated on her nerves, the eerie melody seeming to twist the very air around them. As they neared the grand oak doors adorned with the Navarre crest, Sayra's skin prickled with foreboding. The gold leaf tracing intricate patterns across the wood gleamed dully, as if tarnished by the devastation around it.

With a sickening crack, Vander's kick sent one of the doors splintering inward. The sound echoed through the eerie silence, making Sayra flinch.

The foyer that greeted them was a nightmarish blend of opulence and horror. The grandeur of the space—the sweeping marble staircase, the glittering crystal chandelier—only served to heighten the wrongness of the scene. Sayra's eyes were immediately drawn to the two motionless figures sprawled across the bloodstained carpet at the center of the foyer. Her heart stopped beating as Emrys lurched forward, a strangled sound escaping his throat.

Fighting back the urge to rush to Emrys's side, Sayra forced herself to focus. She and Nessika split off, their movements fluid and practiced despite the tremor of fear that ran through them both. Sayra's eyes darted from shadow to shadow, every darkened corner a potential threat.

The afternoon light streaming through the tall windows felt wrong, too bright and cheerful for the grim scene before them. It cast long shadows across the room, transforming familiar objects into looming, sinister shapes. The ornate furnishings stood as silent witnesses to whatever violence had occurred there, their polished surfaces reflecting fractured images of the devastation.

As Sayra moved deeper into the room, the wrongness of it all pressed in on her. The air was heavy with the metallic scent of blood, undercut by lingering traces of expensive perfumes and polished wood. It was a nauseating combination that made her stomach churn.

Her gaze was drawn upward to the second-floor balcony overlooking them. The intricate marble balustrade, once a thing of beauty, was haunting.

A sudden scuffling sound from upstairs shattered the oppressive silence. Sayra's head snapped toward the noise, her eyes locking with Emrys's across the room. In that moment of shared understanding, a chill ran down her spine. They weren't alone.

With agonizing slowness, Sayra began to move toward the staircase. Each step felt like an eternity, the plush carpet muffling her footfalls.

The hair on the back of her neck stood on end, every nerve in her body screaming that danger lurked just out of sight.

A soft creaking sound echoed through the foyer as Vander and Breane climbed up the other stairwell winding to the second floor. But another noise echoed further up. Sayra froze, her breath catching in her throat. In the silence that followed, she could hear the rapid thudding of her own heart.

Something was up there. Waiting.

Vander spread his arms across the length of the cherry wood banister separating him from the twenty-foot drop into the foyer, his expression disdainful as he watched the scene unfold with his Valkyrie by his side.

A curse slipped past Sylven's lips, drawing Sayra's attention. Emrys was deathly pale, falling to a single knee beside the two bodies. Sayra's eyes stung, her mouth pressing into a firm line. His parents...

Sylven kneeled next to him, brows low as he twisted his face away from the sight. They exchanged whispered words.

Sayra shifted toward the dead, noting the lack of any external damage to their forms. Only dried blood leaked from their orifices. The hair on the back of her neck rose from the obvious conclusion. She faced Nes, exchanging a look that spoke volumes. Her friend dipped her chin. Sayra lowered her head as if in mourning, her soul drawing strength from the relic and a vivid picture of what she wanted the majik to do. Behind her, Sayra sensed the shuffle of boots, dozens of pairs in movement at last.

The trap was sprung once again.

"Stop her," a deep voice warned from above, propelling her mouth to quicken the remaining words. "She's using majik!"

Sayra pled for the relic's power and the unspoken majik to form as feet tramped down the stairs, her mind drawing power from the ley lines far below. Sayra knew what the consequences would be if she failed. There was limited time to act. But it was all or nothing, everything at stake during this pivotal turning point.

Majik thrummed through her skin, flowing from the earth into her veins and out of her body in a lightning-fast burst.

At least eighteen guards swarmed the bottom floor from all angles, the first colliding with the thin veil of writhing translucent flames with a terrible scream. The guard's entire left arm and right foot burned to ash at the brief contact. His body collapsed and convulsed on the ground beside Sayra.

The scream caused Sayra's focus to slip, her mind pulling from her own reserves instead of the ley lines. She cursed, desperately trying to redirect the source while maintaining the unspoken spell.

It encapsulated their small group from the attackers around them. Emrys's face rose to the betrayal before him, his face pointed away from Sayra.

"Now, I simply must dissuade any of you from acting further," Vander warned, his eyes glued to Sayra's. "Let's all be civilized about this, and no one will force my hand. We can all survive this if you indulge restraint."

"*Dra til helvete!*" Sayra shouted, her hand raising in his direction. Go to Hell.

With her finger, she singled Vander out. It pointed with the promise of death, the incoming excruciating spell she'd set upon his very bones. The crowned prince blanched, his eyes tinted with fear at the threat he knew she posed against them all. Sayra opened her mouth to cast the spell, to enact the death Vander deserved for murdering his own people and parents, for Casber's death and Lynn's trauma, and for causing Emrys such anguish at the inconceivable slaughter. Her eyes narrowed on his, her mouth moving to form the word that would spell his death. Vander lurched backward, attempting to escape.

"Sayra, darling." That deep voice distracted her from above, his hands clasped over the railing beside Vander. Kenji assessed her with a collector's eye, impressed by what he saw judging by the delight shining in those autumn-gold eyes. "You won't kill him. You never were capable of such action toward another life, not even to put that poor bunny out of its misery all those years ago when it limped with a broken leg."

Sayra lowered her hand, taking a moment to reassess their situation before she hastily acted.

Though every cell of her being wanted her to damn the consequences, to raze them all from the surface of the earth, a distant voice told her Emrys deserved to know the reasoning behind this destruction. He and Sylven could face dire consequences if she simply killed both Droden and Acacea's heirs. It wasn't her place to act. Not yet.

But that arrogant smile on his boxy face nearly had her lashing out at Kenji.

"What the hell are you doing here?" Sylven exploded, his mind connecting the dots at the same time as hers.

Vander allied himself with the Droden heir soon to take over his own throne. They made some backroom deal involving Vander's ascension to the crown. Though, what could Kenji gain? His father was already at death's doorstep, his own elevation sure to arrive that very year. Vander had kept them alive when he could have contrived a much better course of action for their swift deaths if he wished it.

For now, there was time to bide. Sayra's side held an advantage for however long she could maintain the connection with the unlimited source of majik. But she couldn't separate the spell from her own reserves. It chipped away at her stores, especially after practicing all day on her spellwork.

How much longer did she have?

Chapter Thirty-Five

SAYRA

Her mind continued to work to source her majik from the ley lines, but the more she frantically tried, the more she accidentally dipped into her stores of majik to supply the spell. It was like quicksand, her fear making her slip further and further down.

She gritted her teeth as the guards cautiously approached, forming a perimeter around Sayra's spell. The metallic rasp of swords being drawn sent chills down her spine. Two Arcanists in Droden robes flanked Kenji, their faces impassive masks of loyalty. From the shadows, Akira's wolflike smile gleamed, a predator savoring the moment its prey walked willingly into its den.

"Vander!" Emrys's voice thundered, raw with grief and betrayal. The sheer power in that single word made the guards flinch, a reminder of the prince's strength. It was the voice of a king, more commanding and authoritative than Vander could ever hope to achieve. "Explain yourself. Explain what could possibly entice you to murder the ones who gave you everything!"

Sayra's heart clenched at the pain in Emrys's voice. She longed to comfort him, to shield him from this unimaginable betrayal, but if she moved too much, she feared she'd lose the wrestle with her spell.

Recovering from his momentary unease, Vander brushed down his vest with affected nonchalance. A cruel laugh bubbled from his chest, the sound chilling in its lack of remorse. "You aren't in any position to request such nonsense, little brother."

Nessika's sword slid from its sheath with a menacing hiss, her knuckles white as she gripped the hilt.

Above them, Kenji's eyebrow arched in amusement. "Now, now, Vander. We must provide the explanation, unless you intend to retract your end of our bargain."

Vander's shoulder twitched in irritation at the indirect command. "I'd never dishonor such dealings," he spat, his eyes never leaving Emrys's face. "I'm to be king now, little brother. Our parents were fools. Their aim to reveal the Holy Family's dealings was ludicrous and only spelled our downfall. Had they continued, the Navarre name would be wiped from history and we with it."

"They were our parents!" Emrys's voice shattered, the agony in his words a physical force that made Sayra's chest ache. He rose from the ground, his body trembling with grief and rage. "They loved you!"

"They never treated me as if they did!" Vander screamed, his carefully cultivated facade crumbling as his face purpled with fury. "I was never more than a disappointment when compared to their golden child, their precious second son everyone wished was the eldest." He stalked toward the barrier, each step deliberate and menacing down the stairs. "Every idea of mine was discarded with a patronizing laugh, a wave of the hand at their airheaded son they feared would inherit the throne."

Sayra couldn't help but remember the way Queen Evangelina's face had tightened when greeting Vander, like it had been forced.

Inches from the barrier, Vander halted, his voice dropping to a venomous whisper that only a few could hear. "They planned to do away with the ancient laws, warping and damning tradition so they could set you upon the pedestal instead."

Sayra felt Sylven's shock ripple through their bond, his understanding of Vander's intentions crystallizing with horrifying clarity. His unspoken words echoed in her mind. *Vander is going to kill Rys.*

I won't let that happen, Sayra vowed, her determination hardening even as fear clawed at her throat. A bead of sweat trickled down her temple as she maintained the barrier, her eyes locked on Emrys.

He shifted, his side profile to her. The devastation on Emrys's face was unbearable to witness. His shoulders sagged under the weight of his brother's betrayal, his parents' murder, and the realization that everything he had known and loved was crumbling around him. Tears glistened in his eyes, threatening to spill over at any moment. In that instant, Sayra saw not the composed prince or the powerful Arcanist but a broken young man whose world had been shattered beyond recognition. The urge to rush to him, to hold him and shield him from the nightmare, was almost overwhelming.

She carefully stepped in his direction. Slowly, so slowly.

In the back of her mind, pieces kept connecting.

Her eyes flicked toward Kenji.

Seeing as you and Emrys aren't the best of chaps anymore, fortune may have it be the only deal you'll ever manage to scrounge. You'll come to my court this summer to see all that I have to offer. Kenji had warned them at the formal dinner that he would do anything to secure Sylven's allegiance to Droden and her by default.

Then he later cornered them at the *proelium. Though I imagine you two could put on quite a show yourselves. I've heard whispers of your growing prowess. Your coordination during the combat lecture was remarkable.*

Vander or Akira had been whispering to him, feeding him bread-crumbs that trailed back to Sayra's secret.

Put on your best performance, if I may so request. Vander had told Sayra and the others that right before they left to find Lynn and Casber.

Kenji hadn't appeared surprised at Sayra's display of majik today, nor at the declaration of plans against the Holy Family. They all must have been plotting together for some time; everything Sayra knew had to somehow fit into the larger game they played. If she were willing to wager a bet, Sayra would guess the entire ploy for Lynn and Casber's Horde ambush was a display for Kenji's recruitment. To validate her abilities to the Droden heir.

"You were to be king, Emrys. I was never the intended," Vander murmured, a whirl of insanity crossing his twitching eyes. His fingers tensely picked at his nails, pulling Sayra's attention. "They had to be disposed of and in such a manner we could convince the masses of wards falling to the Horde, the entire city lost in a tragic attack. After what happened at Saint Highburn with the failing wards, it would be entirely plausible."

Her stomach sank further. They used the Horde attack against Lynn and Casber for a multitude of purposes, it seemed. But how? How would they nullify powerful wards with their level of majik? They would need an exceptionally experienced Arcanist to do so.

Ice shivered down Sayra's spine.

Were they working with someone in the Holy Family?

Kenji grumbled above him. "Only sacrificed fifteen Arcanists to *nefas* majik for your ambitions, Vander. Murdering an entire city was no easy feat after you brought down the wards. Blackmailing all those Arcanists was not effortless to manage. I lost another five while putting them down after they set death upon this entire city. *I* made it convincing enough to be passable for a Horde attack. Cut to it."

Kenji forced Arcanists to wield deadly *nefas* majik, knowing their souls would be forfeited in exchange for the ungodly power, and he didn't act ashamed in the least. And Vander took down the wards? That made no sense. How...

The shock had Sayra slipping further into her own majik reserves, a clamminess covering her palms.

"Your price is all but paid, Kenji," Vander said, sternly meeting the Droden prince's impatient eyes.

Her rage spilled over when Emrys lowered his head, his shoulders shaking ever so slightly. "*Fy faen*, Kenji!" Sayra shouted, lifting her chin toward the balcony. "*Why*? Why would you kill so many on Vander's behalf? You aren't this person!"

Greed emerged in those narrow eyes of his, Kenji pulling back to clasp his hands behind him. "One could say there had only ever been one object of my attention, one unattainable object of my desire I could never get my hands on." He smirked, chin dipping toward her. "Perhaps you underestimate what a man may do to get what he wants. Just as I underestimated the whims of a woman who wanted to escape it all." His voice drawled out the last word.

Sickened by the insinuation, Sayra wrinkled her nose, the spell around her inching outward in response to her outrage. The guards exclaimed, retreating several steps as they nearly got scorched. Their fallen brother had long since succumbed to shock, no longer moaning in pain. She wanted nothing more than to burn Kenji and Vander to ash, but that part of her that begged for morality, for honor, still clung to her actions.

"Vander, you cannot dispose of Sayra," Emrys got out. "Even without our parents, you know what must be done. We have a duty to our people to rid of the Holy Family."

Snorting, Vander shook his head. "I've done all I could. At this point, she is out of my hands. She brought this on herself, and so did Sylven."

Behind him, Breane's hand rested on the pommel of her sword. She stood silent, with a blank expression, avoiding any of their sight.

You always seem to come out on top, don't you? Breane had been strange with Sayra recently. It hit her that she knew what Vander was planning all along. Was she a middleman between the Holy Family and Vander who orchestrated much of this? If so, it was cunning and clever how they used their own enemies against each other, toying with Vander's bruised ego and Kenji's greed to eliminate the king and queen of Acacea before they posed more of a threat.

It was possible, especially with the way the Holy Family had been hinting to Sayra there was more to her than met their eyes. But if that were the case, why didn't they kill her? That would have destroyed much of Acacea's evidence of their wrongdoings.

Beside Sayra, Sylven practically vibrated with fury. He stepped on Emrys's other side. "You're a disgusting bastard, Kenji. I haven't the slightest clue how you perceive this nasty ploy of yours to work. Sayra will slit your throat the moment you near," he seethed, his chest rising and falling rapidly.

"You think me lowly enough to be incapable of formulating a sound assurance of my dealings?" Kenji jeered, Sayra's gut sinking at the pleasure twisting his mouth. "I have two safeguards, one being yourself, Sylven. You should never have rejected my offer of employment. Alas, now you'll be nothing more than a prisoner in my cells."

Sayra's jaw ticked, Sylven similarly reaching his own limitations for patience. That bead of sweat on her forehead began to fall, fatigue wearing at her from the spell. It was incredibly powerful... at the cost of immense majik wielding.

Nessika's voice rose, her sword twirling in her hand. "We'll kill you all where you stand if you think we'll bend to these demands. I like our odds against you."

The four of them against more than twenty. Sayra pulled her shoulders back, the challenge rising in her eyes. She would die before going to Droden with Kenji. Would die before anyone she cared for was harmed.

Kenji's tongue clucked, the sound dripping with condescension. "That's where you're wrong," he said, his eyes gleaming with malicious triumph. "I have seven Arcanists in my employ present today, each vastly superior to any academy Arcanist." The Droden heir snapped his fingers, and the cloaked Arcanists fell into formation behind him, Vander, Akira, and Breane.

"They are all *sicarius*. You will not win." His gaze slid to Sylven, a threat in his words. Then, turning to Emrys with a look of smug superiority, he continued, "Besides, Sayra wouldn't ever risk the lives of those she holds dear, isn't that right?"

At Kenji's knowing grin, Sayra felt a surge of rage and fear. Her nostrils flared, lips pressing into a thin line as she fought to maintain her composure. The responsibility of everyone's lives pressed down on her, the immensity threatening to crush her.

"My final reassurance is far superior to the previous methods," Kenji went on, his voice laced with cruel satisfaction. "I have several trusted contacts who will release a missive I've personally written and sealed in case of any unfortunate accidents. Each is addressed to the Holy Family, containing detailed accounts of Emrys's plot with his parents and Sayra's accidental gift with majik."

"Don't play with us. I know at least one of the Holy Family are supporting your cause." Sayra gritted her teeth. "Isn't that right, Breane?"

The Valkyrie's brown eyes grew dark, and her knuckles whitened on the pommel of her sword. Next to Kenji, Akira gave Breane a sideways glance, her face narrowing.

Kenji's eyes glittered with malice, his hand waving away the accusation as he delivered the final blow. "You'll all be eliminated with prejudice in the dead of night or perhaps experimented on by the church. Either way, I couldn't care less."

Sayra felt her heart plummet, dread coursing through her veins like ice.

"All this," Emrys's voice cut through the tension, cold and filled with disbelief as he addressed Vander. "For *power*?"

"Naturally," Vander replied, his gaze boring into Emrys's with unflinching determination. "Anything for my *birthright*."

Sayra could feel the others counting on her majik, their hope a palpable force. But what they didn't know was how close she was to burning out. Her time was limited, her strength waning with each passing moment. The crushing realization they couldn't win, that she had put them all in peril with her lack of majik control, circled dangerously in her head.

Brevn's words resurfaced in her mind. *It's okay, Sayra.* Her brother's dead body flashed before her eyes. Casber's screams and Lynn's cries echoed in her ears.

She had to make a decision. Fast.

Her choices pressed down on her, each option seeming worse than the last. If only she had better control of her majik. If only she hadn't been so reckless. The guilt and fear were paralyzing.

Releasing a steadying breath, Sayra closed her eyes, steeling herself for what was to come. When she opened them again, her voice was torn. "What will happen to Emrys and Nessika?"

It was like a knife cut through the air around them.

Dismay shot through the bond, a hand gripping her arm and pulling her attention to Sylven's determined face. *We will fight our way out, Sayra. I won't let Kenji have you, nor will I permit Rys this loss. They cannot win*, he pleaded, his eyes begging her to agree with him.

Incredible sadness hung in her stomach, Sayra unable to weigh the best option. She needed time to think. But that wasn't a luxury she could afford, not when her consciousness began to gray at the edges.

"I believe the best torment would be for Emrys to witness his failure." Vander's voice dripped with malicious glee, his eyes alight with a cruel excitement. "To live through the loss of everyone he holds dear. He can join his parents in the afterlife for all I care afterward."

Emrys stood frozen, his face anguished as his eyes fixed on the pool of blood at his feet. His parents' lifeblood. The sight seemed to physically pain him. Sayra was close enough to touch him, but he didn't seem to notice.

Vander continued, his voice rising with sadistic pleasure. "Sylven will never be seen again, rotting away for his own arrogance in believing he could assault his king without repercussions. I did warn you, Sylven, that you'd regret laying a hand on me."

Sayra saw Sylven flinch, the consequences of his actions crushing down on him.

"As for my brother's Valkyrie, she is to be executed in this very room. With the love of his life to be wed to another man and his parents to rot in the earth for eternity... Well, I don't think justice could be more poetic."

Emrys's head hung low, the cords in his neck standing out in stark relief as he visibly struggled to contain his anguish. The sight of him so broken, so utterly defeated, sent a lance of pain through Sayra's heart.

She heard Nes's sword graze the floor beneath them, and she knew her friend felt the end upon them. The world seemed to tilt beneath Sayra's feet. They had just escaped a near-death situation with the Horde, and it took Casber's life. She couldn't let the world claim any others. It wasn't an option.

She swayed where she stood, her mind reeling as she tried to process everything. She rested a hand on Emrys's shoulder, a spark racing through her arm as their majik intertwined. He blinked, a cool hand clasping hers as he struggled to regain his composure.

As the horror of their situation settled over her, a desperate plan began to form in Sayra's mind. Emrys was strong, she told herself. He was clever. Resourceful. Given time, he would find a way to overcome this, to rise above the tragedy and reclaim what was rightfully his. If she could play the sacrifice, if she could save them all, then maybe... just maybe... all of this wouldn't be in vain. Her decision pressed down on her. But as she looked at her friends, at Emrys still struggling with grief, she knew what she had to do.

With a deep breath, Sayra prepared herself for what was to come. Her heart ached with the knowledge of the pain she was about to cause, but she pushed it aside. For the greater good, for the lives of those she loved, she would do what needed to be done. In that moment, standing amidst the ruins of everything they had fought for, Sayra made her choice. Even if it meant sacrificing herself in the process.

Everything would work. Emrys would ensure it. Sayra believed it.

Through their minds, she shared her plan with Sylven. She ignored his protests, pleading with him to understand and play along. They would all be together again, but they had to put every bet on Emrys and do what they could to achieve their victory in the end. Despite her assurances, Sylven's hazel eyes were devastated by her decision.

"Emrys," Sayra said quietly beside him, his pain-glazed eyes meeting her silver-lined ones. She leaned into him, her own legs feeling weak. Her voice lowered so only they could hear. "Do you trust me?"

He only nodded, a glimmer of himself returning to those deep gray eyes. The hope tore at her. At what she was about to do.

To Sylven, she said, *Be there for him after this. For Lynn as well. They both will need you and Nes more than ever. Know that you all matter so very much to my heart. This isn't goodbye.*

Sylven's eyes misted.

Emrys's strong arm steadied her as her head became light.

Sayra locked eyes with Nessika's wide ones over her shoulder, giving her a nod of reassurance before facing Kenji. The only one she believed capable of negotiating.

"Kenji, I will willingly go with you. I'll freely bind my hand with yours, without question and without resistance," Sayra breathed, her heavy heart fluttering with mourning at all she'd lose. Who she'd lose. "But only on two conditions and only by oath."

A callous laugh erupted from Vander as he grasped the railing, rocking back on his heels. "What makes you believe yourself to be in any position to declare such ridiculous notions?"

"Hold it, Vander," Kenji interrupted, his eyes glistening with victory. "I wish to hear her prettied words."

"Nessika will be spared," Sayra said. Her breaths came quicker. "She will remain with Emrys as his Valkyrie."

Waving a hand for her to continue, Kenji seemed uncaring of the first demand. A trivial affair for him.

"Sylven, Nessika, and Emrys will not be made prisoners, and none of them will be physically harmed or restrained in any manner."

Ticking his head, Kenji considered before responding. "I would concede to the first demand. Though I cannot abide by the rest."

An incredulous laugh escaped Vander. "I cannot abide by either."

Sayra's heart pounded in her chest, her decision crashing down upon her. She knew she had one chance, one desperate gambit to secure a path to their eventual freedom. Failure was not an option.

Drawing upon every ounce of strength and determination within her, Sayra unleashed her majik in a cataclysmic explosion.

The world around them erupted into chaos.

The roof of the building was torn away as if made of paper, walls crumbling outward in a deafening roar. The very earth beneath their feet began to tremble and quake, guards crying out in terror as they were thrown to the ground. Even those protected by Sayra's barrier were forced to their knees by the sheer magnitude of the majik.

Howling winds whipped around them, stinging their eyes and tearing at their clothes. Ice crystallized on the ruins of the Navarre estate, spreading like a living thing across shattered stone and twisted metal. And through it all, flames rose on every side of the house, a ravenous inferno. The fire crawled over the ruined city, devouring everything in its path. The heat was oppressive. That dark trundle of *nefas* majik lingered beneath her thoughts, whispering it would be too easy to simply kill them all and be done with it.

Sayra pressed it down, down, down.

"I will kill you all to chance our survival if you do not agree to a blood oath this very moment!" Sayra's voice rang out over the cacophony. Her eyes, blazing with an inner fire to match the inferno around them, locked onto Vander and Kenji's terror-stricken faces.

Gone was any trace of the fearful girl she had once been. In her place stood a force of nature, terrible and beautiful in her power. At least, that's what they saw. Inside, Sayra wasn't sure if it would do any good.

"You will repeat my demands if you wish to live," she continued. "Neither Emrys, Nessika, or Sylven will be harmed or detained by you or any other under your command now or later, nor through any manner of trickery, in exchange for my hand given to Kenji."

The maelstrom of elements raged on around them, and she could see the panic on the faces of Kenji's Arcanists as they tried to defuse her majik to no avail. She could feel the drain on her power, knew she was pushing herself to the very limits of her endurance. But she held firm, her gaze never wavering from the men who held their fates in their hands.

But she caught sight of Emrys's face, a blend of betrayal and anguish etched into his features. Whatever came next, whatever sacrifices she would have to make, Sayra was prepared to face it all. But to endure that look on Emrys for a second more...

She turned away from him, moving to pull her hand from his shoulder, but Emrys's arm didn't budge. He wouldn't allow her to carry out the blood oath.

"Not like this, Sayra," Emrys pleaded, such brokenness carving away any trace of hope and happiness he had started to believe in.

Those moments were everything to Sayra. But that was the thing about such moments. They were blips in a person's life. They couldn't truly expect them to last forever, could they? Not when their lives were born to serve a greater purpose.

Sayra's eyes burned, and she opened her mouth to say something, but her throat was too thick with unshed tears to utter a word. *Sylven. Please hold him back*, she thought through the link. When he didn't move, a tear escaped down her cheek. *Please!*

He will never forgive me, Sylven thought back. There was an air of finality to the words, though, and when he moved, so did she.

In a blink, Sylven looped his arms under Emrys's shoulders, pulling him back at the same time as her forward lurch. Sayra opened her spell, stumbling through the translucent barrier and closing it before she could rethink her decision. Her control of the majik slipped further, and with the storm of elements around her, she had to lean heavily on the stairwell railing beside the cowering guards.

A grunt sounded behind her, and she barely caught the tail end of Sylven's struggle with Emrys. Emrys elbowed Sylven around the face. Hard. The impact sent him to the ground, his hazel eyes wincing as he covered his cheekbone with a hand. Further back, Nes had both of her hands over her mouth, tears slipping down her face as she allowed her friend to sacrifice herself. Her head slowly shook from side to side.

With the desperation of a man about to lose his last reason to live, Emrys faced her. For that moment, time around them froze. The shouts, majik, and scene, all of it blurred out of focus, and all Sayra could see was the way his mouth warbled just so.

"I can't lose you too!" Emrys cried out. But he knew it wouldn't change her mind.

They were both stubborn like that.

"I'm sorry," Sayra choked out, her shoulders shaking from a racking sob. She created a slim path free of the elements for them to meet her and perform the rite.

Vander was the first to cave, his value for his own life easily outweighing his distaste for his brother. What use would his newfound power be if he were dead? He stormed down the stairs, careful to avoid the flames Sayra summoned in case they tried anything with her out of the barrier. With a growl, he allowed Sayra to pull her knife and cut their thumbs.

The cuts were jagged. Sayra's vision flickered as she made them, and she desperately tried to steady her breathing. She couldn't let them see how close she was to burning out. She clasped hands with the crowned prince. The spot of blood tingled as the majik took hold. With such self-loathing and bitterness, Sayra repeated her demands once more.

"I swear by *juramentum* to follow your wishes," he yelled, covering his head as a splinter of wood fell upon him.

One down.

The earth groaned beneath them all, shuttering the floor as Kenji finally gave in. He cut his own thumb with a snarl, darkness swirling in the fury of his face. Vander was pushed out of the way, and Kenji took his spot. Vander began to scowl but quickly panicked when the staircase started to crumble beneath him.

Sayra could have sworn she heard someone shouting... someone familiar.

Kenji's voice sounded above the torrent of wind and rumble of stone as their hands clasped next. "I swear by *juramentum* to—"

Her majik dissipated, her mind far too clouded to cling on any longer. The elements around them all stopped at once. Sayra sagged, and her body was fully supported by the miraculously standing handrail. "Then by *juramentum*, I bind you both to my oath that I'll willingly give my hand in marriage to Kenji Haru in exchange," Sayra mumbled, the only words she vaguely remembered with high importance coming to the forefront of her struggling mind.

The majik left her husk, even the fiery barrier in the foyer sizzling out of existence. But Sayra couldn't very well remember the words, the oaths. Everything became blurred, her consciousness fading fast.

Everything swirled around her for a moment until someone caught her. Her head lolled to the side as she was hoisted up, and the last thing she saw would forever be ingrained in her memory.

Across from her, Emrys proved unrecognizable, and his countenance morphed into a living visage of hatred directed at the two heirs. His eyes, usually warm and intelligent toward her, burned with a cold, merciless fury that made him look more daemon than man, a terrifying embodiment of vengeance that promised retribution beyond imagination. Nessika's face squinched in a tearful expression at Sayra. But Sylven, he kneeled beside Emrys, simply being there for the final precious moments they shared together. As if in mourning...

Sayra knew not what was to come, her mind plagued with exhaustion beyond recognition. Knowing her friends and Emrys would be safe, however, made it okay in a twisted way. Her fight against the wave of surging blackness swiftly gave when all she wanted was a few more seconds to see them—seconds she'd cherish and recall when the coming times appeared unmanageable. She breathed deeply, imagining Emrys's cologne, ingraining the warmth of his hands and the sound of his strong heart into her memory.

Sayra's link with the majik then disconnected, her consciousness lost to the unknown.

THE END

If you have enjoyed *Sword of Ruin*, please leave a review. I enjoy hearing back from you, even if it's a kind word or two. Feedback inspires me to continue writing the next book. Keep turning those pages for a sneak peek into some fun extras!

About the Author

Firstly, thank you SO much for reading Sword of Ruin! It's been a dream of mine to write a book since I was in middle school. I never thought I'd accomplish this feat, and I'm so thankful for your support in reading this first published work of mine. My first book was written in 2020, and since then, I've been enjoying every moment of my writing career. Shield of Ruin was written in the beginning of 2022, and since then, has undergone the journey to where the series is today. It will be the first in a line of many books to come!

When I'm not lost in my writing world, you can find me hanging out with my amazing husband and our super lively four-year-old German Shepherd. They are my world! I play tennis for fun, love diving into video games, and there's nothing better than a good hike. Especially in someplace stunning! I've recently made the move to Washington, and let me tell you, it's gorgeous out here. So, that's me. Just living life, enjoying the journey, and hoping my stories find a little corner in your world too!

I'm thrilled to share that the sequel, Arcanist of Ruin, is coming along great! If you'd like sneak peak chapters and other fun updates along the way, join my Discord to stay in touch. If you have any comments or questions, feel free to reach out via my email bookinit@shblodgett.com. I try to respond to every person! In the meantime, please write a review on Amazon. Every review helps boost my book and extends the reach to new potential readers. Plus, it lets me know you want a sequel!

I'm so grateful and appreciative of your support. I hope to share my next story with you soon! If you'd like to explore more about my work, connect with me on social media, join my Discord community, or find direct links to my books and website, check out my Linktree below.

https://linktr.ee/s.h.blodgett

I
LEGACY OF THE DRAGON
BLOOD
AND
BETRAYAL
S. H. BLODGETT

A Sneak Peak into Blood and Betrayal

Book One in the Legacy of the Dragon Series

Rancorous cheering sounded behind Caenrya as she descended from the arena's battlefield. Her feet moved on their own accord as she repressed the wave of disgust and hatred she harbored for the patrons of the underground fighting ring. Revealing even a hint of weakness in her bearing would lead to repercussions for her sister, should her actions reflect poorly on their daimyo. Only a nod from her masked handler reassured her they'd survive another day as she passed through the tunnel. Her bruised fist loosened a hair by the time she was guided into the holding cell.

A metal grate clunked to the floor behind Caenrya. Her black leathers rested against the chilled stone of the room as she was left waiting—always waiting—at the daimyo's beck and call. The daimyo was a calculating man of vast power and wealth, a lord in his own right within a lawless land where no true ruler maintained structure.

Caenrya's final match concluded the evening, and the other fighters lined the endless hallway around her. Only one fighter rebelled in their holding chamber when he refused to obey his handler's order to stay silent. One Caenrya knew to be new. No seasoned fighter would dare the whip, and the sound of the lash almost made her flinch.

Don't react, she recited, suppressing the wave of fear and forcing that indifferent mask to remain locked in place.

Caenrya's handler stood like a statue beside her cell, waiting for their daimyo to collect them after his gambling business concluded.

Once more, the hall fell silent to footsteps. A thundering of them reverberated through the ceiling. She knew then it would only be a matter of minutes before her daimyo collected his winnings for the evening's bets. It was only natural there was much for him to gain. After all, Caenrya was the most profitable fighter in his collection. Having never lost a match in the underground fighting rings, her victories were assured, just as her cooperation was with her younger sister held hostage back at Shikei—the nightmarish bunker where she, and the daimyo's other fighters, were imprisoned. Their sole purpose in life was to earn money for a lord who'd kill them when they proved useless.

It was only a matter of time before she, too, wasn't a financial asset.

One by one, the fighters were claimed by their owners, a handful traded to a new lord or lady through clandestine deals shaken upon over a glass of sake. More than a few jewel-clad people gawked at her in appreciation. Some with outright jealousy that they didn't own her. Caenrya ignored them all and pushed her exhausted frame from the wall when a man's obscenely elaborate silk kimono shone in the minimal lighting of her cell. Without glancing at his face, she knew his up-swept eyes spoke of permanent superiority as he hailed his handler to unlock the steel grate between them and Caenrya.

They were eyes she learned the hard way never to meet.

Without a word, Caenrya fell in behind her daimyo, an intimidating man of extraordinary wealth with a penchant for seeking priceless treasures. His armored guard of four divided themselves to escort their charges through the underground exit. Their emergence garnered reverent whispers as they passed through the exit into the forested mountain range beyond. The daimyo signaled for her to fall in step, and her stomach curled inward as she listened.

"Upon the commencement of the following week, you are to embark on another contract at the behest of the contested lands." The daimyo's deep voice lacked the emotional depth any normal person had.

It was a voice that never ceased to chill her to the bone.

Caenrya distracted herself by wondering which faction she'd be aligning with this go-around within their disputed land. Who was next on her list to assassinate. Her daimyo's loyalties lay with whoever produced the most coin.

The daimyo's silken hair swayed across his lower back as they passed the dense line of pines, the pathway worn by the influx of visitors the arena received every other full moon. "I need not remind you of our arrangement."

Nodding in response, Caenrya wouldn't speak without explicit permission.

The daimyo signaled their departure with a flick of two fingers. They collectively pooled their taiji—a mystical inner energy that ran through their veins—and bounded toward the river weaving throughout the valley. Caenrya once used to relish the harmony of energy that allowed all beings to interact with the earth's natural taiji. Balancing hers against the ground gave her a spring-like mechanic, allowing her to bound vast distances with speed rivaling that of a mountain cat. It made journeys much more tolerable.

Now, though, Caenrya felt indifferent to it as they flew beside the rippling water and only visualized it as another tool of survival.

One day. Caenrya dreamed of a day when she and Verina could escape their soul-crushing lives. Perhaps Caenrya could find a way out, taking Verina with her, and return to the home they were stolen from. Only the faintest of impressions remained in her mind from their life before their capture, but Caenrya adamantly believed it was a better life than they could find here. Every day was spent fighting to survive. Possibly a foolish hope, but it was everything to her.

Even if it meant damning her soul in the meantime.

A clear sky twinkled overhead. Two full moons graced the center of it all with a pearlescent hue. The scuffle of nocturnal animals caught her ears, and the slight scattering of dirt with each leap filled the air as the distance passed in the blink of an eye. Each of the four ronin—the hired guards of the daimyo—kept on high alert. Their eyes searched at a constant pace, and their heads swiveled toward any movement in their perimeter. Weapons of varying types littered their crimson lacquer-dipped plates. Silk cord tied them into a fine mesh of the highest caliber.

Everything about the masked ronin put Caenrya on edge. Especially knowing they'd turn on her the instant she attempted anything deviating from her orders.

Hours passed on their trek back to Shikei before the air tangibly changed. Her shoulders tensed, and her skin tingled at the feeling of being watched. The towering trees around them seemed to lean over her. The ronin leading them slowed, and their group condensed around the daimyo as they stilled beside a copse of pines. One held out a palm, warning them to be quiet and still.

Every internal alarm was blaring with abandon, raising goosebumps along her arms. Her fatigued limbs groaned at the thought of an impending battle. Her reserves were close to being depleted after the countless matches Caenrya had to endure, and it brought a grim edge to her mouth at the thought of an ambush. Truly, it was—

A kunai shot from across the banks of the river. Only a flash of moonlight caught her attention before her body reacted instinctively to the airborne double-sided knife. Caenrya threw herself forward, taking the sharp blade to her shoulder to protect the daimyo. Pain lanced from the deep-rooted injury, and her teeth gritted as the ronin leaped into action.

The lead pulled the furious daimyo into the safety of the overflowing foliage, and the others engaged with emerging black-clad figures. In mere seconds, the sound of clashing metal overtook her surroundings.

Having no weapons put Caenrya at a distinct disadvantage. Her near-empty stores of taiji downright guaranteed anything but a fair fight.

However, it didn't prevent her from joining the fray.

Mid-air, Caenrya felt the shift in her blood as her right hand created the *zen* hand seal—a unique hand movement that activated the taiji in her body. At the same time, she recited an incantation in her mind.

Her taiji's nature shifted, and her body thrummed with a power unique to her bloodline. Pale blue taiji formed a crackling blade around each hand. Her shoulder sung with pain as she blocked the barrage of katana-borne blows one assailant greeted her with. The slightly curved blade sliced through the air, sizzling when it met the resistance of Caenrya's taiji blade.

It took but seconds to determine these opponents were vastly different from those she triumphed over in the ring, even those she felled in war zones.

It was the lack of shock that widened her enemies' eyes at her ability, the grace in which her current ones flowed in unison between attacks within their tag-teamed pairs. And the fact that she was steadily losing ground and being corralled toward where her daimyo had been pushed into hiding.

Her breaths became ragged gasps as she parried between well-timed blows, her footing almost catching on a protruding root.

These enemies were faster. More precise and brutal than nearly any she'd encountered before. Sparks flew as she blocked a nasty blow racing for her healthy shoulder. A grunt escaped her from the angry flare of agony radiating from it.

Minutes passed. Caenrya knew she wouldn't last through the duration of the skirmish. Two of her daimyo's ronin had already fallen, only one remaining at her back to repel the onslaught of four attackers.

Out of the corner of her eye, she caught the flash of flame summoned, a fiery tornado erupting from an enemy's taiji attack around the last of the ronin. His shrieks cut off within seconds. Seconds where she was forced to navigate herself toward the river amid dodging several blows to avoid being caught in the flame.

Caenrya's feet balanced on top of the flowing water, and her movements were purely defensive as they circled her. It wasn't long before a katana cut into her leg, and her taiji faltered.

A distant part of her hoped the death would be fast. That the enormity of her duty would at last be over. She was a shell of a being while working for the daimyo. Only the rare moments she could visit Verina ever brought any semblance of genuine emotion back to her otherwise darkened heart.

But now... Now she'd be ashamed to admit she willingly released her hold on the taiji flowing through her limbs. Ashamed to confess she wanted nothing more than the end of the horrific life she led. She didn't deserve it anyway. Not when a dreadful part of her wished to be rid of the burden of her sister, knowing Caenrya could have fought her way out and escaped ages ago.

When a powerful blow connected with the back of her skull—her vision blacking out—Caenrya's body slackened. A ghost of a smile graced her lips.

She knew then a split second of true contention, an emotion found not in piles of gold coin or a lover's returned smile. Rather, it was within the knowledge her time spent suffering was at its bitter end, her burdens shedding like a snake's skin.

Though it was dampened by a lingering memory of her sister. In that moment, all those years ago, Verina's pleading face made her promise everything was going to be okay.

Deep down, Caenrya knew it never would be, but she would die trying to make it so.

***

Drifting in complete darkness proved to be rather soothing. Such silence made her feel at ease. Caenrya couldn't remember the last time she could let her guard down in such a way. To do so was death, but now that she had fallen to it, it was...

Lonely.

Until a strange presence wormed its way to the edge of her consciousness. It prodded at her steel-clad mind. Caenrya's curiosity allowed her defenses to crumble at the effort the foreign presence put forth. It was then she heard a voice—one unmistakably alive.

"I'm in," a man said. His words echoed in the recesses of her mind. "I'm searching now."

A flash of memory crossed Caenrya's void, a time she'd repressed violently and refused to recall. She knew then she had survived. Not even death would rescue her from the daimyo.

Of *course*.

But a piece of her was relieved. There was still that last thread she clung to, one that whispered she could still save her sister.

Now, though, it was threatened by the man using his taiji to invade her subconscious.

Growling in rage, Caenrya grabbed that vine-like probe with ferocity. Her fist drew it close as she whispered, "I'll enjoy ripping your mind to shreds."

The man's fear leaked through, and his voice was urgent as he shouted at someone to wake the captive. Her. The thought made her grimly laugh at the irony. The invader's consciousness squirmed as her mind struck back, his own mind easily falling apart at her efforts.

From her years of training, Caenrya knew the mind and soul were fragile things. When a person used their taiji to attack with their intangible spirit, they were in their weakest state. Only if a person was assured they were more powerful than their foe could they engage in such an attack.

She was being underestimated.

And. It. Pissed. Her. Off.

A rush of adrenaline laced through her body, and her lungs gasped for air while her eyes snapped open.

Details flooded her sight, from a dreary concrete bunker to an entire company of panicked adults circling the room in a hurry. A balding man was slumped at her left, his glazed eyes unseeing as they faced her pinned form. Liquid rushed through a tube into her arm, metal wound around her leaden limbs. Blaring white lights shone, making the finer details of the white-coated forms and the weapon-clad ronin blurred.

Blinking, Caenrya spotted a bizarre insignia on their person. Some had it over their hearts; others wore it on their shoulders. Six people total.

These weren't ronin. Ronin didn't affiliate themselves with any organization. They were worse.

Shinobi.

By the appearance of their insignia, these warriors belonged to a clan, a crucial and disturbing distinction. As her eyes grew accustomed to the lighting, she picked out the black uniforms identical to those who had ambushed her. She saw emblems of jagged wings over their right shoulders.

Only one figure remained calm at the end of Caenrya's cot, and his stance said more than the set of his face would have. Unflinching with a confidence that spoke volumes. Formal silk attire with royal hues of blue and silver, a cape draping over his left shoulder with the emblem of a jagged wing clasping it to his uniform. The same emblem as on the others. With another blink, Caenrya made out the stern set of his expression, warring on a face that appeared naturally kind.

She ignored the flurry of a white-garbed medical shinobi analyzing the slumped man beside her. "You're wasting your time. My obligations are to another, and no number of honeyed promises or veiled threats will persuade me to fight for you."

For a clan.

There were five sections of divided land on their continent, four of them belonging to individual clans. The section she lived in was the only rogue territory where everyone fought each other to rule. Clans had an established hierarchy, but that didn't make them any better for it.

They certainly never helped the innocent in her territory.

A second passed. Her brows furrowed when the man's steel-gray eyes analyzed her without reaction. His bronze hair was mostly tied in a wrapped topknot up high, a gold wing pinned through the middle. The lower half of his hair fell straight to his shoulders, a neatly trimmed beard wrapping around his jawline. A regal countenance.

A white-garbed woman shook her head, brunette curls bouncing around her heart-shaped jawline. Her voice was urgent as she reported to her lord, "Shogun Arundel, Shinobi Aaric's taiji is too far distressed for me to neutralize. The girl's Kū nature is superior to mine."

Kū nature, one of the five elements of taiji: the mind. Caenrya's strongest affinity.

A pacing black-clad shinobi behind her appeared as if he might launch at Caenrya at a moment's notice. His tanned jaw was locked as he faced the shogun.

A flicker of confusion crossed Caenrya's eyes. Why was she in the presence of a shogun? *This man is the leader of the clan*, she thought grimly. With that morsel of information, the dynamic shifted.

The shogun marked her lapse, folding his arms across his chest as his eyes assessed her.

Tucking away that information, her mind reevaluated the situation.

Caenrya hadn't ever crossed a clan leader's path, hadn't thought them involved with the illicit dealings of the war-torn territory they intruded.

In fact, none of the people in the room blended with her perception of the average criminal.

What was their goal in ambushing them? Caenrya had misjudged them. At first, she thought her ambushers wanted her as their fighter in the rings. But there was more to it. Were the clans now vying for the contested land along with all the other warlords? That would make sense since they had targeted her daimyo, who was one of the many figures of power there.

"You're not a member of the Kriv Clan." A statement, not a question, asked by the shogun.

Caenrya blinked, her brow pinching. Kriv Clan? She knew little of their land's history, but that name had never been whispered to her ears. She greedily clutched to her chest every bit she could glean of the unknown world and would have remembered the clan's name.

Knowledge garnered power, after all.

And right now, she was powerless.

Understanding lit the shogun's eyes. "We refer to the contested lands by the clan that used to rule it. The Kriv. There are enough members from the Kriv Clan remaining among the warring lords, thus it remains titled as such."

An incredulous laugh escaped her before Caenrya could suppress the noise. There wasn't an ounce of humor in it. "I have no clan. I don't belong to any Kriv Clan lord. I thought you knew who you were slaughtering before you ambushed us," she accused with more than a hint of venom in her tone. Caenrya despised losing to *them*. It hadn't been a fair fight. Now what would become of her?

"She's obviously lying," snapped the pacing shinobi, his hand reaching for a tanto blade slung across his black trousers. His ebony eyes blazed with raw anger, and his unbound hair waved about his broad shoulders with each step.

The length of the blade was a third of a katana's, something Caenrya subconsciously noted as her mind devised ways to combat it.

"Rainer." A black-clad shinobi slapped Rainer's hand, her thin mouth a fine line. "If she dies, Aaric has no hope of regaining his mind." The man who tried to probe Caenrya's mind. "Do you wish to make his daughter, Owena, an orphan?" Her auburn head tilted at him with a grim look.

Closing her eyes, Caenrya attempted to focus her taiji.

"It'll do no good," the shogun said, his calm voice drawing closer. "The surrounding graphite-imbued metal prevents the use of taiji."

Her eyes snapped open. Caenrya glared at his squared face in response, her mind circling a method to escape. It appeared she wouldn't be able to rely on her power. "How about this? Release me, and I'll release your friend here. I don't particularly have any fondness for the ronin your people have killed. There won't be any hard feelings on my end."

The shogun gripped a bar on the side of her cot with calloused hands. "Are you a hired ronin?"

Drawing a deep breath, Caenrya tuned out the deadly stares she accumulated around the room. "No," she finally said, a hint of acrimony stretching the word.

"We acquired intelligence that a ring of black-market trading was occurring in the vicinity of your capture. A prominent figurehead of the Kriv Clan was said to be present. If you can trade any further information, then we could discuss an amicable arrangement." The lines deepened on the shogun's forehead.

They moved Aaric carefully into a chair, and the white-garbed medical shinobi monitored his condition closely.

"I've never known anyone from the clan. I've never known much. Even if I had crossed paths with one, I would never have been told," Caenrya responded coldly. Her fists clenched under the metal biting into her skin. "The only thing I do know is that you managed to kill everyone who might have provided such details and captured the single one who is completely *useless*."

Rainer snapped, lunging forward several steps before the two others reined in his arms. Cursing at them, he snarled beside her, "You're lying!"

"Quiet, Rainer," the shogun shot at the man. "She was not responsible for the loss of Serillia. Your team confirmed that your wife passed at the hands of another. We won't get answers without first listening."

They were going to kill her.

An impossible hollowness brought her eyes to the ceiling. Try as she might, there was no reasoning with them when their verdict had already been made. All she could do was disassociate from her body to withstand any torture they tried.

She only hoped Verina would live. Caenrya's throat grew thick.

There was something to be said about devoting her entire life to achieve one tiny dream and for all of it to amount to *nothing*.

"Sit her up," the shogun ordered, motioning to the medical shinobi to adjust the frame.

The brunette medical shinobi avoided eye contact with Caenrya as she elevated the back of her cot, the latter steadying herself for whatever may be in store. Caenrya tensed as the shogun gestured once more, the indication sending a jolt of irrationality through her despite her best attempt not to react.

There was one thing she could never forgive in her years of servitude. The permanent reminder was etched into a story of shame on her back, something she never allowed anyone to see.

Jerking away from the woman, Caenrya bared her teeth in a violent promise. "If you touch my back, I swear I'll enjoy fragmenting your mind." A cornered frenzy lit her eyes.

Everyone quieted, the shogun's expression mellowing as he waved the woman away from Caenrya. "You're a slave then," he determined, knowing full well that each had a brand burned into their backs.

Caenrya only lifted her chin in response. Humiliation and resentment tightened her face.

"Why defend the lord you were escorting if freedom is this close? Why not expose his identity and divulge the information you've gleaned?"

Heartbeats thudded loudly in her ears. Caenrya met his heavy gaze, regaining her composure. "For every day I work in his service—do his bidding—I gain a day where my younger sister lives."

"What if I promised my aid in retrieving her?" That gold wing pin shone as his head inclined, catching the lighting.

Her body froze at the thought. Such a dangerous one.

Damn the shogun and her precarious situation. Damn her shrunken heart for skipping a beat at the thought, at the possibility, as faint and hopeless as it might be.

But the sliver of light must have shown in her distrusting eyes, for the shogun's fingers danced on the bed rail beside her. "In exchange for any details you can offer about your knowledge and experience thus far, however insignificant you might distinguish them to be, I can offer the Duša Clan's full efforts in this exertion."

Duša Clan. She'd never heard of the clan's name before. The shinobi who ambushed her were Duša then.

Caenrya's throat worked for a moment, Rainer's protests barely recognizable over the roaring in her ears. Shaking her head, she cautiously asked, "Why go to such lengths? You must stand to gain something."

"My clan has many enemies, both within our territory and in the surrounding lands. If I can mitigate the threat from any of them, the effort would pay dividends." His tone grew a hair darker, and his spine straightened. "We've lost many good shinobi in ongoing feuds, and if we continue on such a warpath, we'll be left defenseless against the other vultures awaiting our failure. With the Kriv Clan resting on a majority of my clan's border, their civil war is spreading through the edges of my land." Those imposing eyes weighed on hers. "I ask that you join our ranks."

The other shinobi protested along with Rainer. Caenrya's heart sank. She'd be trading one lord for another. But hadn't she already settled on the path she was inevitably fated to tread?

Holding a palm up, the shogun silenced his shinobi. Directing his next words at them, he said, "She already proved to overpower our strongest shinobi in the Kū nature, and she's capable of holding her own against a number of our jōnin-ranked shinobi. Such a bloodline gift would prove substantially advantageous." His thick brows lowered dangerously. "Would the other clans hesitate?"

Licking her lips, the auburn-haired female shinobi sighed. "No, Shogun Arundel."

The others ranged from reluctant to outright spiteful.

Caenrya debated her options, though common sense dictated she could only give one plausible answer.

Throughout her indentured years in the daimyo's care—if she could call it such a thing—whispers of the elusive clans reached the ears of every slave. Some stories were terrifying, detailing the ways many would hunt their own kind for deviating from a single rule or for forsaking their ancestors. Though Caenrya had a gut feeling there was some truth to those rumors, it was said their blood ran thick. Family above all else. A homeland that valued trivial things such as honor and loyalty.

She always resented them for never bothering to show that *honor* and *loyalty* to the victims in her discarded territory. But if there was the slightest chance Caenrya could enter their fold and bring her sister with her... wasn't it worth betting on those forbidden tales she gleaned from other slaves?

After all, she sold her soul once to spare Verina from a life fighting in the rings. Caenrya's life. Why not once more?

"I'll agree to your terms."

Caenrya started from the beginning, her eyes low to the floor. "My younger sister and I were kidnapped at such a young age I can barely remember anything. I don't know where from, but I do know we were sold upon arriving at a bidding event to the daimyo I've worked for." Caenrya fought the urge to touch her pointed ears. She circumvented many truths to prevent history from repeating itself. If these people knew everything...

Caenrya shivered.

"We were too young for fights, but our capacity was measured in various ways. I fought to be the best to leverage my worth. Eventually, I succeed at being the daimyo's prized possession." Her fists tightened. "His highest-earning fighter. In exchange for my efforts, he kept Verina, my sister, out of the fighting pits and separated her from the others." Everyone fended for themselves at Shikei, but she made sure Verina was given better treatment. "As for the daimyo, I learned about his routines. About some of those he made deals with. What he gained from it all."

Her eyes flicked up, catching how everyone was enraptured by her tale. Shogun Arundel nodded for her to proceed.

Caenrya recounted every memory to the tiniest detail, selecting to skip over a few minor things they need not know. But she kept her word, explicating many aspects of her daimyo—her *previous* daimyo—and the constant fighting she underwent at the arenas. She didn't know the daimyo's true identity. Only his face. One she described with a detail only the finest of artists could hope to capture. There were several other faces she'd memorized after frequent appearances at many of the fights she participated in. Some she carried out hits for. Their contracts took her deep into the warring lands, where men fought tooth and nail to climb higher than the rest up that mountain of prestige and power.

No one suspected death to be served by an unremarkable girl, and it was always her target's undoing. It made her daimyo very, very rich.

The shogun's face darkened when Caenrya recounted a number of her contracts. She was careful to leave out anything too damning, skipping over those she thought would raise far too many questions or may have been against one of their clan.

There wasn't much beyond speculation and the general location of her latest arena, as the daimyo had been excruciatingly careful to knock her out whenever they neared Shikei or any other remarkable location. However, from how these people drank up her words, she knew they gleaned something significant.

By the time she wrapped up her story, her shoulder healed by the brunette woman and cuffs unlocked, Caenrya had released her hold on Aaric's mind. They ushered his limp form to the infirmary for monitoring as he came to, leaving only her, the shogun, and Rainer in the room.

For a beat, Caenrya thought they'd double-cross her, laughing all the while at her gullible belief in them. She waited for it too, for a kunai to be sheathed in her heart and her existence to end.

But when the shogun extended a hand to help her ragged form rise from the cot, Caenrya speculated if she traded the devil she knew for the devil she didn't.

THE END OF CHAPTER 1